Safe Harbour

Jane Fenwick

Copyright 1st Edition

First published as an Ebook in 2021

A CIP catalogue record for this title is available from the British Library.

ISBN 978-1-9161957-90

Cover design by Charlotte Mouncey

www.janefenwick.co.uk

For Jo

Also by Jane Fenwick

Never The Twain

My Constant Lady

The Turning Tides

Whitby 1774

Prologue

Gabriel Reynolds looked out over Whitby harbour.

'Man alive, it's heaving today. I'd wager I could get to the other side without getting my feet wet. I never saw so many ships.'

His brother-in-law, Tomas Barker, held on tight to his tricorn as he strode along beside him. 'It looks like rain and the wind's getting up. I think most are waiting to see what the weather will do before they commit to sailing on the next tide. None of the herring fleet has set sail so that tells you something. These old sea dogs can smell when the weather is about to turn.'

'Good job the Eleanor Rose isn't due out for two more days then.' Gabriel stopped and looked up at his ship. He still felt as proud of her now as the day she had been built in John Barker's yard. The collier had arrived the day before from the Baltics and was now being provisioned to sail back to her home port of Alnmouth carrying grain and timber.

Gabriel, his wife Eleanor and their children had returned from Amsterdam two days ago after they had been staying with their friends the Vissers for the best part of a month. Eleanor had been keen to see her family before returning home to Westshore, their house on the seashore at Alnmouth.

Ordinarily Gabriel enjoyed spending time with Eleanor's family at Sandsend. After almost a decade of marriage he now regarded the Barkers as his family too. On this occasion however, he was keen to get home; a large deal was waiting to be finalised and was playing on his mind. It was a deal which would see his tally of ships rise from three to six, effectively doubling his import-export business.

Not that the deal was one he had sought out; indeed it had come about because of an unexpected and not altogether happy turn of events. Gabriel hoped the agreement would be completed to everyone's satisfaction but he worried there would be a problem and so he was anxious to get home and put the deal to bed.

The two men stood together, matched in height and stature, but not in colouring. Gabriel's dark curls ruffled in the breeze, his greatcoat blew out behind him. His chin had dark stubble covering it for unless he shaved twice a day it was the inevitable outcome, much to his wife's chagrin. Tomas' shorter, fairer hair barely moved in the blustery wind. After a sudden blast threatened to tear the hat from Tomas' head he had removed it. He was regretting leaving his coat in the office and wrapped his arms about his body in an effort to keep warm.

'Never cast a clout until May be out,' Gabriel said as he saw his brother-in-law shiver.

He approached his captain Nathan Pearson, a burly Geordie who had worked for Gabriel and his father before him. He enquired after the cargo. With a Geordie accent as thick as his biceps the captain replied: 'First lot er grain arrived not half an hour ago, the rest's not expected 'til tomorrow. It's goin' to be a bit tight to get it all loaded in time, but we'll manage. Don't we allus?'

Gabriel nodded and watched as tubs of herring were heaved on board. Crates were hauled up on pulleys and grain sacks unloaded from wagons. The Eleanor Rose wasn't the only ship being provisioned that day and so the quay was a mass of men, mules and merchandise. A stream of curses went up as a barrel toppled over and rolled back down the gangplank knocking two men over like skittles.

'Have a care Sol, if that there barrel had split it were comin' out of your pay lad.' Gabriel smiled, both he and Nat knew this to be an untruth, but it didn't hurt to keep the deckhands on their toes.

Another crate dangled precariously in the air then a sudden gust sent it crashing against the ship's hull. It rebounded making the dockers duck. A colourful stream of cussing followed, then nervous laughter rang out when they saw they were safe. Gabriel and Tomas stepped back bumping into each other in their haste to be out of range. Tomas laughed as he slipped on a discarded fish head and dropped his hat. 'Lord the wind's skittish today, I nearly went over then.'

'Don't for the love of God fall in the harbour for I'm not keen to dive in after you,' Gabriel told him.

Before Tomas could reply he saw Nat waving his arms over his head and yelling frantic instructions to the crew. The crate was still swaying crazily when another gust took hold of it. Gabriel saw it was heading straight for the two of them. He tried to shout a warning to Tomas but the words were thrown away on the wind. He shot a look at his brother-in-law who had bent to recover his tricorn and was about to raise his head. The crate looked lined up to knock Tomas off his feet. Gabriel hurled himself towards Tomas pushing him to the ground. That and a sharp pain were the last things he remembered.

R

Eleanor Reynolds sat by the fire with her mother. After their walk on the cliff top at Mulgrave House in Sandsend she felt pleasantly tired. The weather had suddenly turned squally so they had retreated to the warmth of the drawing room. The three Reynolds children, Rose who had nine summers and twins Haydan and Ruari, who had seven, were playing on the rug. They were bickering with each other as children who resent being confined indoors generally do.

'Your grandmama will get the impression you're badly brought up. For goodness' sake play nicely all of you.'

Eleanor's mother, Anne Barker, tried not to smile. 'They're like you and your siblings at that age. They long to be outdoors no matter what the weather. You were all just the same.'

'I think it's stopped raining Mama, may we go out again?' Eleanor thought Rose was eager to get away from her annoying little brothers and who could blame her? The boys had begun a wrestling match and were intent on killing each other.

'Perhaps you could go and find Ginny and play in the nursery my love.' The boys stopped rolling around, leapt to their feet and dashed to the window.

'It's only raining a bit now,' Haydan hollered across the room.

His mother remonstrated with him for shouting like a docker then pointed out that even if it stopped raining they wouldn't be allowed out as the wind was blowing a gale. 'You'll be blown off the cliff into the sea never to be seen again.'

'Good,' Rose muttered under her breath making her grandmama smile.

Eleanor was about to order tea when a commotion could be heard in the hall. They rushed out to see what was happening. Gabriel, blood pouring from his head, was being carried up the stairs.

1

Dr Burns wiped his hands on a towel and bundled up the bloodied rags. Eleanor stared at her husband willing him to wake. Gabriel had been knocked unconscious and was yet to recover his senses. He lay on the bed as if in a deep sleep, except he had a livid gash to his head.

Tomas, his arm around his twin sister's waist looked on. 'It all happened so quickly. I bent to retrieve my hat and the next thing Gabriel hurled himself on top of me. The crate was heading my way Nat said. Gabriel is injured because he tried to save me.'

Eleanor squeezed her brother's hand. 'It's no fault of yours Tomas; you don't need to feel guilty, you would have done the same for Gabriel.'

'The wound looks worse than it is,' the doctor interrupted them. 'Often a cut to the head can bleed profusely. A few stitches will see it right. Should you care to step out Eleanor while I sew him up?'

'Yes - no, when will he wake up? He's been unconscious almost an hour now.' She shot an anxious look at her brother for confirmation. He looked at his pocket watch and nodded.

'Sadly I've no way of telling my dear.' Dr Burns began to thread a needle.

The elderly doctor had been treating the Barker family since Eleanor and her siblings were small. He had always had a kind, but no nonsense bedside manner. He was a gregarious Scotsman, stoutly built and jovial by temperament.

He sought to calm Eleanor's fears. 'There is one blessing - at least he won't feel the stitches going in.'

Eleanor didn't share the doctor's levity. 'Perhaps the pain will bring him round?' she suggested. Dr Burns began to sew. Eleanor winced, but resolutely watched her husband's face for signs he was waking. There were none.

Anne Barker crept into the room and took her place by her daughter and son. 'The children are playing in the nursery. They are having their tea shortly, so there is no need to worry about them. I have said their father will be as right as rain in no time.'

'But will he? He's still unconscious. What if... '

Dr Burns finished sewing the gash and looked at Eleanor over his pince-nez. 'My dear I cannot be certain of course, but Gabriel will recover soon I hope. Often it's the body's way of repairing itself, being unconscious, but if by tomorrow he hasn't come round I'll bleed him.'

'Tomorrow! He may be unconscious until tomorrow?'

'It is not uncommon, but who knows he might rally tonight. If he does, do not hesitate to send for me no matter the time.' He picked up his bag.

'Let me see you out doctor. How is your wife? I heard she's been suffering with her rheumatism again.' Anne led the doctor from the bedchamber.

Eleanor reached for her husband's hand and burst into tears; she could hold in her fear no longer. Tomas was quick to come to her aid.

'My dear he's as strong as an ox, he'll pull through. You heard what old Burns said, it looks worse than it is.'

Eleanor wiped her eyes. 'Do you remember what happened to Caroline?' She mentioned a family friend who had been thrown from her horse and knocked out. 'She never recovered consciousness and died. She was just three and twenty.'

'That was different Eleanor, Burns says apart from the scratch to his head Gabriel has no other injuries. Caroline had broken her back from the fall remember.'

For several hours Eleanor continued to gaze at her husband willing him to wake up. At last she was persuaded to leave Gabriel to say goodnight to the children. She returned to her husband's bedside to find her father had kept vigil in her absence.

‘Has there been any change Papa?’

‘I would have sent for you had there been my dear, try to stay calm.’

‘The boys are over excited, what is it with boys and blood? They’ve convinced themselves Gabriel has been fighting a duel. Poor Rose is distraught. She’s such a daddy’s girl.’

‘I’ve sent for a tray for you Eleanor, you cannot go without sustenance, you must eat.’

‘I’ll try, but I’m not hungry.’

A chambermaid brought steamed fish and potatoes. The smell made Eleanor nauseous. She picked at the food before pushing it away untasted.

R

Gabriel opened his eyes and tried to adjust them to the candlelight. A darkened room gradually came into view. He stared up at the unfamiliar bed canopy. Where was he? He tried to look sideways, but a sharp pain shot through his head like a bullet. He lifted his hand to his temple and felt something... a dressing? Had he been shot? Carefully he tried to move his head again and saw a lady asleep on a chair by his bed. He blinked trying to study her face. Who was she and why was she here?

Her long red hair glowed in the light from a three branched candelabra. It was unbound and fell in waves to her waist. She had slid slightly to one side, her head resting on the back of the chair. Gabriel searched her features for recognition; a pale face with a sprinkling of freckles across her cheeks, a nose which had a slight bump on the bridge which didn’t detract from her looks. Who was it that watched over him? An angel? His head felt fuzzy and heavy, confused. The room began to swim and swirl. He fought to stay awake, willing himself to keep his eyes open and focussed on the red-haired beauty. She shifted slightly as she slept, murmured something incomprehensible. He tried to reach out, to touch her but his hand fell back. He was as weak as a kitten. Once more he sank into oblivion.

R

Dr Burns was taking Gabriel's pulse as Eleanor roused herself from sleep. She sat bolt upright as the events of yesterday flooded her consciousness.

'I must have dropped off. Is there any change?'

'No better no worse, my dear. Your mama has gone to break her fast. She told me to tell you the children are fed and watered and that she or Tomas will relieve you shortly. You will make yourself ill Eleanor. Go and eat something and I will do my checks. If he wakes I know how to work a bell pull.' He gestured towards the door with his head.

Eleanor scrutinised her husband's face. His eyes were still closed but he now had thick stubble covering his sun bronzed face. Ordinarily he spent many hours outside at the bay and although it was early spring he still looked sunburnt. Her heart felt heavy thinking how well he looked; aside from the purple bruise and the dressing he looked as he always did - healthy, handsome.

'Very well, I'll check on the children. Rose was so upset last night but I don't want her to see Gabriel like this, she wouldn't understand. How could she when I don't fully comprehend it myself?'

Once she had reassured the children Eleanor went to break her fast with the family. 'Some nurse I am - I fell asleep. What if Gabriel had woken in the night?'

'You were not alone my dear,' Anne Barker sought to reassure her daughter, 'one or other of us stayed with you all night, except for a few minutes when Rose woke. Ginny said she'd had a bad dream so I went to check on her, but I came straight back. She had dropped off again by the time I got there.'

'Rose was always a good sleeper, she takes after her papa.' She threw her napkin aside and frowned at the irony. 'I'll go back to him, I should hate him to wake and not be there.'

Tomas pulled out his sister's chair. 'I'll come too and then I'll go to see Nat Pearson and ask how the loading is progressing, it's the least I can do.'

Brother and sister stood either side of the bed. Dr Burns had finished his examination and was about to take his leave. 'Send for me if he regains consciousness. I will bleed him later today if there is no change. Goodbye Tomas, Eleanor. Chin up my dear.'

After half an hour Tomas left for the harbour. Once alone, fear gripped Eleanor. What if she lost her husband, her soul mate? What if he didn't recover? She would not allow herself to imagine a life without Gabriel; it didn't bear thinking about. 'I must be positive,' she said out loud. 'Gabriel my love, rouse yourself this is too much to cope with. We love you so much. Come back to us, we can't live without you.'

Time passed slowly. Eleanor thought to write to Gabriel's friend and business partner to tell him of the accident. Sir Bendor Percy lived in Dunstanburgh a few miles north of Alnmouth. She knew there was nothing practical he could do to help but it gave her something to do and she thought he ought to know. After all the two men were like brothers.

Later in the afternoon Eleanor's sister Atalana arrived to keep her company. It was a kind thought but did nothing to help Eleanor's mood. The sisters had never been particularly alike, especially in temperament. Eleanor had always been much closer to her twin brother; they shared a special bond as twins often do. Attie was the only one of the family to remain a Quaker after John Barker was thrown out of the Friends for arming his ships. For their part Eleanor and Tomas were relieved to be able to lead more secular lives, while Attie had married Obed Coffin a zealous, dour Quaker. The couple were raising their own twins, Harriet and Edward, strictly and in the Quaker faith. Eleanor thought them *too* strict and tried to make up for it by spoiling them whenever she visited Whitby.

Now Attie sat, upright and stoical, in quiet contemplation across from her. Eleanor found it off-putting. She stood and looked out of the window at the bright, spring day. The sea glinted in the lemon light, gulls soared and dived. She resented the weather and calm sea; they had no right to be clement under the circumstances. She watched as the twins raced around the garden on hobby horses, clearly oblivious of their father's plight. Then Eleanor noticed Rose sitting on a stone bench clutching her favourite rag doll. Her chubby little legs were swinging back and forth as she stared out to sea. Eleanor knew Rose would be worrying about her papa. She was a sensitive little soul and the apple of her father's eye. Silent tears coursed down Eleanor's cheeks.

Never one to be idle, Eleanor grew more and more frustrated as time dragged on. 'How are Harriet and Edward doing with their new tutor?' she asked after regaining her composure and her seat.

'Especially well I think. Harriet has an aptitude for arithmetic whilst Edward has proven himself in Latin. Both twins need to apply themselves however, they are easily distracted.'

'As were Tomas and I; you were always the better scholar were you not?'

'You always had your head in the clouds or else in some romantic novel or other as I recall. I fear Harriet will turn out the same.'

'Would that be so bad?' Eleanor could feel old tensions bubbling to the surface.

'I need to get home my dear. I have a prayer meeting later. We will pray for Gabriel. Do not lose hope, God will provide.'

When Attie had gone it was her mama's turn to sit with Eleanor. This was far more convivial to her. Anne filled her in about local gossip which helped to distract and take her mind off Gabriel's troubles. Her mama suggested Eleanor take tea with the children and at first she was torn not wanting to leave Gabriel, but then reluctantly decided she would. She hadn't been in the nursery long when her father burst in.

'Come at once my love,' he urged, 'Gabriel has regained consciousness.'

R

Gabriel felt himself rise to the surface as if he had been swimming under water and had suddenly run out of breath. This time when he opened his eyes a different lady sat by his bed; an older, paler version of the woman who had been there before. This lady's hair had once been red he thought but now was a pale gold. She had the same shape face as the angel and a few faded freckles scattered across her cheeks. She was reading a book and had not noticed he had woken. She glanced up and gasped.

'Oh thank the Lord you are returned to us.' She pulled the bell. 'Eleanor has only just stepped out to see to the children. How do you feel, are you in pain?' She took his hand and kissed it. 'Oh my dear Gabriel.'

A tall grey-haired man appeared in the doorway and looked at him. 'Well done old man, I will fetch Eleanor. She will be cock-a-hoop.' He promptly disappeared again. Gabriel closed his eyes. There was the pain again, the one he had felt before, though it didn't feel so severe now he was pleased to note.

The door being flung open roused him further; the angel who had been sleeping by his bed rushed in, smiling but with tears streaming down her face. The older man strode in behind her.

'Oh Gabriel my love, we were so worried. How are you? Does your head pain you? You've several stitches, but Dr Burns doesn't think there will be a permanent scar. I don't care if there is now you're back in the land of the living.'

Gabriel looked at the three faces watching him expectantly. He was overwhelmed. His head began to throb.

'I will send for Burns,' the man said turning on his heel.

'Where am I?' To himself he thought his voice sounded hoarse.

'You're in Whitby my love, do you remember the accident?'

'Accident? What accident? May I have something to drink?'

'Of course.' The older woman poured small beer into a glass. He tried to sit up but the room began to spin wildly around him. He lay back feeling nauseous, dizzy. The drink was held to his parched lips and when he signalled he had drunk enough he glanced in bewilderment about him. The room, decorated in blue with velvet drapes and bed hangings, was commodious but not ostentatious. The curtains were open and the sun streamed in. He watched as dust motes danced in the sun's rays. Then he noticed a chubby, red-headed little girl had crept in unnoticed by the other adults. She smiled at him and held her finger to her lips hushing him. Perhaps she was frightened of being asked to leave? He smiled and turned back to look at the angel.

'You were hit on the head by a crate at the harbour. A gust of wind blew it and almost hit Tomas, but you pushed him out of the way and took the blow yourself.' He saw her face screw up in consternation. 'Do you not remember? You were knocked out cold; you've been unconscious for a day and a half.'

Gabriel searched his memory but could remember nothing about an accident. He closed his eyes all the better to concentrate, but still nothing came. Then it struck him forcibly; he could remember nothing at all. A sense of panic surged over him.

'Has Pa gone to sleep again?' he heard a small voice ask.

'Rose. How did you get in here?' The angel spoke softly to the child. 'Papa will get better now. Go and play with your brothers. Tell them you all may have extra cake to celebrate.'

Gabriel opened his eyes as he felt a wet kiss on his cheek.

'You need a shave Pa. Mama will be cross; your face feels like a badger's behind.' She grinned at him as the angel stifled a laugh and ushered the child from the room.

He was lost for words. Who was this child? She had called him Pa? Who were these people and why was he in Whitby? The room began to spin again, he grabbed the blanket as if to stop the turning, but the room continued to shift.

'Ah, here you are back with us Gabriel.' A rotund man was taking his pulse. 'How is that head feeling? I tried to sew as carefully as I could, God forbid I should spoil your handsome face.' He smiled at the angel.

'He can't remember being hit by the crate Dr Burns.'

The angel looked from one man to the other.

'Can you recall anything at all about the accident Gabriel?'

Gabriel? Was that his name? It sounded vaguely familiar, but then he thought someone had called him by that name earlier.

'I know nothing of an accident and furthermore I don't know who any of you are.' He tried to sit up but regretted it.

The doctor peered at him over half moon glasses. 'This is not uncommon with bumps to the head, you possibly have temporary amnesia. It is the brain's way of trying to heal itself and so it blocks out all knowledge, all memories until it is able to cope again.'

'You don't know me my love? You must remember me.'

'I'm afraid not Madam. I'm sorry if my accident has incommoded you and your family.'

'We're *your* family Gabriel. You're not an inconvenience. I'm your wife... surely you remember?' The angel looked at what he now realised must be her parents, he saw the family resemblance.

'No, not at all.' He turned to the doctor. 'How long will this amnesia last? How long will I remain in the dark?'

'Possibly a day or two, could be longer it all depends. I suggest your family try to prompt you to remember. If they tell you about your life, your likes and dislikes, your work, et cetera, et cetera, I am sure it will help jog your memory.'

The doctor's voice was light, carefree as though he was passing the time of day. Gabriel found it disconcerting. Man alive! Here he was, unable to remember his own name and this doctor, this quack, was barely concerned. What sort of a doctor was he? His temper flared.

'How can you be so sure? What if my memory *doesn't* come back?'

The angel sank onto a chair visibly distressed. Even though he had no idea who she was it pained him to see her so distraught, so agitated.

'Please don't alarm yourself... ' Suddenly darkness closed in and blackness engulfed him. Once again Gabriel sank below the surface.

2

Two more days passed. Gabriel floated in and out of consciousness, yet still his memory was lost to him. The visitors to his bedside were becoming familiar, but beyond that he was in a world which was, to him, but a few days old.

By the fourth day he was feeling better in himself. His head ached less than before and he was well enough to rise from his bed. Eleanor asked: 'Shall I send Walters to you? You are in desperate need of a shave, you look like Robinson Crusoe.'

She was a handsome woman Gabriel noted. 'Walters?'

'Jonty Walters has been your manservant for years.' Gabriel was growing tired of having things explained to him. It made him feel like a child, yet he could think of no other way he could manage his days without these constant reminders. It was frustrating nonetheless.

In the dressing room Gabriel looked at the clothes laid out for him.

'Good to see you up and about Mr Gabriel. I've taken the liberty of laying out your usual day wear, but if you require something different then say the word.'

'How should I know what else to choose? I expect my wife has told you I've lost my wits.'

'Surely not, it's your memory that's gone not your brains.' The manservant raised an eyebrow.

'"Brains"! Tell me this Walters, how is it I can remember how to feed myself, how to walk and talk, yet can remember nothing that happened before four days ago? I don't know you, my wife, my children... my in-laws. I don't recognise where I am. I'm told I'm in Whitby and that these people are my family, but it could be anywhere on earth and these people, kind as they seem, are complete strangers to me. And the blasted doctor only wants to bleed me, to what end I'm uncertain. How will blood-letting restore my memory?'

'I'm your manservant not a doctor but presumably he knows best.'

Gabriel slumped before the mirror his long legs sprawled out in front of him. 'The lady who calls herself my wife, Mrs Reynolds, is keen to see me clean shaven. Go ahead, do your worst, though why I can't perform the task for myself is beyond me.'

Walters offered him the cut throat, an ironical look on his rugged, good looking face. Although Gabriel was unaware, master and servant were on friendly terms. Gabriel waved the blade away and sat sullenly while his valet proceeded to lather and shave him. When he had finished Gabriel dressed then combed his unruly curls.

'Tell me, for I obviously cannot ask the lady myself, you've been my man for some time, or so I'm informed, perhaps you know... Do I *like* my wife? Ordinarily do we get on or was this an arrangement, a marriage of convenience? She appears concerned for my welfare, but perhaps she's concerned if I die I'll be unable to provide for her.'

'There was never such a devoted husband and father; you'd do anything for your family and friends. You dote on your children and Mrs Reynolds, well, she's the love of your life or so my lady friend Connie assures me. Connie is your under cook at Westshore,' he added thoughtfully. 'You're a well respected businessman and liked by your crews and servants for being a fair, honest man.'

Gabriel stared at his manservant. 'Quite the paragon, but I must have some faults? At the moment I feel less than amiable, in fact I feel irritable, bad tempered. Is this my normal frame of mind? Do I normally appear out of sorts and as if I could cheerfully murder someone?'

Walters grinned. 'Far from it. It's possibly as a result of the accident - who knows? Under normal circumstances you're even tempered although,' he grinned again, 'you hate being shaved. That's the first time I remember in years you've not grumbled about the time it takes. You'd have grown a beard years ago had it not been for your wife.'

Gabriel looked at his reflection in the mirror. The dressing on his head had been removed and he saw several stitches, not that he remembered getting them.

'Can you imagine not remembering your schooldays, your parents, your wedding day or your children being born? It's remarkable and disconcerting. I'm now expected to go into company and converse with these people, these strangers... about what exactly I'm unsure? They've been told by that charlatan of a doctor to tell me about my life, "fill in the gaps" he said. There are bloody big gaps I can tell you. Man alive!'

Walters tidied away the shaving equipment. 'There's one thing you've not forgotten I notice - your favourite cuss.'

The door opened and Eleanor walked in. He was about to remonstrate with her, he may have been disrobed, then realised she probably came to his dressing room regularly, had seen him undressed, seen him naked.

'That's much better,' she announced. 'You look a little thinner in the face, but now you're up and about you will get your appetite back. Are you ready to break your fast?'

During the meal which he shared with the family, including his brother-in-law, they endeavoured to tell him his life story. Also Tomas was at pains to assure him his ship, which had been moored in Whitby, had set sail on the evening tide the night before. He was astonished to learn he had a flourishing import-export business and owned three ships.

'The grain and timber were all late arriving. There'd been a rock fall which blocked the road by Runswick, but Nat Pearson and the crew worked tirelessly to get it loaded so as not to miss the tide.'

Gabriel's head began to throb.

Eleanor reached for his hand: 'Are you feeling tired?'

'Not at all,' he lied.

'The children have gone to stay with my sister for the time being, I think they'd be confused if you didn't recognise them, especially Rose.'

'I saw her I think, in my bedchamber a few days ago. She has red hair and is a little erm... ' He pulled his hand away. Hand-holding hardly felt appropriate - it felt over familiar, foreign to him.

'Dumpling is your pet name for our daughter. Why she's so plump I can't tell; her favourite pastime is disturbing the peace, she's never still.'

'It's puppy fat my dear, both you and Attie were the same at her age,' her mama said.

The meal ended and Gabriel felt at a loose end. What was he to do with himself? After laying abed for the best part of a week he felt listless, keen to get out in the fresh air. He said as much to his wife, but the woman appeared reluctant to let him out of her sight.

'I'll walk with you my love, what if you were to get lost?'

'Madam, I've lost my memory not my sense of direction. Thank you but I'm sure if I strike out I'll be able to find my way back unless I'm fool enough to walk out to sea that is.'

The moment he saw the hurt look on her face he regretted his outburst. 'I apologise Eleanor, the comment was uncalled for. By all means accompany me, I would be honoured.'

'This situation is difficult for both of us Gabriel, I feel as frustrated as you. We both need to be patient, but of course you should go on your own if that's what you prefer, but remember not to overdo it. Dr Burns says the more you rest the better.'

'No, please come with me. Tell me more about what a well thought of man I am. Better still tell me about you and why I married you. Walters tells me it was not for your dowry.' He saw the tension in her shoulders ease.

'There my love, that's more like your old self, you could always make me smile.'

They donned their cloaks and set off down the path towards the cliffs. It was a typical May day with high blown clouds scudding across the sky, the grey-blue sea shimmering under the sun.

Eleanor began to tell him how they had met. 'We first met under what you may think were strange circumstances. In a rowdy tavern would you believe? The Fleece Inn on the east side of the harbour.' She looked at him expectantly hoping he would remember, but he had no recollection of the event. 'You were in Whitby to order a ship. Unbeknown to me you'd commissioned Papa to build you a collier to expand your business. Of course we never imagined we would ever meet again after our first inauspicious meeting, but Papa invited you to dine at Mulgrave House and you recognised me. I was with my fiancé Captain Seamer, having one of our many disagreements as I remember. Of course I looked very different to how I'd looked on our first meeting, but you were a gentleman and didn't give me away to my family, or to William. It made me love you from the start I think.'

'Intriguing. You say it was an inauspicious meeting yet we married. You can't leave me hanging, please tell me more.' He watched as she stopped and turned to face him.

'Very well, but first here, where we're standing right now is the actual spot where we first kissed. Well, when I kissed you to be fair.'

'Is it really? How interesting, go on.' He could see how he would want to kiss her - she was a striking looking lady. He guessed she was a few years younger than him. Perhaps she had been a child bride?

'I used to have quite a rebellious streak in my younger days, I think it was the result of being brought up a Quaker. All the quiet meditation and endless Friends' meetings bored me witless, made me want to break out and have fun. I used to sneak from home at night and go into Whitby unchaperoned and dressed in my maid's cast offs to blend in.'

'Why on earth would you do that? Had you no care for your own safety, for your reputation?'

'I was keen to sample all life had to offer I suppose, now I'm older and wiser I see how reckless I was. I'd never been in a tavern so I asked a young sail maker who I'd befriended to take me to one, but then things got out of hand.'

'And on one of these jaunts you met me?'

'Not at first, first I met the sail maker as I said.'

'I see where this is heading.'

'You misunderstand; the sail maker was a young girl.' She shot him a look. 'Our romance came later.'

Gabriel deployed an eyebrow. He could easily see why any man could fall for this bewitching creature. She was attractive of course, but she also had an easy way with her, a sense of fun and a self assurance that was beguiling.

'Eva Drage, the sail maker in question, was poor and although she worked long hours she still had to make extra money, by nefarious means you understand, she prostituted herself. She had a widowed sister and a niece and nephew to support. She showed me the sordid underbelly of Whitby, showed me how the other half lived.'

'I'm not sure I want to know anymore. You consorted with common prostitutes?'

She threw her head back and laughed. 'It's not as bad as it sounds. She's respectable now, she's a milliner. The tale has a happy ending. To cut a long story short one night I saw my fiancé William with a, let's call her a *lady of the night*. I decided what was good for the gander was good enough for the goose. Eva made me a wager I daren't, well you can guess what she bet me.' Gabriel, shocked, was not sure he did but allowed her to continue. 'I was all fired up, angry at William's lack of morals, at least that's how I remember it.'

'I hope this is where I come into the story to save you from yourself. You would have been ruined, thrown out by your family, ostracised from society.' They had reached the edge of the cliff and stopped.

'Well I suppose you did save me, but not before... ' She looked self conscious, and then half laughed with obvious delight.

She had an infectious laugh though he wasn't sure what she was telling him was a laughing matter. Gabriel was confused and was about to say so when she added: 'No no, we didn't... you thought I too was a woman of... ' Again she sought to clarify. 'Lord this makes me sound like a strumpet! What I'm trying to say is I came to my senses in time and ran out on you. You see dressed as I was in Charity's old frock you thought I was a woman of easy virtue. I went to your room at the tavern but then as I said, I got cold feet.'

Eleanor was clearly amused and looked for him to return her smile but he felt strangely perturbed by her confession. What sort of woman was she? His wife it appeared was a singular young lady, unconventional to say the least. Was he supposed to approve of her declarations?

'I see.' Gabriel straightened up. 'So when we met again here at Mulgrave House even though you were a respectable, well dressed lady I recognised you. And presumably you were afraid I would tell your father what you'd been about?'

'Exactly so. I was still engaged of course and so were you, to Caroline. She was your childhood sweetheart, but love conquers all as they say and when we met again for a third time we knew we had to be together.' They had wandered down the path to the beach. 'Shall we walk further or are you tired?'

His head was aching trying to take in all she was telling him. His wife had a boldness about her which was at odds with what he thought was right and proper.

'By all means let's walk a little further if you wish. I'm unsure whether it's the sea air which revives me or your tantalising story,' he said with a touch of irony. 'So we married and moved to my hometown of Alnmouth.'

He watched as Eleanor sat on a boulder and unselfconsciously removed first her shoes and then her stockings. He instinctively turned aside. She laughed at him.

'Such a gentleman, but I can assure you my love we know every inch of each other, we have three children remember. And in answer to your question yes we live in Alnmouth in a fine house built by your father. It's called Westshore and it's your pride and joy. Alnmouth is quite a busy port, roughly half the size of Whitby.'

All the while they'd been walking he noticed she held his arm, touched his hand affectionately. He had to remind himself a chaperone wasn't needed - they were married. It was odd, disconcerting but not altogether unpleasant. It was even more peculiar to think he had children with this ravishing creature. He must have lain with her on endless occasions, but he had no recollection whatsoever, more's the pity.'

She began to walk in the surf not caring the hem of her dress was getting soaked. 'All this talk of how we met is making me quite nostalgic,' she sighed. 'If you don't get your memory back then we'll have to make new memories.' She shot him a brazen look. He was surprised to realise he would look forward to making *those* sorts of memories.

R

After supper the men retired with their port. Gabriel was offered a pipe by his father-in-law which he declined. John Barker smiled wickedly.

'You were never one for smoking, strange how you instinctively refused. I thought you would turn it down, but I was curious to see what you would do.'

Gabriel felt his temper tip until he realised John Barker was only being inquisitive, amiable.

'I apologise Gabriel, you must feel like a specimen being examined under a lens, most frustrating for you my boy. I will endeavour to curb my curiosity.'

After another glass of port Gabriel could hardly keep his eyes open. His head, although not paining him, felt heavy; the information he was being continually fed was tiring. For the last week Gabriel had been bombarded with information about his likes and dislikes, his business dealings and about his life in general and in particular. His head was swimming with facts, thoughts and questions. He sought to make his excuses. 'Please make my apologies to the ladies John. I feel in need of my bed I'm afraid.'

Exhausted and alone in his bedchamber he threw his jacket and waistcoat on the bed and sat to remove his shoes and hose. Walters knocked and entered.

'The mistress sent me to help you.'

'I can manage thank you. I'll not need you until the morning, good night.'

He pulled his shirt over his head and flung it on the bed with the rest of his clothes. As his valet left Eleanor swept in. He had noticed earlier she was wearing a green taffeta gown which suited her colouring. Now she looked simply stunning in the candlelight with her red hair glowing and her smiling face. He could hardly believe he was married to this lovely creature. Damn it was frustrating not remembering how they were with each other.

'Papa says you're tired, I knew we'd walked too far earlier. You should have said. You look done in my love.'

'Madam, it's nothing a good night's sleep cannot remedy,' he snapped. Then it occurred to him he was standing in his breeches. Again he felt the absurdity of the situation. She was his wife for God's sake. Surely she had seen him in a state of undress before. Was his old self a bad tempered prude?

Eleanor looked up at him and moved closer, raising her hand to his cheek. He saw her expel a long breath. Unshed tears sparkled on her lashes.

'I miss you so much Gabriel. The old you would have wrapped me in his arms by now and be making overtures. We were always demonstrative, affectionate... passionate. Ever since our first night we've been good together, come back to me my love.' He sensed her concern, but also her disappointment. 'The love you usually give so freely has been withdrawn. Please let it only be temporary, I pray it'll soon return.'

He was at a loss to reassure her but wanted to put her mind at rest somehow. 'I'll do my best.' He could see her strength as she took control of herself. She was worried for him and he was touched, his temper cooled. 'You say we were good together, yet I can't even remember our first kiss, our wedding night.'

'Who mentioned a wedding night?' She laid her hand on his chest and smiling said: 'Shall you be shocked when I tell you we anticipated our marriage vows?' Her eyes danced with mischief.

So not a prude then. He pulled her into his arms and felt her relax against him. 'Perhaps when I recover my memory things will return to how they were before the accident but for now I can't explain, but I'd feel as though... as though I was taking advantage of you.' He took a curl that had escaped from its pins and tucked it behind her ear. She lifted her head from his chest and smiled up at him with such warmth and intensity he almost forgot himself.

'Very well, but at least kiss me. We always kissed one another goodnight, unless you and Bendor had made a night of it that is.' She chuckled. 'And then you'd be too inebriated.'

He wanted to ask if he often took too much liquor but then thought better of it. He already had enough to worry about. Despite himself he could feel his arousal. He kissed her cheek as though she was his sister and not his wife. As they pulled apart he took a step back, saw her sigh.

'I love you so much Gabriel. Try to get a good night's sleep. Although I dearly want to stay with you, I see you need to know me again, recognise me as your wife and lover before that can happen. Sweet dreams my love.'

When Eleanor left he flung himself on the bed in frustration. How could he not remember his own wife? He searched inside his head, but there was nothing hiding in any corner of his brain. It was an empty darkness.

Once again a sense of panic swept over him. A fear gripped him as he closed his eyes sending a chill through his whole body. What if he stayed in this crazy limbo forever? What if the stories his wife and family told him would be all he ever knew? The Barkers said they had never known his parents. Would he never remember them? And what of his school days? He could read Latin and Greek. He had been in John Barker's library and selected books written in French also. How could he remember other languages? He could remember nothing of a tutor, nothing about school. What of his home life in Northumberland? Had he had a happy childhood? Eleanor told him he was an only child, but had he always been interested in ships or had he inherited his father's business as a matter of duty, rather than by choice?

Sleep evaded him. For hours he stared at the ceiling until at last he fell into a troubled, uneasy sleep. He dreamt he was a wicked, evil man who was jeered at in the street. He dreamt he harboured a secret, a dark secret which was buried deep in his unconscious. He dreamt of a fight, a tussle, a gunshot. He dreamt he was a prisoner in the dock charged with murder. He heard men shout “Guilty as charged”. There was a noose around his neck. He woke gasping for air and bathed in sweat.

R

Eleanor sat bolt upright in bed. Gabriel was looming over her.

‘I had a memory, or possibly a dream.’ He sat on the edge of her bed looking as excited as a little boy on Christmas morning.

‘A memory, what was it?’ Perhaps he had remembered their first kiss, their wedding day or perhaps one of the children being born.

‘It was strange. I was riding on a beach in a storm, lightning flashed and thunder roared. I slid off my horse and held her big copper head, then stroked her velvety muzzle.’

‘Gabriel this is tremendous, although not at all flattering you remember your horse over me or the children. The description sounds like your beloved horse Copper. Go on.’

‘The rest is more alarming, a feeling rather than an actual event. I remember I sank onto the sand, put my head in my hands and sobbed, not manly but there it is. All I remember was feeling deep despair, like I wanted to lie down and die.’

‘Oh my love, last night I wished you sweet dreams not a nightmare.’

‘I’m not sure whether it was a dream or a memory but if you think it was my horse?’

‘We weren’t married at the time, but you told me about this. I’d hoped to spare you, for the time being at least.’

‘Spare me what? Tell me. I knew I couldn’t be the saint everyone has made me out to be. Was I a wicked man, had I done something to make me so despondent?’

Eleanor plumped her pillows, sat back and began to explain: ‘We’d met and declared ourselves, but we were taking it slowly so as to be sure we were doing the right thing in marrying; both of us had recently broken our engagements.'

'I was engaged to my childhood sweetheart, Caroline, I think you said. It was a match both our parents were keen on as our fathers were best friends and they wanted to join the two families together.' He parroted what she had told him yesterday.

'That's right, but when you went back to Alnmouth there was an incident.' She swallowed hard. 'Jax, your stable lad, had gone missing. He'd been taken by a French captain who had a fondness for young boys. You rescued Jax and in the process punched the captain who hit his head as he fell. He was killed as a result.' Gabriel was horrified. 'You didn't mean to kill him,' she said to reassure him. 'It was an accident. Although you stood trial for manslaughter you were acquitted. Waiting to go to trial you later told me how devastated you were, how low your mood became. You said you wanted to end it all, but the thought of seeing me again gave you hope, kept you going.' She took his hands in hers. 'My love you're not a murderer. You're not a violent man, far from it.'

'You say "later". I assume you didn't come to me, you must have thought me guilty. Why would you want to marry me when I'd done such a despicable thing?'

'It was the Frenchman who was despicable. You saved Jax. Thanks to you he now works at your stud and has a wife, two children and a happy life. Had you not found him, who knows what would have become of him? As for not coming to you, I didn't come as I didn't know about it until later.'

'Was I imprisoned? Did you come to the trial?'

Eleanor took a long steadying breath. 'I was in Amsterdam. You only spent the night before the trial in prison. You were bailed.' She took another deep breath. 'I didn't know of your plight until William Seamer tried to blackmail me. My father was taking him to court for breach of promise, much to my annoyance. To try to wriggle out of the case he threatened to tell Papa about you. William told me about your past, about the manslaughter case and something else.' Eleanor gasped. 'Oh I could bite my tongue off. Now I'll have to tell you about Libby.'

‘Who? What else have I done? I’m beginning to think I’m not as good as everyone makes out.’

‘It was an indiscretion, a youthful alliance that turned out to have repercussions.’

‘Dear God, tell me, put me out of my misery.’

Eleanor wished she had kept her own counsel, she knew he had never come to terms with not seeing his son again. She would have spared him this if she could.

‘As you wish but this is all water under the bridge and I forgave you years ago.’ She took his hand. ‘You met a young woman when you were still at school. I think you said you were eighteen at the time. You met at the bay when she fell on the ice and broke her arm. You were kind to her and took her home, arranged for a doctor. Her father had died and her brother had gambled away their money then killed himself leaving Libby destitute. She’d no one to look to and very little money. You arranged for someone to take care of her when you went back to school. But then when you left school and returned from Alnwick to start work for your father, you began a *liaison* with her. Like many men have done before... she became your mistress.’

He looked shamefaced, clearly not proud of himself, but neither did he appear mortified. ‘There was a child as a result, Steven. But you didn’t find out until after our marriage. It almost broke us. You saw him once then Libby emigrated to America talking Steven with her and you never saw him again. Even though I didn’t condone men keeping mistresses, I still don’t, I forgave you, stood by you when we thought you were going to see your son regularly, but then no sooner had you met him than he was spirited away.’

She watched as Gabriel stood then began to prowl about the room. ‘Man alive, I begin to wish I’ll never recover my memory. What other horror stories of a misspent life await me should I ever get it back?’

Eleanor pulled him down onto the bed and held him close. ‘Gabriel you’re a good man, and a good husband and father. You have a good reputation, your friends stood up for you at the trial, Bendor especially was a support. Everyone knew you were innocent, they all agreed they would have done the same in your shoes. Libby never blamed you either; indeed I think she loved you.'

Gabriel felt heavy in her arms.

'This is such a lot to take in. I've killed a man whether or not I meant to do so is immaterial, I still took a life. And then I made a life, a bastard, and so I'm a father of four, not three as you said before.'

'I didn't want to lie but, I was wrong to tell you about Steven, I should have kept it to myself for now at least. I know you never say so but you miss your son. You keep your hurt hidden so as not to distress me. You *are* a good person. I'm so sorry my love. This is too much information for you to take in. It's too much too soon.'

He moved to the door stiffly. 'I had a bad night I realise. Perhaps I'll see if I can get some sleep, though I feel I'll never sleep again for all the confounded thoughts swimming about in my head. Why the hell can I not remember such momentous life changing events? Why did you not think to tell me all of this before for God's sake?'

Eleanor saw the annoyance, the irritation suddenly flare. Her husband was usually a man slow to anger, it took a lot to rile him, but now she wondered if the bump to the head had changed him. She sought to calm him. 'I'm sorry, but I was at pains not to overwhelm you. You don't want to break your fast? Are you not hungry?'

'Thank you no. I'll go to my bedchamber, please ensure I'm not disturbed.'

Eleanor sank back on the bed then rang for her maid Molly, a tawny-haired plump girl. When her personal maid, Charity, had married and moved back to Whitby Eleanor had trained up the young woman. Molly had been an unmarried mother, rescued from Hope House a charity Eleanor had helped found. She had taken the girl under her wing and she had proved to be worth keeping, she was loyal and hard working. When she arrived Eleanor was almost dressed. 'Can you do my hair quickly please? I'm in no mood to sit about.'

'Of course, how is Mr Gabriel? Is there any change?'

'Sadly not. I want to try and catch Papa before he leaves for the shipyard.'

'Oh, you're too late I'm afraid, he left as I was coming upstairs.'

Eleanor cursed under her breath. Without breaking her fast she rode to the shipyard feeling out of sorts. As she was shown into her father's office she glanced out of the window at the view over Whitby harbour and out to sea. Again it was a warm sunlit day which ordinarily would have lifted her spirits. Today it did nothing to cheer her.

'I'd hoped to catch you earlier.'

'Is something amiss? Gabriel is no worse I hope?'

She told her Papa part of her earlier conversation with her husband; her parents knew about the manslaughter charge, but not that Gabriel had a son with another woman - she kept this part back. 'I hadn't meant to distress him, but he wanted to know what his dream meant and once I'd told half the tale I had to go on, tell him about the trial. I could kick myself.'

'Try not to berate yourself my dear, none of us knows how to behave around him, these are uncharted waters for us all.'

'And then there's Dr Burns. He's a good man, but he's getting on in years. Do you think it worth consulting with someone younger, a specialist perhaps? Wilson Chaffer has studied the mind extensively over the years and is well respected in his field. You've met the doctor at Westshore you'll remember? He helped Jax after his ordeal. I think if we went home we could consult with him, I trust Wilson and he and Gabriel are such good friends. Perhaps Gabriel would remember him?'

'You may be right my dear though I am reluctant to see you to go. You have only Uncle Brown up there in Northumberland whereas here you have your family for support. Your mama will be worried if you go, and then there are the children. Will you take them with you?'

'They would be confused if their papa didn't recognise them, nothing has changed as far as that's concerned. Yet they aren't happy at Attie's. She looks after them well enough of course, but they've been made to go to the Friends' Meeting House and you can imagine how that has gone down with the twins in particular.'

'Do not fret about them my dear. It will make them appreciate the life they have with you and Gabriel all the more.' He kissed her forehead. 'They will come to no harm and it may even do them some good.'

'I wonder if Tomas and Cora might have them for a while, until Gabriel gets his memory back.' Eleanor, on the verge of tears, was wrapped in the warm embrace of her father.

'He will recover my dear, never fear. Go home and pack and I will ask if the twins can move to Westcliff House if you think they would be happier there. Your sister-in-law will adore having them to stay I know. Or they can come back to Mulgrave House when you leave if you would rather? Allow me to arrange your transport back to Alnmouth if that would be of help.'

Later as Eleanor and Molly packed, Anne Barker was insisting she come to Northumberland too.

'Ordinarily I'd love you to visit, but I should feel easier if you stayed here then the children can come and visit you and Papa. The twins are such a handful; Cora will need all the help she can get and Rose is so bewildered... she misses Gabriel, misses her papa. She'll want both of you in our stead I know. I've told her Gabriel is much better, but that he can't see her or the boys as he tires easily. She thinks, rightly of course, that I'm keeping something from her. She's as sharp as a pin. Please Mama will you do as I ask?'

'Of course I will my dear. Do not worry about the children we will all do our best to divert them.'

'Thank you Mama that is such a relief to me. I'll go and see if Gabriel has woken, he was sound asleep when I looked in an hour ago.'

Gabriel was up and dressed but looked tired and drawn. He hadn't shaved and his hair needed combing.

'You're awake, good. I've had an idea my love.' She smiled reassuringly. 'In Alnmouth you have a good friend, Wilson Chaffer. He's a doctor. I thought we might go home and consult him. He's young and experienced in matters of the mind. I think he'd be of more help to you than Dr Burns. What do you think?'

'He's a head doctor? Madam, are you considering having me committed?' At first she thought he was in jest then saw he was in earnest. Anger furrowed his brow. Eleanor was shocked and horrified at his tone.

'Gabriel! How can think such a thing? Wilson has studied the mind and how it works; he helped enormously with your groom's recovery. He may be able to help you too. I hoped you'd be pleased.'

'He has to be better than Burns. He's a charlatan if ever I saw one.'

Eleanor was unused to Gabriel's censure. It shocked her to hear him berate the trusted family doctor in such a disrespectful way but she swallowed her disappointment.

'Papa's arranging our transport home. Shall I ask Walters to pack for you?'

'So it's all planned. All arranged. No need then to pretend to consult with me, your *husband.* I see I'm to follow my wife's orders.' He glowered. 'Tell me when to be ready and I'll be there.' Without further discourse he left the room.

Eleanor stared after him in bewilderment. The look on his face stunned her temporarily, then she bethought herself and ran after him.

'Gabriel wait.' He stopped at the top of the staircase but kept his back to her. She saw his shoulders drop as he expelled a long, irritated breath. She caught up with him. 'Enough! How dare you speak to me in such a manner? I'm doing the best I can, we all are. I can't imagine how frightening this is for you, but it's doing no one any good behaving like a spoilt child. I've spent all day organising our departure, placating the children who are worried about you and this is how you repay me. I've written to Wilson and told him to expect us. I'm trying to understand, but I don't know what to do for the best.'

'Madam, have you quite finished? I've said I'll be ready what more do you want? I presume you promised to obey your husband on our wedding day did you not? Then please obey me now and leave me be.'

She watched as he almost ran down the stairs and out of the door. It was as if he couldn't wait to be out of her sight.

Eleanor slumped down on the top step and put her head in her hands; never in their entire married life had her husband spoken to her in such a cold way. The rage on his face as he looked at her! They had argued in the past, of course they had, all married couples had disagreements but he had never been boorish. They had argued, but he had always respected her opinion. It had to be said he did so begrudgingly sometimes, but they had always had an equal partnership, always shown deference for each other's point of view. This man was someone she hardly recognised. Would he continue in this vain? Last night when she had gone to his room he was like his old self, warm and loving, kind. But now he was changed again, so different.

She went to her room to finish supervising her packing. She hoped when he saw Westshore, the boyhood home he treasured, it might help him to recover his memory, jolt him back to his old self. Once back in Alnmouth with Bendor, she hoped his mind would get the push it needed to get better. She hoped his temper would return to being even and under control. The sooner they returned to Westshore the better.

3

The journey north by road and sea was uneventful. Gabriel was more like his old self and was for the most part even-tempered and affable. For the last leg of the journey they took one of their own ships, the Alnmouth Boy. Gabriel spent much time with his bemused crew who of course, he didn't recognise. They were tolerant of his questions and answered with good humour and not a little concern. As they docked at Alnmouth, Eleanor and Gabriel stood on deck.

'Sam is with the horses by your office, that's good. At least we'll be able to get straight home without waiting for the horses to be brought.'

'Sam?'

'Sam is the groom we hired to replace Joe. There was a time a few years ago when several of our staff decided to leave all at the same time. My long standing maid, Charity, fell in love with our groom, Joe. They married and moved back to her home town of Whitby. I went to see her last week; she's with child again and incredibly happy. Ivy the housemaid moved to work at Hope House, the charity for women I helped found. Do you remember I told you about her? She delivered the twins.'

Gabriel nodded as they walked along the quay. 'We have two indoor servants Ransom and Carver. Ransom is the butler, he's been with us the longest and Carver is a footman. Dora replaced Ivy as general housemaid, Mrs Madison is our cook and Connie her under cook, is walking out with your man Jonty Walters... possibly. He's a bit of a Jack the Lad. I hope Connie has come to her senses whilst Jonty has been in Whitby with us. Then there's Ginny the children's nursemaid who you've met and last but not least Lisbet and Abner.'

'And what do they do?'

'Not much these days. They were your father's old retainers but then you had a falling out with Abner, he'd hidden smuggled tea on our land so you sacked him. Both he and Lisbet left under a bit of a cloud. She couldn't stay without Abner of course but you always regretted the loss, even though you were quite right to dismiss him. Then five or so years ago Jax found where they were living and told you. You gave them a cottage by the Long Paddock, at the back of Westshore, so they could see out their old age in relative comfort. You all forgave each other. Lisbet does the odd bit of sewing for the children and Abner still loves his smokehouse, so we always have kippers.'

'Very generous of me to take them back,' Gabriel smiled, 'what had Jax to do with it, why did he go looking for them?'

'I believe you asked him to. You were always especially fond of Lisbet. She brought you up when your mother died. She is, shall we say, an acquired taste.'

They had reached Sam and the horses. Both Jet and Copper shook their heads and snickered in recognition. Eleanor stroked Jet's neck and whispered endearments. It was well over six weeks since she had seen her horse and she had missed him. Copper nudged Gabriel with her big, handsome head and snuffled in his pocket.

Eleanor handed Gabriel an apple. 'This is what she's after. You always have one for her, she loves apples.'

He twisted it in his strong hands and fed half to Copper and the other half to Jet.

'Oh Gabriel how is it you know such things? You always twist the apple in half like that, though she usually gets the whole of it. You remember old habits, but can't remember people and places. It's most peculiar is it not?'

Gabriel stroked Copper's neck. 'This is the horse I saw in my dream. I sense we're friends by the way she is with me.'

'You always say an ill-treated animal remembers his beating. You're fond of animals, as am I, speaking of which we have a welcome party.'

A grey whippet and a scruffy looking black terrier appeared tails wagging furiously. The terrier began to bark and turn circles on his hind legs. Gabriel bent to tug the ear of the dog fondly. 'I take it you're part of the family too you old fleabag?'

'Scrabble was resident ratter on your ships, but is retired. His son Scrabble Junior now has the role. Scrabble senior has developed a mellow outlook recently. He has learned that bones don't have to be chased after whereas rats do. He doesn't stray too far from hearth and home these days; he must have known you were returning. Do you remember them? This is Slate. My father bought her for me years ago. She too is long in the tooth.'

'Sorry, I don't recognise either of them, but they know me alright.' Gabriel stroked each dog affectionately.

Once mounted their horses needed no urging, Eleanor and Gabriel began the short ride home. As Westshore came into view Eleanor watched her husband closely to see if he recognised the house he loved so passionately. She held her breath.

'What a fine looking house and so near the seashore, I'd wager there's a view of the bay from most of the rooms.'

Eleanor's face dropped.

'What is it? What have I said?'

'It's what you haven't said my love. The house is Westshore your family home. I was longing for you to remember it.'

R

After dinner Carver announced Sir Bendor Percy. He strode in, grabbed Gabriel by the hand and pulled him into a bear hug as he always did.

'I hear you've been in the wars Gabe. Lord those stitches will leave a scar, that'll spoil your handsome face.' He held his friend at arm's length and grinned.

Where Gabriel was dark Bendor was fair. The two men were of equal height, but over the years Bendor had filled out more than Gabriel who still had a well-muscled physique.

'Eleanor wrote to say you've lost your memory, surely you can't fail to know me? Haven't we known each other man and boy, since we were eleven?'

Eleanor's heart was about to break. There was no recognition on her husband's face. She knew Gabriel was disappointed too. He had told her earlier he felt sure he would know Bendor when he saw him.

'I'm told it's temporary so I'm sure in the fullness of time I'll be urging you to overdo the brandy. My wife tells me we're each as bad as the other and that our drinking bouts are legendary.' Eleanor saw Gabriel smile, but he looked ill at ease as Bendor put his arm around his shoulders. 'I can't tell you how strange it feels when everyone knows all about me, yet I know nothing of the people I meet. You could all be a bunch of reprobates for all I know,' he said trying for levity.

'Ah, see Eleanor, he has the measure of me, even if he says he doesn't know me he recognises a kindred spirit, the spirit in question being brandy or at a push a good Jamaican rum, preferably one that's not had duty paid on it.'

'Would you care to have some time together? You can tell Gabriel about his misspent youth, Grace and I have heard the tales more than once.' She rolled her eyes pretending disdain. 'I'll send the brandy to the library.'

An hour later Bendor came to find Eleanor. 'I must be off my dear. I've a meeting in Alnwick.' His brow furrowed. 'How strange it is to sit and talk to my oldest friend about the past, a past he knows nothing about. He remembers none of it at all! Dear Lord I hope he gets his memory back soon. I can see how frustrated he is, I would feel the same.' He held her hands in his. 'I've assured Gabe everything is running smoothly at the stud and of course you're more than capable of managing the shipping line but if you need anything, any help, let me know. Not that I think you need assistance. You know more about shipping than I ever will. At least he can rest easy knowing his businesses are in good hands. That's something is it not?'

'Thank you Bendor. We're all perturbed; patience has never been one of my strong points.' She smiled up at him. 'It is a blessing the businesses will be looked after but there's the deal with Padraic Turner which Gabriel has in the offing. When we went to Amsterdam the deal was almost done, but Gabriel wanted to check out one or two of the finer points. He didn't discuss it with me so I don't know what was bothering him about the contract, and of course he doesn't remember the contract at all, let alone the details. Tomorrow I'll call and see Saul Coates and hope Gabriel shared his concerns with his lawyer, but I doubt it. If he didn't tell me I can't see him telling Saul.'

'Let's hope Wilson has some ideas about how to get the old Gabriel back to us, for all our sakes. It must be as annoying as hell for Gabriel having everything explained to him. I know it would drive me quite mad.'

Eleanor shuffled uncomfortably. 'Besides his loss of memory how did you find him? Did you notice other differences?'

'Like what? I noticed he looked tired now you come to mention it.'

'How often have you seen Gabriel lose his temper - hardly ever is the answer. It takes a lot to rile my husband and I should know, but since the accident he's on an extremely short fuse. Only this morning I heard him ranting at poor Walters. When I asked Jonty what all the fuss was about he said Gabriel had called him a "bloody fool" for not putting out the clothes he wanted. That's not like my husband; he never loses his rag with servants, especially about something so trivial like which waistcoat he wears.'

Eleanor told Bendor how Gabriel had asked her to remember her vow of obedience when he had lost his temper in Whitby.

'It's obviously a side effect of the knock to the head, but asking you of all people to know your place would be funny in the extreme if it weren't for the circumstances, he must feel exasperated poor chap. Try not to worry Eleanor, all things must pass and one way or another this matter will be resolved. He'll recover I'm sure.'

'I hope so. In the meantime I'll try not to provoke him; an angry Gabriel is a scary proposition. I've never been frightened of my husband. He's the kindest, gentlest of men as you can testify yet - '

'He wouldn't hurt you. Even if you provoked him he's still a gentleman. No gentleman strikes his wife. I can't believe we're having this conversation about *Gabe*. There's no better man, no man more peaceable.'

'Yet he hit out at the French captain.'

'That was different *and* it was an accident. He didn't mean to kill him. In all the years I've known him I've never seen him pick a fight, even when goaded. He was too scared of spoiling his looks.' Bendor was trying to make her smile. 'I can see you're worried Eleanor. Would you like to come and stay at Dunstanburgh, both of you of course; a few days might ease your burden?'

'Gabriel isn't a burden but no, no, I'm over reacting. I've been used to living with a gentle bear of a man and now, well most of the time he's affable, his old self, but then something upsets him and the look on his face. It's something I've never witnessed before.'

'Nor I. Obviously you've told Wilson of this? Do you feel unsafe even with the servants about? Perhaps you should warn them in case he flies off the handle again, ask them to make allowances.'

Eleanor brushed aside his fears as she saw Bendor to the door. 'Where is Gabriel? He will want to bid you farewell.'

'He said he felt tired, he's gone to rest. I presume that's another side effect. I never knew a man who could keep going on so little or no sleep, but now he seems changed, I'm sure it's temporary.' He kissed her cheek. 'Try not to worry. Grace will call in a day or so.'

After Bendor left Westshore, Eleanor collected the mountain of correspondence which had accumulated in their absence and took it to the study she shared with her husband. She began to sort it into piles. There were the inevitable bills from merchants, some outstanding orders to be dealt with from the sail makers and joiners. There were also applications from tutors.

Before going away they had decided to hire a tutor for the children. Rose could read and write of course and was as bright as a button but the twins were a different matter. They too were sharp as knives, but being younger were less inclined to learn their letters.

Eleanor and Gabriel had discussed it and decided a tutor should be hired for all three children. Both were in agreement that Rose would receive the exact same instruction as the boys, though the twins would need a firmer hand it had to be said. Eleanor had been educated by the Friends and greatly valued her schooling. She wanted the same opportunities, if not better, for her own daughter. She believed strongly women should have the same life chances as men.

She read the applications then sat back and squeezed the bridge of her nose with her forefinger and thumb. One or two of the applicants looked well qualified, but one in particular stood out. She would discuss it with... Oh dear, would Gabriel remember or even care what they had decided? He hardly remembered he was a father. It hurt Eleanor he had never asked about his children since the accident, it was as if they didn't exist. To all intents and purposes they were out of sight and out of mind to him. Again this was so different from the man she loved. He cared deeply about them ordinarily. He played with them, was affectionate and even taught Rose to read, she could add up columns of figures and of course he taught all of them to swim. Not many men of their acquaintance gave their children their undivided attention as he did, even after long hours at the bay or stud.

Eleanor, almost at the end of the correspondence, felt her head beginning to ache. She broke the seal on a legal looking document. When she read it she wished she hadn't opened it.

R

As was now the custom, Eleanor and Gabriel slept separately. So when Dr Wilson Chaffer arrived early the next morning Eleanor was unsure if Gabriel was awake or not.

The sleeping arrangements were at Gabriel's insistence, well not insistence exactly more at his request. He maintained until he could remember who she was he would feel strange sharing a bed. This upset Eleanor greatly, though she understood his reasoning. 'Of course you know who I am, I'm your lawful wedded wife. Do you not believe me?'

Gabriel had sighed but she noted, thankfully, he hadn't lost his temper. 'Imagine if the boot were on the other foot,' he had said. 'Would you want to share *my* bed if you didn't recognise me as your husband? I know it must be odd to you and it's not as though I don't want to... I'm a red blooded man.' He had scraped his thumb down his jaw and given her a sidelong look.

Eleanor had tried to see the funny side. 'Do you fear I'll take advantage of you? If that's the case I can assure you it's too late for that.'

When Wilson was shown into the breakfast room he accepted the coffee she offered. 'I'd hoped you would have broken your fast by now, sorry Eleanor to arrive at the crack of dawn. I'm eager to see Gabriel for the sooner I can speak with him the sooner I can begin to help him.'

'I'm sure you will Wilson, the situation is becoming untenable.' She rang for Walters and asked him to tell Gabriel the doctor was here. She had written to Wilson from Whitby, but now she told him in more detail about Gabriel's accident and her husband's subsequent memory loss. She also told him about his recent ill tempered behaviour.

'You say he has flashes of anger? This isn't uncommon in such cases; in fact I'd have been surprised had he not these secondary symptoms. It all depends where the knock to the head occurred. You say it was the temple where the crate hit him. Was there another knock, did he hit his head as he fell to the ground?'

'Tomas said not. Gabriel pushed Tomas out of the way and landed on top of him. My brother broke his fall.'

Gabriel entered the breakfast room and Eleanor waited to see if he remembered his friend. He did not.

'Good morning, I'm Doctor Chaffer. I hope I'll be able to help you recover your memory.' He smiled amiably. 'One thing I can help you with is those stitches. They must be causing you discomfort, they've done their job and can come out now.'

Wilson shook hands with his patient. Eleanor thought it odd to see the two men so formal with each other. Wilson had known Gabriel longer than she had.

'You're the head doctor I take it?' Gabriel was impatient. He sat and poured himself coffee tapping the spoon on the saucer.

'Actually I practise general medicine, but the brain and its function is an interest of mine.'

'An amateur quack then?'

He shot a look of exasperation at his wife. She hoped he wasn't going to be quarrelsome or rude.

'I've studied in London and Vienna, so although I don't profess to know everything there is to know, I've acquired enough knowledge to see results from my work. I'm sorry to arrive so early, but with your permission I'm keen to get started before I begin my rounds.'

'As you say you can begin by getting rid of these damnable stitches, they itch like mad.'

'May I suggest we go to your dressing room? We can talk as I work.'

After two hours Eleanor was wondering why Wilson hadn't come to find her. She went to Gabriel's room, knocked and entered. Gabriel lay on the bed as if asleep. Wilson signalled to her to come in. He talked quietly to Gabriel, then stood and escorted her from the room and down the stairs. She waited to hear what Wilson had to say.

'After I'd removed the stitches I examined Gabriel and then talked to him about a technique I wanted to try. At first he was resistant, quite unlike his usual open minded self, but I expected that from what you'd said earlier.'

'A technique, what sort of technique?'

'You will have noticed Gabriel looked as though he was sleeping, but in fact he was in a deep meditative state. It's an ancient method. A sort of trance-like state is induced and then I make suggestions to his inner mind. It is often quite responsive then. Gabriel wasn't against it once we began, and I'm quietly confident we shall see some improvement.'

'He'll get his memory back do you mean?'

'Not immediately, no. It will take further sessions, but he

responded quite quickly so I'm optimistic. I've asked him to stay quiet for as long as possible. If he falls into a natural sleep then so be it. We shall see. I will call later this afternoon to see how he is.'

When Wilson left, Eleanor crept back into the bedchamber where Gabriel was indeed asleep. She looked at his handsome face. The cut would probably leave a small scar, but his curls would cover most of it. She didn't care a fig, and neither would he. All that mattered was that he got better.

She decided to leave him. She could be of no use sitting by the bed. She went to the study to write to Ginny. Eleanor had decided the house was far too quiet without her children, so she thought to send a letter saying they should return to Westshore as soon as possible. She would somehow have to try to explain to them about their papa's memory loss and hope they would come to terms with it. It was one thing having a husband who appeared absent for some of the time, quite another to be without her children. She missed them dearly. At least if she had them with her it would be a consolation. Eleanor had just finished writing when Lisbet popped her head around the door.

'A've come to see how Mr Gabriel is, we did hear about his accident.'

Eleanor told Gabriel's old housekeeper what had happened.

'An' he can't remember anythin' yer say, not even you an' the bairns?' Eleanor was about to tell her about the prognosis when Gabriel strode into the room. He was smiling broadly.

'Lisbet. Have you come with beef tea? Or have you made me one of your vile tasting concoctions?'

Eleanor was astounded. 'My love you recognise Lisbet? Wilson said your progress may be slow. I'm astonished.'

He looked from one to the other. 'I remember Lisbet scrubbing me under the pump until I was red raw and I remember a time I went missing and I got a clip around the ear when I was found. Why I was keen to go to Berwick heaven knows.'

'You deserved it an' all.' Lisbet chuckled and told Eleanor the story. 'He wanted to go with Jack to Berwick but his pa said he'd to stay an' do his lessons with the tutor, young Mr Scrivens. Do yer remember him?'

'I do, he was a sound fellow, a good artist I think.'

Lisbet continued: 'So this tyke takes the huff and disappears. We thought he'd be back at dinner time, he allus liked his snap, but dinner time came and went an' we started to fret. What if he'd been pressed, or stowed away on a ship? Everybody were out lookin' fer him, on the beach, in the dunes, at the bay but he'd disappeared off the face of the earth.'

Eleanor was overjoyed to see Gabriel laughing like his old self.

'So where was he?'

Lisbet looked at Gabriel who took up the story. 'As Lisbet said I was sulking. It was a scorching hot day so I went for a swim to cheer myself up. When I came back ashore I climbed into the rowing boat to dry off, then the sun was burning hot so I pulled the tarpaulin over to allow me a little shade... and fell asleep.'

'He could sleep for England that lad, he were about eleven at the time. How he never heard folk shoutin' him A'll never know. Then Abner went down to the beach an' happened to think to look in the boat an' there he were! Naked, an' fast asleep. As Mr Gabriel says he got a clip round the ear an' no supper. It were growin' dark by the time we found him. A were in a right lather A can tell yer.'

'To be fair Lisbet you were "in a lather" for most of my childhood.'

They sat drinking tea and reminiscing when Gabriel suddenly looked at Eleanor. 'Yet it's a puzzle why I can't remember our courtship or our wedding day is it not my love?'

Eleanor saw the sadness in his eyes and tried to console him. 'Wilson explained to me how you might be feeling. He said it's like when you put something down and can't remember where you put it. The more you try to remember the more elusive the object becomes. Then if you occupy yourself with something else the memory suddenly surfaces and you remember where the missing object is.'

'Yes the doctor, for I still can't remember he's supposed to be a good friend, says not to try to force the memories. He says in time they'll come back. He counselled me to be patient, but it's difficult, frustrating.'

'But remembering Lisbet is a breakthrough is it not?'

'A'm not easy to ferget am A?' his old housekeeper said a wicked twinkle in her eye.

After Lisbet left, when they were at supper Eleanor listened while Gabriel told her about the treatment. 'I remember laying on the bed and Chaffer talking to me quietly, though I cannot for the life of me remember what he was saying. All I know is I wasn't asleep, I was aware of my surroundings, but I felt my limbs grow heavy. It was as if I couldn't lift them even if my life depended on it. When I came round I felt as if I'd had the best rest of my life. It was most strange.'

'When Wilson came earlier he said he was pleased with your progress so far, though he cautioned there's a long way to go.'

'Another thing I think is a real memory, and not something you've told me is a song. It keeps going around my head, together with an image of a baby in a long, cream, lace gown. One of the children perhaps?'

'What song? Was it about a hat by any chance?'

'How did you guess?'

'On the morning Rose was christened she wore your old christening gown, but she was sick down it. While poor Ginny was cleaning it you put Rose in your tricorn and sang the song, "My hat has three corners".'

'That's it, that's the one.' He took her hand. 'I take it by the look on your face I'm not a good singer.'

'Not especially, but I'm so pleased my love. That's the first time you have remembered your daughter.'

'I think you should send for them to come home. Who knows by the time they arrive I may have recovered.'

'Wilson warned you to be patient, try not to press too hard.'

'I'll try.'

She saw him look thoughtful. 'What is it my love?'

'This must be trying for you. I may not remember most details, but some things are coming back to me... about you.'

'Such as?'

'Such as whatever you're thinking is written for all to see on your face. You aren't good at hiding your feelings. Once or twice since the accident I've hurt you, upset you. I'm sorry if I've been out of sorts. It's been a challenging time for both of us yet now Chaffer has given me leave to *be* it feels as though a weight has been lifted. I'm so sorry Eleanor; I'll endeavour to make it up to you.'

'Good, I should hope so. Would you like apple tart? Lisbet made it especially.'

'Do I like apple tart?'

'I'll let you make your own mind up, but if Lisbet sees you've left any she'll undoubtedly fetch you a clip around the ear.'

'In that case pass the cream my love.'

𝒭

Gabriel was in the conservatory staring out to sea. Standing at his full height he was, tall, handsome and distinguished. He looked lean and strong in his tight fitting riding breeches and long boots. Dark curls touched the high collar of his coat. He pulled on his waistcoat front so it sat on his trim waist.

When he realised Eleanor was behind him watching, he turned and smiled. She stepped closer. She couldn't look away from his warm, smiling eyes. He continued to gaze at her, searching her face, her mouth as if he would kiss her. Then she saw he remembered himself, remembered the gentleman he was and looked away, back out to sea. Eleanor felt the disappointment.

She applauded his principles, but longed for him to take her in his arms and kiss her. She could hardly resist from taking the initiative herself as she so often did.

'I take it I'm a good sailor?' That laconic smile again.

'And a good rower. You rowed for your school along with Bendor.'

'The rowing boat which is pulled up on the beach is sound?'

'It is, we use it often in spring and summer.'

‘Do you have time to... but perhaps you have things to be getting on with?’

‘I’d love to come out with you Gabriel, but I have a meeting regarding Hope House this morning. Three or four ladies will be arriving shortly, another day perhaps.’

Gabriel looked towards the bay. ‘There’s a lady riding this way now.’

Eleanor stood beside her husband and followed his gaze. ‘It’s Lottie Lambton, or I should say Lottie Chaffer. She married Wilson three years ago after an extremely long courtship. She’s a trustee of the charity; she’s coming to the meeting.’

‘She’s the doctor’s wife?’

‘She is though she’s nothing like what you might expect a doctor’s wife to be like. She’s quite singular.’ Eleanor chuckled.

‘Do I like her?’

‘You do, though when you first met you thought her a little outspoken. You were convinced she was too flighty for Wilson, but they’re happy together, opposites attract I suppose. She too has an interest in medicine; she likes nothing better than reading Wilson’s medical tomes. Often at Hope House we don’t call Wilson out for minor problems as Lottie can treat most simple cases. Not that he charges us of course. Wilson does all the work for the charity Pro Bono.’

‘A lady doctor. She is indeed singular.’

‘Well, not a doctor exactly, she’s self taught, not qualified in any way of course, but she’s knowledgeable.’

Lottie saw them and waved as Sam appeared to help her from her horse.

‘Gabriel, so good to see you. I’m sorry I’ve not called before but I was away from home when you came back from Whitby. Nasty scar, was it a butcher that sewed you up?’ She offered her hand to be kissed. ‘I’m Lottie Chaffer, I don’t expect you remember me though some may say once seen never forgot.’

Eleanor saw Gabriel look confused. She realised each new situation, each new person was an ordeal for him. She was never sure what mood he would be in or how he would react. It was beginning to set her nerves on edge. Yesterday he had been sullen and morose. He had snapped and been argumentative over trifling matters he would ordinarily ignore. Today she was relieved to see he appeared undisturbed by yet another stranger in his midst.

'Your servant Mrs Chaffer.' He bowed low. 'It appears I can only remember my horse and my old housekeeper I'm afraid.' He smiled at Lottie in what was his usual charming fashion. 'I look forward to my next session with your husband later today. His optimism gives me hope.'

'A horse and an old retainer? How interesting. Perhaps therein lies meaning though Lord knows what it is. You always call me Lottie by the way.' Lottie raised a perfectly plucked eyebrow. Her dark good looks appealed to most men. Gabriel was no exception.

'I see more attendees arriving.' Gabriel moved to the French window. 'I'll leave you to your business ladies.' He strode out into the garden.

Eleanor looked at her friend and sighed. 'Poor lamb; he doesn't know what to do with himself. He's been to his office and countersigned documents and read though a few more, but it's all Greek to him. Hopefully he'll soon be back at the helm but as yet, well he feels... lost.'

'Time is a healer, take heart Eleanor. Wilson is confident after the first few sessions Gabriel will regain all of his faculties. If love could cure him he would be better already.'

After the meeting and when her visitors had left Eleanor went in search of her husband. Ransom told her he was with Dr Chaffer so Eleanor called for a cordial and sat to wait in the conservatory. She looked out at the sun glinting on the sea; it was such a glorious day. She wished the children were here. They would have been playing, shouting and careering about on the beach. She missed them. Perhaps when they returned they could all go out in the rowing boat. The children might give Gabriel a purpose until he was recovered fully. The thought filled her with hope.

Wilson came to her and said once again the session had been

productive and that Gabriel was resting. 'Although this time he was a little more restive, not quite able to surrender, I gave him laudanum which helped.'

'Yet he was in a bright, sunny mood earlier. Like the Gabriel we all know and love.'

'The mind is a curious thing. What lies beneath the surface is a different affair altogether.'

At Eleanor's insistence they chatted of other matters for a while, then Wilson said he must continue his rounds.

'Before I go I meant to mention something to you yesterday; Susan Stubbs is unwell, a lung condition.'

'Oh no, how sad. Of course with being away and then Gabriel's accident I haven't seen her in a while. I'll try to visit her later in the week.'

'Don't wait too long.'

'Really, she's that poorly? I always liked Caroline's godmother. She's been a great help with Hope House as you know.'

'She won't see another summer I'm afraid. She's also been a benefactor of the hospital. She'll be sorely missed and not just for her money.'

No sooner had Wilson taken his leave than another visitor was announced. Captain Padraic Turner, rakishly good looking swaggered into the conservatory and bowed.

'Eleanor at last you've returned, I thought you quite lost to me.' His lips lingered on her hand for a moment longer than was proper. 'I've missed you of course, but where the devil has your husband been? A month he said and the deal would be struck. It's been over six weeks. Time is money and I've been sitting in this God forsaken place twiddling my thumbs.' His Irish brogue resounded about the room.

'Did you not get the letter I sent telling you of Gabriel's accident? We couldn't leave Whitby any sooner, indeed he's still not fully recovered.'

'I did, but I still expected you sooner than this. Where is he? Can I see him? We need to get the documents signed once and for all. I have them with me.'

Eleanor noticed the captain didn't enquire after her husband's health. There was never any love lost between the two men since they had fallen out over Padraic's flirtatious behaviour when he had made a pass at her years ago. To compound matters the buccaneering captain had married Gabriel's old flame Caroline Hodgeson. Gabriel had never quite forgiven him for it.

One day not many months after her marriage, Caroline had been out riding on the beach when her horse was spooked by a black hound which had run out of the dunes. She had fallen from her horse and been knocked unconscious. Two days later she died from her injuries; she had suffered a broken back. Caroline had lost the baby she was expecting and her life; she had died long before her time. Gabriel had been furious with her for eloping with Turner in the first place and then furious in turn with the captain when she had died. Gabriel had known Caroline all his life and had tried to dissuade her from the match fearing Turner was a fortune hunter. Caroline was heir to Thomas Hodgeson's shipping empire so that when she died her new husband inherited a large fortune. Now Captain Turner was a particularly wealthy man.

Since Caroline's death Turner had spent little time at the Hodgeson's mansion at Eastshore. Some of the time he had been in his home city of Dublin then for more than two years he had been in the Carolinas and then in Virginia. He came back fired up with enthusiasm for the growing trade in tobacco. He was keen to emigrate and start a new enterprise.

On his return he had made Gabriel a proposal; he had offered him first refusal on the shipping side of the business - three ships to add to Gabriel's own fleet. Turner wanted a quick sale so he might invest in the tobacco trade. He had always been a maverick and liked the idea of setting up in a new country.

Gabriel had been surprised at the offer for they both knew Turner hated him. The captain had said he wanted him to have the opportunity as he knew Gabriel had been close to Caroline's father, Thomas. Gabriel wasn't fooled for a second by this statement. He recognised Padraic knew a private sale would be quicker than if he sold on the open market. He suspected there was a reason he wanted to get to America quickly. He had been known to have shady dealings in the past both with the excise men, there were rumours of smuggling runs, gambling and with women.

The sale had almost been completed then Gabriel had decided to take advantage of the cooling off period and said he would sign on his return from holidaying in Amsterdam. Padraic's quick sale wasn't so quick after all and he was put out.

'We can at least conclude the deal on Eastshore,' Eleanor said trying to pacify the Irishman. 'We don't need Gabriel for that.' She was keen to stall him on the matter of the ships. She knew Gabriel was incapable of making an informed decision.

Excluded from the original sale was the Hodgeson's large, but gloomy Tudor mansion. The captain had said he planned to rent it out. Then Eleanor had persuaded him to sell it to her. She knew when the boys were born that the eldest, Haydan, would inherit Westshore. She thought it grossly unfair that Ruari wouldn't have a home of his own; being born twenty minutes later than his brother had disenfranchised him.

Eleanor was a businesswoman in her own right and had sold most of her investments to raise the capital to buy Eastshore for her younger son. In the meantime, until Ruari reached his majority, she would rent out the house and think of it as an asset.

'Do you have the documents with you?'

'Grand Eleanor, I do.'

She sat to sign the papers. Being an astute businesswoman she wanted to re-read the documents first to make sure nothing had been changed. She held the small print at arm's length and read the deed of sale.

Padraic never missed an opportunity to stand too close to her. It was irritating. She finished reading and signed with a flourish. He took the quill and leaned over to countersign.

'At last, she's all yours.' He put his hands on her shoulders and craftily sealed the deal with a kiss.

At that moment Gabriel walked through the door.

'What in God's name - '

'My love - '

Gabriel grabbed Turner by the throat. 'I do believe that's my wife you're manhandling sir.' Their faces were inches apart.

'Stop it! Gabriel please calm down.' She tugged at his sleeve as Turner tried to free himself from Gabriel's iron grip. The captain was turning a nasty shade of puce, his eyes bulging. Gabriel squeezed harder then Turner managed to push Gabriel back. Suddenly Gabriel let go and took two steps back. He looked shocked and astonished at his own behaviour. Turner straightened his neckcloth and tried to his regain his composure.

'Not *that* ill then,' the captain said sardonically. 'What the hell's wrong with you?'

'Perhaps this behaviour is not unusual, this over familiarity with my wife?' Gabriel advanced again. 'Perhaps you cuckold me in my own home regularly sir.' Gabriel shot a look at Eleanor, fury simmering under the surface.

'Gabriel you're not yourself.' Eleanor stepped between the two men as Padraic went to punch Gabriel in the face. The punch missed as Eleanor ducked but it knocked her off balance. She almost fell. Gabriel caught her and moved her out of harm's way but this fresh assault only fuelled Gabriel's anger. He lunged at Padraic and sent him reeling across the desk. His fist hit Turner's chin, then he went for his throat again. Eleanor, frightened, rang for help. There was nothing she could do against his might. She had never seen him so angry.

When Carver saw what was happening he shouted for Walters. The two servants struggled to hold Gabriel, but eventually pulled him off Turner's prone figure. The captain's nose was bleeding and his lip cut. He wiped the blood away on his sleeve.

'Please take my husband upstairs and send for Dr Chaffer... quickly.'

Gabriel continued to struggle and was offering to call Turner out. Eleanor was shaking.

The captain began to recover himself. 'What the hell's got into him?'

'I'm sorry Padraic. What I failed to tell you in my letter is that Gabriel has lost his memory. I'd hoped he would have recovered it by the time we returned. As you witnessed he's not himself, the knock on the head has changed him. You of all people know he's not a violent man, you've provoked him often enough in the past, but he's never offered any weapon against you save words.'

She poured them both a drink, her nerves still unsteady. Turner drank his whisky off in a draught.

'Please Padraic accept my apology on my husband's behalf. Gabriel has been making progress these last few days, but now he's regressed.'

'Are you sure you're safe with him? He needs committing to the asylum if you ask me.'

'I'm not asking you and I thank you to keep your opinions to yourself. Gabriel was provoked. You were taking liberties - again. Had my husband not intervened I would have restrained you myself. You go too far Padraic. Now if you will excuse me.'

Eleanor rang for Ransom. 'Please show Captain Turner out. He's leaving. I'll be in touch regarding the shipping contract though I can't see how the matter can be resolved to everyone's satisfaction at this point in time. Perhaps you need to consider putting the business up for sale on the open market? I wouldn't blame you under the circumstances.' She swept from the room and ran up the stairs to her husband's rooms.

R

'What came over me I cannot say, I saw red when I saw the scoundrel with Eleanor.'

'There's a history between you two, bad blood. Not violence, but he'll never be your favourite person,' Wilson said. 'Once he's on the other side of the world I imagine you'll be a different man.'

'I swore to myself after my encounter with the Frenchman I'd never sink to physical violence again, no matter how I was provoked but I was incensed when he had his lips on my wife.'

The doctor folded his arms and smiled.

'What the devil are you smirking at, what's so amusing?'

Wilson didn't take offence at Gabriel's outburst. 'You said "you swore after the encounter...". You remember making the pact with yourself then?'

'Man alive, I do. Of course I only know of the manslaughter charge because Eleanor told me about it, but she didn't know of the promise I made to myself. No one did.'

'Well then that's progress of sorts. It's another memory to add to your growing list.' Wilson took a vial from his bag. 'With your permission I'd like to give you a sedative, I think you've had enough excitement for one day don't you? Get some rest and I'll call again in the morning.'

There was a pause as the clock struck three. 'If, as everyone assures me, I'm not usually violent then why am I acting this way? You say it's because of my head injury, but will I be this way from now on? Will I always have a vile temper like today? It worries me how I can feel murderous in a split second.'

'I think you'll gradually begin to revert to type. There may be some swelling in the brain, some pressure which is making you behave out of character. If you don't come around in a week or so I may consider trying to relieve the swelling, but it will be a last resort.' He handed him the laudanum. 'Now get some rest and I'll see you tomorrow. Good day to you my friend.'

Gabriel sat on the edge of his bed, his head in his hands trying to understand why he had felt so angry at Captain Turner. He knew why of course, the man was kissing his wife, but the intense feeling of murderous rage had startled him. After a few minutes he heard the door open and looked up to see Eleanor leaning against the closed door.

'Are you frightened of me, do you not dare come too close? Who can blame you? I'm turned into a madman.'

She advanced across the room and dropped to her knees in front of him. She took his hands in hers. ‘I’d trust you with my life Gabriel. I’m not afraid of you, I never have been. I think you went for Turner because you were protecting me, you behaved instinctively.’

‘I can’t honestly say what I was thinking at the time. It was as though I saw him touching you, kissing you and lost control. It was like a huge angry wave had come crashing over me and I was helpless to stop it. I can only apologise.’

‘Is the sedative making you sleepy yet?’

‘A little, I was about to lie down. Eleanor... ’

‘Yes my love?’

‘I shouldn’t want the children to see me fly off the handle like that. Lord knows what Carver and Walters think of me.’

‘Wilson has spoken with them, told them about your injury. They know this is not the real you, they both respect you and know your true worth. I’ll leave you to rest, ring if you need anything.’

‘Eleanor you said there was some deal I was doing with Turner. Is he willing to wait until I recover? If not, I trust you to make a decision for me. If you think under normal circumstances I would sign off on the contract then you have my permission to do so. I can’t for the life of me think why I wanted to hold off. I’ve read the contract of course, it looks sound enough.’

‘Don’t worry about anything. Try to remember what Wilson said, leave it alone and it will come back to you, trying to follow the thought will only make it move further away.’

‘Will you move further away? I shouldn’t blame you after today. I practically accused you of infidelity. I can see now, now I’m rational again, you’re true to me. Although I can’t remember you fully I feel I know you... instinctively I don’t have to explain myself to you because you know me and love me despite my shortcomings. I can see how you make me a better version of myself. I want, no I need, your good opinion. Please don’t leave me. I can see how you’d want to when I act like I did earlier.’

She kissed his hand. ‘I won’t leave you, how could I? I love you.’ She smiled and placed her cool lips on his forehead. He closed his eyes and breathed in the scent of her.

Alone Gabriel began to doze. It felt odd to be abed in the middle of the day, like the rare occasions when he was a little boy and was sick. He remembered Lisbet used to tuck him up with lemonade and tell him stories of pirates and shipwrecks. She was a good storyteller. Again he wondered why he could remember this, but not his own wife and children.

When he woke it was dark, a single candle lit his bedchamber. He saw a shadowy figure move by the bottom of the bed. He tried to rouse himself, but felt heavy-limbed and confused.

'Mr Gabriel 'tis only me, A brought yer a candle. A'm sorry if A woke yer.' Gabriel strained his eyes and saw the large bulk he recognised as Lisbet. Her Geordie accent was unmistakeable. He remembered she had often come to him when he'd had a nightmare. He found her voice soothing.

'How strange you're here. Before I fell asleep I was thinking of the times when I was a small boy and you looked after me when I was ill, told me stories. Oh and made vile tasting medicines from hedgerow plants.'

His old housekeeper giggled like a schoolgirl and plonked her large bottom on the edge of his bed. 'Yer hardly ever ailed as a nipper, thanks to my concoctions as yer used to call 'em. Both er yer enjoyed good health, until of course yer father's heart began to fail. Thank God the end were quick, he would've hated to linger.'

'Tell me about my childhood Lisbet, I cannot remember anything except hazy images. I've seen the portraits of my parents in the library.'

'Yer were a quiet little thing after yer ma passed, it were a sad time. Losin' a ma and a baby brother in the childbed were bad. A tried to cheer yer up, looked after yer like yer were ma own A did. Yer were seven an' a course yer pa was grievin' summat awful.'

'Thank you Lisbet I should imagine it was a weight off my father's shoulders having you about to take care of me.'

'Yer used to play on the sands summer an' winter alike. Yer could swim by the time yer were four. Yer were good at entertainin' yerself, an' Jack an' Abner used to take yer fishin', yer all liked fishin'. When yer were eleven and ready to go away to school it fair broke Jack's heart, A can tell yer. We was all at sea wi' yer gone. Westshore weren't the same until yer came back in the holidays, yer were allus a good lad. Course that's when yer met Mr Bendor, Sir Bendor as he is now. Right rogues yer were in yer youth, there weren't a maid safe in Alnmouth. Then when yer finished at school Jack Reynolds taught yer all yer needed to know about shippin'.'

For an hour or so Lisbet told him about his childhood, about his beautiful mama and his handsome father. How Jack Reynolds had made his money from whaling then set himself up in business and become rich and successful.

'Then he built this house. He were successful in all things except makin' a big family to fill it. He would've loved a house full er kiddies. He'd be that proud er your bairns.'

She told him no matter how busy his father had been he always had time for his son. She also told him about his father's best friend, another widower, Thomas Hodgeson. 'Yer pa trusted me an' Abner to look after yer when he were away on business, but Thomas were like a second pa to yer. He'd come and take yer to Eastshore to play with Caroline, 'cause she were an' only child an' all. She were that pretty, like a little china doll. You weren't that impressed playing wi' a girl, but Thomas' groom had a little lad your age, Charlie 'is name were. Yer used to rough neck wi' him until - '

'He got consumption and died when he was nine.'

'There now, fancy yer rememberin' that. It felt like everybody yer were close to back then died.'

'I haven't seen Abner since my return, is he well?'

'Aye he's a bit worried yer will remember why yer sacked him an' ask him to b - off again.'

'If I could remember why I fired him in the first place I might.'

'He used to tek backhanders from Jack Lawless, 'im from Amble who does smugglin' runs. Sometimes he did the odd tub run if they were short handed. He sometimes hid a cask or two behind the stables, but the mistress did catch him an' telled yer. Yer were in yer rights to get rid er him, A never blamed yer or Eleanor. But course A had to go an' all, A were that mad wi' him.'

They hadn't heard the door open.

'Ah, you're awake.' Eleanor stepped into the room. 'I've waited supper for you.'

'We bin rabbitin' on about the old days. Sorry, A should've known yer would be waitin'.'

'Not at all Lisbet I'm pleased you can share your memories with Gabriel, I'm sure it's a great help to him, you're welcome to join us.'

'Oh no mistress thank yer kindly, but A have mine an' Abner's supper all ready.'

Later at supper Gabriel pushed the food around his plate.

'Are you not hungry? Is there some other dish you fancy?'

'Thank you no, I feel a little odd. Some of the memories Lisbet shared were uplifting, but some were so sad. Losing my mother and father, and infant brother; life can be cruel can it not?'

'And life can be good. The trick is not to look back, but of course you have to do that to know who you are now.' A troubled look swept across her face. She had an expressive face, a face he never tired of looking at.

'Bendor said you were prone to dark moods when you were younger, he said you used to get down until, well until you met me. Apparently after we got together you turned a corner.' Gabriel watched as she flushed slightly.

'My Angel of Redemption. I can see how you would be a tonic.' His wife looked embarrassed and turned a deeper shade of pink and looked especially becoming. He had to admit he had chosen his wife well. In the candlelight her eyes were a most particular shade of blue-green.

'I have a confession. I didn't mean to keep it from you, but it never came up in conversation before, but you've reminded me.' He was a little hesitant.

'What? Have you remembered something horrible about me, something I once said or did to upset you?'

'No nothing like that,' he said smiling. 'I can't imagine you're ever horrible. It's only that when we were in Whitby, when you kept vigil by my bed I came round briefly and saw you dozing. I thought I'd died and gone to heaven, I thought you an angel. Your hair loose in the candlelight looked as if you had a halo of light about you. You looked so serene, like an angel. When I didn't know who you were that's what I called you. My angel.'

'Oh I'm mortified. You regained consciousness and I was asleep! What sort of nurse was I? I knew I'd nodded off but I wasn't aware you knew. Why did you not wake me?'

He noticed how self-effacing she was, ignoring his compliments yet castigating herself for her supposed negligence. 'I was drifting in and out of consciousness I think. The next time I woke your mother was there, my angel had disappeared.'

'I doubt anyone has ever called me angelic before,' she sighed, 'but I'm here now my love and I promise I'll never leave you. We'll be each other's protectors, each other's guardian angels. We'll steer each other to safe harbour, I promise.'

R

A few days later Eleanor was riding on the moorland behind Westshore. She had given Jet his head and was tearing up the ground as she was wont to do; the next she knew she had landed on the ground with a thud.

'Ouch.' She rubbed her ankle, then quickly realised it was her wrist which pained her most. She sat for a moment knowing from past experience not to jump up too soon in case she took a dizzy spell. Eleanor was an experienced horsewoman; this was not the first fall she'd had, she doubted it would be her last. She was upset to see Jet with his front fore held aloft. She was about to get up when she heard a noise and saw Gabriel riding towards her.

'Well met my love. I think Jet caught a rabbit hole. I'm fine, well my wrist hurts a little, but poor Jet looks lame.'

Gabriel jumped down and rushed to her side. She held out her good arm so he could help her up.

'What the hell were you doing? Have you no sense woman? What would you have done had I not come along? Do you forget you're a mother?'

Eleanor was sore and didn't feel in the mood for a lecture. She had already felt the lash of his tongue at breakfast when the coffee he had asked for was cold. Apparently it was her fault the servants were lax. She was used to his mood swings of late, but now more than ever when she was in pain, she resented his rebuke. His behaviour was in stark contrast to how the old, loving, caring Gabriel would have behaved. It was too much. She began to struggle to her feet. He attempted to help her but she shrugged him off.

'I can manage, unhand me.' She pulled away and limped towards Jet and took hold of the reins, talking softly to her injured horse.

'You don't mean to ride back?' Gabriel scoffed. 'Your horse is lame, as are you by the looks of it.' He scowled. 'I asked earlier if you were to ride out. You said not. You should not ride alone on the moors, unchaperoned it's asking for trouble.'

'I changed my mind. I wasn't aware I had to ask permission.'

'Madam you're infuriating.'

'And you're a bully.' She turned Jet and started to lead him home.

'You can't possibly walk all the way to Westshore.' He mounted Copper and held out his arm. 'Don't be so stubborn, climb up.' He waved his hand irritably urging her to take it.

'Go to Hell,' she shouted. She carried on walking biting her lip to stop the tears which threatened to fall. It wasn't the pain in her arm, but her husband's unfeeling attitude which hurt most.

He dismounted, tore the reins from her fingers, scooped her up in his arms and plonked her unceremoniously on Copper's back. He tied Jet to Copper and climbed up behind her. Eleanor struggled to get free as he put his arms tight around her to hold the reins.

'Stop writhing woman, you're so pig headed. It will take you the best part of an hour to get home on foot. Sit still damn you.'

'I'd rather crawl on my hands and knees than ride with you.'

To her annoyance he had too firm a grasp of her. He ignored her protestations and pointed Copper in the direction of Westshore. Eleanor had no choice but to comply.

By the time they arrived at Westshore her wrist was throbbing. She didn't wait to be handed down but sprang from the saddle and marched into the house shouting instructions to Sam to take good care of Jet.

In her room Eleanor sobbed into her pillow. The strains of the last few weeks were too much to bear. After a few minutes she heard the door open; if Gabriel had come to give her another lecture... but to her relief she saw it was Lisbet carrying water and bandages.

'Let's have a look at yer... oh yer cryin'. Is it that bad ma love?'

Eleanor wiped her eyes and blew her nose. 'No it's not my arm so much as Gabriel's attitude.' She told the old woman what had happened.

'A never known him to be unfeelin'. A saw you ride into the yard an' when A asked him what had gone on he said... well he weren't happy let's leave it at that. It's as the doctor says, he's makin' progress but some days he has a set back.'

'A set back! In the past if I'd taken a fall Gabriel would have been so attentive, so caring... but not now.' Lisbet continued to bathe the cuts and bruises and set about bandaging her wrist. 'As it is he hasn't even been to see how I am. It's as though I'm married to two different men. I want my old husband back.'

As the words left her mouth Gabriel stepped into the room, his face anguished.

'I'm so sorry. I don't know what comes over me, a mist appears to descend. Eleanor my love, can you ever forgive me?'

'No she can't yer great lummox, get yer gone afore you need bandages an'all. Comin' in here beggin' forgiveness; if she ever talks to yer again it'll be a day too soon.'

Just then there was a knock on the door and Ginny stepped aside as the children rushed in, almost knocking Lisbet over.

'Mama, Papa, hello Lisbet, we're home.'

'So I see.' Eleanor began to cry afresh, but these were tears of joy. The boys hurled themselves onto the bed.

'Have you hurt yourself?' Hayden looked admiringly at the bandage while Rose began to climb into her father's arms.

‘Pa are you recovered? Have you missed your Dumpling?’ She planted a wet kiss on his lips. ‘I’ve missed you. Did you take care of Podge?’ She mentioned her beloved pony.

Eleanor looked at her husband and held her breath.

‘Of course I have Rose. Now I’m better I intend to take care of you all, especially your mama. Now you children have returned we are a house full once more, all together here at Westshore.’

4

The early summer became warmer which was not always the case on the North East coast. More than a month had passed since Eleanor's fall, her sprained wrist was mended and so was the rift between husband and wife.

Gabriel had begun to act like his old self once again. He said he felt more in command of his emotions, calmer and more at ease with himself. Eleanor could feel the change, sense his relief. Memories had begun to surface and he could remember not only hazy images but whole events. The fog was lifting and he could see some, if not all, of his past more clearly.

Eleanor, grateful Gabriel's moods were less erratic, began to relax. Her husband was on more of an even keel now although he still felt minor irritations, usually about the misty areas where his memory failed him. But now he was more able to damp down his anger, his temper was less prone to flare up. He was beginning to behave more like his old self. He began to talk to the children, play with them, reconnect with them. It was a tremendous relief to Eleanor.

Yet still there was one area of their life which was unresolved. They were still sleeping in different beds. It was true they had become closer again, the odd touch or light kiss but no real intimacy. Their relationship was more the way a brother would behave with a sister. Eleanor was beginning to feel impatient.

Wilson had said the more Gabriel was prompted to remember familiar things such as sounds, tastes, sights and the like, the more it would help his recovery. She noticed he responded well in some instances but not in others. She decided an experiment was called for. She had been tolerant long enough.

One evening after a particularly hot, sticky day Eleanor took extra care dressing for supper. Since their return from Whitby they had not been out to dine or sup, refusing invitations as Gabriel still found it a strain to be in company. Often he didn't remember events and said he would feel strange, rude if he lost his way in conversation. Grace and Bendor had come to dine of course as had Lottie and Wilson. Gabriel was at ease with this intimate group. Bendor also called often on his own out of concern for his oldest friend. But for what felt like months Eleanor and Gabriel had lived quietly, soberly, or so the usually effervescent Eleanor thought.

Tonight she dressed in a bronze gown which had been a Christmas gift from Gabriel a few years ago. The dress was a particular favourite of his because he said the colour suited her. She knew he liked it because it was quite revealing, having a low neckline and short sleeves. She left her hair unbound and sprayed rose scent in her hair and on her wrists.

Gabriel still tired easily and often needed to be abed before it was even dark. Eleanor often sat up after he had retired and read or went for a walk if the weather was fine. The early summer nights were long and balmy. In the past they'd made the most of them. After a quiet supper they prepared for an early night.

'Are you not to take a walk on the beach as you usually do when the weather's warm?' he asked.

'Not tonight, I thought I'd come up now.'

They didn't need candles to see them up the stairs. Outside the master bedroom they stopped and Gabriel kissed her cheek. A brotherly kiss, chaste and without passion. She suppressed her impatience. Her husband had always been a man with strong appetites, in this they were well matched, but since the accident it appeared he had forgotten about this aspect of their marriage. She proposed to remind him what he was missing.

'Goodnight Gabriel.'

'Good night my love, I hope you sleep well despite the heat.'

She entered her dressing room and quickly disrobed dabbing more perfume on her wrists. She turned her ear to the adjoining door and listened waiting until she heard Walters leave the room. She hesitated. Earlier when she had had the idea to seduce her husband she thought it a good plan. Now she was unsure. What if he rejected her? Thought her a strumpet? Failed to be aroused. She took a deep breath and opened the door.

Gabriel was about to get into bed. He stopped and looked at her in surprise.

She moved towards him, put her hands on his chest and glanced up at him expectantly. She felt him catch his breath.

'Eleanor... '

'Don't talk just kiss me, hold me, love me. Gabriel I've missed you so much.'

R

The next morning Gabriel woke early and decided to take advantage of the warmer weather. He raced down to the sea and threw himself into the surf. Dawn was breaking and the sky blurred with gold, orange, lilac and vermillion. He breathed in the salt laden air and felt at peace. It was like welcoming an old familiar friend back into his life.

He had been swimming hard when he turned back to look at Westshore. He could feel it was his natural habitat being in the sea. He sensed he always swam out in order to look back and admire his home, not in a covetous way, but in a way which made him feel secure, safe. Swimming was as usual to him as breathing. An ordinary thing but to remember such a feeling was exhilarating.

His thoughts turned to Eleanor. In his mind's eye he saw her face, her hair, her body. He had a vision of her wet and swimming with him, slithering about him, her nakedness gleaming in the sun, her hair like spun gold. She was a mermaid weaving her magic around him, enticing him, inviting him, calling to him like a siren. Yet this was no siren calling him to flounder on the rocks; last night had been a call to home, a call to safe harbour. He remembered their hot, passionate bodies reunited at last.

Suddenly Gabriel knew all there was to know. It was as though a veil had been lifted and he could see his past, his present and his future. Eleanor was all of this and more. He swam hard for the shore and raced up the beach struggling into his breeches as he ran, then he took the stairs two at a time. He burst into their bedchamber.

'My love I remember, I remember everything. My memory has returned. It's all fallen back into place like, like... I can't explain it. All I know is I love you Eleanor.'

He watched as she attempted to sit up, but he was upon her. Kissing, caressing, laughing. She wriggled, amused, happy.

'You take my breath away Gabriel.' She squirmed under his weight. He was devouring her, stroking her face, her hair, her body. Suddenly he looked into her eyes and was stilled. 'Last night I believe you seduced me... and now I'm going to return the favour. Let me have you again my love. Now that I know you once more I have to reacquaint myself with all of you, every bit of you.'

She lifted back the covers and welcomed him home.

R

Life was good and in July friends gathered to welcome Gabriel home at a garden party Eleanor had decided to throw. It had been spontaneous and was a great success.

Gabriel's life now continued as before. He had taken back the reins of the shipping line with alacrity. The business had continued to do well under his wife's supervision; in fact she had made some minor changes of which he approved.

One morning he was at his offices at the bay when Padraic Turner was announced.

'Is it safe to come in or might you try to throttle me again.' His snide remark could not cloud Gabriel's day.

'I apologise unreservedly. Please take a seat Padraic; I'm pleased you could attend today. Can I offer you some refreshment?' He poured his visitor an Irish whisky. 'As I said in my note I'm now fully recovered so perhaps we can resume negotiations. Unless that is you have found another buyer in which case - '

'Another buyer would be hard to come by at short notice as you well know. Your wife,' he stopped and smiled elliptically, 'urged me to look elsewhere for a buyer when you were indisposed, but I decided to wait in the hope the deal could be salvaged.'

'Good, then we're of the same mind. However there's a stumbling block, a fly in the ointment, and that's the Alnmouth Girl.' Gabriel came straight to the point.

'The Alnmouth Girl? What about her?'

'The deal we agreed was for three of Thomas' ships was it not? The Swiftsure, the Fear Not and the North East Star.'

'The ships belong to me now or had you forgotten? What of it?'

'I want to make a change. Switch the Alnmouth Girl for the Fear Not. They're the same tonnage, the same speed and are of similar age. They're both merchantmen but without the change I cannot countenance the deal.'

Padraic Turner downed his whisky. 'Why the hell should I swap ships? I think I've been patient in waiting this long. As you point out they're the same, oh but I see they're not the same to *you* are they my friend? It would be like splitting twins, sending one to the other side of the world and leaving a sibling behind. The Alnmouth Girl and the Alnmouth Boy.' Turner laughed. 'I never had you down for a romantic Gabriel. Did your father never tell you there should be no room for sentiment in business?'

Gabriel knew Turner would mock his soft-hearted stance. Now he had recovered his memory he knew why he had held off on signing the contract; Turner was right, he had been reluctant to see the Alnmouth Girl sail out of Alnmouth Bay for the last time never to return. Turner had said he planned to sail her to America then use her to ply tobacco around the world once he got his export licence. Gabriel couldn't bear to let her go, not only because of the memory of Caro, but also for her father, Thomas. Gabriel and Caroline were never meant to be together but the two ships had grown to symbolise the union, the friendship between the two families. He wouldn't let the Alnmouth Girl go without a fight; he owed it to Thomas and to Caro's memory. He knew there would be a battle; as soon as Turner saw the chink in his armour he would pounce and try to raise the stakes.

Gabriel twirled a quill idly between his finger and thumb. He stared at the man sitting opposite him and smiled. 'As you rightly surmise it would not please me to see the Alnmouth Girl leave her home port, but don't get the idea I'll be enticed into paying over the odds. However, I'm a reasonable man and could see my way to making a small concession for your latitude. What say I donate a sum to any charity you support in addition to the swap?' Gabriel already knew the answer to this proposal.

'Charity? The only charity I subscribe to is the bank of Padraic Turner.' He stood. 'We either sign today, the original deal, or I'll be forced to pull out and find another buyer. Have you not wasted enough of my time by God? I've been tolerant so far, so I have, but will tarry no longer. I'm in no big hurry but,' he leaned across the desk, 'I'm eager to be off, away from here to start a new life, a new adventure, there's rich pickings to be had as I witnessed when I was in Virginia last year. I don't mean to stay here a minute longer than is necessary.'

Gabriel continued to turn the quill. 'Don't be too hasty my friend, if we can agree terms today you can be on your way whenever you like. I expect you have a cargo lined up to ship out to America; you wouldn't sail her with an empty hold. That wouldn't make any sense.'

Padraic's temper flared. 'Of course I've a blasted cargo ready. I've been waiting these last six weeks to set sail. All the time you were in Amsterdam and then in cloud cuckoo land! America has need of essential items that only the Motherland can provide.'

'By essentials I take it you mean wines and spirits and other goods on which tax hasn't been paid?'

Turner sat back down. 'Are you accusing me of smuggling? What do you know of my affairs? Only two weeks ago you could barely remember your own name.'

Gabriel had touched a nerve but he felt perfectly calm; the Irish Rover not so. 'Let me inform you that if you load your cargo on the

Fear Not and sail out of the bay by Friday week at the latest, I'll turn a blind eye. If however the Alnmouth Girl sets sail with a cargo of contraband goods then I'll be forced to alert His Majesty's Customs like any law abiding citizen. Sir John Riddleston, the magistrate, is a friend. I have eyes and ears at the bay and they'll tell me the minute you start provisioning, day or night. Those eyes and ears have been quick to bring me up to date about what's been going on whilst I've been absent. The North East Star has been especially busy in France I hear.'

His rival stood, then began to pace the floor.

Turner barely suppressed his outrage. 'You're welcome to try to stop me. 'Tis surprising how sailors can be bought, you of all people should know what turncoats men can be when money's involved. There's a lot of hungry men on this coastline.'

'Do as you wish.' Gabriel put down the quill and stood to show his visitor the door. 'Good luck with getting a quick sale. I heard Josh Henderson is retiring and putting his ship up for sale in the near future. The Fair Wind is a good little craft; I may make a bid for her myself. Your offer came out of the blue and as it was never my intention to expand so quickly, the smaller vessel would suit me for now.' Gabriel watched as Turner's face changed colour. He thrust his point home. 'It appears it's a buyer's market at the moment. A ship doesn't come up for sale for an age then four come along all at once. You may be well advised to sell the three ships separately perhaps, though it may take longer, but in the end you could make a better profit. It's a thought.' Gabriel opened the door. 'I wonder if our deal falls through the locals will be suspicious? They'll wonder why. My family has long been respected in these parts whilst you, a relative stranger, are known to sail close to the wind. They may speculate the price was too high or that - '

'Don't think you can blackmail me, I'll take my chances.' Turner reached the door in four strides and slammed it shut behind him.

Gabriel let out a long breath. He had expected him to make a stand. He knew Turner to be a hot head. He was no businessman; his negotiating skills consisted of brawn rather than brain. He was more used to turning a quick buck than building a venture on firm foundations. He feared Caro's fortune would slip through the man's fingers in no time at all.

When he had inherited Caroline's fortune Turner had been reluctant to take advice from her stewards and factors. He had gone abroad, supposedly to America. Gabriel suspected he had spent some time in Ireland settling old debts... or possibly gambling or womanising or all three. Who really knew what the blackguard got up to?

Gabriel was sure of one thing. The deal would be done to his satisfaction or not at all. When Turner had first offered to sell the shipping line to him he was unsure whether he wanted to expand at all. It was a huge commitment to raise the money for such a big deal, but the more he thought of it the more he liked the idea. Not only would he be taking over Thomas' ships he would be safe-guarding the future of his twin boys.

He suddenly smiled to himself as he saw his wife's indignant face in his mind's eye. She would insist Rose be included. *All* their children would inherit equal shares. Now he thought about it he agreed Rose too should have a chance to inherit. He thought how his life had changed since meeting Eleanor; she had altered his way of thinking and now thanks to her he had a legacy to leave. The Reynolds name would live on. It pleased him to think if he could secure the Alnmouth Girl, Rose would succeed to the title. The thought warmed him that she would be the next "Alnmouth Girl".

As for Turner, he would bide his time and wait. After all he wasn't the one in a hurry.

R

Later that day Gabriel was hard at work in his office at the bay when a visitor was announced. His face broke into a wide smile when he saw who it was.

'Charles, this is some surprise, I didn't know you were ashore you old seadog.' He grasped his old school friend's hand, then pulled him close and slapped him on the back.

'And I'm here for good this time. I've left the navy after nigh on twenty years can you believe?'

'Never! At last they've found you out to be a charlatan who couldn't navigate his way to the end of the bay.' They shook hands. 'I never thought you'd pack it in, become a landlubber.'

'Me neither, but there you are. I have my reasons.' Charles grinned showing even, white teeth. He was a head shorter than Gabriel and stockier; his flaxen hair fell over his high, aristocratic brow.

Gabriel offered his friend a drink and a seat in that order. When they were both settled Gabriel moved behind his desk. They talked of Charles' last voyage to The Americas and of old friends, acquaintances and family.

'I saw Claude some months ago,' Gabriel said, 'but we were at the opposite ends of a ballroom and somehow we never got to speak. You know how it is at these events. It was at a wedding I think, but for the life of me I cannot remember whose.'

'My brother loves to socialise. His wife has recently given birth to their *sixth* child would you believe, another girl. I think they mean to keep going until the longed for male heir arrives.'

'Eleanor and I have stalled on three and Bendor has two so you've some catching up to do Charles.'

'I said earlier I had my reasons for leaving the navy; I'm to be married later in the year.' Charles looked sheepish as his long fingers swept his fair hair from his forehead.

'Married! That's tremendous news. Who's the lucky lady? You must be the last of us to be snapped up by the parson's mousetrap.' Gabriel refilled their glasses. 'What's her name, do I know her? Who are we to toast?'

'So many questions. You don't know her as she resides in Norfolk. Her name is Violet, Violet Crow. I've come here today to ask if you'll stand up for me, be my best man. We've known each other since school and I think it fitting an old friend should be by my side on such an auspicious occasion.'

'I'd be delighted, honoured. It's about time you gave up your wild ways you old rogue.'

'Who says marriage will change me?' He laughed then said: 'But before the wedding there's the traditional stag night, you wouldn't want to miss that. It'll be at Harry's or so I hope, I've not seen the old devil yet, but I know he'll oblige if he can, if not Claude will host, but all this is some way off.'

'I'll let everyone know you're home to stay, Bendor will be happy for certain. I'll write and tell him you're back and we can all sup together, catch up. But tell me about your future wife. Who are her family, is she pretty? Fair or dark? Not a redhead I hope. Redheads are trouble Charles, take my word for it.' Gabriel refilled their glasses. 'Is the wedding night eagerly anticipated or have you dodged the chaperone? You were always good at stealing the ladies away from their protectors.'

He saw his friend's face drop. Charles hardly looked excited about the prospect of his marriage. 'Violet is... well the marriage is arranged of course, younger son and all that. She wasn't my first choice, but needs must as they say. Claude has given us South Point, the old place at Amble, do you remember it? Good of him I must say. I rode over yesterday and while I expected it to be in a bit of a state I hadn't realised just how bad it would be; the roof leaks like a sieve, pigeons are roosting in the eaves and damp is rife throughout. It would probably be cheaper to knock it down and build again, but Claude wouldn't agree to that. Violet's dowry, her not inconsequential offering, will of course pay for the building repairs. There's not a hope in hell it will be habitable by October, that's when the wedding will be by the way. The only stipulation her cousin made, she has no near relatives save a distant cousin, was that I quit the service. He didn't want her left alone for months or years at a time. Understandable I suppose as she's an only child.' Charles resumed his usual optimism and looked more cheerful. 'So I'm going to be back in the neighbourhood my friend, lock up your wives.'

'So long as you leave mine alone.'

'How is the lovely Eleanor, well I hope?'

‘Very well, as are the children.’

Gabriel had suspected Charles would have to go down the arranged marriage route; the Noble family were minor aristocracy and impoverished landowners. When last he had spoken with Claude he was bemoaning yet another poor harvest, the third in a row. North Point, the family seat, was at least in a better state of repair than Charles’ new abode.

‘It’s a good job you didn’t turn up a few weeks back my friend, because if you had I wouldn’t have recognised you.’ Gabriel succinctly explained about his accident. ‘But it’s tremendous to have you back; wait until I tell Eleanor, but you still haven’t told me about Violet.’

‘You’ll meet her later in the year and can make your own judgement. There’s to be a sort of welcome to Northumberland get together before the wedding. As I say she hasn’t any near relations so the wedding is to be at North Point. Until South Point is put to rights I’ll have to lease somewhere to live, I couldn’t countenance living with Claude’s brood... Cecily is a strange woman, Lord, imagine living there with all those children. I don’t know how he stands it. I should scurry back to sea after a week.’ He finished his drink. ‘If I find somewhere close I can supervise the building work, keep the men with their noses to the grindstone, but even then I doubt if South Point will be ready before Christmas.’

‘You’ll be glad you came to see me today Charles as I may be able to assist you in finding a house to lease.’ He told him about Eastshore. ‘Come to supper soon, Eleanor would love to see you.’

R

Back at Westshore Gabriel slaked his thirst then went out to the wood shed. He took off his waistcoat, rolled up his sleeves and began to chop logs. It was something he liked to do on occasion, it stopped him getting fat and lazy he joked. After ten or so minutes his shirt was sticking to his back. He dragged it over his head and threw it on top of his waistcoat, then mopped his brow.

Eleanor, back from a ride, saw him and standing a little way off watched as the axe split the wood with apparent ease. His strong shoulders and back worked rhythmically, his muscles rippled with the effort. From the corner of his eye he noticed her. Eleanor knew, even after all these years of marriage, he could still make her heart beat faster. She strolled over to join him admiring his healthy, tanned body gleaming with perspiration.

'What are you grinning at?' she asked.

'You, am I not allowed to be happy to see you?'

'Of course, but I've seen that look in your eye many times.'

He wedged the axe in a log, then made a grab for her and pulled her into his arms.

'Get off, you're hot and sweaty.'

'Do you prefer it when it's you who's made me this way and not hard labour?'

'I'm a little over-heated myself after my ride.' She stopped struggling as he began nibbling her neck.

'You smell,' she said laughing and pushing him away again.

'Thank you my love, sweet of you to mention it, but I don't care and by the time I've finished neither will you.'

'You sound sure about that.'

'I am. Anyway where have you been?' He whispered in her ear. 'Shouldn't a wife be at home waiting for her Lord and Master's return?'

'If you think that Gabriel you married the wrong woman. As it happens I've been nowhere in particular, just riding for the pleasure of it, it's such a wonderful day.'

'Are you tired?'

'Not especially, why what did you have in mind?' she asked knowing exactly what he was about. All through their married life, save for the time after the accident, they had enjoyed a healthy relationship. Neither ever tired of the other in that regard, in fact they were more attuned than ever now.

He began to kiss her, she began to surrender. She pulled away a little and looked about her. 'Not here - the children... '

'Are at Lisbet's for tea, Sam is at the farrier and it's the kitchen staff's afternoon off.'

'In that case,' she laughed as he led her into the small barn, 'heaven in the hay awaits us.'

R

'After you recovered your memory it was a busy time. You were obviously keen to reacquaint yourself with people and places and there was much socialising, which is how it should have been, it was fun. We all enjoyed ourselves. And then there was the business.'

After their earlier exertions they were sitting in the conservatory.

'Are you going to start cracking the whip and make me buckle down to earning a crust?'

'Not at all,' Eleanor shook her head smiling, 'but there's something I wish to speak with you about. Now our lives are more or less back to normal there's something I need you to see, something I didn't want to show you before as I thought it may... spoil the mood. But now I think I can wait no longer as an answer is long overdue.'

She took a letter from her pocket and held it out to him. 'When we returned from Amsterdam and Whitby there was much correspondence to deal with which needed your attention. I dealt with what I could, but this is addressed to your father.'

She passed the letter to him. He read the name aloud. 'Jack Reynolds Esquire.'

'I opened it, but I was none the wiser for doing so.'

Gabriel unfolded the missive. 'All it says is to contact the firm of Truscott and Timbers as they have information which needs to be passed on to my father, how odd.'

'I wrote to the solicitors of course and told them Jack had passed away and that you, his only son, had been involved in an accident. I didn't say you had amnesia of course, just that you were unwell and would contact them at your earliest convenience. I also asked if they could give a hint about the matter in question.'

'And did they reply?'

‘They did.’ She passed him a second letter. ‘All they would disclose was that there was a letter addressed to your father which they’d been keeping. A letter the solicitor wasn’t at liberty to release until a certain event had taken place. That event has now happened apparently.’

‘How mysterious. The firm are in Berwick I see. I’ve no desire to race up to the Borders at this moment in time, but I’m intrigued and I imagine you are too.’ He often accused her of being inquisitive; he knew this mystery would have piqued her interest.

‘I’ll write and ask them to forward the letter. They sound like two old fusspots making something of nothing. Why the need for drama, just send the damn letter. What harm can it do now Father’s dead and gone?’ He shrugged. ‘Is there anything else you’ve been keeping from me?’

‘Not anything I’m aware of except, oh yes there was the handsome sailor who asked me to run away to sea with him.’

‘But you weren’t tempted because you know when you’re well off.’ He suddenly sighed and then stifled a yawn. ‘I feel perfectly well all day, but as the evening wears on I have to admit to feeling tired, perhaps I overdid it earlier.’

‘Chopping logs do you mean?’ she raised a brow. ‘Perhaps it’s a sign you aren’t fully recovered... or is it an indication you’re getting old?’

He ignored the jibe. ‘I think I’ll have an early night. At my time of life one can’t be too careful.’ He bent over like an old man and leant on an imaginary cane.

‘I’ll put these on your desk,’ she said taking the letters from him. ‘Then I’ve one or two things to attend to before bed, you go up I won’t be long.’

Gabriel stood in the hall and lit a candle to see him to bed. He was about to go up when Abner appeared.

‘Abner, what is it? Has Ransom locked up?’

‘Not yet, yer got a visitor.’

‘A visitor? At this hour?’

‘That fool Ransom sent her round to the side door, poor lass got lost in the dark. A see'd her stumblin' about on ma way back from ma usual constitutional. A think she's a lady. Looks like she's bin on the road, bin travellin' a long way by the looks. She's a bit mucky that's all. Talks proper like.'

'For the love of God have you all lost your senses? Is she in the kitchen?'

'Aye, as A said Ransom sent her there.'

Gabriel lost patience and headed for the kitchen. A young girl was standing by the fire, her dusty cloak pulled about her. Mrs Madison thin lipped with disapproval glared at the late arrival.

'You may go to bed Mrs Madison; I'll deal with the matter.' Reluctantly she turned to leave, but not before signalling to Abner he should go home. Gabriel half smiled. Abner had never taken orders well, even from his employer, so he wasn't about to start now. The old man stood his ground.

Gabriel turned his attention to the young lady. She was soberly dressed, but dishevelled. Her dark hair had lost most of its pins and her boots were scuffed.

'Good evening, how can I be of assistance to you Miss... '

'Rebecca Argyle. Good evening sir, I'm looking for Mr Jack Reynolds. I was led to believe he resides here.'

The letter addressed to his father flitted through his mind. Surely this was too much of a coincidence. Twice in one day his late father was sought.

'I'm sorry to say you have had a wasted journey Miss Argyle, my father died some years ago. I am your servant and his son Gabriel Reynolds.' He bowed.

The girl's face dropped as she dipped a curtsy.

'Then I'm lost sir.' She turned to leave. 'This is indeed a blow I'd not envisaged, I'm sorry to have interrupted your evening.'

The girl was on the verge of tears. 'Please take some refreshment, you look weary.' He asked Abner to make tea. 'Rest awhile, come have a seat. Have you travelled far?'

'From Berwick sir,' perching on the settle she looked relieved not to be thrown out, 'and it's been a long, arduous journey.'

Again he thought back to the letter Eleanor had shown him.

'As my father is unable to help Miss Argyle is there anything I can do to assist you? Are you able to tell me why you're looking for my father?'

'It is a delicate matter sir.' She glanced at Abner who was scalding the tea leaves.

'You can speak freely in front of Abner.' The old man served the tea; she cradled the dish in her hands.

'As you wish sir but this may come as a shock to you. I have reason to believe we may be related.'

'Really? That's news to me. I only remember an aged aunt and you don't appear to be her.' He smiled hoping to put the girl at her ease. He saw her bite her bottom lip and then her face flushed.

'I think Jack Reynolds may have been my father sir.'

Gabriel and Abner looked at each other. Abner raised his bushy, grey brows.

'I'm sorry, but this can't be the case Miss Argyle,' Gabriel said incredulously, 'my mother died when I was seven and I'm an only child. There must be some misunderstanding; Reynolds is a common enough name, and to my knowledge I have no other relations.'

'I had a letter from a solicitor, Truscott and Timbers of Berwick saying my mama had died and that she'd left me a letter to be opened after her death.'

Gabriel stared in amazement at the pretty girl who all at once appeared familiar to him. 'You didn't reside with your mama?'

'I've been away at school since I was eleven sir. My parents have a house in Berwick, but they have lived in France for several years. I never saw them, not even in the school holidays. I spent all my time at a boarding school near Berwick. In the letter it said the man I thought was my father, John Argyle, was in fact not my real father. I think it fair to say Mr Argyle was not exactly fatherly towards me so it came as no surprise. I haven't seen him in years and he never wrote. Then I received news, from the solicitors, of Mama's death.'

Gabriel smiled triumphantly. 'I don't believe my father ever went to France Miss Argyle, therefore he cannot have met your mama. As

I said there must be some mistake; Abner do you remember my father ever going to France?'

Abner shook his head. 'He were allus in Holland but never in France. Never did any business wi' the Frenchies as far as A knew. But he did go to Berwick; every month at one time when yer were a sprog.'

'And would that time have been about seventeen years ago?' the girl asked looking expectantly at Abner.

He scratched his head hoping to tease the information free. 'A suppose it would er bin now a come to think on it, used to go on business he did. He had an interest in a lugger up there as A remember, but she were lost an' he stopped going then.'

'Mama says she met your father in Berwick. I believe they had an affair.' She stated the fact baldly, but blushed to the roots of her hair.

Gabriel was astounded but recovered himself quickly. 'Hold on there Miss Argyle. My father was devoted to my mother. He would never have carried on with another lady, a married lady at that.' Gabriel looked at Abner for confirmation, but saw a look of uncertainty on his old retainer's face. Gabriel began to do mathematical calculations in his head.

Rebecca helped him out. 'I think this would have been after your mother died sir. I have almost seventeen summers.'

Gabriel's head was swimming. By his calculations this affair, if the girl was to be believed and he wasn't at all sure she was telling the truth, would have taken place when he was away at school. He had no idea where his father went or indeed what his father did at this time. Was it so unreasonable that a good looking man such as his father would have lived a celibate life after Alice died?

The young girl continued haltingly: 'If you would give me leave I will try to explain Mr Reynolds.' Gabriel nodded and took a seat.

'My parents' marriage was arranged. It was a misalliance as these sorts of marriages often are. Mr Argyle was older than Mama, a lot older. Her name was Louisa. He was bad tempered and argumentative whereas Mama was a sweet natured beauty and an heiress. He married her for her dowry I imagine. John Argyle was furious when my mother couldn't give him children, like most men he craved a son and heir. Then when she did eventually have a child, me, I was the wrong sex. This made him even angrier, even more belligerent. He made both our lives a misery... actually that's not quite true. He refused to acknowledge me, hardly ever saw me, and hardly spoke to me. It was poor Mama who bore the brunt of his wrath. He was always an ill-tempered man, but with my birth he became even more cantankerous.'

'So you think your mama found solace in my father's arms? *My* father?' He still couldn't believe it.

'In her final letter Mama said Mr Argyle accused her of having an affair which she of course denied for fear he would disinherit me and injure her. He refused to admit I was his child, said I was a by-blow. He was always a jealous man, often in jealous rages because she was admired by all who met her. Both he and Mama were fair-haired and I was always so dark so he was disbelieving from the start. That's why we went to live in France I believe, his suspicions ate away at him. Mama was half French and her uncle left her a chateau in Le Havre. My father wanted to separate her from her lover, your father.'

She stopped and took a breath. 'Until I was eleven he publicly kept up the pretence that I was his daughter, but privately he wouldn't recognise me. He called me a, well you can imagine what name he used. Then he sent me back to Berwick to a ladies academy and forgot about me. It's from there I've run away.' She looked wary as if he would pack her back off there this very moment. 'It was another way to punish my dear mama, separating us as he'd separated her from her protector. I was the only light in her life, her only reason to live she said. If it's any consolation to you sir your father didn't know of my existence; he didn't abandon us. Mama broke off the affair despite your father being the only man she had ever loved. She knew they could never have a future together and she needed to protect me.'

Gabriel was all at sea. He heard the door open and Eleanor came to stand by him.

'I'm sorry my love, I didn't realise you had a visitor.'

He heaved himself wearily from the chair, the weight of the girl's confession sat heavily upon him. If what she said was true, then this young woman was his half sister. He tried to pull himself together.

'Miss Argyle allow me to introduce my wife, Eleanor.'

Rebecca Argyle stood tentatively and curtsied. 'I apologise for arriving unexpectedly Mrs Reynolds, but I've had a long journey. I'll go now and leave you in peace.'

'Do you have somewhere to stay tonight Miss Argyle? Perhaps one of our servants can escort you. It's late for a young lady to be abroad alone,' Eleanor said.

'I'm afraid I don't have lodgings, I used my last coins to get here but - '

Gabriel was quick to come to her rescue. 'In that case you must stay the night here at Westshore. You look exhausted, you must be hungry too. We can speak further after you have had a good night's rest if that would be agreeable.'

Gabriel saw the questioning look on his wife's face as he sent for Dora then issued orders to have a room readied and food prepared. The young girl, who may or may not be his relation, thanked him profusely.

Later in their bedchamber Gabriel told Eleanor about the girl's claim.

'Lord Gabriel, can it be true?'

'Your guess is as good as mine, but I expect she's alone in the world. Her father sounds a stranger to her. She could hardly count on him if what she says is true. She didn't know my father had passed.'

'Did you ask to see this letter from the dead Mama?'

Gabriel sighed: 'Eloquently put my love.'

'I'm sorry but she could be anyone, an imposter, though it's unlikely I would concede.' She furrowed her brow. 'If you *were* to have a sister Miss Argyle is exactly how your sister would look. The colouring and especially the eyes are the same as yours.' He threw his clothes on the floor and climbed into bed. 'What are you going to do about her?' Eleanor asked eyes wide with astonishment.

'She's run away from school. Now her mother has died she fears...

I don't exactly know what she fears. Not being sent back to her father that's for sure as he's all but disowned her.'

'The poor thing.'

'I was tired before she arrived and now my head is spinning with questions. There may never be answers to some of them I fear. It has to be true.' He looked shocked. 'Do I have a half sister? Abner knows more than he is letting on. He gets that glint in his eye when he's hiding something. I'll quiz him in the morning. I must admit I never thought my father looked at other women after Mama died, but I suppose it's unrealistic to think that way. I can't image wanting another woman if I lost you and I presumed Father had felt the same, but apparently not.'

'Forever is a long time to live alone. You always say men have needs, but beyond that people need friendship, companionship, someone to confide in. It doesn't mean he didn't love your mama any less; it doesn't diminish what they had together. This woman may not have been the love of his life, but she could have fulfilled some purpose, given him a reason to live.'

'I thought I, as his son, was that.'

'Of course you were, but as I say there are other reasons for having a *liaison* other than the obvious.' Eleanor laid her head on his chest and he felt easier.

'You have a way with words my love. Blunt and to the point, but down to earth in your outlook as always; I suppose you're right. Father was but five and thirty when he was made a widower, still relatively young. And I was away at school.' He was thinking out loud, trying to justify his father's actions, though he had no right to judge he realised.

'If this is true and if, as Miss Argyle says, her mother was married to an ogre then perhaps Jack felt compassion for the poor woman. They both fulfilled a need in the other.'

'Perhaps.'

He knew even though he was tired, sleep would evade him. Eleanor lay in his arms, he heard her breathing slow as she drifted off but sleep escaped him for many hours.

R

Gabriel rose early and marched down to the far end of the paddock. Abner and Lisbet had lived in a grace and favour cottage at Westshore since their return from exile. The little cottage had been refurbished and the whitewashed exterior shone brightly in the early morning light as he went in search of Abner - and answers. He noticed the neat rows of vegetables growing in the garden as he crunched up the cinder path. Gabriel knocked and waited. He heard Lisbet's shuffling gait come to the door.

'Hold yer horses, where's the fire? Oh Mr Gabriel, you be up early. Are yer wantin' Abner? Step inside if yer boots are clean.'

Gabriel ducked his head and entered the neat and tidy kitchen. The smell of freshly baked bread assailed his nostrils and made his mouth water. 'No one bakes bread like you Lisbet.' He didn't wait for an invitation to sit at the table. She cut a slice from the warm loaf and passed it to him smothered in homemade butter. She pushed a ham towards him.

'Help yerself.' She went out through the side door and called Abner's name.

When the old man limped in he showed no surprise at his early morning visitor. 'A knew yer wouldn't be able to rest easy. A can guess why yer've come.'

'You didn't look surprised at last night's revelations. What do you know of the matter?' He washed down the bread and meat with the strong coffee Lisbet had poured for him.

'A knew yer pa had met somebody; he telled me about her. She were half French like the little lass said last night. Yer were at school then and he'd met this lady who were the wife of a landowner in Berwick. He said she had a terrible life wi' him.'

'And he had an - ' He shot a momentary look at Lisbet who pretended to sweep crumbs from the table into her apron and then disappeared outside.

Abner continued: 'There were summat goin' on aye. Her husband were a real ol' tartar. A doubt there were any love lost in the marriage. Besides that Jack telled me he were tryin' to help her get away from her husband cause she were afeared er him.'

'To be with her here at Westshore do you mean? How could that be if she was still married?'

'Naw, a think the affair were short lived, but he wanted to help her as a friend. Her husband were violent he said. Seem to remember Jack had arranged to meet her wi' a carriage. She were supposed to slip away when everybody were abed, then she were goin' to get a passage on a ship to France where she had relatives. She were leavin' her husband, but not to be wi' Jack. From what yer pa said she would've come to him if he'd asked her though.' Abner slurped his tea. 'He still loved yer ma. He liked this woman well enough, but nobody could replace Alice in Jack's eyes. He allus said there'd never be another mistress at Westshore until the lad growed up an' wed. He were right an'all weren't he?'

'Why did you never tell me this after Father died?'

Abner shrugged. 'To what end? What purpose would it serve? Jack never knew she were wi' child A know that. He wouldn'a let her go to France on her own if he'd known. Yer pa were honourable.' He drained his tea. 'Not that she did go.'

Gabriel looked confused. 'You talk in riddles Abner.'

'That night he went to rescue her he waited and waited 'til the cock crowed, but she never came. Whether she couldn't get away Jack never knew. Her maid used to act as go between so he waited two days at the inn, but never got no message. Then he came home.'

'I expect that's when her husband got wind of the affair and took her off to France to separate them.'

''Spect so, an' now yer've a half sister. Jack would've bin that pleased to have a daughter.'

'I'm not so sure about that. You say the affair was short lived. Would he have taken the child, but not the lady? I think not. Dear Lord, this is all so unexpected, so confusing. I never expected my father to... '

'What, lead his own life? He were still a young man when yer ma passed don't forget.'

Lisbet appeared in the doorway. 'Yer pa were a good man, he would've done right by the bairn had he known. That role falls to you now Gabriel.'

He might have known Lisbet would be eavesdropping.

'Abner telled me about the girl turnin' up last night. Shall yer tek her in?'

'Who knows? She hasn't asked for anything and besides there's Eleanor to consider in the matter, Westshore is her home too. I'm not sure what the girl wants exactly, we wouldn't turn her away, but the situation is delicate and needs careful thought.'

Back at the house Gabriel went to the breakfast room, poured himself a strong black coffee and sat beside his wife. He told her what Abner had said.

'Shall you write to the solicitors?'

'I already have. I couldn't sleep and dare not wake Abner at the crack of dawn. After a swim I wrote asking if they would either send the letter or bring it at their earliest convenience.'

'You were restless all night.'

'I'm sorry if I kept you awake, but the matter was on my mind as you can imagine. If all this is true then I have a half sister. It's unbelievable.'

'About that Gabriel; it's early days I know, but I wonder what she wants now her mama has passed.'

'I don't know what her intentions are, we shall see.' He drank more coffee. 'I thought about it this morning whilst swimming. I've had it swilling around in my head all night. We may be jumping the gun, thinking she would ask for support from us, but... I feel responsible for her, if it is true that is. As you say she may want to go back to Berwick, but I got the feeling from our conversation last night that she wasn't keen. If she does stay, if you wouldn't mind... oh it's such a lot to take in. I shouldn't think she would go to France to be with her father.'

'Of course she may want to go back to school now she knows Jack has passed, but if she doesn't and you think to acknowledge her as your sister, then I will support your decision. We know nothing of her financial situation however. Perhaps her mama left her well provided for?' Eleanor thought for a moment. 'I too have been thinking about all this. We don't know for certain that it is true of course, I assume the solicitors, or the letter, will confirm or deny her story. Eleanor pushed her plate away, the food half eaten. There's so much to think about, but until we know for sure there's nothing we can do. I know you Gabriel and know you will do the right thing by her.'

Just then Rebecca entered the breakfast room, a timid smile on her face. She was a pretty girl, dark haired with lively features, a snub nose and Gabriel's blue-grey eyes. Her colour was high.

'Come in, please join us and take a seat. Good morning did you sleep well?' Gabriel pulled out a chair for her. He noticed how her dark hair escaped its pins and how it curled at the back of her neck. Her dress though once pretty, was faded and ill fitting. She appeared to have out-grown it. She was going to be tall like him and his father that much was obvious.

'Thank you yes; I can't thank you enough for taking me in last night. I realise it was a great imposition and I must have been quite a shock to you both turning up at such an hour and looking as I did.'

'Not at all.' Gabriel was keen to put her at her ease. 'Actually you *were* quite a shock; I can't lie, but a welcome one.'

'I can assure you my husband is usually a little more eloquent than he appears right now. I think what he's trying to say is he would be pleased to get to know you better. Perhaps you might consider staying with us, at least until we hear from Truscott and Timbers.'

'I wrote to them this morning,' Gabriel said. 'Hopefully we shall hear from them soon, but as my wife says please feel free to stay with us in the meantime.'

'That would be so kind, thank you. I hinted last night I'm a charity case I'm afraid, I have little more than what I stand up in, but perhaps I can pay my way. I can sew and turn my hand to most practical tasks, I don't look for handouts.'

Gabriel noticed how Rebecca dropped her eyes shyly as she passed the napkin through her fingers. She was perhaps by nature quiet and thoughtful. He noticed how the night before it had taken all her courage to tell her story. The fact she was in desperate need had loosened her tongue he suspected, made her tell her sorry tale to strangers. He felt for her plight.

'You will be our guest, Eleanor knows I always wanted a big family and it appears to be growing as we speak. I didn't mention it last night but we have three children. You'll meet them soon I expect.' He wanted her to feel at home he was surprised to realise. The more he looked at her the more certain he was they were indeed related.

Eleanor added: 'You'll hear them before you see them so at least you'll have advance warning and be ready for the onslaught.'

Rebecca selected a roll and began to butter it. 'I love children I would like lots of my own one day.'

Gabriel shot a fleeting look at his wife and smiled. 'It must run in the family. I too always longed for a house full of children. We have a daughter Rose, and twin boys Haydan and Ruari, the latter are boisterous I might add.'

'At the academy we were being readied to take our place in society. Trained to be a companion, governess or... ' she blushed. 'I would have preferred to teach children, be a governess given the choice.' Rebecca again lowered her eyes self consciously.

Eleanor spoke up: 'I take it the third option was marriage to some old, rich wrinkly.' She shuddered.

'My wife doesn't mince her words you'll soon realise.'

Rebecca summoned up her courage. 'You're right in your assumption Mrs Reynolds.' Again she stared at the table. 'I've only ever had one friend in the world and that's what happened to her. She was married off. Lizzie was so clever and sweet, but a month ago the Principal sent for her and told her to pack her things ready to leave the next day. She was to be married to a man old enough to be her grandfather. We tried to get her away that night, but we were closely watched. It was impossible.'

The speech clearly affected the young girl. She continued to stare at her plate.

'I take it that's one reason you ran away?'

'It is. Once I knew Mama could no longer send for me, rescue me, there was nothing else for it. I couldn't bear the same fate poor Lizzie endures.'

'Do you feel able to tell us how you escaped?' Eleanor reached out and squeezed the girl's trembling hand.

'Of course, it's the least I can do. Then perhaps you'll understand why I arrived so late. She sipped her tea. 'We always go to church on Sundays, and I knew this was my only chance to get away as we were watched constantly. The teachers were as cruel as the Principal; we were punished for the simplest misdemeanours. Lizzie was once locked in the cellar all night without food or a candle for daring to look at a visitor who came to the school. I'm sorry I digress.'

'Please, if it distresses you then we won't press you.'

'Thank you sir, but I want you to see it wasn't some girlish whim which has led me to your door. It was fear. Mama promised she would try to come for me, but when she died my hope of being liberated died with her. I knew I had to get away. I feared plans would be made for me if I waited much longer, so when my chance came I took it.'

Gabriel cast a look at Eleanor. He could see his wife was touched by the girl's plight, as was he.

'In church I pretended to have a coughing fit.' For the first time Rebecca smiled and Gabriel noticed how her whole face lit up. She really was an exceptionally attractive girl.

'I knew the Principal, Mademoiselle Troudeau, would be furious. She glared at me and when I didn't stop she hissed I should wait in the churchyard so as not to disturb the other parishioners. As soon as I was outside I ran as fast as I could; the night before I had hidden a small bag with my few belongings under the hedge by the school gate. I ran to retrieve it then followed the signpost south. I daren't go by road so then I cut across fields to avoid capture. I knew what would happen to me if I was apprehended. The only thing of value I had was a gold chain and locket which my mother had given me. I pawned it to raise the money to get the mail coach as far as

Dunstanburgh.' She stopped and took a long steadying breath.

'How did you get from Dunstanburgh?' Gabriel asked.

'I walked all day towards Alnwick. Thankfully the only pair of boots I own were school issue. They're not pretty but they're sturdy.' She took one foot from under the table and showed them the scuffed, black boots.

'As you say they're at least serviceable and stood up to the wear and tear,' Eleanor said. 'You don't mean to tell us you walked all the rest of the way.'

'I had only enough money for bread and cheese so I slept the first night in a barn. The next morning as I was sneaking out a young man was loading milk churns onto the back of a wagon so I begged a lift as far as Lesbury. Then I walked the rest of the way.'

'No wonder you were exhausted. My maid will take care of your blisters for I'm certain your feet must be cut to ribbons. You poor girl, no wonder you looked half starved and ready to drop last night.'

After breakfast Eleanor took Rebecca to her own room. She sent for Molly to bring hot water. Whilst Rebecca soaked her sore feet in rose oil Eleanor instructed her maid to bring slippers for Rebecca to wear. 'I think they may be the wrong size, but they'll do until we can get new ones. As for clothes, well mine may fit you but again we'll have to make do for the moment.'

'Thank you Mrs Reynolds, you're too kind.'

'You're safe now and we're family... well at least I think we are. Call me Eleanor.'

5

Two days later a messenger arrived at Westshore saying Messrs Truscott and Timbers would arrive on Monday.

'I wonder if they'll be fuddy duddy old gentlemen,' Eleanor said, 'Truscott and Shiver-Me.'

Rebecca, who was now a little less shy, was amused. With Eleanor's help the young woman was beginning to come out of her shell.

'What?' Gabriel said. He was only half attending as he had his head in a shipping periodical.

'Shiver me timbers,' Rebecca explained the jest.

Gabriel rolled his eyes. 'Worthy of Haydan or Ruari my love, but hardly side splitting.'

The door burst open and the two boys raced into the room.

'Look what I found,' Haydan said thrusting a large rusty key in front of his Papa.

'*We* found it, not you alone,' Ruari corrected him. 'It was washed up on the beach, I wonder what it opens. It's from a wreck is it not Pa?'

Gabriel took the proffered key and examined it. 'Quite possibly, can you search for gold in future? This is hardly of any use or value.'

The boys looked downcast.

'Perhaps it's the key to a treasure chest,' Rebecca suggested taking the key from Gabriel's hand. She knelt on the turkey rug and rubbed some of the rust off onto the hearth. 'Look here, I think there's something scratched into the metal.'

The boys leaned in to look. So far they had not taken much notice of their house guest. She was a girl and so not of interest to two lively five year olds.

Gabriel went to fetch the quizzing glass and passed it to Rebecca.
'Look I think it says "Black"... I can't quite read the rest.'

Haydan peered hard. 'I can't see anything except scratches.' It was hardly surprising; both boys could barely read yet.

Eleanor asked to hold the key and held the glass over it. 'I can see it says "Black" something, the sea has washed away the rest.'

'Blackbeard! It must have belonged to Blackbeard! Haydan leapt into the air, a side table was upended in his enthusiasm. The adults all knew there was nothing at all written on the key. The two boys were so eager for adventure they would believe anything.

'It might lead to gold Pa? If only we can find the treasure chest.' Ruari's face was bright with anticipation. The twins fled from the room without a backward glance leaving the door wide open as they went.

'What imaginations they have, that should keep them occupied for an hour or two.'

'I still can't tell one twin from the other. They're adorable, but identical,' Rebecca said.

'In looks they're the same as you say, but as parents we can tell them apart. Their temperaments are so different.'

'Haydan is generally first in line and the loudest, which is one clue,' Gabriel explained. 'I think he's more like Eleanor in personality, whilst Ruari is quieter and more thoughtful.'

'Like you?' Eleanor huffed. 'I don't think that's such a flattering remark to me. "First in line and loud", thank you husband for the compliment.'

He tried to dig himself out of a hole, but didn't quite succeed. 'I only meant that as an only child I grew used to entertaining myself. When I was their age I was quiet and a little reserved, whereas you had siblings with whom to play. As you've often said, you had to fight for your position being a girl and the youngest.'

'I thought you were a twin Eleanor?'

'I am, but I was born second and Tomas never lets me forget it. We're close. I miss him so much, I don't see him as often as I'd like. I have an older sister too, Atalana, Attie. I love my sister of course, but we're very different both in looks and personality.' Eleanor glanced at her husband. 'You look a lot like Gabriel, but as yet I don't know you well enough to comment how alike you are in personality. We're all on our best behaviour are we not? All except the boys that is, they're never well behaved. Are you a gambler Rebecca with a fondness for brandy like my husband?' She smiled at the young girl.

Gabriel refused to rise to the bait. 'I agree you definitely have the Reynolds colouring, but you perhaps favour your mother too. The shape of your face and nose is different to mine.'

'Mama had the same snub nose and bone structure. She was an extraordinary beauty, I could never hope to match her in looks, but I try to be as kind as her. She was always thoughtful. The only image I had of her was in the locket I was forced to pawn.'

'Oh, how sad to have lost it. I'm sorry for your loss Rebecca, you must miss her.'

Gabriel could see Eleanor was taking a shine to the girl; she was bringing out the maternal side of his wife's nature.

'It's so long since I saw her and not to be there at the end was distressing but I thank you both for taking such good care of me since I arrived. It's grieved me not being able to show Mama the respect she deserved even though I've not seen her this last six years. Thank you Eleanor for the loan of the mourning clothes.' The gown fit where it touched, but served a purpose for the time being. Rebecca continued: 'Father wouldn't allow her to come back to England to visit me; I only got the odd letter when she was able to get one sent via her maid. I think Agnes was let go by my father. Another maid, who reported to him I expect, was appointed because I've not received a letter from Mama for over two years. She must have felt even more isolated and alone without Agnes. I didn't know whether she was alive or dead until the solicitor's letter arrived and then of course it was the worst possible news.'

'It must have come as a shock to you. I don't suppose the Principal at the school was a comfort.' Gabriel sneered. 'It will be interesting to see what the letter to *my* father says and indeed to know who it's from; I expect it's from your mama of course. Perhaps we'll know more soon.' Gabriel stood and put his hand on the young girl's shoulder. 'Eleanor and I want you know you have a home here for as long as you need Rebecca, we hope you know that. We were discussing the matter last night. We don't want to pre-empt the visit from the lawyers, but we believe the situation needs careful handling. If you are my father's daughter, then perhaps it's unwise to have you introduced as my half sister. There's your reputation to consider. Eleanor and I don't care about such things, but if you're to be accepted in society then we need to decide how you will be known. Although I'd willingly acknowledge you as my half sister it may not do you any favours. It might serve you better to be known as a distant cousin perhaps. We could say I've been appointed your guardian and you've come from France. That way people may be disinclined to question your roots, but as I say we are getting ahead of ourselves are we not? I wanted to mention it as friends often drop by, so it's as well to get our story straight.'

'You're so kind to think of me and I can't thank you enough. You don't know me from Adam yet you offer me a place to stay and... ' She appeared overcome for a moment. 'I understand you're trying to protect me and I thank you both for your kindness, I see there's no other way. I must deny my birth if I'm not to be a disgrace to myself and to you, I will of course be guided by both of you.'

Eleanor rang for tea. 'It's not Gabriel and I who would be vilified my dear, but you do see how it would look? For our part we, and indeed our friends, don't care for convention, but your reputation is at stake and must be defended at all costs. Unless you decide to run off with Sam the head groom and then he won't give a jot where you come from which is how it should be, but we don't want to ruin your chances.'

Gabriel smiled wryly and shook his head. 'We think it best if we stick to one story, it will be less confusing. I expect our close family will know the truth, but all others will be told you're my ward. Do you agree Rebecca? Then if in future you decide to move on, or marry, no one will be any the wiser.'

'Of course, but will your family not despise me? Did you not say they used to be Quakers Eleanor?'

'I did, but it's neither the Quaker way nor my parents' way to despise anyone. They'll accept you for who you are; a young girl who through no fault of her own has been cast adrift with only her own resources to rely upon.'

'It's true, Mama left me nothing for she had nothing to leave. *He* took the lot, including her life.'

The mood had turned sombre. Tea arrived and Eleanor passed around the cakes. 'Tomorrow we'll go shopping. You need something half decent to wear that fits. My dressmaker will have at least one mourning dress off the peg I hope. She will also have slippers that fit before Mr Shiver me Timbers and his side kick arrive. Those boots are an offence to the eye and should be burnt forthwith.'

R

When Mr Truscott and Mr Timbers were announced the next day, Gabriel and Eleanor were waiting for them in the study. It had been agreed Rebecca would be sent for if needed. After all Gabriel didn't know what to expect; there may be something from which Rebecca needed to be shielded. He had known her for only a few days, but already he felt protective of his half sister, if indeed she was his relative that is. She had no one to look out for her excepting John Argyle and from the little he knew about the man he was hardly likely to help her.

The two lawyers, one tall and thin the other short and round, sat across from Gabriel and Eleanor. The introductions had been short and business like which Gabriel thought boded well for the meeting. He hated to waste time; he had a business to run.

Mr Truscott, the rotund, florid one, extracted papers from a brief case.

'We have been holding this letter for some time.' He laid the sealed missive on the desk in front of him. 'As you have proved you are the legitimate heir of Jack Reynolds the missive now passes to you sir. We were instructed to convey it after Mrs Louisa Argyle's death and not before; we were notified of her death last month. We have been trying to deliver the letter, as you are aware, but were hampered in our task. Firstly by finding Jack Reynolds was also deceased, and then by your own ill health.'

Gabriel looked at the letter lying on the desk. 'I'm sorry for the delay, but as you can see I'm well now.' Gabriel could feel impatience growing. It was hardly his fault his father had passed and he himself had suffered amnesia.

The gaunt looking Mr Timbers added: 'Sir, we have other news to convey. Sad news I am afraid.'

'Go on, tell me.'

'The lady's husband, John Argyle, recently returned to Scotland from France to take care of his wife's affairs, to settle her estate. We acted for him on behalf of his wife you understand. Indeed he had been to see us only the day before he was killed.'

'Killed?'

'Yes sir. An unfortunate accident befell him I am afraid. He was crushed to death by a carriage and four.' The man delivered the news matter of factly. 'In our last meeting with Mr Argyle he changed his will, disinherited his daughter for a Mr Fredrick Cooper, a distant cousin.'

Gabriel stared at his wife. 'As you say this news is most unfortunate. Why I wonder would he change his will in favour of this cousin?'

'It is not a lawyer's place to ask such questions sir. I have no idea.'

Mr Truscott picked up the letter in his fat, stubby fingers and passed it to Gabriel. 'This then concludes our business here today sir. We have delivered the letter into your hands as directed. If you have any other questions then I am afraid we do not have the answers.'

Gabriel thanked the lawyers, offered them refreshment which they declined then rang for Carver to show them out.

R

'That was short and sweet.' Eleanor said.

Gabriel turned the letter over in his hands. He read his father's name written in a flowing, feminine hand. He broke the seal and read the words of a woman who until four days ago he hadn't known existed. He sensed Eleanor watching his face intently.

The letter, essentially a love letter from Louisa Argyle to his father, explained some of what he had been eager to know since Rebecca's arrival. Firstly, it explained why she had been unable to meet Jack on the night they had arranged her escape; it was as they'd surmised, Argyle had got wind of the plan and locked her in her room. She described her husband as a "vile jealous man, who would stop at nothing to keep her apart from those she loved".

The letter also professed her undying love for Jack and explained why she had not written before. Again it was as they'd expected; her husband had kept a close watch over her since their arrival in France. He had also kept her away from her only relative, a maternal uncle. He had told her mother's brother she had suffered a nervous breakdown and could see no one. She was essentially kept a prisoner in her own home.

The contents of the letter made Gabriel uncomfortable. It was never meant for his eyes and it felt intrusive and voyeuristic reading the private thoughts of a woman he had never met. He was especially uncomfortable about the parts where she declared Jack was the only man she had ever loved.

Secondly the letter stated she suspected the child she had borne was Jack's. She had been too frightened of her husband to tell Jack about his daughter at the time, knowing nothing could be done. She hoped in doing so now he would try to do something for the girl. She told the same story as Rebecca; that Argyle suspected the baby wasn't his, that he denied the baby privately and made his wife's life a misery.

Eleanor watched as he read. Having read it he handed it to her. When she had finished she looked up at him, sadness in her eyes.

The poor woman and poor Rebecca. 'What a monster. How could he be so cruel, I hate to say it but he got his just desserts being run over and crushed.'

'Eleanor! It's not like you to be so testy.'

'Well, he sounds craven. How much of this will you tell Rebecca?'

'She knows most of it of course, but perhaps not the full extent of the mental cruelty Mrs Argyle describes, the man was indeed unfeeling, worse now I come to think of it, he was deliberately spiteful. I think we should spare her the details, for the present at least. It was his way to separate his wife from anyone she cared for, including her maid. It's a lot to take in is it not?'

'It is, but I agree, Rebecca need not know all. From what the letter says he kept the poor woman confined for most of the time. Yet when she did attend parties with him he made her life a misery for weeks afterwards accusing her of infidelities and calling her degrading, foul names.'

Gabriel thought of a time when he had been jealous. He had thought Padraic Turner was making a play for Eleanor and they had quarrelled over it. He was thankful their marriage was built on love and respect, not jealousy and vindictiveness. 'Death was possibly a relief for the unfortunate woman, an escape from a living hell. Not being able to see or communicate with her daughter or even a companion must have been devastating.'

'Perhaps, but despite her fortune it looks like Rebecca's mother had nothing to leave of any real value when she died, except her love for her daughter of course. Argyle had tied all her money and land up securely on their marriage and now the bullying brute is dead. Good riddance,' Eleanor said vehemently.

'As an only child Rebecca would have expected to inherit. Yet the day before his death Argyle wrote a new will leaving his fortune to a distant cousin if what the lawyers say is true. The final insult. It's a substantial sum I imagine; in fact it will be a fortune. The lawyers said Argyle was one of the leading importers of liquor in Scotland and he owned vast tracts of land. Poor Rebecca, she has nothing.'

'It was good of Timbers to impart the news of the change of will otherwise we would have thought Rebecca an heiress. As you say the girl is to be pitied. Ill fortune seems to have dogged her young life.' He watched as Eleanor's brow furrowed. 'But this new will Gabriel. Should Rebecca contest it? *We* know who her *real* father is but - '

'Do we really? We only have the word of Louisa Argyle and she may have been mistaken, though as you say Rebecca looks every inch a Reynolds.'

Eleanor leaned back in her seat and thought for a moment. 'Louisa said she and Argyle couldn't have children. That was the main reason he was disenchanted with her, he blamed her, wouldn't accept the fault might be on *his* side. He was angry with Louisa for not producing a son and heir, then Louisa does the deed with your father and suddenly she's with child. As she suspected, the error lay with Argyle; after all there were no other children after Rebecca. I'd wager he suspected as much himself, but from the little we know of him he wouldn't own the defect. He was too arrogant, too proud, serves him right. He made Louisa's and Rebecca's lives hell. I hope that's where he is now and getting a good roasting to boot.'

'So you think she should contest the will? On what grounds my love? Rebecca could be rich in her own right if the will was overturned, but would she want to try and would it be a fool's errand? It would be even more imperative her ancestry is kept secret if she decides to fight this in court, for that's what will happen, it would of course go to law. There would probably be a long drawn out battle too. The new recipient, this cousin, is hardly likely to step back willingly.' Gabriel thought for a long moment. 'Would it not seem well, untruthful, unethical, given what we know of Rebecca's circumstances and what we think is the truth regarding her birth? She'll want for nothing while ever she's with us if she chooses to stay that is. Is it worth the trouble raking up the past?'

'It does feel deceitful, but what's to be done? If she contests the will and wins the case then her parentage will be confirmed beyond question and she'll be an extremely rich young woman.'

Gabriel rubbed his chin. 'True enough. Perhaps I'll talk to Saul

Coates, in confidence of course. He'll know how best to proceed. I for one would let sleeping dogs lie, but it's not my fortune. I'll not speak of this to Rebecca until I've spoken with Saul, do you agree?'

'I do, but by fighting this Rebecca would be righting the wrong which was done to her poor mama. In her shoes I should contest it no matter how long it took. If Argyle was one hundred percent certain Rebecca was not his own flesh and blood he should have disowned her long ago, which he almost did but he didn't totally cut her off. This shows perhaps he harboured some doubts.'

'Rebecca has known nothing but heartache and hardship in her short life, to pursue this matter may be inviting more trouble to her door, to our door.' He reached for his wife's hand. 'Rebecca isn't like you my love; she's more reticent, retiring. For the first time in her life she appears to be experiencing a happy family home. I think she feels safe here, with us. Would she want to spend the next few years and her youth fighting for her birthright, especially as we all suspect the truth of her parentage? *My* father it appears is her real parent and in his absence it's my responsibility to take care of her. In fact it will be an honour to do so.'

'I suppose you're right. I too would welcome her into the family, if she decides to stay. Saul will be the best person to advise us, but in the meantime you need to decide what to tell Rebecca. She'll be wondering why we don't send for her to tell her what news Truscott and Timbers delivered. You must take care how you tell her what the lawyers said, as you say she's a sensitive girl.'

R

Later that day, after Gabriel had been to see his man of law, he asked to see Rebecca in his study. He fiddled with a quill turning it around in his fingers then dropped it on the blotter and scratched the stubble on his chin.

'As we guessed there was a letter addressed to my father from your mama. It's what you might call a love letter and so I don't feel it altogether appropriate for you to read it at present. Indeed I felt like a voyeur myself; it was extremely touching in parts.'

'I see. Did she add anything that was not in my letter, other than loving sentiments that is?'

'Not really I'm afraid, but something else came to light from the meeting with Truscott and Timbers. They were not "fuddy duddy" as Eleanor suggested. In fact they imparted information about John Argyle which you may or may not find distressing. I know you had little regard for the man, but at least he kept a roof over your head and paid for your education. He could easily have disowned you and thrown you out onto the streets.'

'Yes I suppose that's true but was it not Mama's dowry which paid for my upkeep. I like to think that's the case.'

'Perhaps you're right.' Gabriel admitted. 'I'm sorry to have to tell you but John Argyle is dead Rebecca. He came back to Scotland only to be run over by a carriage and was killed.'

For a long moment Rebecca was silent. He watched as she took in the knowledge then she lifted her eyes to his and said: 'Good.'

'There's more bad news I'm afraid.' Again he picked up the quill. 'The day before he died your father disinherited you, left you penniless in favour of a cousin, a distant cousin at that.'

Saul Coates had advised Gabriel he should put the facts before the young woman and let her decide whether to contest the will or not. He agreed there would be a difficult court battle, made worse for Rebecca as she was sixteen and had no near relative to guide her. Of course, Gabriel could not stand up for her without giving rise to speculation about her parentage, although Saul suggested the issue wasn't insurmountable; Gabriel could indeed be passed off as her guardian.

Several emotions played on his half sister's face. Finally she said: 'Then it's as well I can find work for myself... as a governess. I'll not presume on your kindness for longer than needs be Gabriel. You and Eleanor have been so good to me, but I'm not your responsibility. I shall stand on my own two feet and try to find suitable employment. At least that awful school has been good for something. I shall look for work.'

Gabriel came around the desk and took her hands in his raising her from the chair. 'Rebecca you're my half sister and I couldn't be parted from you on any account. I don't feel obliged to take you in, I'm privileged to do so.' He kissed her hand. 'I always wanted a little sister and now I have my wish.'

'But - '

'You must decide your own future of course, but both Eleanor and I would like you to reside here with us at Westshore. If you decide to contest the will then so be it, we will try to help as best we can. Think it over carefully my dear.'

'I shouldn't want to contest it; I don't want anything which belonged to the man.'

'You said before it was your mama's money which paid for your education, is it not also your mama's fortune you would be fighting for? Well partly at any rate.'

Rebecca looked Gabriel in the eye and flushed a little. 'I understand what you say, but the chances of me winning the case are slim I would think. On what grounds would I challenge the will? Presumably my father was of sound mind.'

'Apparently so, but he obviously didn't possess a conscience.'

'As you say I'll think it over, but I can't see I'll change my mind. I got more than a fortune when I found you Gabriel; you and Eleanor are the family I never had.'

'I hope in time we will be.' He saw how shy she was, but she also had spirit he realised. 'You don't need to find work Rebecca, I'll take care of you for as long as you like. If you wish to continue your education and perhaps go to be finished then I would be happy to fund it. When the time comes I'll also provide you with a dowry. My father would have done the same. It's the least I can do.'

'I don't know what to say. I can't possibly... perhaps you need more time to think about all this? I'm quite capable of finding a position.'

Gabriel shook his head. 'Stay as long as you like my dear, if you have a burning desire to be a governess then so be it, but I hope you'll stay here at Westshore.' He hugged her close.

‘I too have always wanted a big brother. I’ve lived a lonely life so far and can see what a happy home you have here. I would honoured to share it with you all, but I can’t presume can I?’

‘I think you can Rebecca.’

‘Then thank you Gabriel, I can’t believe my good fortune. It feels as though I’m dreaming and I’ll wake up to find I’m back at the academy.’ Her eyes filled with tears. ‘I’m longing to get to know you better brother mine.’

R

‘Where are you going?’

‘Shopping. The poor girl has only the clothes she stands up in and a few rags in a bag she brought from the academy.’ A bee came in through the French window and landed on an arrangement of white roses and pink peonies. ‘Rebecca has never had a decent cloak or gown as far as I can see. The few clothes she owns are too short or too tight. She’s almost seventeen and still growing. Her only day dress is positively indecent. Would you have her going about showing her ankles?’

‘Of course she must have whatever she needs, buy whatever she wants, charge it all to me. She’s in need of spoiling.’

‘Luckily Molly is a dab hand at sewing, as is Rebecca, between them they’ve altered one of my mourning gowns to fit her until the clothes we order from the dressmaker arrive. Of course when she comes out of mourning she’ll need summer bonnets and slippers, ribbons and other fripperies a lady can’t live without. I’m also taking Rose for a fitting as she too is bursting out of her clothes.’

‘For the love of God I’ll be bankrupt.’ He took his wife in his arms and held her tight. ‘It’s just as well I prefer you naked,’ he whispered in her ear sending a shiver tingling down her spine. ‘At least *you* don’t need new clothes.’ He brushed his lips against her neck, then found her lips and kissed her softly, searchingly.

They heard a sound by the door.

‘Sorry, I tried to warn you I was here by coughing a little, but you didn't hear,' Rebecca said.

'Ah, sorry we sometimes act like newlyweds.' Eleanor stepped away from her husband.

'No apology needed I assure you,' Rebecca said blushing scarlet. 'It's so refreshing to see a couple who love and respect each other as you two obviously do. It's something I've never witnessed before.'

'They're always kissing.' Ruari came in behind Haydan, both were pulling a face. The boys headed for the bee.

'Have you found the treasure yet?' Gabriel asked changing the subject quickly. Eleanor knew it was times like this Gabriel wished the children could be seen and not heard.

Rose rushed at her father. 'Here I am Pa, I'm your treasure am I not?'

'You are Dumpling. I hear you're off to buy new clothes.'

'We are thank you Pa. I want a yellow gown for the summer, like the sunshine.'

'The sun's not yellow it's gold.' Haydan stuffed a biscuit in his mouth.

'Where's Ginny, we need to get off, the carriage is waiting.' Eleanor kissed her husband goodbye. Haydan made a slurping sound by kissing the back of his own hand. Eleanor judiciously ignored her son.

'I'm here mistress, but I'm afraid Haydan's in trouble again. Perhaps his father would like to know what bother he's been up to now. Tell your papa what you stole from the kitchen.'

Eleanor hid a smile. 'I'm sure he would. Come Rose, Rebecca, let's go into town and leave the man of the house to lay down the law,' she grinned then threw over her shoulder, 'stealing is punishable by chopping off a hand Haydan, did you know that?'

'It wasn't me.' She heard him plead as she took her hat from the table in the hall. Sam was waiting for them and handed them both into the carriage, before lifting Rose up and putting her down inside.

'Thank you Sam, you're so strong,' Rose said settling herself besides her mama.

'He is indeed,' Eleanor said dryly. 'Do you ride Rebecca?' Eleanor asked when they were on their way.

'I've not ridden for years. Of course there was no need at school, but I did ride a little in France.'

'You can have lessons with me Becky. I have lessons at the stud and sometimes with Sam. I can do a rising trot can't I Mama?'

'You can my love, but I don't think it polite you shorten Rebecca's name.'

'But Mama I've Becky's permission. She said she wants a new name for her new life.'

Eleanor noticed the young woman blush again; she blushed easily Eleanor noticed. Young men would find it most beguiling.

'I don't mind at all, in fact I should like it when we're together at home. Of course you may not think it appropriate when we're in society.'

'Whatever pleases you Rebecca, so long as you're happy.'

The fittings took an age and then they had to visit the haberdashers, all of which was provoking for Eleanor. She had something on her mind and was anxious to get the errands finished quickly. Finally with their shopping completed they were making their way back to their carriage when Padraic Turner appeared before them.

'Good afternoon Eleanor, you look especially attractive today.' She noticed him look Rebecca up and down. The man had terrible manners. Could he not see her companion was in mourning?

'Allow me to introduce Miss Rebecca Argyle, my husband's ward. You know Rose of course. He bent down to kiss Rose's podgy little hand. Eleanor knew it was all for show, but Rose was flattered by the attention nonetheless.

'This is Captain Padraic Turner, a family friend.' Eleanor was not sure the description suited him. The captain cast his most winning smile at Rebecca and kissed her hand... for just a moment too long. Eleanor pursed her lips. Again the poor girl blushed.

'Where has Gabriel been hiding this ravishing beauty?' Turner had turned on the charm offensive. No wonder Rebecca appeared flattered; he was enough to turn any young girl's head.

'I'm sorry we can't stop to chat, but Rose has to get back for her lessons, will you excuse us please Captain Turner.'

'Ah but I'm sure you can wait a moment, pass the time of day with an old friend. I swear I'll not take up more than a moment of your time.' Again the dazzling smile, Rebecca flushed anew.

'What news of your new adventure? When do you sail?' Eleanor explained: 'The captain is emigrating to the New World shortly Rebecca.'

'If your husband had only come to his senses sooner I should have been long gone. As it is I'm hoping for a more reliable buyer for the ships. Who knows when I'll get away now? But what news is this? I didn't know your husband had a ward.'

This was not how Eleanor wanted to present Rebecca into society. Not his society at least. 'As I say Padraic we're pushed for time today. I'm sure we'll meet again before you sail, goodbye.'

He made a great fuss of handing them into the waiting carriage. 'Perhaps I could invite you ladies to tea. Would you like that Rosie Lee?'

Rose giggled. 'Oh yes sir I would, will there be cake?'

'But of course. I'll check my diary and let you know the date.'

As the carriage pulled off Eleanor saw the look on Rebecca's face. It was clear she was enthralled with the captain.

Eleanor said: 'That's one invitation we'll decline; he and Gabriel aren't exactly sworn enemies, but let's just say they don't get on. It's a long story and now they're in the middle of a business deal so I think it best if we ladies keep out of it.'

'I see. He has a wonderful accent, where is he from?'

'Ireland, Dublin I think. He has a silver tongue; sensible ladies give him a wide berth.'

As they pulled up outside Westshore Eleanor noticed the dreamy look on the young girl's face; it appeared she may have an eye for older men.

R

Back at Westshore Eleanor prepared to go out again. She was about to mount her horse when Rebecca appeared.

'I was coming to ask if you'd like to go for a walk, but I see you're busy.'

'I'm sorry I've business to attend to, a boring matter, but I'm afraid it cannot wait. We could go when I get back?'

Eleanor felt her cheeks warm as she kicked Jet on. It wasn't exactly a lie, but it wasn't the whole truth either. On her return from the dressmaker she had sent a note to Eastshore asking to see Padraic. He had returned a short reply saying he was at home and was looking forward to her visit. Eleanor curled her lip at his pert reply; the man was the limit.

'It was a welcome surprise to get your note Eleanor. Especially as earlier you couldn't wait to see the back of me. Have you come to tell me you're leaving that swine of a husband and are running away to Virginia with me?'

She wrung her hands together dramatically. 'I have. I simply can't imagine living without you Padraic... take me away from all this.' There was more than a touch of sarcasm in her voice. 'You are a fool Padraic, and I resent you calling my husband a swine. I came to ask when Eastshore will be vacant, you must know I'm keen to let it and the agent needs a date when the house will be available. I'm sure there's somewhere you can stay until you sail. A lady friend would be willing to let you lay your head perhaps?' She raised an eyebrow. 'Technically Eastshore now belongs to me, and I'm keen to see a return on my investment.'

She watched as he turned the gold ring on the little finger of his left hand; she recognised the wedding ring he had given Caroline.

'You'd have me walk the streets? You're a harsh businesswoman Eleanor.'

'I doubt it will come to that. I'd wager there'd be a long line of ladies offering you a bed... I mean a roof over your head.'

She was surprised when instead of his usual ribald retort, they often used to bandy words together, he looked crestfallen. There was sadness in his eyes. He turned away quickly.

'Will you take tea?' He summoned the maid without waiting for a reply.

Eleanor held her tongue until tea was served. 'Is there a problem Padraic?'

She knew how mercurial he could be and hoped he wasn't going to spin her some yarn to try to get an extension on his stay. She already thought she had been lenient enough letting him live at Eastshore since the sale was finalised. At the time he was hoping to be sailing to Virginia within a matter of weeks so it was but a little imposition. Gabriel had been against him staying on, but she had overruled her husband. Had she not liquidised most of her own assets to buy the house? It was *her* decision. She hoped she wasn't about to regret it.

'Not a problem as such. I know we agreed the furniture and fittings were to be included in the sale so they will remain in situ, and my own belongings are packed and ready to be shipped, but... there's Caroline's things... '

She looked questioningly at his painful expression.

'Will you please come with me? I'd rather show you than try to explain.'

He moved to the door. Under normal circumstances Eleanor wouldn't have dreamt of following him upstairs, she knew him too well, but she sensed this was no a trick. She saw it was taking all his strength to compose himself. His normally cocky confidence had evaporated like a sea fret on a sunny day. He opened the door to what was obviously Caroline's dressing room.

Eleanor was shocked. It was as though her friend had stepped out of the door a moment ago. The dressing table was tidy with her brushes and combs laid out in serried ranks, her trinket box gleamed in the sunlight and her dressing robe hung on a hanger by the door. There wasn't a speck of dust; the room was as she had left it.

Eleanor swallowed hard when she saw the wretched look on Padraic's handsome face. 'But its years since Caroline passed. Why have you not sorted all this out?' she whispered.

He let out a long, slow breath. 'I couldn't face it, couldn't throw anything away. It would have felt disrespectful to dispose of her things. What was I to do with all this?' His voice was hoarse as he glanced about the room.

He stepped through into the connecting bedchamber and opened another door. Inside were all Caroline's clothes; dresses, gowns, riding habits, rows of them, all neat and covered with linen. The smell of cedar wood drifted on the air.

'A maid comes in every few days and makes sure the rooms are cleaned. Moths have been kept at bay; her things are as she left them on the morning she rode out to her death.'

He sank onto the bed. Eleanor noticed a gossamer thin nightgown lay artfully on the counterpane.

He looked appealingly at her. 'Will you oversee the removal of her clothes and her more intimate possessions? I can't think of anyone else who would take more care than you. I know Lottie would, but I would prefer if you could help. I'm sure you'll know what to do. Take what you like; do what you like, but please clear it all away. Make it go away.'

Eleanor was moved beyond words. She and Gabriel had often argued about whether Padraic had married Caroline because she was a beautiful heiress or because he had truly loved her. Gabriel had never had a high opinion of the captain while she had preferred, to some extent, to give him the benefit of the doubt. Now she saw the answer; he really did love Caroline.

'Of course I'll help you Padraic. Why did you not ask before? You know I would have done this for you.' She sat beside him on the bed and took his hand in hers. 'I think it's a good idea you'll leave Eastshore, leave England I mean. A fresh start in a new country will do you good.'

'Why do you think I've hardly been here since Carla died? The memories were too hard to bear. Can you smell her perfume? I can, every time I come in here.'

Eleanor breathed in the familiar scent Caroline favoured. It was one she had made up in London. It had a warm base note of sandalwood and violet mingled with a fresher lemony top note. It was as if she was in the room, watching them.

Eleanor choked back tears. She missed her friend too. 'Oh Padraic why torture yourself? If only I'd known but you seemed... '

'To be coping?' His laugh was hollow. 'There's nothing anyone can do. Can you bring her back? Or the baby? We'd only just begun our journey together and we had such plans, lots of plans.'

She squeezed his hand, but could think of nothing sensible to say; platitudes were superfluous under the circumstances. She felt as if she really didn't know the man, the real man at all. She had never guessed at his depth of feeling. Gabriel would be more than a little surprised.

It had turned into a wet day, a weeping day. The branches of the trees dripped long after the rain had ceased. Back at Westshore Eleanor went to her bedroom, it was the only place she could think of where she wouldn't be disturbed. The children were with Ginny, Rebecca was about somewhere possibly waiting for her to go for a walk, and Gabriel wasn't due home until later. She lay on the bed and thought about what she had seen and heard at Eastshore.

She wasn't sure how long she had been there, but the light was fading when the door opened and Gabriel came in and sat on the edge of the bed.

'Are you unwell? Can I get you anything? Rebecca says she's not seen you for hours. She thought you were still out, but I saw Jet was back in his stable.'

She sat up. 'Not ill. I went to see Padraic to ask him when he might vacate Eastshore. Oh Gabriel!' She launched herself into his arms sobbing.

'What in God's name! Did he make a play for you again? Did he compromise you? I'll kill him.'

'No, no nothing like that.' She dried her eyes and between sobs told all.

Gabriel's shoulders dropped. 'I was wrong; he really did love her then.'

'And still does. You of all people should know that when someone dies love doesn't die with them.'

She swung her legs from the bed and sat beside him as she had done earlier with Padraic. 'He said that was the reason he'd been away from Alnmouth since Caroline died; he couldn't stand being at Eastshore without her.'

'I never liked the pet name he gave her - Carla. I thought it affected.' Eleanor narrowed her eyes, exasperated. 'But I'm gratified to know Caro knew real love however.' They sat in silence for a few moments then Gabriel added: 'They would have had a happy future together if he really loved her. Turner has few of the refinements of polite society, but he has charm in spades, and it appears real love for Caro.'

'Yes, a real and abiding love. He's heartbroken.'

'His charisma means he's been accepted, to some extent, in Alnmouth society.'

'It's true, even Dolly Harper accepted him and she's a notorious snob. Perhaps it was because of Caroline? He took on the mantle of respectability being married to someone who was well liked and respected.'

'Yet if what Bryony Swift said is true he used to be a smuggler.' Gabriel sneered. 'In my opinion Padraic has always had a sense of entitlement, a self assurance which allowed him access where others would be denied. I wonder if Caro knew about his dealings with the trade. Still, I never thought I'd say this but, I feel sorry for the man. I was mistaken, regarding Caro I mean. I see that from what you say it was a love match. If I put myself in his shoes and God forbid it had been you who'd died, I too would feel the same, about a new start I mean, but is it not running away?' He put his hand on his heart. 'Is it not in here where Caro lives? The departed live here in our hearts and in our memories, not in the bricks and mortar of a house, we take our loved ones with us wherever we go.'

'I agree but I can see why he wants to start afresh. There's always something to remind him here in Alnmouth. A favourite walk they shared, her favourite flower blooming in the garden, her perfume. Gabriel it was so heartbreaking. I could smell her, feel her presence.' She shuddered. 'I wonder does he go into her rooms each night. It must be hell for him. He obviously puts on a show to the rest of the world and a good show at that. Perhaps that's the reason he wants to sail out on the Alnmouth Girl. It will be one last thing to take with him, one last reminder of Caroline.'

She saw her husband scrape his thumb down the stubble on his chin and heard the rasp.

'Then he shall have her. I'll write and tell him I've changed my mind. His need is greater than mine, I see that now. With the obstacle of the Alnmouth Girl removed he can begin to move on, start again in the New World.' Gabriel held her in his arms and rested his chin on the top of her head.

'It's times like this when I cherish you most, don't ever leave me Eleanor.'

'And don't you ever leave me my love.'

There was a silence, this time a long one.

'Yet one day it will happen. One of us will inevitably leave the other. Selfishly I hope I go first. You're stronger than me, you'll manage, cope.'

Eleanor shook herself and pulled free. She stood abruptly. 'Don't be foolish Gabriel. It's true of course one day death will part us, but spending our precious time on earth being gloomy won't make a jot of difference. Caroline wouldn't wish any of us to waste our lives being fearful. Come, I'm hungry it must be nearly supper time.'

Gabriel followed her down the stairs. 'Ever the pragmatist,' he muttered. 'As I said you'd get by without me far better than I'd manage without you.'

6

Rebecca Argyle began to settle into life at Westshore. Both Gabriel and Eleanor were becoming fond of the young woman and the girl herself was happy and content with her new life. Despite hating her school days, Rebecca had been a good student, therefore she was a well educated young lady and possessed many interests and accomplishments.

One thing Rebecca was particularly good at was needlework. She had soon won Rose over by making the child's favourite rag doll a new outfit complete with a felt hat and tiny shoes. She had also helped Rose to get started on a sampler. It had surprised Eleanor that her daughter was keen to learn to sew. She had never had the patience, or the skill it had to be said, to perfect the art.

Rebecca was also a great reader and on wet days could often be found curled up with a book of poetry in the library. Eleanor had also lent her several romantic novels which she had devoured. Rebecca was keen on flora and fauna too; the beach became a favourite place, and after a session of beachcombing she would look up her finds in a dusty old tome which had belonged to Gabriel's mama. She had even managed to get the boys interested in books by showing them how to find the names of the different shells and seaweeds they found. Haydan was particularly keen when Rebecca agreed to catalogue his finds. The twins were reluctantly beginning to learn their letters, but this research was giving them the impetus to want to learn more quickly. Their parents were amazed.

Rebecca's greatest accomplishment however, was the spinet. She had tested the instrument which had been sitting unused in the corner of the drawing room since Alice Reynolds died. As the spinet was another skill Eleanor had never mastered it had not been played in years. When Gabriel realised his ward could play he sent for a man to clean and retune it; in time he hoped she would teach Rose to play too. He remembered fondly how his dear mama used to play for him. Now sometimes in the evenings Rebecca played and Eleanor sang. Singing was the one thing Eleanor could do musically although she was purely self taught. Gabriel listened with growing admiration for his womenfolk as he had jokily taken to calling them.

The one achievement in which Rebecca did not outshine Eleanor was riding. She had ridden as a child but was now out of practice. Sometimes Eleanor supervised her on the lunge rein and often Sam, the head groom, took her into the paddock and put her through her paces. She was quickly becoming a capable horsewoman. She wasn't yet good enough to go out and about on her own Eleanor thought, but Rebecca was keen not to be a trouble to her new family. Sometimes Eleanor's maid Molly, or one of the grooms would accompany her, but often she would promise not to go too far and ride alone. Rebecca was still exploring her new surroundings and, Eleanor realised, she sometimes liked her own company. And who could blame her when the twins were in high spirits; Westshore was often noisy with their screams and loud voices. Eleanor too needed her own space on occasions.

When on a glorious sunny day Rebecca thought to take a ride Eleanor suggested she take a groom along as she couldn't chaperone her, she was expected at Hope House to look over the monthly accounts. Sam was free so he saddled the horses and they set off towards Boulmer.

'Have you always worked with horses Sam?' Rebecca asked as they rode through the surf. He had told her the horses liked to paddle.

'Yes since I was a lad in Yorkshire. I moved to Northumberland for a better position shortly after I married. I was under groom for a wealthy land owner. He kept a stable full of thoroughbreds besides carriage horses. It was a good job.' He reached out and pulled on her reins. 'Look out ahead Miss Argyle.' They rode around two large blue jelly fish.

Sam, in his early thirties, was quite a handsome man. He was strongly built with broad shoulders. Rebecca thought he had an aristocratic profile; he had a strong jaw with an aquiline nose. He wore his thick, dark hair tied back in a queue.

'So why did you leave? Oh I'm sorry, how rude of me asking such a personal question.'

'It's of no matter. Mary, my wife, became ill. At first we thought the illness would be of short duration and she would recover, but as it turned out that wasn't the case. She died three months after contracting a condition which started out with her vomiting, and then she had terrible headaches and stiffness in her joints. Later the disease progressed so she was fighting for breath.' Sam looked out to sea. 'I'm sure it was a relief for her when she died.'

'I'm so sorry. I knew you were a widower but... the poor children.'

'Thank you, I never expected to be a widower so young, and of course this left me with Beth and Davy to look after. They were little then, and knowing no one who could look after them while I was at work I hired a woman. I worked long days so I was hardly at home. I relied on her, she was a sort of housekeeper, I paid her well but she drank the money away and one day I came home to find her out cold, drunk, and the children still in their nightclothes, unfed.'

'Oh my goodness, how awful.'

'I had to give up the post of course and find work with less hours, or more flexible hours at least. That's when we moved to Westshore. We have a tied cottage at the back of Lisbet and Abner's. It works well thanks to Mr and Mrs Reynolds being so understanding. It's been a blessing because Lisbet often looks after Beth when my lad's at school.

'If ever Lisbet is unavailable I can always keep an eye on her. They're both lovely children, so well mannered; they're a credit to you Sam.'

'Thank you Miss, Beth is the image of her mama.'

'She's a pretty girl.'

Rebecca tired easily in the saddle not being used to long rides, she knew if they went much further she would be sore the next day.

They turned for Westshore chatting companionably all the way. Sam was easy to talk to and Rebecca found she liked him.

Eleanor was in the yard when they returned.

'You didn't fall off then?' Eleanor smiled up at Rebecca.

'Miss Argyle has a good seat, but we took it steady, no galloping today.'

A few days ago Rebecca had ridden her new horse, Hero, for the first time; she had almost had a fall when he decided to increase the pace without prior warning. Sam had cut in front of Hero to slow him down and disaster had been averted. Rebecca had been most grateful Sam had been there to come to her assistance.

The two women left Sam to rub the horses down and went to the drawing room where Eleanor ordered tea.

'Have you balanced the books?' Rebecca asked between mouthfuls of buttered crumpets.

'It doesn't take long. They're quite straight forward.'

'They are for someone like you who's used to such things. I wouldn't know where to start.'

'If you ever want a lesson you only have to ask. One day, when you marry, you'll be mistress of a household and you'll need to know the merchants and servants aren't swindling you. Being able to balance the books helps.'

'You talk as if it's a foregone conclusion I'll marry. What if I don't, what if no one offers for me?'

'Do you think it likely a pretty, educated, personable girl like you will go begging? I've seen how the men are drawn to you like moths to the proverbial. You'll be a heart breaker I'm sure.'

Rebecca blushed at the compliment and changed the subject. 'Perhaps I could help out sometimes at Hope House? I don't mind getting my hands dirty, I'd help in any capacity.'

Eleanor thought for a moment. 'Some of the women and girls are a little rough and ready if you know what I mean; some have been dragged up as Lottie often says. Some are more innocent than others of course, but none of them deserve to be left without support of any kind. We opened a school last year, but the teacher we hired though good at her job, found she couldn't handle some of the girls. Perhaps you could take a class or two, teach some of the younger ones their letters and numbers. A lot of them can't read either. If they had basic lessons in reading, writing and arithmetic it would give them a chance of securing better paid work.'

'I should like that. When can I start?'

'Whenever you have spare time but as I say the girls are a handful sometimes.'

'When I was riding out with Sam earlier he was telling me about how his wife died; such a sad story. I said if ever he needs help with the children I'd help out. I wonder if Beth can read. He told me she's nearly six so if she can't I could teach her. Perhaps I'll suggest it to him.'

'What a good idea. You could borrow some of the children's books for her to make a start. He's a lovely man, a hard worker too. Gabriel hired him because he had experience with carriage horses. Gabriel knew he was well qualified and he came with excellent references, but what clinched it was when Sam told him why he had to leave his last employer. Gabriel is such a softie and I love him for it.'

'Such a shame the children haven't a mama, I know only too well what that's like. Of course I had a mama, but hardly ever saw her once I was at school.' Rebecca looked wistful. 'Sam is such a warm, caring man. I'll go and ask him now if Beth needs help with her reading.'

No sooner had Rebecca left the room than Gabriel appeared. 'You're home early,' Eleanor said as he bent to kiss the top of her head.

'Can a man not come home when he has a fancy to see his beloved wife and children?'

'I only meant I'd not expected you yet, nothing more.'

'I like to keep you on your toes, make sure you're not up to anything you shouldn't be.'

'Gabriel, I'm rationing myself to one small sigh a day, don't let me waste it on you. What on earth would I be getting up to with children and Rebecca in the house? You do talk nonsense.'

'Is there tea left in the pot?' Eleanor poured him a dish. He sat next to her to drink it. 'I saw Rebecca in the stables talking with Sam. Is he another who is smitten with her? They looked cosy together. I suppose a good looking girl like Rebecca will always have a following.'

Eleanor told him why she had gone to see Sam. 'He's the sort of character to attract her. He's already a hero in her eyes I expect. He saved her from a fall the other day, he's her champion. He's not bad looking either which helps. He's also a young widower who suffered greatly when his poor wife died leaving him with two motherless children. It's the stuff of novels. Young lady meets man from a different station in life, everyone tells her it cannot be, but they fall in love, surmount all the obstacles, marry and live on her money. The children adore their new mama and they all live happily ever after. It's the theme in many a romantic novel.'

'I wouldn't know. You don't think Sam would set his cap at her do you? He's a fine fellow, but well, I hope she'll do better for herself than a head groom.'

'Obstacle number one; her dastardly guardian forbids the marriage.' Eleanor laughed at the look on her husband's face, but was prevented from teasing him further when Rebecca returned.

'May I borrow a couple of books please Eleanor?'

Gabriel butted in: 'If they're romantic novels then no; your head will be filled with silly nonsense.'

Rebecca looked puzzled.

'Ignore him Rebecca; he's got the wrong end of the stick again. Becky wants to borrow books suitable for Sam's daughter. I told you she's going to teach Beth to read. I should take the alphabet one first my dear, teach Beth her letters first. It will be in the nursery I expect.'

'That's kind of you Rebecca - to think of others.' Gabriel helped himself to a scone and loaded it with cream and jam.

'It's the least I can do; everyone has been so kind to me since I came to Westshore. I'm to help out at Hope House too, teaching the young girls.' She left in search of the book.

'She's a sweet nature has she not? She's thoughtful and caring.'

'She is. I only hope she'll be able to cope at Hope House. Some of the girls are... well let's just say they're not ladylike.'

'It will do her good to mix with people from different walks of life, show her that not all have an easy life... not that she's had an easy time of course.'

'I agree. Our children are so lucky and it's hard not to spoil them, but at some point they'll have to learn not everyone shares their good fortune. But then again they're only young, plenty of time before they have to be introduced to the harsh realities of life, not that you or I have ever suffered hunger and loss like so many hereabouts.'

Ruari appeared in the doorway of the conservatory. 'Is there cake left? May I have some please Mama?'

'Certainly not young man,' Gabriel said. 'Your mama thinks it about time you learnt the harsh realities of life. You can have dry bread and water from now on and only then thrice a week.' Gabriel saw the look of abject horror on his son's face, beckoned him to the table and handed him a slice of seed cake. 'Perhaps we'll start tomorrow,' Gabriel said laughing. Ruari took the cake gingerly and looked to his mama.

'Papa is joking Ruari, or at least I think he is... eat up, we'll try your brother on the new regime instead.'

R

Eleanor was sad to see how low Susan Stubbs had fallen. It was clear from her laboured breathing she was gravely ill.

'We've been abroad and then a family matter has kept me busy or I should have called sooner. It was Doctor Chaffer who told me you were ill. How are you feeling today Susan?'

'As you can see my dear, not good which is most frustrating.' Perspiration moistened her top lip. 'I remembered you were going to see your friends the Vissers.' Susan fought for breath. 'Oh how I wish I could travel, but I fear the only journey I will be undertaking is in a box to the churchyard.' She smiled wanly. 'Don't bother to protest my dear; at least I have had a good innings unlike my poor goddaughter. Caroline was taken long before her time.'

Eleanor was never good in a sickroom and struggled to find cheerful topics to talk about. When she had told Susan about Amsterdam and the subsequent visit to Whitby, carefully omitting Gabriel's accident as she thought it not an appropriate subject, she made to leave. She could tell the poor woman was struggling to stay awake. She promised to call again in a day or two.

'Before I go I ought to mention something about Caroline which may be of interest to you, but if I'm tiring you it can wait.'

'You had better impart your news today Eleanor, lest it be too late.'

Eleanor explained how Captain Turner had asked her to empty Caroline's personal effects from Eastshore. 'Caroline's possessions are packed away. Is there a keepsake you would like, a trinket perhaps?'

'Soon it will be someone clearing away my belongings. I think not to make them more work my dear.' She chuckled bravely. 'I am surprised it has taken Captain Turner so long, but I understand from Miss Swift you now own Eastshore. It is nice to think it will belong to someone with a connection to Caroline and her father. I was not at all surprised the captain seeks adventures abroad, but I admit I am surprised he loved her quite so much that he kept her rooms as a shrine.' She fought for another breath. 'How extraordinary.'

Eleanor's eyes brimmed with tears as she made her way downstairs. The last few days had been trying, hard on her nerves, now this. She was about to leave when the drawing room door opened and Bryony Swift appeared.

'Good morning Mrs Reynolds, I imagine you're much shocked by Mrs Stubbs' rapid decline. Before you went away she was well, now she's not long for this world, or so the doctor says.'

'I'm sorry to see her so reduced; she was always a vibrant, cheerful lady.'

'And kind, so very kind. If not for her who knows what would have become of me. She kept me on when others would have turned me out.'

When Bryony Swift had, for a short time, been Eleanor's personal maid she had been difficult to manage. She had been given notice after she had made a deliberate and shameless play for Gabriel. Bryony had a colourful past, which included having an illegitimate child with Captain Turner before he was married to Caroline. The baby boy had been adopted by Eleanor's friends the Vissers, when Bryony had abandoned him at Westshore. Mats, as he was named, now lived in Holland.

'With Susan's help and guidance you have turned your life around have you not? You're a great help at Hope House too I hear. It's good of you to give up some of your free time for the charity. I expect you'll have more time on your hands soon though I'm sure you wouldn't wish it.' Eleanor glanced up the stairs where Susan Stubbs lay dying.

'She has a good nurse, but I like to look after her myself as much as I can. I read to her in the mornings when she's a little brighter.'

'That's kind of you. What shall you do when... will you stay in the area?'

'It depends if I can find work, who knows what the future holds.' She shrugged philosophically.

Eleanor turned to go then stopped. 'We have been in Amsterdam - to see our friends.'

'Mrs Stubbs told me.'

Eleanor thought Bryony would be keen to know how her son was doing. She wasn't mean spirited enough to deny her the information. 'Would you walk out to my carriage with me Miss Swift?'

A footman opened the carriage door and let down the step. Eleanor reached inside and brought out a flat parcel which she handed to Bryony. 'My friend, Abalone, is an artist. She sent this for you with her kind regards.'

Bryony peeled back the paper carefully to reveal a watercolour of a small boy. She let out a sob.

'He's the image of his father!' she cried.

'He is and he's a lovely little boy, light hearted yet thoughtful. My friends dote on him and he in turn loves them and his older sister. As you say he looks like his papa, but he has your eyes I think.'

Bryony was too overcome with emotion to reply.

'I must go. I hope to call in a day or two to see Susan, but if the worst should happen before then please let me know.'

On the journey home Eleanor thought about how it must be for Bryony Swift separated from her son; never seeing him, never holding him in her arms, never kissing him goodnight. How could she bear it? Then a thought struck her. Did Padraic know he was a father? If Bryony wanted Turner to know then she would have told him. Perhaps he didn't know? Eleanor thought he trusted her and when he had spoken so intimately last time about his love for Caroline, he would surely have added the child to his list of losses. She turned the notion around in her head.

The twins along with Rose ran to meet their mama as she stepped from her carriage. They were disdainful of the many hugs and kisses she bestowed upon them but she was not to be put off. She held them tight as though she would never let them go.

7

Eleanor and Rebecca sat either side of the fire. The wind roared down the chimney and rain hurled against the windows. Gabriel poured them all a drink. They were awaiting their guest, Captain Charles Noble.

'You'll like Charles Rebecca, he's so amusing and so handsome in his regimentals. I always thought you'd look dashing in uniform my love.' Eleanor looked her husband up and down.

'Would you have me enlist just to look dashing?'

'Perhaps not, I'd miss you too much, but the next time we go to a costume party perhaps you could go in a uniform.'

Gabriel handed Rebecca a cordial. He winked at his half sister. 'Eleanor always had a soft spot for Charles. If she'd not seen me first I think she would have taken him, impoverished as he is. They could have lived on her money.'

'As he is about to do now with someone else's dowry. You do exaggerate Gabriel, all I said was I thought him amusing. He has a wicked sense of fun, unlike some who *think* themselves amusing but aren't.' She looked pointedly at him.

'What's that supposed to mean?'

'It means you *think* you're witty while Charles actually is.'

The playful bickering was nipped in the bud with the arrival of their guest.

'Good evening all. I could have swum here. The night is turning into a wet and stormy one, I'd forgotten how the weather here in the North East can be as fickle as a woman, present company excepted. I'm soaked. Was it not a glorious sunny afternoon earlier?' He strode over to Eleanor and kissed her hand. 'I'm glad to see some things don't change, you look as young and gorgeous as the last time I saw you.'

Eleanor was flattered as was the intention. Charles noticed Rebecca. 'Forgive me you must wonder what the cat dragged in; Captain Charles Noble at your service.'

'Charles, this is my ward Miss Rebecca Argyle. Rebecca has been at school until recently. She lives with us now, but it's a long story so let me get you a drink while you dry yourself by the fire.'

Gabriel noticed as he handed him his drink, Charles didn't have a hair out of place. Probably some naval greatcoat abandoned in the hall had kept him dry and pristine.

'I'm disappointed you're not in uniform Charles, I was telling Rebecca how dashing you look in it.' Eleanor made room for him to sit beside her.

'Let me know when you can pop over and I'll dress up especially for you,' he said cheerily.

'Don't come here with your amorous advances Charlie boy, not unless you want to fight a duel, and we both know how that will end. You never did know one end of a sword from another.'

'Which is precisely why I should choose pistols; you were always a bad shot Gabe.'

'Lack of practise; you know I never shoot, though many friends offer me the chance to have a go at their pheasants or pigeons.'

They continued to chat amiably with Gabriel and Eleanor making sure Rebecca wasn't left out of the conversation. Gabriel told Charles a little of how his ward came to be at Westshore.

'I'm sorry for your loss Miss Argyle. A double blow losing both parents so close together,' Charles said. Gabriel hadn't elaborated about John Argyle's lack of care and attention towards his daughter. 'It's such a shame you didn't enjoy your schooling; we enjoyed our schooldays enormously did we not Gabriel?' He looked knowingly at his friend. 'Though most of our education was gained outside the classroom - oh, forgive me Miss Argyle, I forget myself.' Colour immediately infused Rebecca's face once again as Charles turned his smile on her. He continued: 'I can't imagine how awful it must have been for you to feel so isolated, so alone in the world. You showed great fortitude in escaping from the place. Not many young ladies possess the guile to evade detection, for I'm sure they would have come looking for you.'

'When you're a virtual prisoner sir, and awaiting a sentence you'll risk anything to get away.'

'Rebecca even had to pawn the one valuable possession she had; a locket which was a gift from her dear mama. It had her mama's image inside. Such a shame she had to part with it,' Eleanor said.

'But the money it raised got me away from that awful place and here to safety with you both. Mama would understand.'

'Still, when one loses a cherished possession it cannot be easy. You're philosophical for one so young my dear,' Charles said as he led the young woman into supper.

Once seated Eleanor pounced; Gabriel knew she was dying to find out about Charles' fiancée. She had already been quizzing him for details. Gabriel had protested saying he knew little about Miss Crow. She hadn't believed him. Now she went in for the kill.

'When Gabriel told me you were to be married I asked him what your future wife was like. Of course he was worse than useless in supplying information. Tell me about her for all I know so far is her name.'

Gabriel remembered the face his wife had pulled when he told her Violet's surname was Crow. She had decided Violet was a pretty name, but Crow was a name she thought the poor woman would be glad to shed on marriage. Violet Noble she decreed was far preferable.

'You will meet Violet at the welcome party, but I'll tell you something to be going on with shall I?' He winked at Rebecca. 'Violet lives in Sheringham in Norfolk, she only has a distant cousin, both her parents died when she was young, and she used to be a pirate... wears a patch over one eye,' he teased.

Eleanor sighed in frustration. 'Fair, dark or a redhead?' She wasn't easily deterred.

'Grey and straggly.'

Eleanor sighed again in pretend impatience. 'Eyes?'

'Two, one bloodshot the other covered with a patch as I already told you.'

Charles raised an eyebrow making Rebecca laugh. She was clearly enjoying herself.

'Be serious Charles. Is she tall, medium or small in height?' Eleanor stood her ground.

'About the same height as Queen Charlotte.'

'How tall is that? You talk in riddles. Very well I see you aren't going to tell us anything pertinent. Perhaps you want her to be a lovely surprise for us. That I suppose is your prerogative.'

Gabriel laughed loudly. It wasn't often his wife was bested. She shot him a look, then laughed as well.

'I hear you're in need of accommodation Charles. Did you know I've become a landlady?' she joked. She told him how and why she had bought Eastshore. 'Of course I had to have my husband's signature on the deeds, being a mere woman, but it's my money that bought Eastshore,' she said proudly. 'Poor Ruari by being born minutes after Haydan is seen by society as the spare heir,' she huffed, 'most unfair in my humble opinion.'

Charles listened with interest then said cheerily: 'The term has been levelled at me also. I know Eastshore of course, but I didn't know Turner was heading to the Americas. I think the house will suit us as a stop gap. I don't need to look her over for I remember her well so if you'll have me, and Violet too of course, as tenants then where do I sign?'

'*Her*,' Gabriel mocked, 'it's a house not a ship. You'd better start getting used to being on dry land had you not?'

Before he could answer Eleanor thought of one last question. 'Does Miss Crow like to ride Charles?'

'I couldn't say. Do pirates have the need to ride? Do you ride Miss Argyle?' Charles turned his attention to Rebecca. He was being deliberately evasive. 'Most ladies today are extraordinarily accomplished I find.'

'I haven't ridden for some years but Gabriel has been kind enough to furnish me with a horse. Another kindness I can never repay.'

'From what I see Gabriel is enjoying having your company Miss Argyle, and who can blame him? And anyway he can afford it... he's not a pauper by any means.' Charles, as always, was good company, they were all enjoying themselves.

Eleanor stood to leave the table. 'Come Rebecca we'll leave the men to their port, their banter *and* their secrets.' She leaned into Gabriel and said sotto voce: 'Bring me information about Miss Crow or sleep by yourself tonight.'

Left alone Charles said: 'You're so lucky. Eleanor's a good sport and an attractive woman. She's borne you not one but two sons and a daughter. She's your perfect match in every way.' His face clouded over.

'I take it Miss Crow wouldn't have been your first choice Charles?'

'As you say she wouldn't have been first in line if I'd been able to pick and choose, but needs must and I dare say we'll make it work. Others have done the same before us. Look at Claude and Cecily.' He mentioned his brother, the heir to the Noble dynasty, such as it was, and his wife. Their marriage too was arranged though Cecily's dowry was nothing compared to Miss Crow's offering.

'I feel for you my friend. However, you do realise that by your evasiveness my dear wife's imagination is now set free and running wild. She'll think you're hiding a rare jewel.' He raised an eyebrow. 'Is Miss Crow so unsatisfactory? If she is I feel even sorrier for you for I know what it is to marry for love.'

'Rub salt in the wound why don't you?' Charles helped himself to a fine tawny port Gabriel had put by him. 'Between you and I, for I shouldn't want to sound disloyal but,' he thought for a moment, 'I should say she's on the plain side and not a little socially awkward.'

'Shy you mean?'

'No, not shy. Rebecca's shy, Lord she's nothing like your ward, who's charming by the way.'

Gabriel had decided not to tell Charles about Rebecca's true parentage for the time being lest she should feel embarrassed, though Gabriel knew he would tell Charles in due course. He trusted him with the information, but realised this wasn't the occasion to impart her sad story.

'She's... how to describe Violet's looks and character?' Charles furrowed his handsome brow. 'She's sallow skinned, thin, appears to have a huge chip on her shoulder, is cold and unfriendly and has a surprisingly high opinion of herself.'

'Oh! I see.' Gabriel was taken aback. 'Quite a combination, but tell me does she have any redeeming features? How old is she may I ask?'

'Nine and twenty last month so if there's to be an heir we'd better not tarry.' He shuddered. 'She does have some good points I concede. She rides well, paints, and plays the harp. Without meaning to sound ungallant I'm not looking forward to the honeymoon. You'd better fortify me on the stag night my friend.' Gabriel topped up their drinks. 'That said, I don't think she's enamoured with my good self either. I don't kid myself she's madly in love with me. I think I'm what you might call a means to an end; it was either me or the shelf. I think she's looked down from that particular vantage point for too long for it to be comfortable any longer.' He shrugged. 'I think perhaps she thought she was marrying a naval man who'd be at sea for half the time. We've both been scuppered on that front thanks to her interfering cousin.'

'Has she no good traits, personal attributes that is, no features which attract you?'

Charles guffawed loudly. 'She's a voice like a strangled cat if that's what you're after. Seriously though she has nice hair, extremely dark, black you'd call it and I suppose when she smiles, which isn't often, she has good teeth. Lord I sound like I'm describing a horse not my future wife.'

Both men had taken to the bottle liberally and were now a little intoxicated.

'Unless I'm not to sleep alone tonight give me more than that Charles for God's sake. Of course I won't share your more choice description of your future spouse, but dark hair and good teeth won't cut it. Eleanor will give me my marching orders.'

'Let's hope Miss Crow does the same to me, but not before I'm in full possession of her dowry.' The look they exchanged wasn't without irony. Both fell silent and stared into their drinks.

'Very well, tell Eleanor my future bride has a strong personality, rides to hounds most days in the season and is a fine shot. Did I mention she likes archery?'

'That should do the trick.' Gabriel led Charles through to the library where the ladies awaited them. 'If I'd had to tell her Miss Crow did embroidery and sings prettily I'd have been in the dog house. Archery you say? That should impress her. I think Eleanor will want to befriend Violet, you know how friendly and sociable she is. She undoubtedly remembers what it was like when she was new to Alnmouth society. Caro and Lottie took her under their wings. Eleanor will want to show Violet about and make introductions I expect. But please promise me she won't teach Eleanor archery. I've already been shot at once before and I don't fancy my chances should Eleanor decide to take a pot shot at me. When my wife puts her mind to something she generally succeeds.'

R

The night of the welcoming party for Miss Violet Crow was a mellow, warm evening. Violet was to stay at North Point for two weeks to get to know her intended a little better as Charles and Violet had only met thrice before their betrothal. Three dozen or so friends and family gathered in their finery at North Point to welcome the lady.

This was also to be Rebecca's first introduction to Alnmouth society. Prior to this there had been a supper party at Westshore so Gabriel's "ward" might be introduced to Bendor, Grace, Lottie and Wilson; they were privy to her circumstances, but sworn to secrecy to safeguard the young woman's reputation. Eleanor had hoped it would help ease Rebecca's nerves on the night of the party. It would be a grand affair of that she was sure.

Rebecca herself was excited but anxious she would say or do the wrong thing. She had never been to a formal supper party before being only sixteen. To boost her confidence Eleanor thought she should leave off her mourning clothes. She had helped Rebecca choose a pretty white gown sprigged with pink rosebuds especially for the occasion. The young girl was tall for her age but she had a natural grace about her. Add to that her pretty face and lustrous hair and Eleanor guessed she would net many admiring glances.

Eleanor, Gabriel and Rebecca were shown into the ballroom of Claude Noble's impressive, yet shabby mansion. Eleanor had passed by the house on the way to Amble many times but had never been inside.

'Are you not impressed my love?' Gabriel whispered. 'Perhaps now you can see why poor Charles has to marry up. If you think this old heap faded you should see South Point. It's ready to fall down the next time we have a gale.'

Built in the Palladian style the proportions of North Point were elegant. The sash windows let in the early evening sun but, Eleanor guessed, they would also let in the wind and rain which wouldn't be so welcome. The plaster work was exquisite but was missing in several places. Paint work was scuffed and drapes faded from the sun; moths had made merry with the upholstery. Everywhere one looked there were signs of neglect. It was clear money was in short supply for repairs, but what the house lacked in smartness it made up for in taste. The furnishings may have seen better days but whoever had last decorated clearly had a good eye. There were good pieces of furniture and the silverware, of which there was much, gleamed brightly.

'I like it. I'm not saying I'd like to live here, far too draughty I'd wager, but I can see it has charm. It's lived in, comfortable.' She spotted Charles and her eye wandered. 'There's Charles, oh but he's not in uniform again. I don't suppose he'll wear it now he's not serving.' She sighed. 'The lady he's talking to must be Miss Crow, she's so elegant. She suits both him and the room. She looks aristocratic.'

Gabriel glanced across to where his friend was talking to a blonde-haired beauty. Charles was laughing, clearly enamoured with the young woman by his side. She wasn't at all what Gabriel was expecting. 'I agree my love; they look well together... but then it can't be his intended for she isn't - '

'What? Eleanor turned to Rebecca. 'My husband is contrary is he not? You agree they look good together and then frown.'

'Yes, because the lady doesn't fit his description.'

Charles was leading the lady over to them, all smiles. 'Welcome one and all. Allow me to introduce you to my cousin, second cousin I should say. We haven't seen each other in years, we've been catching up.' Names were exchanged and pleasantries made.

Eleanor was disappointed. 'But where's your intended Charles? Has she abandoned you already?'

'Unfortunately Miss Crow's carriage broke an axle and the accident has made her late. She's arrived now thankfully, but it's meant she's not had the luxury of time to ready herself though I'm given to understand she's about to make an appearance. Ah here she is now; please excuse me, I must escort her in to meet our guests.'

Eleanor craned her neck to see Captain Noble's betrothed. She shot a look at Gabriel. 'Oh... she's not what I expected.'

Violet Crow was tall, taller than her future husband it had to be said. Not only was she tall she was also angular. She had broad shoulders and wide hips. Sharp features were accentuated by black hair pulled back severely from a long, oval face. Her eyes appeared permanently narrowed and her lips pursed. As she walked beside her future husband she looked awkward and ungainly.

She was wearing an insipid yellow gown of watered silk edged with black lace. It wasn't of the latest style and did nothing for her skin tone which was edging towards olive. In her hair she wore three tall feathers, which, Eleanor thought, looked a little peculiar, not being quite vertical and not quite at a jaunty angle either. They prevented Charles from standing too close to her; indeed he was almost poked in the eye by one when she turned away from him to speak to her future sister-in-law. Charles had led his betrothed over to where Claude and his wife Cecily were waiting to welcome her.

Miss Crow's outfit was not a becoming ensemble. For an heiress she looked positively dowdy. The only jewellery she wore was a fine gold chain around her long neck, a neck that would never be called slender as the receding chin spoilt the effect somewhat.

'I'm not sure I would have chosen that particular gown, it does nothing for her,' Eleanor whispered to Gabriel, 'not that I'm the arbiter of good taste of course, but it's not becoming. That particular shade of yellow is hard to carry off.'

'Mmm, perhaps.'

'I can see black lace edging might look well on dark green or scarlet but on acid yellow! Oh I feel mean now, I shouldn't judge.'

'As you say my love, you shouldn't judge.' He half smiled but Eleanor knew despite his lack of comment he agreed with her opinion.

Charles brought Violet over and introductions were made.

'I was sorry to hear your journey was more eventful than you would have liked Miss Crow,' Gabriel said kissing long bony fingers.

'Yes it was a bore.'

'But you're here now and that's all that matters.' Eleanor smiled encouragement.

'I am, as is self evident.'

There was a long moment's silence before Charles added: 'The roads in dry weather are terrible hereabouts. Then again when it rains they're as bad I seem to remember, they turn into mud baths do they not?' The friends discussed the state of the roads and how dry the weather had been until Eleanor managed to change the subject to a more entertaining one.

'When you've settled in and got your bearings you must come to tea Miss Crow. We live not too distant. We'll be neighbours.'

'Thank you Mrs Reynolds for your kind invitation, as you say when I have become acquainted with my surroundings I will no doubt venture out whether the roads be dust bowls or puddled.'

Rebecca caught Eleanor's eye and bit her lip.

'Eleanor was once new to the area but she soon settled, did you not my love?' Gabriel intervened.

She nodded. 'I can introduce you to some of the ladies. We're a small set, but friendly and sociable all the same.'

Once again the conversation stumbled to a halt.

'Come Violet, allow me to introduce you to more of my friends, please excuse us.' Charles bowed and led Miss Crow away. Gabriel spotted Bendor and Grace who were making their way over.

'Is that the bride-to-be?' Grace asked as the couple moved out of earshot.

'It is. She's a little overawed I think, not surprising really. I remember what it was like to be the newest face in Alnmouth. It's a small place where everyone has an interest in newcomers. Being peered at and critiqued from behind fans isn't for the faint hearted I can assure you. She'll soon get used to us hopefully.'

Grace leaned in so only Eleanor could hear. 'I imagine any critiques you received were complimentary. I know this is unkind, but that gown is a fright. Is that the best the dressmakers of Norfolk have to offer? I know we're behind the times up here in sleepy Northumberland, but at least we get the latest fashion plates. That gown is the limit.'

'She was late arriving; perhaps the dress she'd planned to wear couldn't have the creases knocked out of it in time?' Eleanor felt she needed to defend the poor woman.

'And that one could? Meow. Oh, I'm sorry I should be a little less critical Eleanor, you're quite right of course,' Grace said. 'Charles is such a good looking, well dressed man, and they look so odd together, so mismatched.'

Eleanor was only half listening. She was noticing Rebecca watching the betrothed couple. As Charles introduced his fiancée around the room Rebecca's eyes followed them; had the star of Bethlehem been followed so assiduously the Three Kings wouldn't have missed Jesus. Miss Crow wasn't the only one who looked on edge, so did Becky. Had the young girl taken a liking to Charles? If she had she had backed a loser. Nevertheless Eleanor had to admit he was good to look at, he certainly drew the eye. What a lucky lady

Violet Crow was. She wondered if she realised it.

When the dancing began Gabriel surprised Eleanor by first dancing with her and then dancing twice with his ward. He even offered to dance with Violet, but she demurred saying she wasn't a dancer. Gabriel said neither was he but still he couldn't persuade her to take to the floor.

Violet danced one dance, the cotillion, with her husband-to-be; she was right Eleanor thought she wasn't a good dancer. This strangely enough brought out the protective side of Eleanor's nature. Where was it written that all ladies had to dance well? Plenty of men trod on her slippers yet no one criticised them. Some ladies had all the accomplishments polite society expected and some did not. Eleanor, never one for conventionality, didn't care that Miss Crow wasn't a dancer or that she didn't care about fashion. What did it matter? Live and let live, she was sure they would soon be firm friends.

As the evening wore on Violet had been introduced to the guests and now she sat with her future sister-in-law and observed the proceedings. Charles, who had been dancing with his cousin, then came to join their group which now also included Lottie and Wilson.

'Would you care to dance Miss Argyle?' Charles offered his hand as the young girl blushed prettily and was led to the dance floor.

Eleanor watched as the pair made small talk and took up their positions. She saw Rebecca giggle at some aside he made. The young girl was enjoying her entrance into society by the looks of it.

'Rebecca and Charles make a handsome couple do they not?' Grace remarked. 'A far better match in my humble opinion than Miss Crow. Rebecca looks charming Eleanor, the gown is modest yet manages to be alluring. She's acquitting herself well, there's more than Charles captivated by her I think. Oh, to be sixteen again.'

'He's far too old for Rebecca,' Lottie said. 'Is he not twice her age?'

Gabriel agreed. 'She's a child! You're right Lottie, Charles is more than twice her age. I believe he's four and thirty or thereabouts and she's sixteen, far too young to be thinking about men.'

Rebecca tripped lightly about the dance floor looking innocent and sweet. 'As you say my love she's sixteen; just the age when a young girl's fancy turns to the opposite sex.' Eleanor smiled at her husband's naivety. 'Ah, I remember it well.'

Rebecca looked up at Charles with a coyness that was natural and becoming in a young girl at her first dance. Eleanor noted how he smiled back amiably. They did indeed make a good looking pair. For a time when she was younger, Eleanor too had a liking for older gentlemen; men her own age had appeared gauche and boyish. She could see the attraction.

'Well my love shall we?' Gabriel asked.

'Shall we what?' Eleanor hadn't been listening.

'I asked if you fancied a turn on the veranda as it's warm in here, you were miles away.' She allowed him to lead her out.

'What's amiss?'

'Nothing, I was just thinking.'

'Always a dangerous pastime where you're concerned, thinking about what pray tell?'

Lottie and Wilson came to join them saving Eleanor from having to explain that she thought his ward had a small fancy for Captain Noble, a fancy that could not end well under the circumstances. Still, she told herself, Rebecca was young and inexperienced; she had not been in society before. She was probably impressed at an older man's attentions and Charles was a charming man, no wonder she was flattered. Any young girl's head would be turned in his company.

Before supper Lottie and Eleanor excused themselves. In the lady's withdrawing room they saw Miss Crow sitting before a mirror trying to stop her hair from coming undone. She wasn't faring well. The troublesome feathers lay discarded on the dressing table before her.

'Is your maid not available to help you Miss Crow?' Eleanor asked.

'I sent her for her supper.' The newcomer pushed a handful of pins into her hair, then looking flustered, quickly stood to leave.

'My maid could assist you, she's outside,' Lottie offered.

'Thank you, but please do not trouble yourself.' She dropped a stiff curtsy and fled the room.

'She was a bit off-hand was she not?' Lottie said. 'The gown really is awful and her hair, lovely as it is, so silky and thick, looks dreadful dressed in that particular style. Who but a dinosaur would think the style becoming? It doesn't suit her at all, far too severe. In my opinion she needs curls about her face to soften her strong features.' Lottie patted her own perfectly coiffured tresses.

Eleanor knew Lottie and knew these comments weren't meant nastily, it was just her forthright way. She often made comments about how people looked, and not just ladies, she could be equally scathing about the gentlemen when the mood took her.

The door to the ladies withdrawing room opened and a stern-faced Miss Crow returned. 'I left my feathers behind,' she said snatching them up. 'Is this what you mean by "friendly and sociable" Mrs Reynolds?' She shot a venomous look at both of them. She had clearly overheard Lottie's criticism, but before Lottie could apologise Violet Crow fled the room once more.

R

Back at Westshore Eleanor was sitting up in bed.

'Shall you mind if I leave the window open?' Gabriel asked hovering in case she asked him to close it.

'Leave it if you've a mind, but the moths will singe their wings on the candles. It's distressing to see them be so foolhardy.'

He pulled the shirt over his head and climbed naked into bed beside her. 'It's warm this evening. We can blow the candles out if it bothers you.'

'I think we better had. They always fly too close to the flames.'

Gabriel blew out all but one candle. 'From what you said earlier Lottie flew too near the flames. She'll need to apologise to Miss Crow.'

'She will though what excuse she can make I'm not sure. I too feel guilty by association and feel the need to offer an apology. Earlier in the evening did I not also make unkind comments about her dress, albeit not in her hearing but that's no excuse. It was mealy-mouthed of me and I regret it.'

'You were only being your usual plain-spoken self, and as you say your comments were made out of earshot.' He blew out the last candle.

'Still I will try to make amends somehow, it's the least I can do. She must hardly feel welcome now.'

'As you say, not a good beginning.'

Eleanor searched for sleep but found it eluded her. A guilty conscience regarding Violet Crow kept her awake for some time. Rebecca's obvious fascination with Captain Noble was also on her mind.

Before bed Eleanor had popped her head around Rebecca's door to wish her a good night and found the girl staring out of the window at the moon. She had been surprised when Rebecca had gushed: 'Tonight was the best night of my life and I'll never forget it. I never knew dancing with a handsome man could feel so wonderful.'

Eleanor had smiled, remembering her first dance; she'd had quite a crush on Henry Fishburn and had been thrilled when she had been singled out by him. She thought him worldly and sophisticated, she remembered being flattered. With hindsight he was only five years her senior but he had appeared so mature.

But now, in the darkness of her bedroom, Eleanor felt a little disconcerted; *her* first dance partner had not been double her age and about to marry to someone else.

R

Two days later Eleanor was shown into the drawing room at North Point. The reception she received could only be described as icy. She sat with the bride-to-be whilst tea was poured by a decrepit looking maid. An uneasy quiet fell upon the well proportioned room.

'How are you liking Northumberland, are you settling in Miss Crow?' Eleanor asked tentatively.

'The Nobles have been especially accommodating thank you. I'm sorry Mrs Noble is not here to greet you, one of her children has need of her.'

Eleanor breathed deeply. She couldn't put off the reason for her visit any longer. 'It is you whom I wish to see Miss Crow. I came to offer my apologies. I'm deeply sorry you had to witness my rudeness the other evening.' Eleanor waited while Miss Crow sipped her tea then looked directly at her. The look was one of disdain.

'It is of no matter Mrs Reynolds. Ladies, I often find, can be unkind. I do not care for the opinions of a doctor's wife and I said as much to Mrs Chaffer when she called to make amends yesterday. I did however acknowledge that as Charles is friendly with her husband we shall be forced into each other's company and therefore for appearance's sake I accepted her act of contrition.'

Eleanor was at a loss to how to reply, but quickly recovered herself.

'In Mrs Chaffer's defence may I say she isn't malicious, merely a little candid. Although you may find it hard to believe she's a kind and caring person. However, it's for myself I wish to make amends. I'd intimated to you we were friendly in these parts and your experience so far must prove otherwise.' Eleanor ploughed on even though Miss Crow sat bolt upright with a condescending look on her face throughout her speech. 'My husband and Charles are also good friends and we too will, without a doubt, be thrust into each other's company. I hope you won't think you have to tolerate me because of the attachment. If you can see your way to accepting my apology I'll do my utmost to rectify your first impression of both myself and the ladies of Alnmouth.'

Violet Crow showed no sign of softening. She had clearly made bluntness an art form. 'Charles is uncommonly fond of your husband I realise, and as we are to be tenants of his for the foreseeable future I accept your request for forgiveness. If you did say anything untoward I did not hear it so it would, perhaps, be wrong of me to judge you too harshly on this occasion.'

Eleanor felt her hackles rise. She was never good at saying she was sorry but in this case had admitted it had needed to be said. But now to have her apology so roundly dismissed and in such a patronising fashion was irksome to say the least.

'Thank you Miss Crow for being so gracious,' she said bristling. 'You're mistaken however in thinking you are to be my husband's tenant; in actual fact you'll be mine. *I* own Eastshore not Gabriel.'

'How singular.'

Eleanor waited for her to continue, but no more was forthcoming.

'Have you seen Eastshore yet?'

'Charles and I rode over yesterday.'

'If there's anything you need please don't hesitate to let me know, I hope you'll be comfortable there.'

'It will serve in the short term. It is not what I am used to of course, but as it is only until South Point is ready it matters not. We shall spend some time at my estate in Norfolk so we may not be in Northumberland over much after our wedding.'

'As you say it's not forever.' Eleanor was annoyed with the woman. Eastshore wasn't to Eleanor's personal taste either, it was far too dark and gloomy, but to have it so criticised by this woman was beyond provoking.

Eleanor finished her tea and made her excuses to leave. She left Miss Crow still looking as if she had sucked a lemon. It had been even more of an unpleasant visit than she had anticipated.

Back at Westshore she found Rebecca in the conservatory staring out to sea. She joined her.

'Why the long face?'

'I'm a little... pre-occupied.'

'May I enquire what about?'

Eleanor saw Rebecca hesitate. 'It's... the other night was such a lovely evening; the house, the ladies in their fine gowns, the gentlemen in their finery... I've never met anyone so... '

'Do I detect you're a little smitten my dear?'

'Smitten. With whom?'

Eleanor tilted her head. 'With a dashing naval officer of course. He's handsome is he not - Charles that is? It's perfectly acceptable to cast your eye in a gentleman's direction so long as you realise that in this particular case it can come to naught. No harm in looking and admiring I always think; makes a dull day bearable but there are plenty more fish in the sea. You're young and have your whole life before you. Good Lord, I sound like my mother! When I was your age she warned me off so many unsuitable young men.' Eleanor remembered, too late, it had only made them more attractive to her. She hoped this would not be the case with Rebecca.

The young girl continued to look out to sea. Rose wandered in and stood before them. 'Why do you both look sad?'

'We're not sad Rose we were talking.'

'About something sad?'

'I told you we aren't sad we were talking about Captain Noble.'

'I like him. He doesn't make me sad, he kissed my hand.'

'That was Captain Turner my love.'

'No it wasn't, although he did kiss me too. I like being kissed by handsome men, though none are as handsome as Pa.'

Eleanor smiled at her daughter, she was starting young. Then it registered what she had said: 'When did you meet Captain Noble for him to kiss your hand?'

'We saw him yesterday riding on the beach. He did kiss my hand didn't he Becky?'

Rebecca's face was crimson.

'I didn't know you had met with Charles? Were you unchaperoned Rebecca? Gabriel won't be happy if you were alone with the captain or any man for that matter. You know he's at pains to protect your reputation.'

'I asked you to come with me, but you said you were busy so Rose and I went for a walk. We saw him only for a short while on the beach here at Westshore.'

'Then you should have taken my maid with you. The sooner we get you a personal maid of your own the better.' Eleanor looked at her daughter. 'Rose please go and find Ginny it's almost time for... tell Ginny to entertain you.'

When Rose had remonstrated and finally been convinced she should do as she was told Eleanor turned to Rebecca. 'Was this an accidental meeting, please tell me it wasn't planned?'

'It was mere chance. Charles, Captain Noble, happened to be riding back from a meeting. He stopped to pass the time of day, nothing more.'

'Here on our beach it would pass unremarked, but you shouldn't be seen alone with *any* gentleman in town. I don't care a hoot about such things but Gabriel does. Under the circumstances, and with your background, you can't be too careful. It's wrong people are so narrow minded, but some are quick to judge.'

Gabriel arrived holding his daughter's hand. 'I found *madam* here wandering about the stableyard. Have we not asked her to stay away from the horses?'

Eleanor gave her daughter a withering look. 'Indeed we have. I sent her to Ginny.'

Gabriel sat next to his ward and looked hard at his daughter.

'I thought I heard Ginny in the stableyard.' Rose made her excuse.

'Why is your apron pocket moving of its own volition?'

'What does that word mean Pa?'

'It means of its own accord, without you moving it.'

Rose plunged her hand into her pocket and pulled out a tiny ginger kitten.

'Ah that explains it. I take it Flossie has had her kittens?'

'She had three but the others died.' Rose looked tearful.

'Even more important then you put her kitten back my love. She'll be missing him. He's far too little to be away from his mama for long.'

'How do you know he's a boy? I already called her Tilly.'

'Most ginger cats are Toms, but it's too early to tell. You may have to rename him. Now run along and put him back where you got him from.'

'But you said not to go into the stableyard.'

'Rebecca, would you mind taking the kitten back from whence it came, then take Rose to the nursery and ask Ginny to keep an eye on her.' Eleanor gave her daughter a warning look.

When they had gone Gabriel looked askance. 'Is something the matter? Were you not a little brusque with Rebecca?'

'Was I? I think I was put out with Rose. I recognise the argumentative trait I had as a child. I was always quick with a clever excuse.'

'*Had* the trait, you still own the characteristic do you not?'

Eleanor grimaced. She didn't think it necessary to tell him about the meeting between his friend and his ward. Chance meeting or otherwise she knew he would think her lax in her chaperoning duties. She was in no mood for another dressing down. The one she'd had from Miss Crow was still smarting.

8

Eleanor stood at the water's edge and breathed deeply. She felt calmer, less restive than she had felt since her talk with Padraic about how he had not quite coped with the loss of Caroline. The sea, as always, worked its magic. Clearing Caroline's belongings had been a morbid task and one she was pleased to have dispensed with.

The shingle washed the shore, the spume rinsing her boots and wetting her skirt. The tide was retreating and the sun going down. Despite the solemnity of the task Eleanor was glad to have been of assistance to Padraic and to the memory of her dear friend.

'Ahoy there,' the man she was thinking of called out. He strode down the beach to join her then stood tall and erect beside her and looked out to sea, his hands clasped behind his back.

Earlier she had sent a note saying the task was complete. 'There's nothing left in Caroline's rooms save the furnishings.' She saw his shoulders sag.

'I'll be forever in your debt, you know that Eleanor.'

'It was a privilege I can assure you. When do you sail?' She was keen to change the subject.

'Any day; there's nothing to keep me here now. I've come to say my goodbyes.'

'Let's hope you don't sail too close to the wind in your new adventures. You've weathered one storm and now it's time for a new beginning, a calmer beginning. Let us know when you make land won't you? Take care of yourself, and the Alnmouth Girl, for my husband's sake.'

'When I first saw you in Whitby I thought I'd met my match, before that is, I knew someone else had got there before me.' He smiled ironically. 'I thought at one time you could have been the one for me, but now I realise you're far too independent for my taste. I like my women less... self-determined. Carla was, and is, the only woman I'll ever love. Truly love. You and I would never have managed, though it would've been fun trying. Our temperaments are too similar Eleanor; we would've been forever fighting, scrapping, though the making up would have been gratifying.'

'Caroline was the type of woman who liked to depend on a man and although at the time I wasn't sure you were at all dependable Padraic, now I see I was wrong in my assumption. I believe you would have had a good life together.'

'Ah, but it wasn't to be... You'll tend her grave as you promised?'

'Of course; we both will.' She turned to look at Padraic's handsome profile, his square jaw and straight nose. He looked back at her and smiled the slow, laconic smile that made even his harshest critics waver. In some ways she would miss him, he was a loveable rascal, more loveable now she knew how he felt about Caroline. 'Who knows, you might meet someone to love in Virginia. I hear gentlemen in the New World are in short supply. You might just pass muster, you're not such a bad looking fellow.'

'A compliment is that Mrs Reynolds?' He cocked his head to one side. 'I doubt very much I'll find another Caroline Hodgeson no matter how far I travel. I'm off to the other side of the world, but I'll never find such a gentle and generous soul as my Carla.'

Eleanor was overcome. 'Perhaps not, but that doesn't mean you have to live the rest of your life alone.'

'No lady wants to be second best and for the first few years at any rate I'll have little time for romance. I'll be working hard to establish myself.' He moved closer and took her hands in his. 'Thank you for your friendship Eleanor, I once said your husband was a lucky man and I was right.' He kissed her on the lips. 'Goodbye Eleanor, if you ever want to invest in tobacco I'm sure we can come to an accommodation.' He turned away and without a backward glance marched determinedly towards the bay.

Eleanor shook herself trying to lift the feeling of gloom which had wrapped itself about her. A cool breeze sprang up making her shiver.

Over the past week she had neglected her accounts. She headed for the study hoping for a distraction.

She had been attending to her ledger for an hour when she heard raised voices, it was the twins. Eleanor tried to add up a column of figures three times but the twins hollering and shouting put her off. She stepped into the drawing room to find the boys rolling about on the floor. Haydan had his arm held high trying, and succeeding, in keeping a large spiky shell out of his brother's reach.

'What *is* all the racket about?'

'It's mine,' Ruari yelled, 'I found it.' The twins continued their tussle unabated.

At that moment Ginny appeared. She deftly took the shell from Haydan's grasp. 'And now it's mine. Apologise for disturbing your mama and then go to the nursery and wait for me there. You should be ashamed of yourselves; this is no way for young gentlemen to behave.'

The boys scowled at each other, apologised to their mama then did as they were bid.

'Sorry I only turned my back for a moment and - '

'Don't apologise, you need eyes in the back of your head with those two. I thought Rebecca was with them?'

'She went for a ride about an hour ago.'

'Oh, has she taken Molly along?'

'She went on her own, said as she wouldn't be too long.'

'I see, which way did she go... towards Boulmer?'

'Towards the bay I think, she generally goes that way.'

Eleanor went back to her accounts. That was twice, no three times, this week Rebecca had ridden out alone. She wondered where she went. The stretch of beach towards Boulmer went on for mile after glorious mile, but it was only a matter of two or three miles to Alnmouth. Eleanor wondered what the attraction was in that direction. She thought she might have an inkling.

R

'What a shame Violet has gone back to Norfolk, for Charles I mean.'

Eleanor looked thoughtful. 'Imagine marrying someone on so small an acquaintance, a couple of weeks is not long to get to know someone but still Charles is a likeable chap. I expect she has much planning to do for the wedding. Is he missing her?'

'How would I know? He's said nothing to me.'

'Violet likes to hunt.' Eleanor made a face. 'She was out in the field most days when she was here Charles said. He doesn't hunt does he?'

Gabriel shook his head. 'Apparently they're not to have a honeymoon. Miss Crow said she'd prefer to stay at home in their new house, if it's finished of course. She doesn't want to miss the hunting season.'

'How odd; I love my home but I'd still like to see more of the world. Imagine giving up one's honeymoon.'

Gabriel was about to leave for the bay so changed the subject deftly. 'Have you a busy day lined up?'

'It's the reading of Susan's will this morning.'

'I'd forgotten. I suppose you feel duty bound to go with Susan being a patron of Hope House.' He kissed her cheek and made to leave. Eleanor watched him ride off, Scrabble Junior accompanying him running in and out of the gentle waves. She wasn't looking forward to her morning.

At midday Eleanor and Lottie took their seats in the library at Lesbury Lodge. It was cold and grey outside but the room was stuffy, overheated. The two friends glanced about nodding to acquaintances.

Saul Coates sat behind the imposing desk and coughed to get the attention of the assembled company. Eleanor and Lottie knew from what Susan had said she would leave an annuity to Hope House. They had thought it only polite to attend the reading because of it.

Saul began to read from Susan's will in a suitably mournful voice. Eleanor looked about her only half listening. It transpired the majority of her fortune was left to her nephew, a Mr George Black. Eleanor thought he must be the man sitting front and centre. She could only see the back of his head which was sandy-haired and thinning. He was to be a wealthy man as he was left not only Lesbury Lodge, but various stocks and shares and monies laid down at the bank exceeding thirty thousand pounds.

'He'll be a catch for someone,' Lottie muttered irreverently, 'if he's not married already of course.'

Hope House was left a generous yearly income which pleased the pair. Next came a few small legacies then Saul explained that Susan had added a codicil to the will some six months before she died.

'I have over the last few years been attended by a constant companion,' Saul read. 'Throughout my time in Lesbury Miss Bryony Swift has waited upon me with due care and attention and I would say we have become not merely companions, but friends. She was an especial comfort to me when my dear goddaughter was taken from us all too soon. In recognition of her devotion to me I leave her the sum of five thousand pounds in the hope she will never be in need again.'

A murmur passed around the room. Eleanor saw Bryony for the first time; she too was sitting at the front, but off to the side so Eleanor could see only her profile. Miss Swift looked moved by the revelation.

'That's an interesting development,' Lottie said. 'Both of them came to Hope House on a weekly basis and Miss Swift has kept up the visits since Susan's death. I think she deserves the money. What say you?'

'I agree, as you say both were extremely supportive of our cause.'

The reading was concluded and sherry was handed about by a footman.

As the assembled group began to mingle, Eleanor caught her first sight of the newly rich nephew. He appeared to be in his early thirties, with a serious expression that didn't seem fixed solely for the reading of wills. His pale face was close shaven, and oval rather than round. He wasn't what Eleanor would call handsome, although his features were perfectly regular. Saul Coates introduced them.

'Allow me to introduce Mr George Black.' Saul did the honours as Eleanor and Lottie bobbed and he bowed. They expressed their condolences. 'Mr Black is from near Berwick, though still this side of the border,' Saul said as he helped himself to another glass of sherry.

'Is this your first time in these parts Mr Black?' Eleanor asked.

'Indeed not Mrs Reynolds, I have visited my aunt on two or three occasions since she removed to Lesbury. I believe the last time I came, when she was fading, you were abroad. She said how she would have liked me to meet you and your husband. She had a high regard for you both, and you also Mrs Chaffer and the charity work you both do.'

Eleanor noticed when he smiled his eyes sparkled and his face came alive. He appeared better looking when he smiled she thought although he wouldn't make a girl's heart beat faster; well not until she heard how much he was worth at any rate.

They chatted for a while, then Eleanor noticed Bryony sitting alone in a corner. She excused herself and went to join her. 'Good morning Miss Swift. How fortunate you were remembered by Susan in her will. I know she thought well of you, you deserve a reward for your devotion. You were a good companion, especially towards the end.'

'Thank you. I knew of course she was to leave me something for she told me when she added the codicil, but I never expected it to be so much. This will make all the difference to me. I can hardly believe it.'

'It's enough to house you for the rest of your life if you're careful. That must be a comfort to you.'

'It is. I haven't had time to think yet, the amount is somewhat large. Mrs Stubbs was a lovely lady, so kind and so generous.'

'She was and she believed in you when no one else did. I think she was a good judge of character.' Eleanor meant what she said; although Bryony had given up her son she had done it with good intentions, even though at the time it had caused heartache for all concerned. Eleanor admired Miss Swift's fortitude. She had not had an easy existence but with Susan's help she had managed to turn her life around.

Back at Westshore Eleanor was telling Gabriel about the reading of the will.

'He's a lawyer you say this man, White did you say he was called?'

She looked skyward. '*Black*; yes he's a man of law. I wonder if he'll come to live at Lesbury Lodge and practice hereabouts.'

'You didn't ask him?' Gabriel mocked. 'You're losing your touch my love.'

'I thought not to bombard the poor man at a will reading so I've invited him to dine before he returns north. I'll ask him then. He appears nice, but then he would be if he's related to Susan. He's her sister's boy apparently.'

'And is he married?'

'Again I didn't think it appropriate to ask.'

'Eleanor! You really are slipping. Your title of font of all knowledge is in danger of being lost.'

R

'Where's Rebecca? I haven't seen her to talk to properly for days.'

'She took breakfast in her room earlier, said she felt a bit under the weather, a slight headache. She said she might ride out if it stays dry but it looks like rain again.' Eleanor wrinkled her nose. She suspected the young woman was avoiding them, but didn't want to worry Gabriel. Since finding out about Rebecca's accidental meeting with Charles, Eleanor was suspicious the young girl had taken more than a fancy to him, she suspected a *crush*.

Eleanor had noticed Rebecca's changeable moods of late; she was a girl who changed her humour as often as she changed her gowns. She had tried to talk to the young girl about her infatuation with Charles but each time she felt she had made matters worse.

One day Rebecca had wept and pleaded to be left alone, pleaded with her not to tell Gabriel about the "chance" meeting. On other occasions Becky was light-hearted and cheerful, full of the joys of spring and passed Eleanor's concerns off as nonsense, said she had not thought about Charles in days.

Lately Eleanor thought Rebecca was trying to avoid Gabriel in particular, as if she had something to hide. Eleanor knew that at Rebecca's age she had probably been just as temperamental, just as capricious. Was she really so melodramatic at sixteen she wondered. Possibly she was. It was difficult to remember. But it was hard to keep abreast of the young woman's moods. Eleanor hoped Rose didn't turn out to be so unpredictable.

Eleanor had tried to be sisterly towards Rebecca, tried to listen, to advise, but what could she say? Charles was twice Rebecca's age and about to be married. It was no good hanging about Westshore like a love struck puppy is what she had really wanted to say but held back knowing Rebecca hadn't had a mother to guide her. She saw the girl was naive and full of dreams. She hadn't wanted to be the one to burst her bubble.

In addition Eleanor felt guilty she had not told Gabriel about his ward's infatuation with Charles. Secretly Eleanor was hoping it would pass, it must pass, it was folly to think otherwise. This attraction Rebecca had for a man who was about to marry someone else was, after all preposterous, impossible. And yet Gabriel was oblivious to the situation. It was hardly surprising as he was always busy. Men didn't understand how young girls could be madly in love one minute and disdainful of the attachment the next. It would fade this infatuation, she was sure of it. In time Rebecca would move on and find a more suitable man to revere.

Little did Eleanor know things were about to come to a head.

After Eleanor had dealt with her correspondence she ordered tea and threw more coal on the fire. It was a cold dreary day. She shivered as she set about her accounts.

Ransom brought a note alongside the tea. It was addressed to Rebecca. Who would be sending Rebecca a letter she wondered. Eleanor turned it around in her fingers wishing there was some way of seeing the contents without actually opening it.

But then Eleanor paused for thought. Was Charles honourable? Would he seek a dalliance with a pretty girl? By comparison Violet was a poor second to a young, nubile girl like Rebecca. Eleanor knew what men were like. She hoped Charles was better than most. She hoped not to be wrong about him. But now there was a letter, a letter most likely from Charles, for who else would be writing to Rebecca? Surely he wasn't encouraging her? Eleanor would think differently about him if he was and so would Gabriel.

Eleanor knew Charles was marrying Violet for her dowry to replenish the Noble coffers. It's what the aristocracy did, but she had thought him more admirable than this... if that is, he was having a last fling before he tied the knot. If he wanted a diversion he should have looked further afield. She let out a long breath. This couldn't continue. Eleanor admitted to herself it was time to tell Gabriel about her fears, if only to have her worries squashed. Gabriel could speak with his friend and attempt, if her suspicions were true, to rescue Rebecca's reputation before it became tarnished for good.

The door opened and Rebecca looking excited stepped into the room. 'Ransom says there's a letter for me Eleanor.'

'There is.' She handed it to the girl who after a cursory glance at the handwriting said a brisk thank you then slipped it into her pocket. She turned to leave.

'Is that from who I think it's from? If it is I feel I must tell your half brother, you must know he won't condone your behaviour or Charles' for that matter.'

'Please Eleanor don't tell him, not today.'

'No Rebecca, Gabriel will already be furious and not only with you. I've kept this matter from him as I thought you would get over this nonsense, but now things have taken a more serious turn have they not?'

Rebecca let out a sob and ran from the room.

'Becky come back here young lady, we need to talk about this - '

Haydan burst through the door almost colliding with the young woman as she dashed from the room.

'Mama come quick, Ruari's been stung by a jelly fish. His foot is swelling up and he's crying. I tried to pee on it like Pa said to do if ever we got stung, but he screamed like a girl.'

Eleanor called for Sam as she ran down the beach where she found

Ruari laying on the sand sobbing. A translucent blob was being washed out to sea as the tide went out. The groom lifted the child and carried him back to the house and laid him on the kitchen settle by the fire. Lisbet was on hand straight away.

‘’Tis just a little sting Master Ruari, let me have a good look. There’s no need to send for Doctor Chaffer, A can fettle it.’ She bustled to the pantry much to Mrs Madison’s annoyance and set about covering the red mark with a pungent green paste. Ruari accepted the biscuit she gave him. ‘It’ll be right as rain in half an hour. Does it feel better? Has it stopped stingin’?’

‘Somewhat,’ he said through a mouthful of biscuit. ‘Thanks Lisbet.’

Eleanor breathed a sigh of relief. She knew her son was going to be alright. It would take more than a jellyfish sting to put him off his food. Then something caught her eye through the kitchen window; Rebecca riding off at a gallop.

‘Sam go after Miss Argyle and bring her back. Someone has to save the silly girl from herself. Lord, Gabriel will be fuming,’ she muttered under her breath.

‘Fuming about what? Where’s the fire?’ Gabriel came in as Sam rushed past him.

‘Ruari’s been stung by a jelly fish, but Lisbet’s sorted him out.’ She saw the worried look on his face. ‘He’s eating his way through the biscuit barrel so no need to fret my love.’ She looked apologetic. ‘It’s not him you need be upset about, it’s Rebecca.’ Eleanor took her husband’s arm and guided him through to the sitting room away from flapping ears. ‘Don’t be cross but I think Rebecca has gone to meet with Charles. I should have told you about all this before.’

‘“All this”... Charles? Why would she go to meet Charles? What’s going on, I don’t understand?’

Before she could explain, Charles Noble was announced. Eleanor looked from one man to the other, a puzzled look on her face.

‘Charles. Speak of the devil and he shall appear,’ Gabriel said. Eleanor saw the baffled look on her husband’s face. He wasn’t the only one perplexed.

'Oh! It's nothing for you to worry about Gabriel,' Eleanor said trying to backtrack. She must have made a mistake, perhaps the letter was from someone else after all. Perhaps she too was being fanciful as well as Rebecca. Her cheeks felt warm.

Gabriel narrowed his brows. 'I wasn't worried until you told me not to worry.'

'Have you seen Rebecca?' Eleanor asked Charles.

'I haven't, I came to see Gabriel, on a delicate matter.'

Gabriel's face was a picture of confusion. 'Will someone please tell me what's going on?'

Charles threw his hat on a chair and took a letter from his pocket. 'I'm afraid it appears your ward has developed a schoolgirl infatuation for me Gabriel. I swear I haven't encouraged her, quite the opposite in fact. After I saw which way the wind was blowing I sought to put her off, let her down gently if you will, but that only fanned the flames. I even invited her to tea, with Claude and Cecily of course, to try to show her I had no untoward intentions.'

Eleanor was agog. 'And did she come?'

'She did not. And now Rebecca is beginning to make a bit of a nuisance of herself. I came to see you today Gabriel because the silly girl is going to ruin her reputation if she's not careful.'

He handed the letter to Gabriel who quickly scanned it.

'I'm sorry Charles of course I knew nothing of this.' He shot Eleanor a look. 'In her defence Rebecca has known little affection in her life and I fear she's misinterpreted your friendship, your kindness as something more. How embarrassing for you.'

Eleanor was fit to burst with curiosity.

'I received it this afternoon,' Charles explained. 'I swear Gabriel it's all her little fantasy, I should have nipped it in the bud, taken it more seriously perhaps, but well, I never knew she felt this way. I wrote back to your ward an hour or so ago telling her I was coming to see you as I was worried for her character. I told her I had to put a stop to this for everyone's sake.'

Gabriel looked to Eleanor. 'Where is Rebecca, is she about?'

'She rode off minutes ago. I sent Sam out to look for her. I thought she was going to meet you Charles, I'm sorry I've misread the situation, I too thought it a light attachment.'

'You knew something of this? Did you not think I should know my love?'

She saw the accusing look on his face. 'Can we argue about this later Gabriel? If Becky hasn't gone to meet with you Charles then where has she gone? She rode off like the wind.'

'I think I might know where she is. She suggested we might meet, of course I didn't intend to keep the assignation, I came straight here. She said she'd ride to Eastshore. There's a sheltered cove down from the house, she hoped we wouldn't be seen there.'

Eleanor could imagine the machinations of the romantic little fool; meeting her lover on a secluded beach. It was straight out of a romantic novel, possibly one she had lent her.

'I'll go and bring her back,' Gabriel said. 'I'm sorry Charles, thank you for the warning. Why has she got it into her head she's in love with you? Silly girl! Surely she knows nothing could come of this. We'll talk to Rebecca, sort this matter out. Thank you for coming to see me.'

'I'm only sorry I didn't come sooner but I thought it would run its course. I'll head home. I'd come with you to look for her but I don't think that would be helpful do you? Let me know when you find her.'

R

Eleanor sat on the edge of Rebecca's bed. The young woman's eyes were red-rimmed with crying.

'Is Gabriel angry?'

'Not so much angry, more concerned. He's been at such pains to safeguard your reputation and if this gets out there will be a price to pay. In a small place like Alnmouth people talk. If you've been seen together some may come to the wrong conclusions.'

'I'm so sorry but I love and admire Charles so much and I thought he had feelings for me too.'

'Did he give you reason to think he had more than a friendly attachment to you?'

'Yes... no, well perhaps. Maybe I misunderstood his intentions.'

'He's about to be married! Have you met with him?'

Eleanor was worried that earlier Charles had been less than honest.

'Not on purpose but... our paths have crossed on more than one occasion.' Eleanor waited for Rebecca to explain. 'He came to Westshore and we took tea when you were out and Charles had mistaken the day he was supposed to meet Gabriel. He was so entertaining, so handsome and kind to me. He makes me feel special, grown up.'

'But he's engaged.'

'I know.'

'And he's twice your age.'

'I know that too, but he's so worldly wise, sophisticated. And there's this.' She lifted a gold locket from beneath her gown.'

'I don't understand. Is that new? Was it a gift from Charles?' Eleanor was horrified.

'Charles remembered the story of how I'd had to pawn my locket, so he sent a manservant to scour the pawn shops in Berwick to look for mine, and he found it. I'm so grateful to Charles. It was such a thoughtful, dear thing to do. Now I'm reunited with my mama's image and all thanks to Charles. If he didn't have some regard for me why else would he go to so much trouble?'

'I don't know, but you didn't think to tell us about this Rebecca?'

'He only gave it to me yesterday.'

Eleanor was reeling. 'And you say you've met on other occasions?' Eleanor asked wondering what Gabriel was going to say when he found out. Was his friend as innocent in all this as he made out? *He* was old enough to know better, at least Rebecca had the excuse of being young and inexperienced.

'Earlier this week I was riding by Eastshore and Charles was talking to the gardener; now he's moved into the house he's much closer to Alnmouth. 'I've seen him about often, well not often but... he asked me did I want to look around the garden which slopes down to a sweet little cove. We walked a while in the garden then went down to the beach.'

'You know you should have refused. You shouldn't be alone with a man, it's not fitting. Did he behave... did he try to kiss you, did he behave inappropriately?'

'His manners were impeccable; he was the perfect gentleman.'

'I know how hard this will be for you my dear, but you must forget about him. No good can come from thinking about him. Now try and get some sleep, things will look different in the morning. Good night Rebecca.'

'I'm sorry to be such a bother. Good night Eleanor, tell Gabriel I'm sorry and deeply ashamed.'

R

'I'm not blaming you Eleanor. I can see why you didn't tell me about Rebecca's feelings for Charles.' It was the next day and Rebecca had yet to make an appearance. 'As you say, at her age young girls fall in and out of love as often as they change their bonnets.

'I didn't realise she was so impressionable, so susceptible to flattery. When she first met Charles I could see she had taken to him, but then she also cast her eye at Padraic Turner as well, not to mention she admires Sam. It's what young girls do. I was in and out of love every week of the year at her age I remember. I almost hope she decides to go to finishing school, my nerves can't cope.'

'I'll miss the silly little minx if she does. Despite her dramas I've grown fond of her, but perhaps under the circumstances a year at finishing school might be a good idea; put some distance between her and the object of her desire, or is that objects, plural.'

'When I spoke with her earlier she was still professing undying love for Charles. And I don't think he's as innocent as he made out. Men are susceptible to flattery too you know. Charles getting back her precious locket made him a hero in her eyes, which must have convinced her he had feelings for her.'

‘It’s the kind of gesture Charles would think do; he always was thoughtful. I remember he wrote such a good letter when my father died, said all the right things. He’s a good man.’

‘But old enough to see what was happening. Another reason Charles was attractive to Rebecca is because he’s unattainable, he’s even more fascinating to her because deep down she knows he’s not for her. It’s a rule, in love that is, that we always want what we can’t have is it not?’

‘I only ever wanted you my love. And you weren’t unattainable.’

‘Ah, but I was initially. I was engaged to William remember.’

‘So you were, I’d forgotten that.’

Eleanor bit back a pert remark. ‘I thought to organise a small party for Becky and some of the younger people hereabouts to take her mind off her broken heart. A party would introduce her to new people like Mary Coates. She’s the same age as Becky, perhaps it would do her good to meet friends her own age. Mary is going to be finished in Switzerland so if Becky did decide to go they might go together. There are a couple of young boys of a more suitable age we could invite too like George and Mark Suggs and the Brophy boy.’

‘It can’t hurt. Perhaps she’ll cast her eye at the children’s new tutor. How old is he? He looks barely out of breeching pants to me.’

‘He does have a baby face, I wonder does he even shave yet. I know it’s because he’s fair-haired but you’re right he’s young looking for one and twenty.’

Jeremy Pater had arrived the day before to take up his duties amid all the mayhem of Rebecca’s escapades. He was a quiet, studious young man of medium height and slim build. With a shock of fair hair and his limpid blue eyes which were fringed with pale lashes he was too insipid looking to be handsome. His pale, almost translucent, smooth skin laid testament to the fact he spent far too long indoors poring over his books. Despite his unprepossessing looks he appeared to be a pleasant young man and had good qualifications and references.

Mr Pater had been impressed with the library at Westshore when Eleanor had suggested Rebecca show him the shelves of leather-bound books at his disposal. Becky had dutifully shown him about, but had made her escape as soon as was reasonably polite. Strangely enough he was one man to whom she wasn't drawn.

'It's been so quiet about the house this morning with the children at their lessons. The twins weren't keen to begin of course.'

'I'm not surprised. Sitting still is not their favourite pastime. Sitting still, listening *and* learning may prove a bridge too far.' Gabriel took up his newspaper.

'Ginny said they were both feigning tummy aches after they'd broken their fast. Rose on the other hand skipped along happily enough, but then the kitten she'd taken to class was expelled so she might not be too keen either by the end of the day.'

Eleanor went in search of Rebecca to tell her of the proposed party. She found her sitting in the summerhouse looking mournfully out to sea. She outlined her plan.

'You like Mary do you not? Felicity is a little older than you both but she may come to the party too. I thought to invite a dozen or so guests.'

'That would be most kind Eleanor. I should enjoy a party, but would it not be a lot of trouble? I already feel I've caused enough bother.'

'Not at all my dear, it will be fun. Very well, I shall arrange it for next week in that case. You can help with the arrangements; it will be good experience for you.'

Rebecca was all smiles.

'Another thing I've been meaning to talk to you about is a lady's maid. You need one not only to help you dress, but to chaperone. I'm not always able to spare the time and it would mean you could go out and about more without risk to your reputation. Gabriel insists.'

'I'm not happy to put you both to further expense. I'm content to share Molly with you as we've been doing so far.'

'Molly has enough to do and I have someone in mind. I wouldn't foist someone on you that you couldn't get along with however. It's important you like her, we ladies spend a lot of time together with our maids. I still miss Charity, she's Ginny's sister, and the first maid I had. At the end we were firm friends.'

'Did she die? Oh, how sad.'

Eleanor wondered at Becky's over active imagination. 'She didn't die! She moved back to Whitby because she fell in love with one of our grooms. They married and now she has two children. Speaking of Whitby, Gabriel and I have decided to go and see my family for Christmas; they're dying to meet you. Gabriel says he's too busy to escort us, but he'll be able to come for a couple of weeks, we'll stay for a month or so. I should like you to see my home town.'

R

The party was not the success Eleanor had hoped it would be.

'Rebecca liked the party but she wasn't particularly attracted to any of the young men,' Eleanor told Gabriel after the guests had left. She climbed into bed.

'I thought that was the idea; to introduce her to *younger* men, men of her age not men twice her age like Charles.'

'It was but when I asked her if any had caught her eye that was the response I got. Oh well, never mind, I tried. I think she enjoyed the distraction anyway, the dressing up and the society. Mary Coates and Becky liked each other so all wasn't lost. I remember being matched up with young boys too and resenting it so I know how she feels.'

Gabriel climbed into bed beside her. 'Were you a flirt even then? I bet you were.'

Eleanor smiled enigmatically. 'I might have been, I remember rehearsing at any rate.'

'And now you're a seasoned campaigner.'

'Chance would be a fine thing, who is there hereabouts to flirt with may I ask?'

'You'll miss Turner when he goes.'

'Very funny.'

'Why the dreamy look then?'

'What dreamy look?'

Gabriel waited. He knew there was more to come.

'I was thinking - all this business with Becky has brought back memories. Part of growing up is falling in and out of love is it not? The will you, won't you fall head over heels.' She sighed. 'I remember my first love or what I *thought* was love. At school we used to call it having a pash on someone.'

'Did you now? It's a good job I came along and saved you from your madcap ways. When your mama thought you safe abed you were running wild in the evenings seeing a seamier side of life. Was this when you were Becky's age, when you had your first *pash*?'

'I would have been fifteen.'

'You started young. Was William your first beau?'

'Lord no, he was *much* later, after I'd disgraced myself going to Amsterdam.'

'Then who was it? Tell me about him. Was he handsome like me?'

Eleanor spluttered: 'Not exactly.'

Again he waited for her to go on.

'It was at school, the Friends' school that is. We used to steal away at break times to a secluded part of the garden.'

'I see. It was part of your Quaker education was it this extracurricular activity?'

'Something like that. It was the first time I'd ever kissed anyone. It was the merest brushing of lips but it was... intense, exciting, dangerous. I still remember it fondly.'

Gabriel smiled. 'Do you indeed.'

'It never went any further. Before the kiss there was the anticipation, poems were written and love tokens exchanged, but then the next day, after the kiss, I changed my mind.'

'But you said it was love.'

'I decided I didn't like her after all.'

'*Her!*'

'Your face Gabriel,' Eleanor burst out laughing. 'You went to an all boys' school; did you not have a *pash* for a boy?'

'No I did not! I climbed over the school wall to get experience of *women*. I had no thoughts for boys.'

'You and Ben... you two didn't ever... explore? You and he have always been close. I thought all boys experimented when they were young?'

'We did not, but now I come to think about it we did have our admirers... younger boys.' Gabriel smirked. 'Are you saying all girls experiment, I never knew that. Sometimes Eleanor I think you can't shock me anymore and then you don't just shock me, you stun me.'

'You're so easy to shock my love,' she said giggling.

'Why have you never told me this before?'

'A lady has to have some secrets.'

'Apparently not now you've told me about your illicit, misspent youth.'

'Are you sure it was misspent?'

'Perhaps not; all experience is valuable is it not?' he said as he brushed his lips tenderly on hers and beginning an exploration of his own.

9

Gabriel looked closely at his wife who was toying with her food. 'You're quiet my love.' She appeared unusually subdued.

'Susan's death and the reading of her will upset me more than I'd anticipated, that on top of clearing Caroline's rooms has affected me, brought my mood low.' She put down her knife and fork leaving her dinner almost untouched. 'It's all been so unsettling lately. Before we left for Amsterdam Susan was well, busy as always. Her failing health was sudden, and her death so unanticipated, yet Wilson says it was a lung condition and not unexpected, she didn't tell anyone about it, kept it to herself. When I saw her last she was fighting for breath, but so brave poor lady. She'll be missed.'

'Remember Thomas' death? It took both Caro and I some time to come to terms with him dying so suddenly.' The dinner table took on a gloomy atmosphere. 'Where's Rebecca? Did she dine earlier?' Gabriel asked. He knew Rebecca sometimes ate with the children to give himself and Eleanor time alone. She was a thoughtful girl, but now he suspected she was keeping out of his way. Perhaps she was embarrassed about her recent conduct.

'She said she had a headache and would take something later in her room if she felt up to it. I think she's gone for a walk.'

'She does appear to suffer from headaches. We should mention it to Wilson so he can look her over. I hope she won't be incapacitated tomorrow, it would be a shame if she missed Charles' wedding.'

He saw a look on his wife's face he thought he recognised. 'Is there something else amiss?'

She stood up quickly. 'Gabriel! Tomorrow the man of her dreams is to marry someone else. I expect she's not looking forward to the ceremony as much as the bride. Will you excuse me my love, you've reminded me I need to pick flowers to decorate Becky's bonnet for the wedding. Her gown is lovely, such a pretty shade of lilac, she'll look radiant I know, although red eyes aren't becoming on any lady, even young pretty ones.'

'Let's hope the bride looks radiant too,' Gabriel said with a touch of irony.

'I couldn't possibly comment,' Eleanor replied as she left the room.

R

Later the same day Gabriel, Bendor and Wilson joined Claude and Charles and a few other male friends for what promised to be an entertaining stag night.

'So why did you three not come to sup with the rest of us? Are you such crotchety old men you feared you wouldn't stay the course?' Charles asked.

'Sadly we all had duties to perform first,' Wilson explained. 'I had my rounds to do and I believe Gabriel and Bendor have been buying horses again, but we're here now so let the celebrations begin.'

Claude was already well oiled. He and Charles had supped at Lord Acton's and were now looking forward to the entertainments Harry had laid on.

'You should have first pick Charles, after all it's your last night of freedom. Who takes yer fancy ma boy?' Claude surveyed the room eyeing the women like a child eyes sweets in a sweet shop.

'After you Claude, I'm a little fussier than you are I believe. Perhaps I'll save myself for my wedding night.'

His brother roared with laughter and mopped his round, red face as he scanned the room again. 'Very well, if you insist ma boy, no point in standing on ceremony eh? May as well strike while I've still got the energy, and before the drink takes hold and renders me incapable.' He beat a path to an auburn-haired beauty who greeted him with a warm smile and a kiss on his flaccid cheek. The rest of them watched as the pair left the room arm-in-arm.

Charles shook his head and laughed. 'Lord knows where he gets his energy from, he's ten years my senior, but he's still active if you understand my meaning. I'd have thought he'd plenty to entertain him with his own wife, but apparently not. She's another one full of vim and vigour.' Charles also appraised the room. 'He's got a mistress holed up too would you believe and I'm almost certain Cecily knows about her; some woman who he's been keeping for years I think. He named a lady they all knew. 'Cecily's no angel either; she too has a gentleman, or so I suspect. The last brat looks nothing like Claude. The girl has bright red hair for God's sake!'

'Is that what you'll do Charles, take a mistress? Most of the people we know are in a relationship with someone who isn't their wife, or husband in some cases. I think we three are the exception to the rule,' Wilson said looking at Bendor and Gabriel.

Charles shrugged noncommittally.

'I know Miss Crow isn't your first choice,' Bendor slapped him on the back, 'but maybe some pretty thing here will be willing to service your needs on a regular basis?'

Gabriel looked derisively at his best friend. 'You sound a regular man of the world Bendor, not the pipe and slippers man you actually are these days.' Bendor took the criticism in good part knowing the statement to be true.

'I agree it's different for Charles but we three are happily married men and would never dream of playing with fire. All three of us would be literally cut off in our prime if the thought even passed through our heads, but it's not our wives' censure which stops us from straying,' Wilson said.

'Hen pecked the lot of you.' Charles nudged Gabriel in the ribs.

'On the contrary; love and respect is what keeps us true to our wedding vows, unfashionable perhaps, but the truth nevertheless.'

'Our good fortune lay in being able to pick and choose in the marriage stakes in the first place. I'm only sorry you can't do the same Charles,' Bendor was suddenly struck with concern for his old school friend.

'Don't worry about me,' Charles said good humouredly. 'I'll not be in the Doldrums for long, I may be getting hitched, but there are other fish in the sea. Fish who are happy to be snapped up by a handsome chap like me. I'll not go without, never fear.'

The three moved to the card tables to play faro, Gabriel of course lost and Bendor had to be restrained from over speculating as always but Wilson, who it transpired was an expert card player, made the biggest winnings of all. After several hours the party began to break up. A petite blonde who had draped herself about Charles' broad shoulders for the past hour was cast aside; he showed no inclination to take up her tempting offer.

'You aren't going to partake for the last time as a single man Charles? Not that I'm encouraging you,' Gabriel said looking at the blonde who still hovered nearby.

'I think my tastes are a little more, shall we say, refined these days, I intend to pay heed to my wedding vows, for the foreseeable future at least.'

Gabriel, taken aback at the turnabout, made no comment. Claude had not reappeared when the three men left for their own beds. Charles said he would wait for his brother.

'See you in church Charles,' Bendor shouted through the carriage window as the three friends set off for home, 'unless of course you change your mind.'

R

'What a lucky man I am to be able to escort two lovely ladies to church this fine morning,' Gabriel said as he handed Rebecca and his wife into their carriage. Eleanor was excited at the prospect of a wedding. Rebecca, however, didn't share her enthusiasm.

'Does your head still trouble you my dear,' Eleanor asked as they took their seats and set off.

'I'm well thank you, a little nervous. Going into society is still new to me remember, I don't want to let either of you down.'

'Don't be silly how could you do that?' Gabriel smiled encouragement. 'You'll overshadow the bride I shouldn't wonder.'

Eleanor took a well aimed kick at his foot.

'What's that for?'

'You're likely to get us into hot water with thoughtless comments like that. Miss Crow has only just forgiven me *my* faux pas; don't for goodness' sake make matters worse.'

The wedding was to take place at St Lawrence's Church at Warkworth. Eleanor looked about her and nodded to several acquaintances. The bride was, as is customary, late.

'Gabriel and I came to a wedding here when we were beginning our courtship,' she told Rebecca as she looked up at Gabriel wistfully. 'It was a lovely tryst.'

'Tryst? As I remember it you argued with me through most of the reception about how down trodden women were. When Eleanor gets in a debating mood she's not to be turned,' he told Rebecca. Gabriel moved off and took his place by Charles' side.

The bride arrived and accompanied by her cousin made her stately progress down the aisle. Eleanor thought she looked charming but kept the thought to herself lest she upset Rebecca.

Their wedding vows exchanged the happy couple made their way back down the aisle. Gabriel, standing up for Charles, was escorting the eldest of Claude's daughters. Eleanor thought how handsome he looked. She saw the young girl blush as he bowed, before taking her arm.

Charles was smiling broadly and Miss Crow for once wasn't scowling. The guests began to follow on. As their row was about to spill into the aisle Rebecca sank heavily onto the pew.

'Are you unwell? You've lost all colour my dear.' She threw a worried look at her husband. 'You go ahead Gabriel, I'll wait with Rebecca, we'll be out in a moment.' Gabriel looked concerned, but carried on dutifully.

'As you wish my love, I'll ask Sam to bring the carriage around,' he murmured.

'I'm fine, I felt a little faint.'

Eleanor narrowed her eyes at the young woman. 'Are you sure that's the reason Rebecca? It couldn't be you're overwrought with emotion?' Colour suddenly flooded the girl's face. 'Ah I see, I suspected as much. Charles is still in your thoughts I take it. You must see nothing can come of it, especially now. How could it? He's a married man.'

'I know I've told my heart the same, but it appears to be deaf and takes no heed of me.'

Eleanor looked about the empty church. She was shocked at the declaration; she had hoped Rebecca was over Charles. Since the letter, Eleanor had had long conversations with the young woman and thought she had made her see sense. It appeared she was wrong.

What to do she wondered. In Rebecca's place she would not have wanted to witness the man she *thought* she loved marry another woman. She wasn't such an old matron that she couldn't still remember what first love felt like.

'Do you want to return to Westshore? I can say you've been taken ill, no one will be any the wiser.'

'Oh, Eleanor I've let you down, I knew I would despite what Gabriel said. I can't face smiling and pretending I'm enjoying myself, not with Charles in the room. Please don't tell Gabriel, he'll think me a silly, besotted girl and send me back to school.'

'He'll do no such thing; he's too fond of you, as am I for that matter, but this cannot go on Rebecca, you must see that. Charles hasn't encouraged you; how could he? We discussed this and agreed you mistakenly took his friendliness as something more. You have to get over him. Come, the carriage will be waiting, leave the talking to me. Go home and get some rest and put all thoughts of Charles Noble from your mind.'

Out in the churchyard most of the guests had set off for North Point and the wedding breakfast. Gabriel was talking with Bendor and Grace. Eleanor explained Rebecca felt unwell and was going to return to Westshore.

'I'm sorry to hear that my dear,' Gabriel said to Rebecca. 'What a shame you'll miss the celebrations. Wilson has already set off or else I'd have asked him to check you over.'

'It's just a megrim, no need to fuss my love.' Eleanor gave Gabriel a look she hoped he'd understand.

Bendor suggested Gabriel and Eleanor share their carriage. Gabriel made sure his ward was comfortable then Rebecca returned home to Westshore.

R

Sam handed Rebecca from the carriage, but as she stepped down, head lowered, she stumbled. He caught her. 'Are you alright Miss, I've got you.' He held her elbow to steady her.

'Thank you Sam, it was my fault, I wasn't looking where I was going.' She looked up at him and saw the concern on his handsome face.

'I'm sorry you're not feeling well, such a shame to miss the wedding. You look so pretty - I'm sorry I forget myself Miss Argyle.'

'It's of no matter Sam but thank you for the compliment.'

He was still holding her elbow; when he realised he let go and stepped back. 'I hope you feel better by and by Miss.' He moved off and began to unshackle the horses from their traces. Rebecca watched his strong shoulders and straight back make easy work of uncoupling the pair from the carriage. Rebecca turned and went into the house.

In her room Rebecca changed out of her gown, unpinned her hair so that it fell in ripples down her back and looked out of the window at the sea. She thought about going for a walk, but couldn't summon the energy. She then tried and failed to rest, laying on her bed she felt listless, out of sorts. She picked up the novel she had been reading, but it didn't hold her attention; she read the same paragraph three times, but still didn't know a word it said.

For what felt like hours she stared at the ceiling, dry eyed, but with an empty, hollow feeling inside. She missed her mama. How she wished she could talk to her, ask for counsel. Tell her how she felt about Charles.

Some hours later she gave herself a stern talking to and with a new resolve set off for a walk along the beach. She lifted the hood of her cloak to stop her hair from blowing in her eyes as she headed for the shoreline. The tide was out and the sea as grey as the sky. She walked purposefully as if she had somewhere to go, but she merely thought to tire herself, she feared she would lie awake all night otherwise. She had been walking for over an hour when she decided to turn back. As she turned she saw a man walking towards her, a stranger perhaps; she shouldn't have walked so far unchaperoned. Then she realised it was Sam.

'You shouldn't walk alone Miss Argyle, most likely no harm would come to you but you never know. I saw you leave Westshore and thought to keep my eye on you. Begging your pardon Miss, I hope you don't think me presumptuous.'

'Not at all, it's good of you to think of my welfare.'

They walked side by side. 'Are you feeling better? You have more colour in your cheeks I'd wager.'

'Yes thank you, my headache has gone,' she fibbed growing redder. She hadn't had a headache in the first place, but couldn't say why she'd had to come home from the wedding. She felt foolish now, immature.

'I can walk at a distance if you prefer to be alone Miss. I don't want to get in your way. So long as you're within sight of me you'll be out of harm's way.'

Rebecca thought what a considerate man the groom was to think of her safety. 'Not at all Sam, please call me Rebecca. I'm not such a lady you need to defer to me; I'm a silly girl who needs to grow up. I'm sorry for putting you to so much trouble. You possibly have much to be getting on with back at the stables.'

'Not until later when I have to return to fetch Mr and Mrs Reynolds from the wedding. I often have a walk in the evening. The nights are drawing in are they not? Soon that pleasure will be lost to me.'

Rebecca looked at the darkening sky and realised it was later than she had thought. It would be dark by the time they got back to Westshore. What a fool she was. The night was moonless; she would have been walking in the dark in another half hour. She was doubly grateful for Sam's care and attention.

'You must get lonely without your wife. The long, dark nights can be trying I expect.' A gust of wind tugged at her hood.

'Once the nippers are abed yes, the nights can be long and drawn out, but I try to keep myself busy. I have a fancy for carpentry and in my leisure time I fashion small pieces for the cottage; I've made a stool, a side table and wooden toys for the children. I made both of them a hobby horse, you might have seen Davy and Beth galloping about on them?'

'You made those? My goodness you're so clever, they're handsome.'

'Made all the better by Lisbet. I could make the horses easily enough, but it was Lisbet who furnished the manes and the fancy stitching to fix them in place. Beth calls her horse Dobbin, not so original, but she loves him. Davy's horse is named Flash because of the stripe down the horse's nose, that and the fact he says the horse moves like a flash of lightning.' He laughed and she saw how handsome he was in the near darkness, how strong and powerful he looked. He was the sort of man who would protect his loved ones to the death she imagined. How lucky his wife had been to be loved by such a man and how heartbreaking she had died so young.

As they made their way through the dunes Rebecca's hood slipped from her head. She suddenly shivered.

'Are you cold?'

She noticed a sprinkling of stars litter the heavens. 'No, not cold. Thank you for watching out for me Sam.' She was glad it was dark for she could feel a blush creeping up her neck. 'Perhaps you'll show me what piece you're working on sometime?'

'I'd be honoured. I'm making a little corner cupboard for Davy's room. I could show it to you now, oh but you're possibly wanting your supper.'

'I'm not hungry, please lead the way, I'd love to see it.'

R

After the lavish wedding breakfast Gabriel, Eleanor and their friends gathered on the veranda. Lottie, Grace and Eleanor sat chatting together whilst their husbands discussed the latest issues of the day including a government scandal and the troubles in France.

'I must say the bride looks quite delightful,' Grace said a look of surprise on her face. 'Her gown is much more fashionable than the yellow monstrosity she wore at the welcome party and the way her hair is styled suits her.'

'All thanks to me,' Lottie said looking smug.

'I don't understand.' Eleanor and Grace looked puzzled. 'Why thanks to you? When I went to North Point to make amends she was particularly scathing regarding *your* comments Lottie. What have you to do with how she's turned out today?'

'She certainly didn't hide the fact she thought me no better than I should be when I went to apologise. I admit I felt ashamed of the way I'd behaved and said so. However, I think Mrs Noble a bit of a snob. When I pointed out I was not merely a doctor's wife but had also been an heiress she soon changed her tune.'

'Really?'

'I sent a letter the next day suggesting she needed help with her appearance if she was to be a credit to Charles on her wedding day. Well I worded it better than that obviously, more tactfully.'

Grace and Eleanor were dumbfounded. 'Diplomacy has never been your strong point Lottie,' Grace giggled, 'I should love to have seen the missive. You mean to say she didn't bite your head off?'

Grace and Eleanor were scandalised but thrilled at the same time.

'On the contrary, she bit my hand off. I suggested the old crone of a maid she had should be pensioned off and I then offered to lend her Jenny on a trial basis.'

'Jenny?' Grace asked, 'who's Jenny?'

'She's a young girl at Hope House who was a lady's maid before the master of the house had his way with her and got her with child.' A look of anger flashed across Lottie's face. 'She needed work and Violet needed a young, up to date maid with experience of how to style hair in ways that didn't make her look matronly. Then Violet and I met again, cleared the air and she said she'd be grateful for any advice I could give her. I think she wanted to please Charles. She's not as disdainful of the match as I'd first thought.'

'Well who would have thought it? I must say I did wonder that she didn't admire him a little, he is as they say noble by name and noble by nature... and incredibly good looking too.' Grace too was an admirer apparently.

Lottie continued: 'She showed me the gown she was to wear and whilst it wasn't a complete disaster it wasn't exactly captivating. I suggested some alterations, a nip here, a ruche there and, more radically, a lowering of the neckline. She was a little hesitant at this recommendation, but I managed to persuade her Charles would be delighted to get a glimpse of what would be on offer later.' Lottie roared with laughter in a most unladylike fashion. 'And the result is as you see; sophisticated and stylish.'

'I must admit you have managed to hide her bad points and enhance her good ones which is exactly what we all aim to do, but I have a question. Does she know Jenny's background?' Eleanor asked looking anxious. She knew not many would hire an unmarried mother and Violet didn't strike her as munificent.

'She doesn't. She didn't ask and I left it up to Jenny to decide whether she disclosed her past or not. She chose not to I assume, and as the baby is cared for at Hope House it will not be an encumbrance to either of them should Violet choose to hire Jenny permanently.'

Gabriel came to stand by his wife's side and held out his hand expectantly. 'Would you care to dance my love?' The three ladies looked astounded. They all knew Gabriel usually danced only when pushed.

'Thank you I would.' Eleanor allowed him to lead her to the dance floor. 'To what do I owe the honour?'

'Can I not dance with the most beautiful woman in the room?'

Self mockingly Eleanor glanced about the room as they took their positions. 'Where is she?'

'Have I not said before how beautiful you are?'

He bowed and she curtsied and the dance began. As he moved towards her Eleanor caught the scent of his cologne drifting on the warm air. She wondered how, after all this time and with three children, he still had a magical effect on her, still made her feel special, loved. The dance drew them apart and back together, their hands entwined. He spun her expertly, effortlessly this way and that, his arms encircling her waist. They turned and pirouetted. When they were back to back he glanced over his shoulder and smiled. Eleanor felt eighteen again. Her knees were weak. He leaned in and stole a kiss.

The dance ended and they linked arms and moved to go through to the refreshment room to join the others. 'Have I told you how much I still love you Mr Reynolds?'

'Not recently Mrs Reynolds, but it's good to hear. Have I told you how I love you and how I still desire, no not desire, crave you night and day?'

'My love you're already on a certainty,' she smiled happily, 'you don't have to convince me.'

Charles was before them. 'You two look like young lovebirds.' He smiled. 'Anyone would think it was your wedding day. Should you not be disdainful of each other's company after years of marriage?'

'On the contrary Charles, we grow more deeply in love every day.'

Eleanor was slightly embarrassed. 'What is this heady brew you're serving Charles? It must be a love potion for my husband has turned romantic all of a sudden. Most unlike his usual self I might add.'

Gabriel was unabashed. 'Cannot a man admire his wife?' Then he too looked embarrassed by his outburst. 'Congratulations on your marriage Charles, I hope you will be as happy as Eleanor and I.'

They all glanced over to where Violet was being flung haphazardly about the dance floor by a ruddy faced Claude. 'Poor Violet, she didn't want to dance in the first place. What Claude lacks in refinement he makes up for with enthusiasm,' Charles chuckled.

'I'll rescue her,' Gabriel said as he moved off once more to the dance floor.

'I don't know what's come over him. As I say there must be

something in the champagne. May I too add my congratulations Charles? I hope in time you and your bride will come to love and respect each other. Marriage is a wonderful institution when one finds the right partner. I know you weren't completely free to choose, but you're easy going and amiable, you'll make the best of it I'm sure. Violet will come to appreciate you and you'll learn to admire her. Who knows what the future holds.'

'Thank you Eleanor. I think we already have some respect for each other, but only time will tell if anything more develops. Although, as you say, I wasn't entirely free to choose I did have some small choice in the matter. She did have some characteristics which drew me to her; I didn't marry her solely for her money I can assure you.' Eleanor followed his eye as he watched Violet dance with Gabriel. In her husband's arms she almost appeared graceful. 'Her personality is not of the kind to simper and, to coin a phrase, she's no shrinking Violet.' He grinned at his own wit. 'I couldn't have married a shy, empty headed chit of a girl. At least Violet has character, knows her own mind. We'll make it work I'm sure.'

Gabriel brought Violet back to her husband and they all took supper. The wedding was a great success. Only time would tell if the marriage would follow suit.

Later, back at Westshore, Gabriel enquired after Rebecca's health.

'She's a little better, hopefully after a good night's sleep she'll be as right as rain.'

'Is there something you're not telling me Eleanor? I take it Rebecca is still pining for Charles. She didn't have a megrim did she?'

'My love you're so perceptive.'

'I'm injured by your comment. I dislike your sarcasm,' he said trying not to smile. 'As you say I'm sure tomorrow she'll be back to her usual self.' Gabriel took his wife in his arms and pierced her with a look. 'Earlier I remember you saying I was on a promise?'

Eleanor pretended to search her mind. 'Did I? I think perhaps you may be right.'

'Good because earlier I was reminded of our wedding day and

especially our honeymoon. The years have not diminished you Eleanor Barker, quite the reverse in fact.

Eleanor smiled. 'I adore being Mrs Reynolds but I miss the young, rebellious Eleanor Barker.' She giggled. 'I bet Violet won't miss being Miss Crow!'

ℛ

'Are you ready Eleanor?'

'I am. I hope it doesn't rain. I don't want to be standing about in the damp all morning.'

It was the day Padraic Turner was to sail for the New World. The day the Alnmouth Girl was to leave the bay for the last time. Eleanor had said she wanted to go with Gabriel to see the ship off; she had of course already said her goodbyes to the Irishman.

'I must confess I'll be glad to see the back of Turner, but I couldn't miss seeing the Alnmouth Girl leave port. It feels odd I'll never see her again. It feels like another link with Thomas and Caro has been severed. I know Eastshore is now in our family and that I own the three other ships that belonged to Thomas but I can't help but feel, not sad exactly, but a little sentimental; the Alnmouth Boy will be lost without his twin.'

Eleanor squeezed her husband's arm as they watched Padraic approach.

'Come to make sure I'm really going Gabriel?' He mocked.

'Something like that.' This was no time for pettiness, he let the remark pass.

Turner bowed to his rival then kissed Eleanor's hand. 'We may not have seen eye to eye in the past but,' Padraic looked contrite, 'I've much to thank your wife for Gabriel. Thank you Eleanor, only you know how much you did to help and I appreciate it more than you'll ever know.'

'I'm only glad I could be of assistance.'

'And thank you Gabriel for giving up your claim on the Alnmouth Girl.' He shook hands with his old adversary then said: 'You don't need me to tell you you're a lucky dog. Cherish your wife every day.' He looked up at the ship which awaited him. 'If only Carla had lived she'd have been excited to be starting a new life and a new adventure in Virginia, but sadly it wasn't to be.'

With that he leapt up the gang plank; the ship was ready to sail.

'Do you really think if Caroline had lived she would have gone to the Americas, left Eastshore forever Gabriel?'

'Who knows? The old Caro I knew would never have left these shores, but for ill or good he changed her. None of us will ever know.'

Suddenly the heavy bellied clouds burst, Gabriel looked up at the sky and rain lashed the deck as the Alnmouth Girl and Captain Padraic Turner left the bay for a new life across the ocean.

R

From behind a pile of crates and barrels a chestnut-haired young woman watched wistfully as Padraic Turner sailed out of her life once again. This time it was forever. Bryony Swift wiped a tear from her cheek as he stood on deck and stared resolutely out to sea. She wrapped her cloak about her and shivered as the rain soaked her.

The father of her child was leaving forever; not that he hadn't given her the opportunity to go with him. In the past she would have jumped at the chance, but not now. She had changed, life had changed her, she had grown up.

He had been to say goodbye and offered her free passage to a new life and with Susan Stubbs' recent death she had been more than tempted. After all what was there left for her now? Once again she was without employment, without her darling son and without protection. But she did have five thousand pounds and that made all the difference in the world.

She knew if she took up Padraic's offer it could have been a new start in a new land. She also knew it would be running away from her past. If she went with him he offered no guarantees; there had been no marriage proposal, no promises. She may have changed, but he, it seemed, had not.

In the end Bryony had decided to stay close to Alnmouth. At least if she stayed she might get word of her son from time to time. She now knew Eleanor Reynolds was more friend than foe. Who knows one day she might take a trip of her own, go to Amsterdam and see her son? She would not of course uproot him. She loved him too much to be selfish, but she might see him from afar, know him a little if, that is, she removed to live in Amsterdam. With her nest egg anything was possible. She didn't know how or if she was brave enough, but it was something to dream about, something to hope for.

She watched as the Alnmouth Girl cleared the harbour. The rain continued to fall steadily. She turned her back on what might have been and set off to walk back to Lesbury.

10

Mrs Violet Noble was shown into the morning room at Westshore, much to Eleanor's surprise. She had paid Violet a call twice last week only to be told the lady of the house was out hunting.

'I was sorry I missed you last week Mrs Reynolds. I thought to call and thank you in person for your thoughtful wedding gift. So lovely, thank you.'

Eleanor had the distinct impression she had no idea what the gift had been. She probably got someone else to write the thank you note they had received.

Violet's riding habit had seen better days. It was mud splattered and patched at the elbows. It was another acid shade Eleanor noted, this time of green. The lady was fond of strident colours though they did her no favours.

'You don't hunt Mrs Reynolds?'

'Please call me Eleanor, no I've never taken to the sport.' Eleanor thought it not much of a sport when the sides were so unevenly matched. 'I'm a keen rider however, and ride out most days, usually on the beach.'

Mrs Noble looked about her. Eleanor sought to fill the awkward silence by ordering sherry and biscuits; tea would not be stimulating enough under the circumstances.

'How is married life suiting you? May I call you Violet?'

'Of course. Married life is... different to how I expected it to be. I am used to pleasing myself, coming and going at will without having regard for anyone else. I see this is not how my life will be from now on, though Charles is not my gaoler you understand. As I said it is merely different.'

Eleanor remembered the first few months of her own married life, remembered how thrilled she was to be cherished and loved. Remembered how she was eager to please her new husband in any way at all. It was the happiest time of her life… until the miscarriage that is and even after that and with all the trouble over Steven she had never regretted her marriage. Their travails had brought them closer, more in love than ever.

'I'm sure you'll both learn to adapt; as you get to know each other better you'll reach an understanding.'

Again silence. Eleanor poured herself more sherry, Violet declined another glass making Eleanor feel like a lush.

'How are you getting on with your new maid, Jenny isn't it?'

'She has left my employ; indeed she would never have been hired by me in the first place had I known her background. Mrs Chaffer failed to inform me of the girl's disreputable past for some inexplicable reason.'

'I see. Jenny was taken advantage of by her employer who should have known better than to degrade his servant. She isn't the one to blame.'

'Is that what she told you and Mrs Chaffer? Are all the girls hereabouts victims, have some of them not got their eye on the main chance? She didn't pull the wool over my eyes I can assure you.'

Eleanor was about to remonstrate, stand up for poor Jenny, but then thought better of it. From what she remembered Jenny was an attractive young woman; could it be that Violet's main objection to the girl was her looks. Violet didn't want her new husband's eye wandering perhaps. Either way Eleanor knew Violet was entitled to her opinion... even if it was wrong. Eleanor made a mental note *not* to invite Violet to fund raise for Hope House.

'Is Miss Argyle not about?'

Eleanor was surprised by the bluntness of the question. The woman certainly had no artifice. In some ways Eleanor liked that about her unless as now it left her struggling to find a suitable answer. Did she know of Rebecca's fancy for Charles? She hoped not. 'She's run an errand for me, gone into Alnmouth. Did you want to see her particularly?'

'On the contrary, it is of no matter. I must be off, Charles will be wondering where I am. Goodbye Eleanor and thank you again for the silver candlesticks.'

'We bought you a silver breakfast set,' Eleanor muttered to the woman's retreating back. Violet Noble wasn't an easy woman to like Eleanor acknowledged. Yet she couldn't help but be intrigued by her. In her own perverse way she too was an unconventional woman. Next time she saw her she would ask Violet to teach her archery. Now that was a sport she might enjoy.

ℛ

George Black sat beside Rebecca at the supper table at Westshore. Eleanor had been keen to invite Susan's nephew to sup. She was eager to learn more about him. Had he plans to move to Lesbury Lodge was one question to which she was keen to know the answer. Was he a married man was another. She had thought about it and couldn't ever remember Susan telling her much about her nephew, or perhaps she had and Eleanor had forgotten. Her memory was sometimes at fault she admitted.

As the plates were being removed from the first course Gabriel broached the question he had been primed by his wife to ask. 'Are you a married man Mr Black?'

'I'm a widower sir. Tragically my wife passed seven years ago. After having a tooth pulled she became ill, possibly with blood poisoning.'

'I'm sorry to hear that, how harrowing for all concerned.'

'It was a great tragedy, especially as we have a daughter. Sophia, will be seven this July. She was a babe in arms when Constance passed away. Sadly for her she will never know the wonderful woman that was her mama.'

'Is your daughter in Lesbury with you?' Gabriel asked. The dinner had taken a decidedly cheerless turn.

'Please call me George,' the lawyer said. 'She is, along with her governess. We thought to stay a while in Lesbury as my daughter has never seen the sea before; indeed she has not seen it yet. I have been busy since my arrival with my late aunt's affairs. Sophia would be thrilled with the position of your stunning home.'

'Then if you're to stay awhile you should bring your daughter to play with our children on the beach. We have twin boys and our daughter Rose is a similar age to Sophia. She would be most welcome and you too of course if you'd care to accompany her.'

'Thank you, most hospitable of you. We would be pleased to come.' He looked at Rebecca who blushed before the man had even spoken a word to her. 'I thought I heard you were from my neck of the woods Miss Argyle. I know Berwick quite well.'

'I am sir. I was at the Berwick Academy for Young Ladies.'

'I have heard of the establishment, indeed I am considering sending Sophia there in the fullness of time. It has a good reputation I think.'

Rebecca looked at her plate, then blushing even more summoned up all her courage. 'That all depends on what you want for your daughter sir.'

'I would have her receive a good education of course, and as she hasn't siblings I thought she might make friends. Although Miss Cosgrove is an excellent governess she cannot summon other children for Sophia to meet. I fear my daughter is lonely at times and will be increasingly so in the future. Going away to school would do her much good I think, though I would miss her.'

Rebecca cast a look at Gabriel. She was deciding whether to tell Mr Black exactly what sort of establishment the academy was or whether to hold her tongue. Over the past weeks she had revealed what type of schooling she had received at the academy; whilst the teaching had been sound enough the regime and range of punishments had been harsh, often cruel. Gabriel was appalled to find such places existed.

'If you don't mind my saying sir you appear to be a caring and loving father.'

'I hope so; we are devoted to each other. My mama too dotes on the girl.'

'Then may I suggest you take my advice when I say, respectfully, that if you care about Sophia then send your daughter anywhere else *but* the Berwick Academy for Young Ladies. I wouldn't presume to know you sir, but I think you the type of gentleman who has his daughter's best interests at heart. To be frank I don't think Sophia, or any young lady for that matter, could be happy there. I wouldn't monopolise the conversation at supper by expounding further, this is neither the time nor the place, but Mr Reynolds will I'm sure tell you what he knows of the school. All I would add is please don't go on reputation alone. For years I endured the place. I have no vested interest so you may rely upon my judgement Mr Black.'

With Rebecca's impassioned speech over the rest of the meal passed enjoyably. Gabriel, always a sociable man, liked having someone new with whom to talk. The atmosphere had been uplifted by George Black's seemingly irrepressible good nature and dry sense of humour. Initially he had come across as a man of a studious disposition, but as supper progressed he had been an entertaining guest who, although was undoubtedly bookish, was also a man with a love of life. Gabriel thought it a remarkable trait having lost his wife so young and so tragically. He also thought, somewhat irrationally, he was starting with a toothache, he was sure of it. He would walk over to Lisbet's cottage for oil of cloves in the morning.

When the ladies left the gentlemen Gabriel mentioned Saul Coates. 'He's a good lawyer as well as a good friend.' He passed the crusted port to his guest. 'He's been of great assistance to me in the past.'

'When my aunt was alive she invited Mr Coates to supper on two of the occasions I visited Lesbury. Knowing him to be a man of law she hoped we would have that in common at least, but as you say I found him to be gracious and a man of some intellect.'

'What kind of law do you practise George?' Gabriel asked. He liked the man and could see that he too was intelligent, but not boringly so like many learned men.

'I deal in property law, but of course I deal with wills too. Wills as well as marriage settlements are the bread and butter of any country lawyer's practice.'

'My wife will be interested in your reasons, the law's reasons that is, why she, as a lady isn't allowed to buy property in her own right, even though she has her own money and is of sound mind.' George understood the irony.

Gabriel explained about her acquiring Eastshore and the motive behind the purchase of the property. He went on to say how put out Eleanor had been that the final signature on the deed of sale was his and not hers.

'It is a quirk of law which most men would not rush to change. I see from what you say your wife has a strong personality.' He steepled his fingers together as Gabriel had seen Saul Coates do many a time; he wondered did they teach this action at law school.

'Bess of Hardwick, a lady who had the knack of marrying rich men who pre-deceased her, was a lady of wealth and property. You may have heard of her? She was ahead of her time I think. There are ways and means around this problem if one cares to look I am sure. She certainly knew how to find a way, though ultimately a man probably inherited her vast fortune at her death.' He smiled to himself.

Luckily Gabriel had heard of the lady as Bendor said his family were related to the Devonshires. All aristocracy were related in one way or another Gabriel knew.

'It is a pity we didn't know each other at the time,' George concluded, 'I could have looked into your wife owning Eastshore in her own right.'

'Please don't tell her.' Gabriel grinned. He could see a costly investigation ahead if Eleanor got to hear of this.

They talked of other matters then George Black returned to the subject of the Berwick Academy for Young Ladies. 'Your ward was distressed I should even consider sending Sophia to the school. Can you enlighten me further Gabriel? Miss Argyle obviously has her reasons for speaking out so vehemently.'

Gabriel related Rebecca's experience of the establishment's draconian methods.

'In the end and after her mama had died she ran away. She feared being groomed to be the bride of some unscrupulous, older man. Rebecca did a brave thing in running away in my opinion.'

Of course Gabriel only told of Rebecca's life there, he wasn't about to disclose his and Rebecca's real relationship; that was no one's business but their own.

'Indeed she was brave, poor girl. She has suffered greatly. It certainly gives me pause for thought; perhaps I will put off sending Sophia away at all.'

When they rejoined the ladies George was amusing and light hearted. Gabriel could see his wife was warming to the lawyer. She cross examined him at length on why the law was so against women, but he bore the interrogation well.

'If ladies were ever allowed to practise at the bar Mrs Reynolds I would certainly hire you as my attorney had I the need,' he said good humouredly. 'You have the quick mind required of a lawyer, but also a strong sense of right and wrong. You would fight well for the underdog I believe, and win quite possibly on merit alone. Any judge *you* came before I am sure would find in your favour; he would undoubtedly see you as altogether more attractive than the majority of old, bewigged barristers who come before him.'

'I believe like men we should be judged on merit and not on looks George, whether we happen to be male or female.'

George agreed. He was a good diplomat Gabriel thought.

'And you Miss Argyle I believe, from what your ward tells me, may decide to go away to finishing school.'

'Yes, though I'm so well settled here at Westshore I'm not sure I'll want to go when the time comes.'

'Will you play for us Rebecca,' Gabriel asked. 'My ward plays the spinet George, very well as it happens.'

Rebecca took her place and George said he would turn the pages for her. Then accompanied by Rebecca, Eleanor sang a popular ditty to finish off the entertainment.

Although Gabriel knew Rebecca was still a little nervous in mixed company, George talked to her in such a manner that he put her immediately at her ease. He too was musical and as they discussed the merits of particular composers, the young woman began to unwind. She then told him how she loved her new home and surroundings which pleased Gabriel. He was glad she was settled for he had a growing appreciation of his half sister.

George said: 'I too have taken a strong fancy to the area and I feel sure when my daughter finally gets to see the sea she also will be disposed to stay in Lesbury.' He smiled amiably. 'When I was here earlier in the year Mr Coates and I talked of the benefits of having a partner; neither of us has one you understand. Over the last week or so we have revisited the idea and have thought of joining together and forming a partnership. He's not getting any younger, his words not mine I hasten to add, and I would be able to spend more time with Sophia. I also thought I'd like to take up sailing though I have never tried before.'

Before the supper party came to a close Gabriel could sense both his wife and Rebecca were charmed by the lawyer. Gabriel tended to concur; George Black was an agreeable fellow he decided, and would be a welcome addition to society hereabouts if he did indeed decide to relocate to Lesbury.

R

The next day along with her father and governess, Sophia Black, beribboned and smiling, came to see the sea at Westshore. Rose being of similar age to the lawyer's daughter was pleased to have someone new with whom to play. She took her new friend onto the beach and showed her how to make sandcastles. Despite the cold westerly wind that blew, both little girls did not notice and hit it off immediately. The grown-ups, sheltering in the conservatory, were chatting cordially. Gabriel had been detained at the bay so it was Eleanor, Rebecca and George who talked happily. When Rebecca said she would go and fetch the girls in for refreshments George offered to go with her as it was years since he had been on a beach.

Eleanor watched the pair walk down the garden path and wondered if perhaps George hadn't taken a liking for Rebecca. He was certainly attentive but as he was such an amiable man it was hard to tell.

After tea had been taken they decided to walk on the seashore. Although chilly it was at least dry. Scrabble and Slate's days of running on the sands were over, but Scrabble Junior and Pebble came along and enjoyed being chased by the children. The adults walked towards the bay with Miss Cosgrove running on ahead with the children who were meandering betwixt the sea and the dunes with the dogs bouncing around and barking.

'I have never seen Sophia so animated. She clearly loves the beach... it is so bracing,' George shivered.

'If she loves it in autumn she'll be enchanted in the spring and summer. We often swim together.' George looked sceptical. 'All our children can swim. We taught them when they were tiny, in fact Rose and the twins first bathed in the sea when they were babies; they have no fear, but they do have respect for the sea. They know not to go out of their depths and know never to swim without an adult present.'

'Really, then they're more proficient than I for I cannot swim.' He looked at the cold North Sea and shivered again.

'Then if you decide to learn to sail you may wish to learn to swim first,' Rebecca suggested. 'I couldn't swim until recently but now I love it, well I did before it became too cold. Gabriel is much hardier than I for he swims all year round.' George and Rebecca walked towards the sea as Eleanor stopped to help Ginny get a grain of sand from her eye.

'Do you think he likes Miss Argyle?'

'Don't all men?' Eleanor said. 'She captivates everyone she meets. He's a little old for her don't you think? He's possibly twelve years her senior I would think.'

'That's not too old, in fact I think that a good age difference. He's mature, stable.'

'Unlike Rebecca.' Eleanor laughed thinking of the girl's past liking for Charles. She watched as the sea suddenly turned quarrelsome and almost wet Rebecca's slippers. George rescued her at the last minute catching hold of her elbow and steering her clear.

Eleanor turned and saw Gabriel riding along the rough track at the top of the dunes. She waved to him as he navigated his way down onto the beach and then dismounted. He offered the girls a ride back to Westshore on Copper. George, who had rejoined them, looked dubious.

'You needn't worry George,' Gabriel said, 'Copper is as docile as a lamb. I shouldn't risk my own daughter's neck otherwise. I intend to keep hold of the reins in any case.'

Gabriel lifted first Sophia and then Rose onto Copper's back and they turned for home. George offered Rebecca his arm.

11

Eleanor was gratified Whitby looked at its best as she showed Rebecca about the town. They were in Whitby to spend Christmas and to introduce Rebecca to the family. Gabriel was to follow in a week or so as he had pressing business affairs to deal with in Alnmouth.

Eleanor's parents made Rebecca welcome and the young woman was carefree and enjoying her visit. Eleanor had shown her about and introduced her to Eva Drage, the milliner she had befriended some years ago. They had both purchased bonnets and were now on their way to visit Eleanor's twin brother Tomas and his wife.

'Cora, you look well I'm pleased to see.' Eleanor's sister-in-law had given birth to her second child the week before, a sister for Matilda whom they had named Martha.

'You always were a good fibber Eleanor, but thank you for not telling me to steer clear of the harbour in case I get harpooned. I look like a whale and you know it. How did *you* get your figure back, especially after the twins?'

'It takes time, but don't worry you look blooming. Where's the baby? I'm dying to see her.'

'Ring the bell my dear and she'll be brought down to us, it's too much effort for me to get up. She looks just like my sister Grace; chubby and dark haired,' Cora said unabashed. 'Aren't you going to introduce me to this lovely, *slim*, young lady?' Cora said with pretend disgust.

Eleanor had already warned Becky about Cora's sense of humour. The introductions were made and baby Martha was being admired when Tomas came home from the shipyard. Brother and sister embraced warmly. 'Oh, how I've missed you Tomas.' Eleanor hugged him tight.

'And I you sister mine, but at least this time we meet in altogether better circumstances.'

'I was going to ask how Gabriel does,' Cora said handing Martha to Eleanor. 'Is his memory back to normal?'

Eleanor cooed over the infant. 'He's well thank you. Sometimes he forgets the odd thing but then don't we all.'

Eleanor introduced Rebecca to her brother.

'You look alike, well sort of,' Rebecca said. 'It's odd you being twins, I had never met twins before I met Haydan and Ruari.'

Throughout dinner Tomas, always good company, was on top form. Being a father for the second time clearly suited him. Eleanor could remember a time when she thought he would never settle down; he always had an eye for the ladies.

'Have you heard the news of your old beau Eleanor? William has been caught at last.'

'Mama never said! I fear she's another one who's becoming forgetful. Who's the lucky lady?' Eleanor raised a sardonic eyebrow.

'Sonia Simpson as was. Her husband fell overboard and now she's a rich widow. William specialises in rich widows does he not?' Cora asked rhetorically.

'He died of influenza Cora as you well know,' Tomas said. 'You'll soon see Rebecca that my wife's mind works in a wondrous way.' He continued: 'The engagement party is tomorrow night. Our parents have an invitation, as do we, but Cora isn't up to it are you my love? Why not let me escort you and Rebecca too of course. William won't mind I'm sure, in fact he'd be pleased to see you.'

'I'm not persuaded about that Tomas, no love was lost between us at the end, but a party sounds exciting. There's bound to be lots of my old friends there, what do you think Rebecca should you like to go to a party?'

R

The next evening Eleanor, escorted by her brother and accompanied by Rebecca, was shown into the withdrawing room at Sonia's parents' home by the harbour.

Eleanor looked about her hoping to see familiar faces, almost at once she noticed her old beau in earnest conversation with his father. Trust William to be talking business at his own engagement party she thought. She didn't know for certain he was of course, but she would have laid odds on it. He was standing in front of a window and was unaware she was watching him.

Over the years William Seamer had filled out; indeed in profile his jaw looked saggy and his belly protruded. He was still handsome and as always he was dressed impeccably, but somehow he seemed shorter, rounder than the last time she had seen him. His hair was receding and greying at the temples but it added a distinguished air to his countenance. She was surprised he wasn't wearing a wig or powder to cover the grey. He had always been vain. She noticed his face was red, whether from the sun or too much port it was hard to say. At that moment he glanced about the room and they locked eyes. He made his way over smiling ironically.

'Well well well, this is some surprise. I heard you were in Whitby, but I never thought to see you come to congratulate me on my engagement. How are you Eleanor?' He kissed her hand. 'You look as pretty as a picture as always.' He bowed to Tomas and then his oily eye slid over Rebecca. No doubt he was gratified when the young woman blushed to the roots of her hair. Little did he know the poor girl blushed at the drop of a hat. He would think she was impressed by his manliness. Eleanor was far from stirred. What good fortune *not* to be married to him.

'Congratulations on your engagement William. I hope you'll be happy, I can highly recommend the state.'

Sonia was at his side at once. 'Eleanor as I live and breathe, it's been so long. Of course I was living in Scarborough for the last five years so we wouldn't run into each other when you were visiting your parents. I hear you have three children. Is your husband recovered from his accident? It was the talk of the town.' The words tumbled from her smiling lips.

Pretty, petite and auburn-haired Sonia was an old friend of Eleanor's. They had always got along together. They had been quite close for a time, but then Sonia had married and moved away and they had lost touch. William was left talking to Tomas as Eleanor and her old friend caught up on news and gossip.

As the evening wore on both Eleanor and Rebecca were escorted onto the dance floor, mostly by Eleanor's old friends, but then a tall, handsome young man in naval uniform asked if Rebecca would favour him with the minuet. Of course the young girl coloured prettily as he led her away.

'Who's that Tomas? I don't recognise him.'

'He's Eskdale's grandson, Kit.' Tomas smiled as he saw Eleanor's face.

'Christopher! My goodness he was a child when I saw him last, I feel so old.'

'He'll be eighteen or thereabouts I believe. He's been away at sea, in the navy, for the last few years.'

'He should take Rebecca's mind off her heart pain.' She told her brother about Becky's unfortunate infatuation with Charles Noble.

'Lord Eleanor, how many times were *you* in love at her age, but then as I remember you were an early starter.'

'Is that not calling the kettle black Tomas? You were such a rapscallion, but now look at you, a happily married man with two lovely children.'

'You see my cynical one; a leopard *can* change his spots.'

Eleanor was enjoying herself; being with Tomas, catching up with friends and relatives and being back in Whitby were all making her happy. She was looking forward to Gabriel joining them. She knew Christmas was going to be special.

When it was time for refreshments she realised she couldn't see Rebecca. 'Have you seen Becky?' She asked Tomas as he joined the group, part of which included Eleanor's parents.

'She was dancing with Kit I believe,' Anne Barker said, 'she'll be safe enough with him, such a lovely, well brought up boy.'

'So was my brother but that didn't stop him from behaving badly with the ladies,' Eleanor said ironically as she searched the room ignoring Tomas who had begun to remonstrate with her.

'Ah here they are.' John Barker smiled as Rebecca and Kit joined them. 'Come on you two let us find a table, I could eat a horse and go back for the rider.' They went in to take supper.

In the carriage on the way home Eleanor leaned in to Rebecca and whispered: 'Does Kit Eskdale meet with your approval?' Eleanor thought she already knew the answer to this particular question.

'He's charming, so interesting. He's already been all over the world and he's not much older than I.'

'And so good looking in his naval uniform.'

'He is but I felt... like a child talking to him. I was tongue-tied and empty-headed. I asked him how his ship was... Can you believe it? I could think of nothing to say but nonsense. It was as though my lips betrayed me, yet he was chivalrous and tried to put me at my ease by making a joke. I could think of nothing rational to say as he took my hand and led me to the dance floor. He's so handsome and such a good dancer.'

'You look good together.'

'And yet when he was near I felt in a storm of foolishness. I don't know what came over me. I doubt he'll ever think of me again.'

Eleanor sat back in the carriage and smiled to herself. She begged to differ on that point. She was sure Kit Eskdale would have thoughts for no other lady from now on.

R

'I'm going to visit Charity and her new baby and then I'm going to Attie's for the afternoon.' It was the next morning and Eleanor was talking with her mama. 'If, as I suspect might happen, a certain young naval officer should call on Rebecca don't, for goodness' sake, leave her unchaperoned. I don't want a repeat of her previous behaviour.' Eleanor told her mama discreetly what had happened with Charles Noble.

Anne Barker laughed. 'How times change. It seems not five

minutes ago since it was I trying to chase my tail to keep up with your antics and now you're the model of respectability. Worry not my love, I've asked her to join me for a walk so if he does call it won't appear too obvious if I tag along too.'

'You make me sound as if I had loose morals.'

Anne smiled. 'I meant no such thing, but you did perfect the art of losing chaperones my dear. Poor Attie used to tear her hair out.'

Eleanor rode into Sandsend to the little fisherman's cottage which Charity shared with Joe and her two children. 'If you only knew the half of it Mama,' she muttered to herself smiling.

Later Eleanor and her sister dined alone then sat in the withdrawing room which looked down the harbour and out to sea. 'I'm glad we had a chance to talk today Eleanor. I think we had started to drift apart and it has been bothering me. Family is important and not just because I am a Quaker. I know we write to each other but the only thing we talk about is the children.'

'You're right of course but it's difficult to maintain a sisterly relationship when we meet so infrequently. I'll try to include other news in future. I too am glad we've cleared the air.'

Eleanor and Attie had had a frank and open discussion about their relationship. Attie had apologised for not being more of a sister to Eleanor and Eleanor had taken her share of the blame saying she knew she didn't write often enough.

Attie had admitted she had let her husband Obed dictate terms for too long; a sentiment Eleanor had long thought to be true, but didn't say so. As sisters their attitudes towards their husbands were completely at odds. Attie obeyed hers loyally and unquestioningly whilst Eleanor only complied with Gabriel when it suited her.

Attie had also apologised for never visiting Eleanor in Northumberland. 'All the years you have been married we have never ventured to Alnmouth. I see now that is partly my fault. All invitations have been declined; excuses were made because Obed thinks the children will be influenced by the way you and Gabriel live.'

Eleanor had been indignant until her sister had explained further. 'I think he felt if Harriet and Edward saw how free your children were, compared to them that is, they would be resentful. Bad enough you spoil them when you visit Whitby but... '

'So is that the reason the twins have never been allowed to visit us too? I suspected it was the case, but I wasn't certain.'

'I feel disloyal to Obed saying it but he's so devout and for so long I have gone along with him, followed where he has led. But now I miss you and want to see more of you and Gabriel and the children of course. Children grow up so fast and I feel I hardly know them. When they stayed with us when Gabriel had his accident, they were adorable. Rose is so sweet and sensitive and the boys are clever and so funny. Harriet and Edward adore them. We should all see more of each other.'

'Then come for Easter. Perhaps all the family could come; our parents, Tomas, Cora, little Matilda and Martha. It would be wonderful.'

Attie looked crestfallen. 'I doubt Obed would agree to that. We keep all festivals quietly as you know, but let me think about it, as you say having all the family together would be diverting. If I cannot persuade him to come at Easter we can arrange another time. I will not let him put me off again I promise.'

After their talk the sisters made their way into the town. It was something they had rarely done on the previous times Eleanor had been to Whitby. Eleanor had an errand to run for her mama so they set off on this cold but sunny afternoon.

'It's true what you say about Rose. She's nothing like me; I think she takes after you more than I. Had I not witnessed her birth I'd think her an interloper.' Eleanor cast a wry look at her sister. 'She's a thoughtful child who feels things deeply, she's sensitive. She loves her papa to distraction. I swear if we were both drowning she'd save him and not me,' Eleanor said with feeling. 'She enjoyed going to the Meeting House with you when she was in Whitby last. The boys would rather gouge their eyes out with a fork than sit in quiet contemplation, they're more like me I think, but Rose enjoyed the peace and quiet. There's not that much peace to be had sometimes when the boys are about. Rose loves to read too, in that respect she's like me, but she's not wilful or headstrong like I was.'

'Or argumentative.' Attie returned the wry look.

'I've mellowed. I find I have other means of persuasion at my disposal these days,' Eleanor added sagely.

'Would your husband agree I wonder? That you have mellowed.'

'Possibly not,' Eleanor said laughing.

They turned into Church Street where several Quakers were leaving the Meeting House. Eleanor didn't recognise anyone. Of course it was years since she had stepped foot inside the place; it held no fascination for her, never had in reality though she had enjoyed her school days there.

'Ah, here's someone I think you should meet Eleanor. The lady and her son are new to Whitby, let me introduce you.'

A slim, dark haired woman of perhaps forty dressed in the familiar black garb all Quakers favoured was heading towards them. She was accompanied by a similarly dark haired boy who looked about the same age as Attie's son Edward.

'Good afternoon Mrs Hague allow me to introduce my sister, Mrs Eleanor Reynolds.'

'Good afternoon Mrs Coffin, Mrs Reynolds. I'm pleased to make your acquaintance ma'am.' They each curtsied.

Eleanor thought her accent strange, regional but which region Eleanor was unsure.

'Mrs Hague has been living in America until recently.'

That possibly explained the accent Eleanor concluded.

'We have returned to these shores after living abroad for some years. My husband, who was English, wanted to go into business with his brother who lives in Whitby and as there is a large Quaker community here we decided to settle in the town.'

'Sadly shortly after arriving Mr Hague died. He contracted TB,' Atalana added.

'Oh I'm sorry to hear that Mrs Hague. Please accept my condolences.'

Eleanor glanced at the fatherless boy. Not only had he moved half way around the world, which would have been a big upheaval for a child, he had also lost his father; she felt for him. Yet there was something about him which made Eleanor look twice at the young boy.

'The Friends have been a great support in our hour of need. Your sister in particular Mrs Reynolds has been a comfort and a blessing.'

'Not at all,' Attie remonstrated, 'I have done only what anyone would do, and besides our boys are almost of an age and enjoy each other's company do they not? Perhaps Steven would like to come to tea tomorrow? I know Edward would be thrilled.'

Steven...

Eleanor looked again at the boy. The eyes... those eyes were so like...

'My sister has twin boys Mrs Hague, twins run in our family. She also has a daughter, she is a sweetheart is she not my dear?'

'What sorry... yes she is. Whereabouts in America did you live Mrs Hague?'

'Nantucket Island. My husband was a whaling captain but he wanted us to return to these shores after he gave up the business. The industry isn't what it was and in any case, it's a young man's game, my husband was quite a bit older than I. We decided to come back to England to be near his brother who owns a rope making business here. They were going to join forces and expand, but sadly the venture had barely begun when he contracted the terrible condition that killed him.'

'Eleanor are you unwell? You look pale my dear.' Attie took her sister's arm.

Eleanor's head was spinning. 'You say you *chose* Whitby. Does that mean you weren't originally from hereabouts? Do I detect a hint of a Northumbrian accent?' Eleanor tried to keep the rising panic from her voice.

'Oh, I forgot to say Eleanor, you are correct, Mrs Hague hails from further north. She originates from Alnwick.'

Eleanor felt her knees give way.

'You do look queer my dear, shall we make our way home? Will you excuse us please Libby?'

ℛ

Gabriel arrived at Mulgrave House five days before Christmas. The warm welcome he had hoped for was not forthcoming. Eleanor waited for her husband to process her news, the news his son had returned to England. Gabriel held his head in his hands.

'I can hardly believe it. My... Steven is here in Whitby you say? Are you sure Eleanor? Could there be some mistake?'

'I could be wrong,' she said derisively, 'but the lady was called Libby and her son, who looked the right age to be *your* son, was called Steven. And as Libby Hague comes originally from Northumberland and has been living in Nantucket Island, then I think you'll agree it's more than a coincidence.' His wife walked the length of the room, clearly agitated. 'Gabriel if you had seen him he is the image of you. The eyes, his dark curly hair, even the shape of his face. He's such a handsome little boy. If you want to know what the twins will look like in five years time then look no further. They look like, well, like brothers which technically they are I suppose; half brothers at least.'

Gabriel was reeling from the news. 'You say she's a widow? Of course we never knew her married name. When I wrote to her, when Steven was first born, she was still Libby Lawson. She only ever referred to the man she was emigrating with as a "Quaker sea captain". She didn't disclose his name, why would she? She always was a private person.'

Eleanor sat twisting her hands in her lap, a habit she had when she was anxious or upset. Was she wishing it was his neck she was wringing?

'I'm sorry this has happened,' Gabriel said trying to placate. 'Who would have thought she would turn up here? Of course she didn't know you were from Whitby, she knew nothing about you. I expect when Atalana first introduced you to her, Libby wouldn't have thought anything of it either; Reynolds is a common enough name is it not? So *she* doesn't know who you are,' Gabriel mused.

Eleanor spat out: 'Do you want to see him Gabriel? Of course you do.' She answered her own question. 'I won't stand in your way, I didn't when he was a baby and I won't now.' Tears fringed her lashes.

'I'm so sorry all this is being raked up again. It's been years and still the recriminations wash up on the shore like driftwood after a wreck.'

'You scuppered the ship Gabriel,' she shouted, 'you and her.' Eleanor swallowed a sob. 'I wonder what the Friends would think if they knew Mrs Hague's background?'

He tried to take her in his arms but she pushed him away and moved to stand by the window. She looked out to sea trying to gain control of herself. 'On second thoughts the Friends would think nothing at all. The teachings say not to judge lest we be judged, or words to that effect. I'm sorry Gabriel; I didn't mean to be horrible. I know this is all water under the bridge but now, with the boy back in England, how will it change our lives? Is he going to be back in *your* life, and if so in what capacity? Are you going to be his "godfather" as we thought before?' She tried to calm herself by taking a deep breath. 'Lord, I thought all this was in the past, washed away on the turning tide.'

'I've no idea how things will change. I can't pretend I've never thought about him. You know I've never forgotten him although I've been at pains not to rub your nose in my past indiscretion, but I do want to see him. How can I not? I met him once when he was a few months old and now he's a young boy. How can I not want to meet him? Know how he thinks, behaves, know how he's turning out? You always say children change so quickly and you're right. I've already missed so much of his life.'

'It would be strange, knowing you as I do, for you not to want to know him, but think of *our* children. How does this affect them?'

'I haven't had time to think about it, but I do know it won't affect how I feel about them. How could it? I'm not about to disinherit the twins in favour of Steven if that's what you think.' Eleanor pursed her lips. He knew she was trying not to say something she would later regret. 'I shouldn't think Libby was about to look me up, why should she? She's never asked for anything from me so why would she start now?'

Question after question reared its head. He hated putting Eleanor through more turmoil. He had arrived in Whitby only a few hours ago anticipating a pleasant family visit, a happy Christmas, now this.

'Because my love, she's now a widow with a growing son to take care of, why do you think?'

Gabriel shook his head. 'As I said she hasn't come looking for me. Had she wanted me to help her she would have come to Alnmouth, looked me up. You say she has a brother-in-law so perhaps he'll offer any help she requires, not that I wouldn't help her if she asked of course, I'd do anything for Steven.'

'But how do you know she won't come looking for you? Now her husband's dead she may have been about to come asking for... something. Her brother-in-law may have a family of his own to support.'

'Did she look down at heel?'

'Well no, but it's hard to tell, as she was dressed from head to foot as a Quaker, Steven too.'

'Atalana must know where Libby lives. Somehow I'll have to find out without telling your sister why I need to know. Then I'll go and see her, ask her if I can meet Steven.'

'I know where she lives; Attie pointed out the house to me on our way home. It's called Prospect House, it's in Bagdale.'

'In that case I'll go and see her tomorrow.'

'Do you think you should send a note first? Will it not be a shock for her if you turn up on her doorstep completely out of the blue?'

'Of course, I'm not thinking straight. I'll write. Eleanor allow me to apologise.'

'Don't keep saying you're sorry Gabriel, it doesn't help. I said years ago I didn't like the situation and I still don't, but we cannot undo what's been done. I love you and I trust you to do the right thing... for *all* our sakes. This time you not only have responsibilities to me you also have children who depend on you. Think carefully before you meet your son.' She moved towards him and added tenderly: 'Has it occurred to you that Libby may not want Steven to know the truth about his parentage? She may not allow you to meet him. Don't get your hopes up my love.'

'Man alive what a mess. She would be quite within her rights to keep her secret of course, though she didn't stop me from seeing him all those years ago.'

'But that was before, he was just a baby. He has known no other father other than Captain Hague. He doesn't know you exist.'

Eleanor's mother entered the room.

'Will you excuse me Anne I have a letter to write?' Gabriel beat a hasty retreat.

'Is anything amiss?' Anne was a shrewd woman and picked up on the tension in the air.

'Gabriel has a deal in the offing which is making him uneasy. It will be fine when he's met with the client and discussed terms.' It wasn't exactly a lie. Gabriel would be anxious until he had seen Libby. They both would.

R

The next morning Gabriel was shown into the morning room at Prospect House. He was surprised how little Libby had changed and told her so, much to her delight. She professed he too looked little changed. Besides appearing a little drab in her Quaker clothes Libby was the same as the last time he had seen her all those years ago. Then too she had been plainly dressed, but nonetheless she had been attractive, almost beautiful. Now he looked closer he did discern a difference; her face was softer, less careworn.

There was an initial reserve on both sides, but then as they took coffee they began to unbend a little, they remembered how they had always been easy in each other's company.

'May I offer you my condolences on the loss of your husband Mrs Hague?'

'Call me Libby; we're not such strangers are we? Even though we haven't met for a long time and never imagined we would ever see one another again, surely we can still be friendly?'

Gabriel asked Libby about her life and in turn told her a little about his, about his children and his growing business. And then they couldn't ignore the elephant in the room any longer. Tentatively he broached the subject of his son.

'Is Steven here, in the house I mean?'

'He's at school. He goes to the Friends' school on Church Street; he's a day pupil there.'

'Of course, I didn't think.'

'Gabriel, I know this is a difficult situation. I never thought to see you again and until I got your letter I hadn't made the connection with your wife. I hadn't realised Mrs Coffin's sister was your wife is what I mean to say. Of course the name registered with me, but Reynolds is not an uncommon name. Before we go any further can I say something, something I'm not sure you will want to hear?'

Gabriel's heart plummeted. He remembered Eleanor's words about not getting his hopes up.

'I want you to know I'm not here to upset you or your way of life.' Gabriel saw his old flame draw a deep breath.

'Any meeting you have with Steven has to be on my terms Gabriel, I want to make that perfectly clear.'

'I will respect your wishes.'

'Will you? I'm not sure you will like what I propose.' Again she took a deep breath. 'When we got to America Cyrus adopted Steven legally. Papers were drawn up. It was all done properly you understand. My son has known only one father, indeed he doesn't know he's adopted. We thought to tell him the truth, well a version of the truth, when he's older, but now with my husband's passing... if I agree to let you meet him it will be as a family friend, nothing more. Not as his real father that is.' She continued haltingly: 'Now more than ever I don't want my son to know about the circumstances of his birth. He's lost one parent and I don't want you to suddenly appear and try to fill the void. It wouldn't be fair on anyone, least of all Steven.'

'I see.' He realised she had given this much thought since he wrote to her yesterday. He hesitated then said: 'When I met Steven, when he was a baby, Eleanor and I had thought perhaps we could be known to him as godparents. Could this not be the case now?'

'I don't want such a close connection Gabriel. We can manage on our own thank you. We have all the family we need at the Meeting House and my husband's brother is kind and understanding. He too is a Friend. My husband, though not as wealthy as you of course, left Steven and myself comfortably off. We have this house and enough to give us a reasonable standard of living. Cyrus made sound investments when he was whaling thinking if he was lost at sea we would be provided for. He hoped we would have enough to maintain our standard of living you understand. In addition my late husband wanted Steven to have a good education, and so he set aside monies to that end. He will have the opportunity to go to public school. He also wanted his son to go to university, get his degree.' She stopped to catch her breath. She had spoken quickly but with considerable feeling. 'Once you were kind to me Gabriel, I had nothing back then, but now I'm able to provide for Steven thanks to my husband's hard work and diligent financial planning. I know you would want to endow him with more perhaps, I know you're an extremely wealthy man, but I don't want your help, your charity. We don't need it. You helped me once when I was in deep distress and I'll be forever grateful, but Steven and I can more than manage as you can see. You were always thoughtful, considerate and helpful. Ours was an unusual arrangement... and besides, there's your wife and your own children to consider in this matter.'

Gabriel had not known what to expect before coming to see Libby, indeed he'd had little time to digest the fact his son was not only back in England but here in Whitby. Yet what Libby proposed wasn't at all what he had wanted he realised. Gabriel had hoped to be introduced to Steven as his "godfather", he had wanted to be able to provide not only financial support, but also to be a father figure, someone close who would guide and protect. He was surprised how vehemently Libby had opposed his suggestion; after all Steven was his son too, his own flesh and blood.

Then he remembered how obstinate she had been when he offered to find her work all those years ago. She had wanted to do things her way, arrange her life on her terms. It seemed nothing had changed in that respect. He had to admit he admired her for it even if it didn't suit his plans.

'But you'll let me see the boy? You won't deny me that surely?'

'I will but you'll be introduced as an old friend, perhaps a business acquaintance of his father's. I don't like lying, but some story will need to be invented.' She shuffled in her seat. 'As your wife's family live hereabouts perhaps when you're in Whitby you can call on us. However,' and here she looked him directly in the eye, 'Gabriel there must never be any hint from you about your true relationship with Steven. I know I can trust you.'

Gabriel wasn't sure if the last statement was a question or a warning. He moved to the window. He could see the top rigging of the ships in the harbour. He watched as a Dutch flag flapped in the breeze. He didn't doubt his son had been legally adopted, but was he to give up all claims on the boy and only know him as an acquaintance? Then he realised it was more than he had ever expected; he had never thought to ever set eyes on his son again so who was he to argue with the terms of their meetings? Yet...

'Of course it will be as you wish Libby.' Her shoulders relaxed and she smiled warmly. 'I'm only here for a few more days, may I see him before I go back to Alnmouth? Would it be convenient?'

'Of course, if you call at four this afternoon you could meet him then. I'll speak with him, prepare him, say you did business with Cyrus when we lived in Northumberland.' Suddenly she looked wistful. 'I've missed the North East. I loved the coastline thereabouts, the climate too. It was often unbearably hot in Nantucket especially in the summertime. I was keen to return to these shores it has to be said, so when my husband's brother suggested they went into partnership together I encouraged Cyrus to take him up on the offer.' Libby suddenly looked pensive. 'It's true I was often lonely in Alnmouth, but you were always a good friend to me.' She saw he was about to protest. 'No, don't say it Gabriel, you were a young man, you didn't take unfair advantage of me. I needed you as much as you needed me after my brother let me down so badly. Let us remember the time with fondness, because without your care and support who knows what I would have become.'

'It was all so long ago, we're both different people now. I never knew you were religious back then, of course I knew you weren't a Friend.'

'Nor was I. It wasn't until I met Cyrus that I was introduced to the Quaker way of life. It's a liberating, non-judgemental path. I don't find it restrictive in the least, indeed I find it freeing. I know from your sister-in-law your wife's family were also Quakers.' She suddenly flushed. 'Atalana and her husband must never know of our connection, we will give it out as we've discussed; you're a family friend of Cyrus'. Atalana is kindness itself, but her husband, for all he acts devout, is not as tolerant as he pretends. Oh dear what was I saying about not judging?'

'We think alike on that score. My brother-in-law is an acquired taste and not one I've yet been able to stomach for long. Thankfully we don't see much of him.' Gabriel prepared to take his leave. 'It's good to see you Libby, but I must be on my way and leave you to the rest of your day. I'll come back later as you suggest. I must admit I'm a little discombobulated at the thought of meeting Steven again. Last time he was so small, a baby, now he's older I don't know what to expect.'

'He's a lovely boy, but then I would say that wouldn't I? He's tall for his age I think, some think him older than he actually is because of it. Don't worry Gabriel I'm sure you two will get along just fine.'

Gabriel turned in the direction of the harbour, but was unsure where his legs were taking him. It was true he was eager to meet Steven but also a little anxious, unsure of how to approach the situation. He was to act a part and wasn't sure he could carry it off with confidence. Somehow what Libby proposed felt like a false note, a lie, discordant, not as he would have wished it to be, but what could he do but agree her terms?

He headed over the bridge, turned left and found himself at the bar of The Fleece Inn where he ordered a large brandy. He took it down in one, ordered a second then went to sit by the window. He realised, to his amusement, he was sitting in the very seat where he had first met Eleanor. So much had happened since that first auspicious meeting. He came to his senses, drank off the brandy and left the bar. What was he thinking? He knew his wife would be anxiously awaiting his return.

Eleanor met him by the beck at Sandsend.

'Well? How did it go? Did you see Steven?' She was on edge. Why else had she not waited at Mulgrave House? He could kick himself for making her wait a minute longer than need be. It was selfish, but he had needed to organise how *he* felt, not that he had.

He told her, morosely, sullenly what Libby proposed. The brandy had worn off now and he felt strange, not exactly deflated but not content with the situation somehow. Eleanor walked quietly by his side as he led his borrowed mount back along the sand.

'Do you think she's being unfair?' she asked.

'Not at all. Then again yes... ' Once more there was an unquiet moment. Gabriel looked out to sea and saw the swell of the tide. Waves were climbing the shore as the wind began to pick up.

'I was thinking as I waited for you,' Eleanor said, 'what would I do in her situation?'

'And what conclusion did you reach?'

'I think I would have come to the same decision as her.' He saw her hair blow across her face. She tucked it behind her ear. 'You have to understand that Steven's world has been turned upside down recently. He's possibly left friends behind in America and now he's lost the only father he ever knew. He's had to adjust to a whole new way of life here in Whitby; a new school in a new country with new people to get to know. He's learning to live in a different culture. He may have not wanted to come to England, have you thought of that? He was born here but of course he was only six months old when he left these shores. He's possibly left behind all that is familiar to him.

None of us like having change imposed on us, although I may be wrong and he might have been happy to come to England. As for his mother, she's made a decision and she's put her son's needs first, as any mother worth her salt would do. And as hard as it is for you, it's as it should be I feel. At least she's not refused to let you see him.'

Gabriel drew in a steadying breath. 'I suppose that's true, yet I cannot help but want more.'

'More? You never expected to see Steven again so anything you're given now is a windfall surely?'

'It's as you say my love, but not to have him know me as his father is hurtful, hard to accept. I know it could never happen of course, I see her reasoning but... I'd hoped, well you know what I'd hoped. I see how Libby couldn't burden the boy with the news I'm his real father, not burden exactly, but he's a child and to tell him *I'm* his father is out of the question; he doesn't even know he's adopted. I see her thought process, but I'd wanted to be more than a "family friend" who seldom sees him and has no influence in his life.'

He heard his wife sigh. 'Selfishly I'm happier knowing we won't be treated as godparents; we have enough to deal with bringing up our own children. They're my first priority Gabriel.'

'And mine too of course.'

She put her arm through his. 'Before yesterday you were happy, now you're discontent. Try to see a more balanced view. You have more than you ever anticipated, try to be grateful.'

R

At four in the afternoon Gabriel, keen yet apprehensive in equal measure, was shown into the drawing room of Prospect House. It overlooked a terraced garden which sloped down to the estuary. The top masts of ships could be seen in the near distance. His son sat at a small writing desk. He looked up as Gabriel was announced.

'Allow me introduce you to Mr Reynolds my dear. This gentleman was known to us when we lived in Northumberland.' Not a lie exactly but it was stretching the truth somewhat.

'Your servant sir.' The boy bowed respectfully.

Gabriel remembered Eleanor had said she thought Steven looked like an older version of the twins, but he wasn't prepared for how much his son looked every inch a Reynolds.

Steven was indeed tall for his age, straight backed and slender, long boned; almost wiry. His nose and mouth were the same as his own, the same as Haydan's and Ruari's for that matter. The child's hair was dark and curly. It was like looking at his younger self.

Libby led them to a round table set with pretty blue and white china. There were plates of scones, cakes, pastries and jellies. They sat down to eat and drink tea. An ordinary thing to do made extraordinary by the fact he was seeing his son for only the second time in his life. Gabriel couldn't take his eyes off the boy, but realised it would be odd if he stared at his son any longer.

He collected himself. 'How do you like England Steven?'

'I find it exceedingly cold sir.' The boy shot a look at his mother and grinned. 'And wet.'

'I'm afraid Steven has been used to a more temperate climate, not that it didn't rain in Nantucket, but perhaps not as often. I hate to tell you this my dear boy, but this is only the beginning of winter. In January it gets even colder and wetter, we might get frost, ice and snow. And it's always windy; gales are not uncommon on this coast.'

'Have you settled in at school, have you made friends? It must be hard leaving acquaintances behind in America.'

'The masters are kind and I have made two or three new pals. I miss my friends from home, not home now of course but I'm happy Mama and Papa thought to come to England to be near Uncle Joseph.'

The conversation turned to Steven's likes and dislikes. Gabriel noticed Libby's proud face as her son spoke confidently and without reservation.

'I would like to be an explorer,' Steven said. 'I should like to travel the world looking for new species of flora and fauna and study their habitats. When I go to university I plan to study biology and geology.'

'At your age I'm not sure I knew what I wanted to be. No, that's not quite true; I wanted to be a pirate. My father owned a shipping line which I've now inherited, so I knew I would do something to do with ships. Being a pirate sounded more exciting than imports-exports.' He watched his son closely. 'I have three children, twin sons and a daughter. None of them are interested in shipping, but then they're very young.'

'I doubt you can gain a degree in piracy sir,' his son joked. 'Perhaps when you graduate they give you your very own Jolly Roger?'

Gabriel realised the boy had a different accent, an American accent presumably. Libby's own accent was changed, not quite English anymore. He liked the boy, he was easy company. Self assured but not arrogant.

After an hour or so Libby said: 'Steven you'd better take your leave. Steven has a tutor twice a week to help him with the classics. He'll need Latin and Greek if he's to study botany.'

The boy got down from the table and bowed to Gabriel. 'It's been a pleasure to meet you sir. Perhaps next time I could be permitted to meet your sons, I've never met twins before; I would find it interesting.'

Steven made to go, leaving the door open as he left. 'What is it with children and doors?' Libby tried to look cross.

'The twins are the same, and if they do remember to close them they loosen them from their hinges because they bang them so hard.'

'Speaking of your boys, I don't think that's a good idea Gabriel, your children meeting Steven that is, not yet at any rate, when he's older perhaps.' She suddenly said: 'Oh dear look, he's left his exercise book.'

'Shall I try to catch him up?'

'No no, he'll manage I'm sure, please don't bother Gabriel.' Libby looked him in the eye. 'All this is quite bemusing is it not? The less lies Steven is told the better. I dislike lying to my own son, though I see there is no alternative. You're his natural father but I'm his mama. It's confusing for me having you back in my life again.'

'It is unsettling I admit - for all concerned.'

'Steven appears mature I know, but he misses Cyrus, misses his friends. Your wife must be a tolerant lady; it can't be easy for her either.'

'She's broad-minded, but as you say it's hard for her to accept. Our... *friendship*, mine and yours happened before I knew her of course, but the repercussions have affected her nonetheless. Thank you also for your tolerance Libby. I appreciate it more than you will ever know.'

R

Back at Mulgrave House Eleanor was preparing to dress for supper when Gabriel came to her dressing room. After she had dismissed Molly he told her how the meeting had gone; she had half expected him to feel a little down hearted. She wasn't wrong.

When he had finished she said: 'Yet you don't look happy my love. What is it that troubles you? You say he's a lovely boy and Libby has agreed you can see him next time you're in Whitby so why the long face?'

'I don't know.' He was looking at her but not really seeing her. He glanced at the swell of her breast as her dressing robe fell open but he looked away, sat on the chaise. 'I'll go and change although I don't feel particularly sociable this evening. How many are we for supper?'

'Just the family - and as Rebecca is quite taken with Kit Eskdale Mama has invited him too.'

'Who?'

Eleanor explained how Rebecca had come to meet the young sailor.

'Does this mean she's over Charles?' Gabriel was still distracted she could tell. He was listless, out of sorts.

'Quite possibly, I told you young girls can be fickle. I said she'd get over Charles.' She stood and put her hands on his chest, started to undo his neckcloth. She kissed him tenderly hoping to help him relax. He was pent up, unmoved.

Eleanor wanted to rebuild contact but he couldn't quite let her in. His thoughts were concerned only with Steven. She searched his face but couldn't break down the wall of discontent and resentment he had built up around him. It wasn't resentment against her she realised or Libby for that matter, but it kept her on the outside. Just for a moment when he had come back his eyes had changed, warmed when he had seen her as they always did, but now they were distant again. She was unable to keep his interest. Not since the accident had he been so remote. She needed to keep him away from dark thoughts, thoughts which she understood to some degree, but Gabriel was lost to her in this mood. It was a change, an unwelcome change and she hoped it would not be lasting.

He stepped away. 'I'll go and shave.'

'There's ample time yet.' She stroked his back, yet again he was unresponsive.

'In that case I'll go to the nursery. Rose said earlier she has something to show me.'

'Gabriel.'

He turned back irresolute; she knew he wasn't really here, in the room. His guard was up.

'Be patient my love. Don't expect too much and you won't be disappointed.'

Gabriel shrugged then left her.

R

Christmas at Mulgrave House was a joyous occasion. With all the family together Eleanor couldn't have been happier - except for one thing. She knew Gabriel had Steven on his mind and that was putting a damper on the proceedings. For the most part her husband was cheerful, good humoured, playing with the children, drinking too much brandy with Tomas and spoiling Rebecca with gifts. But occasionally, when no one was watching, she saw him drift off, he was somewhere else, somewhere even she could not reach.

The long winter evenings were spent with family and friends. Kit along with his grandfather, called on a number of occasions and Eleanor saw Rebecca was keen on the young sailor and that equally he had a liking for her.

Yet always in the background there was a shadow, the shadow of Gabriel's eldest son presided over the proceedings like a spectre at the feast.

12

Back in Alnmouth her husband was brooding. Why she didn't quite comprehend. Well, she did understand but her stubbornness wouldn't let her admit it. In regards to Steven, Gabriel now had more than he ever thought to have; contact with the son he had lost years ago, yet he was less than satisfied.

She tried to distract him, to entertain him, to understand him, but it was all to no avail. It was as if he wilfully disregarded her attempts to cheer him, to show him how fortunate he was with his life with her and their children. His frustration became her frustration; he had retreated like the tide.

Gabriel began to leave early for the bay and come home later than he had ever done since the children were born. For days they had hardly spoken, save for the day to day ordinary talk and even that was an effort for him. It was after midnight when he crept into their bedchamber.

'You're still awake; I thought you'd be asleep by now.'

You hoped so I'm sure. She bit back the unkind words.

'Have you eaten? I asked Mrs M to leave you a cold supper.'

Again.

He climbed wearily into bed.

'Charles came to the office as I was leaving. He needed advice about licences for some ship he's bought. By the time we'd gone through the papers, he's no idea what he's doing of course, it was late and so we supped at The Hope and Anchor.'

'You didn't think to send a note. I waited on supper for you.'

'Sorry, I was distracted.'

Again.

He blew out the candles.

‘How is Charles getting along with Violet?’ Eleanor turned in the darkness to face him.

‘He seems content strangely enough. I think there’s a growing fondness between them from the little he said.’

‘I find that hard to believe.’

He didn’t reach out for her as he usually would. Didn’t touch her, pull her into his arms, rest his hand on her thigh. Her pride was injured so she stayed on her side of the huge bed. She wished lately the bed was smaller.

‘Does Charles know about Steven?’

‘He doesn’t know. I never thought to tell him.’

The silence echoed around the room. She waited for him to continue and when no more was forthcoming she said: ‘Are you hankering to go to Whitby? Do you want to see the boy again?’

Silence.

Eleanor swallowed her pride and moved closer.

‘There’s no point in going to see him again so soon. It would look strange would it not? I do want to know more about him and I’ve been thinking of ways in which that could be brought about. It’s been much on my mind since we returned.’

‘I know it.’

‘I had thought that in time, I could ask Libby and Steven to come and stay here at Alnmouth for a visit.’ Eleanor was glad it was dark; if her husband could only see the look of horror on her face. She didn’t trust herself to speak. ‘But I can see this isn’t a good idea. I’d imagined, idiotically, that if perhaps I could see Steven two or three times this year, in Whitby of course, then I could ask them to stay for a week or two. Use the pretence of Libby returning to where she used to live when Steven was a baby. Show Steven around a little. Then I saw how many lies would have to be told. We’d have to lie to our children, to our friends, to the family. Only Bendor and Grace are privy to the secret of Steven’s parentage, but if the boy was to visit it would be too difficult. I don’t want to tell lies. I’m also keen to shield you and the children from this as much as possible of course.’ She shuffled away from him trying to see his face now her eyes had become accustomed to the dark. 'Bad enough you've lied to your sister, but I wouldn't want either of us to lie on purpose.'

Eleanor had lied by omission; kept up the pretence to Attie she didn't know Libby's background. She felt guilty about it. 'And there's Rebecca of course. She would have to be lied to also.' She heard the air expel from his lungs slowly.

'Why can't you be content with how things are Gabriel?' Her frustration threatened to erupt. 'Why complicate things more than they need to be. It's clear Libby doesn't want you to be overly involved in her son's life.'

'*Her* son's life. He's *my* son too. I know, I know but yet I *want* to be more involved. I understand Libby is protecting Steven and you obviously don't want me meddling but, well he's my son. I would have to be made of stone not to think of him. Now I know him a little it somehow feels worse.'

Another long, unquiet silence filled the room.

'If you push too hard you may push her in the wrong direction Gabriel. She's made it perfectly clear how she feels. You have to come to terms with it. Come to terms with knowing him yet having no influence over him. When he's an adult it will be different. Then he can choose whether to know you better. As a friend of his father's of course unless - '

'Unless when he's of age he can be told the truth you mean?'

'Libby would not countenance that. Would you?' She knew the answer. 'You can't go against her wishes even when he's grown up. That would be disloyal, disrespectful. Up until now she's been more than fair, since they returned to England I mean. Tread carefully my love, how would you feel if she felt the need to move away because you interfered?' He started to interrupt but she stopped him. 'I'm only thinking what I'd do in her shoes. I'd want any meetings on my terms, but if I felt cornered I'd protect my son like a she-bear. I would leave without a forwarding address if necessary. All I'm saying is don't rock the boat, gain her trust and see what happens in the future. You have a family who love and adore you, don't jeopardise that Gabriel. I've been patient while you come to terms with your son's re-emergence, but don't make us second best.'

'I would never do that my love, you know that. I promise you I'll do nothing to risk our happiness.' He reached out for her, pulled her close, kissed the top of her head. She felt safe for the first time in weeks.

R

Sir Bendor Percy leaned on the fence that enclosed the large paddock at the stud he owned with Gabriel. The two friends watched as their prize dam munched the sweet grass. 'She's in foal again. Good news is it not?'

Gabriel nodded. 'It most certainly is. Falladore's foals always sell at a premium.'

'That's good news I've given you Gabe, why then do you look like I've delivered bad? You appear distracted my friend, not your usual self. What troubles you for I know you well enough to know something's amiss? Your head isn't paining you again?'

'No, no, I am well thank you.'

Gabriel hadn't seen his friend for weeks. Ben and Grace had taken a trip to France for more than a month and then Gabriel had been in Whitby. Therefore Bendor knew nothing of Gabriel's travails regarding Steven. He told his best friend about his son's resurgence. He explained how Steven was back in the country and back in his life. He also shared his feelings about having little or no contact with him for the foreseeable future at Libby's insistence. It felt good to unburden himself to his oldest friend. He knew Eleanor had struggled to understand him; she was too close to the situation, too concerned he was becoming overly involved. Bendor would be more objective he hoped.

'Back for good you say, that's some surprise.' Bendor shrugged. 'I feel for you but it's Libby's decision how much of a role you take in Steven's life is it not? She's his mama when all is said and done. Sadly you must learn to live with it even though I see how it pains you my friend.' Ben tore at a piece of long grass then chewed it thoughtfully. 'I own it's odd you've met him, yet won't play a big part in his life, but that could never be, you must see that. Even if you'd been introduced as his godfather your influence would have been limited. You say the boy doesn't even know he's adopted?'

'Libby says they planned to tell him when he was older.'

'I see. Then be glad the boy is in good health and well provided for and get on with your life here in Alnmouth. It's hard I know, and I'm glad it's not me having to wrestle with this situation, but there it is.' Gabriel sighed not at all happy with Ben's response. 'How does Eleanor feel about this turn of events?'

'As always she's being supportive, though Lord knows why because I've been difficult to live with since we returned from Whitby. She thinks I should be happy Steven is in my life again regardless of the restrictions.'

'I'm in complete agreement with her. You have more than enough to be grateful for so don't go causing problems. I know that's easy for me to say, but you never thought to see your son again and now you have and will do so again. I remember all too well the black moods you used to suffer, don't go brooding and pushing Eleanor away is my advice; she's been more than patient from what you've told me.'

'I know, I know, but I can't help but want to be in my son's life more, more than being known as some business acquaintance of his father's. He's such a special boy; intelligent, well mannered... he looks like me and the twins.'

'He's a lucky boy then, except for looking like you.' Bendor grinned. 'Life rarely gives us all we desire Gabe, but Eleanor deserves your attention now... and Rose and the twins. Don't return to your old ways of wallowing. Eleanor will kick you out and I'll not take you in.' He tried to make light of the situation. 'Who knows what the future holds my friend, Libby may change her mind in time. You turning up on her doorstep would have been a shock for her.' He put his arm about his best friend's shoulder.

Gabriel knew Bendor was right but still he had hoped for... what exactly he was unsure. He changed the subject and told Bendor about how Eleanor had invited his brother-in-law for Easter.

'In that case I'd be more concerned Obed Coffin decides to take you up on the offer.' He shuddered. 'Now that *is* a worrying development. Whatever was your wife thinking inviting *him*? Do you suppose he'll join in on one of our drinking games? I think not.'

'I may invite myself to Dunstanburgh,' Gabriel said grimacing. 'Imagine him looking down his long nose the whole time. I know Eleanor and know she'll cut back on the celebrations not wanting to upset her sister's husband. She'll think if she puts on too much excitement she'll be stopped from seeing the children at Westshore again. Rations will be cut *and* when they'll be most needed. Liquor will be seriously curtailed I imagine. It will be plain fare and cordials all round.'

'I don't think it's an option to jump ship, you'll have to put up with it *if* they decide to visit. Easter is a long way off yet. It's not been decided finally you say, there's time for him to change his mind, after all he's never darkened your doorstep before.' Bendor checked the time on his pocket watch. 'I need to be on my way, I told Grace I would be home to go to the costumier. Yes Gabriel it's that time of year again when we're expected to dress up and make fools of ourselves to please our wives.'

Gabriel knew it wasn't Bendor's favourite event of the social calendar either but they consoled themselves with the business they might do there. Half the county now attended The Hope Ball.

'Cheer up you old misery and count your blessings,' Bendor said punching his friend on the shoulder.

Gabriel watched Bendor ride off. Nothing had changed but still he felt better having discussed his son with his old friend even if Bendor agreed with Eleanor. He moved to the small paddock where Rose had been practising her riding. As he leaned on the fence Jax, his head groom cum-under-manager, came to stand by his side. They had been friends for a long time and were easy in each other's company.

'Rose has outgrown her pony don't yer think? It's a good job he's a sturdy little thing otherwise she'd squash him,' Jax said smiling.

Rose noticed she was being watched and waved.

'Look what you're about Rose,' her father shouted. 'And don't go near the cavaletti jumps.' Gabriel turned to Jax. 'She rides well, but you're right, Podge is on the small side for her now. Poor Podge won't make it over the jumps with her on his back.' They both grinned, but affectionately not disparagingly.

'She's more than ready to start learnin' to jump,' Jax suggested.

'So she tells me on a daily basis.'

'The twins could learn on Podge, he's always had a good temperament.'

'I'm not sure even Podge would have the patience to cope with the twins. Lord knows we'll have to think carefully before putting them in the saddle. As yet they've not shown an interest in riding.'

'That's because they're happy to be traipsed about in a carriage like little princes.'

'Perhaps you're right.' Gabriel conceded then changed his mind. 'They run everywhere... at speed and without due regard to their safety or anyone else's for that matter. They're a hazard.'

'Where's she off to?' Jax asked as Rose headed for the lower paddock. They both watched as Rose demonstrated a rising trot. Podge complied well enough.

Jax cleared his throat. 'We have news. Sarah's with child again, she expects in the autumn.'

'That's tremendous news Jax. You'll have caught up with us then.' Jax already had a son and a daughter. 'I was going to offer you the larger cottage here at the stud. Now with a growing family you could do with the extra space I would imagine, your current cottage is on the small side is it not?'

'As you say wi' another on the way it'll be useful to have more space. Sarah will be that pleased when A tell her. Thanks, we appreciate the thought.'

Neither man had been watching Rose while they talked. When Gabriel turned his attention back to his daughter his face changed.

'What in God's name?'

He leapt over the fence with Jax close behind him. Rose and Podge were heading for the training jumps. Although they were tiny Rose was expressly forbidden to jump at all and she knew it. Hadn't he just said so?

'Pull him up Rose. Stop this minute,' Gabriel cried.

Whether Rose heard or not he couldn't say but she carried on regardless and was heading for the first of the three juvenile jumps. Rose lined Podge up, wrongly as it happened. The little pony pricked up his ears, possibly in surprise at what he was being asked to do. He stopped dead, tipping Rose over his head unceremoniously. She lay inert on the other side of the fence.

Gabriel was at his daughter's side in seconds. He knelt down to inspect her. 'Stay still, don't move. Do you feel pain anywhere?'

Her eyes shot open and with a mischievous grin she said: 'I can't tell, but I don't think so.'

'Try to sit up, careful now. Are you dizzy?'

'Not more than usual. Lisbet's always says I'm dizzy, but I don't think it's a compliment.'

'Now Gabriel saw she was uninjured he was furious.

'Wait until we get home young lady, your mama will hear of this.' Rose got to her feet and dusted the dirt from her jacket. Jax held Podge's reins as Gabriel took his daughter by the hand and frogmarched her out of the paddock.

Back at Westshore Gabriel told Eleanor about his disobedient daughter. Eleanor tried not to laugh. 'She's certainly getting a bit above herself recently, she always used to do as you bid, but lately she's becoming headstrong.'

'It was obvious what was going to happen. From the minute she lined poor Podge up she was always heading for a fall.' Gabriel didn't see the funny side.

'All's well that ends well my love, but she needs reprimanding, she's testing you Gabriel. You need to make her understand when you say no you mean it. She thinks she can charm the birds from the trees.'

'Like her mama.' He poured himself a brandy.

Eleanor tugged the bell pull. 'No time like the present my love.'

Gabriel had been about to shirk his responsibility, put off the lecture for another day or better still pass the buck to his wife. Eleanor had other ideas. 'You know she only has to look at me with those big, innocent eyes and I'll be putty in her hands.'

'Do *not* let her get away with it Gabriel. She's the one who needs pulling up.'

Rose sauntered into the room and stood before her parents. She was eating an apple. It was clear she was not expecting a telling off.

'I forgot to give Podge the apple I'd taken for him so, as Uncle Obed would say, waste not want not.'

Gabriel saw his wife purse her lips together. She turned away and sat by the fire signalling he was in charge.

Gabriel pulled himself up to his full, imposing height. 'Rose you deliberately disobeyed me this afternoon. You have been told, more than once, that you are not allowed to jump, not yet anyhow and not on Podge. You haven't been schooled to jump so it was clear to me you didn't know what you were doing.'

'Actually I didn't jump. Well Podge didn't anyway and I more or less flew rather than jumped.'

Rose was blithely unaware the trouble she was in. Gabriel pressed his fingernails into his palms to stop himself from smiling, his daughter was a little character, but then he recalled how the incident may have had a more serious outcome. His precious daughter could be abed injured. 'You could have broken your silly little neck don't you see?' He didn't raise his voice but he glared at the errant child through narrowed eyes. 'When I say don't do something I mean it Rose. You defied me. This time, luckily for you, neither you nor Podge was hurt. Not only did you put yourself at risk young lady, you put your pony at risk too. A good rider takes care of her mount and doesn't risk injuring him. Your pony has to trust you to make the right decision and today you did not. There was no way poor Podge could have jumped safely from that angle.' Gabriel saw his daughter's head drop. She put the apple in her pocket. He knew she loved Podge to distraction and his point had hit home. 'Today you've let Podge down, let me down and let yourself down. I'm disappointed in you, very disappointed indeed.'

She looked up at him through lashes that sparkled with unshed tears. Her bottom lip trembled.

'I'm sorry sir. I'll never disobey you again.'

Gabriel saw his daughter's resemblance to her mama; he wavered but then stiffened his resolve. Rose had to learn her lesson. He had never chastised her before, never really had cause as she had always been a biddable child, but Eleanor was right; she was getting too big for her boots. He had to behave like a stern father, show his daughter he meant business.

'You will go to your room and stay there until the morning. There'll be no supper for you tonight young lady.'

'Yes sir,' she sniffed, 'goodnight then Pa, Mama.' The dam burst and tears spilled down her chubby cheeks.'

'That's enough now... I accept your apology, now run along.'

She wiped her eyes on her sleeve and walked from the room. Gabriel let out a long breath as the door closed behind her.

'Well done my love. Neither I nor Rose thought you had it in you. Thankfully I think you got through to her.' Eleanor was amused. 'The "being disappointed" was a nice touch, that always got me as a child when I was scolded by my father.'

He poured himself another brandy. 'Why was that so hard I ask myself? I tell the twins off every day, until I'm blue in the face sometimes, but one trembling lip from Rose and I'm reduced to a wreck.'

'It's the father - daughter bond. It never goes away so you should learn to get used to it. Even now if I think I've let Papa down I'm mortified. Mama soon learnt that if I'd been naughty she left it to him to sort out. I took much more notice of my papa than I did of her.'

'I see I've been played again. You were cross with her too, but knew she would listen to me more than you.'

'Quite possibly my love, but nevertheless I'm proud of you. You were masterful.' She rolled her eyes but smiled affectionately.

Gabriel sat beside his wife and thought about Bendor's words earlier at the stud. Bendor had suggested that maybe he was pushing Eleanor away. He thought perhaps his friend was right. Since their talk he had come to see he had been unfair to her, he had unintentionally shut her out. After he had left the stud he called at the jewellers on Northumberland Street. Fattorini's wasn't a shop he frequented often preferring Spencer and Cobb in Alnwick, but with the Italian's help he had picked out a pretty pair of opal earrings. He wasn't sure if they were a peace offering or an apology or a way of saying he appreciated her forbearance. Now he took them from his pocket.

'I happened to see these in Fattorini's window.' He opened the box to show her the gift.

'Oh, Gabriel are they for me?'

'Who else?'

'Thank you, I adore them, look how they catch the light. They shine all the shades of the sea at sunset, so bright and fiery.'

'Opals are a perfect stone for a redhead are they not?' he said with a hint of irony. 'But since we came back from Whitby you've managed to curb your natural tendency, Lord knows how - I've not been easy to live with I own. I've found it hard to live with myself so I know you must have struggled. Thank you my love for putting up with me. I mean to try to regain some perspective.'

'And I too for I know in my heart you would never do anything to endanger our marriage.' Now he saw unshed tears glisten on his wife's lashes.

'You have nothing to reproach yourself for my love. I'll try my utmost to make it up to you I promise.'

'There's nothing to make up Gabriel,' she said. 'Your feelings are hurt, I see that but together we will come through this.'

As they sat by the fire he held her hand in his. He touched her wedding ring with his forefinger. 'It was a happy day when we wed Eleanor. Our marriage is everything to me. Know that even if you think you can't penetrate my dark mood you're always there with me at the core of my very being giving me strength and solace. You're the light of my life and I love you.'

13

Gabriel reached out for his wife. He thought she was awake but until he stroked her thigh and felt her quiver beneath his touch he wasn't quite sure.

'Good morning.'

She looked so lovely with her tousled hair and sleepy gaze.

'Are you getting ideas this early in the day Gabriel Reynolds?'

'I don't know what you mean,' he said rolling towards her then kissing each eyelid in turn.

'Do you suppose other couples are amorous in the mornings?' Eleanor asked yawning.

'How would I know? What a strange thing to ask.' He kissed her again, softly, then ardently.

'Don't men discuss such things when they're in their cups? I thought men talked about their likes and dislikes?'

'Stop talking Eleanor and kiss me.'

She did as he asked then moved closer so they were as one. He ventured under the covers.

'Where's Ginny with our breakfast?'

The couple froze. Gabriel was the first to look up. Rauri, in his nightshirt, stood at the bottom of their bed looking annoyed. Neither of his parents had heard him come in.

'What are you doing Papa? Have you lost something? Only I wondered why your head was under the covers when I came in.'

'Explain to me why I wanted children?' Gabriel muttered under his breath.

Eleanor rearranged her nightgown and sat up. 'Good morning Ruari. How long have you been standing there? Never mind. You're up too early. Ginny will be along soon. Go back to the nursery and wait, it wants twenty minutes to seven and she doesn't bring up your breakfast until seven.' She whispered in an aside: 'Remind me to ask Mr Pater to teach the boys how to tell the time.'

Ruari was unmoved. 'Your clock is slow. It's gone seven already I know because I checked with Rose to make sure and it's almost seven thirty and I'm hungry.'

Gabriel reached for his pocket watch from the night stand. 'So it is, our clock must need regulating.'

'That's odd then,' Eleanor said, 'where is Ginny? She must have overslept. That's most unlike her. Ruari go to Ginny's room and knock on her door, ask if she's overslept. She may be unwell.'

'I've already done that. When she didn't answer I opened her door and she wasn't there. Can I go and see if Mrs M has made my breakfast I'm starving.'

Gabriel pulled the bell. 'Go back to the nursery, Ginny will be along soon.'

Haydan arrived. 'I'm dying of hunger, where's Ginny?'

'Neither of you know the true meaning of the word I'm pleased to say. Go and get dressed and wait. Patience is a virtue.'

Dora, the maid of all work, arrived as the boys, muttering under their breaths, shuffled off back to the nursery.

'Has Ginny made the children's breakfast? Does she know what time it is?' Eleanor asked.

'Mrs Madison were about to send me up with it ma'am. Ginny's not about, she's not bin seen all mornin'. When she din't appear at her usual time Mrs Madison told me to go and wake her but she weren't in her room. Her bed's not bin slept in or else she made it as soon as she got up. Nobody's seen her today. Mrs Madison's not happy ma'am.'

'I can imagine,' Gabriel muttered.

'Dora, send Molly to me and can you see to the children please. I wonder where Ginny can be. This isn't like her. In all the years she's worked here I've never known her to miss bringing the children their breakfast, I hope nothing's happened to her Gabriel.'

Dora went off to do as she was instructed. Gabriel threw his legs out of bed and scratched his head. 'So much for any thoughts of an early morning tumble, remember the thought for later my love.'

'Gabriel! I'm worried, where can she be?'

'Maybe her clock's wrong too. Perhaps she was up early and went for a walk on the beach, it's a lovely morning by the looks of it. I think I'll go for a dip - cool my ardour.'

Molly could be heard pouring water into a ewer in Eleanor's dressing room. 'I'll get dressed quickly and then go to see what can be done.'

He saw how worried Eleanor looked and realised he too should be anxious for the nursemaid's whereabouts. 'I can be dressed quicker than you; I'll go and see who saw her last and when.'

The staff gathered in the kitchen. Mrs Madison looked as though Ginny had disappeared on purpose just to inconvenience her.

'Good morning all. Has anyone seen Ginny this morning?'

Most shook their heads but no one spoke up. 'If not this morning then who saw her last night? She put the children to bed at the usual time I expect so who saw her later?'

Dora came into the kitchen having given the children their breakfast. 'A saw her go into the scullery at about nine sir. She said she were goin' to wash grass stains out of master Haydan's breeches.'

'I saw her later than that sir. She wished me a good night at about ten just as I was retiring.' Mrs Madison continued: 'Your breakfasts going to be late at this rate, I can't get on with everybody in my way.'

'Don't worry about that Mrs M, finding Ginny is of more importance as I'm sure you will agree.' She didn't look convinced but the look he gave his cook silenced her.

'I think we need to set up a search party, something may have befallen her last night or early this morning. Sam can you gather the men and start towards the bay, I'll take the boys and look north.'

Ginny suddenly appeared in the doorway.

'Ginny! Thank goodness you're safe we were about to send out a search party.'

'Did you not get the note I sent Mr Gabriel? That Smith boy is worse than useless,' she added as Gabriel shook his head.

He saw the look on her face. 'Come through to the breakfast room my dear. Mrs M please let Mrs Reynolds know Ginny is found and bring tea.'

'Sit down Ginny,' Gabriel said once they were alone. Eleanor rushed in and hugged the girl.

'Are you alright? You look like you've been up all night. What's happened?'

Dora set down the tea then scuttled out quickly.

'I'm afraid it's bad news. I sent a note earlier but it seems you didn't get it. It's Abner. He's... I went for a walk and found him. He's dead I'm afraid.'

Before either of them had time to catch their breath, there was a brief knock at the door and Lisbet bustled in. Disregarding the others in the room she made a bee line for Gabriel.

'Abner's not bin home all night. He went to The Hope and Anchor as usual and he's not come back. A never wait up, who knows what time the old rascal comes home usually, but now A'm that worried he's bin set upon. He could be dead in a ditch fer all we know. A never noticed 'til A saw his nightshirt still folded on his pillow. Often he's up afore me an' in the smokehouse but A looked an' he's nowhere about.'

Gabriel put a protective arm around his old housekeeper's broad shoulders. 'I'm afraid you're going to have to brace yourself Lisbet. Ginny has news of Abner. She was about to tell us what happened. Sit down.' He led Lisbet to a sofa by the fire. 'Ginny can you tell us what you know?'

Ginny looked pityingly at Lisbet. 'I'm that sorry Lisbet but Abner has passed.'

'Passed! How, where? Oh my good Lord.'

'Take your time Ginny, here drink this.' Eleanor passed her a cup of sweet tea. She looked like she was in need. She also offered one to Lisbet but she refused.

'I sometimes go for a walk afore bed and last night when it turned fine I decided to get some air; a little stroll along the top road by the dunes.' She sipped her tea and looked at Lisbet who was on the edge of her seat.

'Any road, I was halfway to the bay when I heard a noise in the dunes. At first I thought it were a courting couple, you know, getting... anyway I carried on for a bit then I thought to turn back. It was dark then and the full moon had risen. Then I saw a pair of boots sticking out of the dunes. At first I thought it some drunk, then I heard someone cry for help, quiet like, not hollering. Then I saw it was Abner and I realised he was unwell. In the moonlight his lips looked a funny colour, tinged with blue like he'd bin drinking ink. He recognised me and said how he felt tired an' needed a little rest. I asked him if he could get up if I helped him but he said not. For a few minutes I sat an' talked to him. Asked if he had a pain, but he said he only felt weary to the bone. He didn't look well an' he were sweating even though it were a cool night. I put my cloak over him an' thinking he had a fever I said I'd run an' fetch Dr Sharpe, but Abner wouldn't have it; said he didn't want me to leave him, said he din't trust doctors.'

Lisbet let out a sob. 'He were afeared er dyin' on his own. He must've known his end was nigh.' Gabriel squeezed her hand.

'Did you stay with him all night?' Gabriel asked.

'Well no, because after about half an hour he dozed off so I thought I'd run to Dr Sharpe an' get him to come to help Abner but when I got to Pease Lane he'd left to go to Amble. I wish I'd set off sooner.'

'You weren't to know Ginny. You did what you thought best,' Eleanor said hoping to reassure the nursemaid.

'Any road I decided to press on an' go to Wooden House, but as bad luck would have it Dr Chaffer was out on a call as well. Mrs Chaffer said she would come and see. You know as she has some skills learnt from her husband. We took the carriage and two servants so we could bring him home. When we got there he were still asleep, or not conscious at any rate. Mrs Chaffer said to take him back to Wooden House 'cause she'd access to medicine there and her husband might be home soon which, in the end, he were. So Mrs Chaffer made Abner comfortable an' gave him some medicine an' after about an hour Dr Chaffer came an' took over but he said there was nothing he could do. We sat with Abner all night Lisbet, he weren't on his own. He slipped away peaceful like around dawn.'

Gabriel took Lisbet in his arms as she sobbed quietly into his shoulder.

'After that Mrs Chaffer said to get some rest for a couple of hours then she'd send me home in the carriage which she did. But Dr Chaffer sent the Smith boy with a note, paid him to bring it. The little tyke deserves a whipping. I didn't think you'd be worrying, especially you Lisbet. The doctor said in the note Abner had passed.'

'Thank you Ginny, now go and get some sleep, you must be done in.'

'I'm alright; I think I'd rather keep busy if you don't mind.'

'Don't worry about the children.' Eleanor stood then sat back down again.

'In that case shall I walk you back to your cottage Lisbet? I'll sit with you if you want company.'

Lisbet blew her nose. 'Yer a good lass Ginny an' A thank yer fer lookin' after Abner in his last hours.' She looked at Gabriel. 'A just want him home, see him fer the last time. A need to lay him out maself.' She wiped her eyes. 'At least it don't sound like he suffered. Lord bless us he would've bin eighty next year. We bin together close on sixty year. Can yer bring him home to me Gabriel?'

'Of course, I'll go myself. You go with Ginny I'll take care of everything, don't you worry.'

R

After the funeral Gabriel walked Lisbet back to her cottage. 'Are you sure you won't stay at the house? You know you're welcome to stay as long as you like. Move back in for good if you'd prefer.'

'Thank you, but A'll stay where A am if you don't mind. A got all mine and Abner's things around me here.'

Gabriel thought the old woman had aged twenty years in the past few days. 'The offer is an open-ended one, so if you ever change your mind just say the word. I don't want you to be lonely.'

'A got plenty of friends here in Alnmouth, A'll manage. A can't thank yer enough fer all the funeral arrangements an' the wake an' all. Yer gave him a grand send off, he would've enjoyed it.' She half smiled at the thought.

'It was the least we could do. On another matter will you be alright for money? If not you only have to ask, you know that. I realise Abner sold his kippers at the bay so you won't have the income from that anymore. How will you manage?'

'A'll not starve lad. We've a bit put by. You and yer pa were always generous employers, but on the subject of money A want yer all to come to the cottage on the morrow; to hear Abner's will read.'

'Abner made a will?' Gabriel asked incredulously.

'He did that. A never knew 'til last winter when he had a bout of bronchitis an' he thought he were about to shuffle off. A've not read it maself. A promised the old man A'd not do until, well until now A suppose.'

Back in his own drawing room Gabriel sank heavily onto the sofa. The wake had taken place in the morning room as only a couple of dozen people had been expected. In the end closer to seventy people had attended. Either Abner was more popular than they had imagined or else people had come on from the church to support Lisbet; having lived here years she knew most of Alnmouth. Gabriel thought it mattered not either way just so long as Lisbet was pleased and she was, especially with the turn out. She thought it only fitting for a man who had almost reached eighty years on this earth that so many should come to pay their respects.

He told Eleanor about Abner's will.

'So tomorrow afternoon we're to go to the cottage to hear the last will and testament of Abner Boatwright! Who will read it? A lawyer?' Eleanor asked astonished.

'I wouldn't imagine so. He never had a man of law, why would he? I can't imagine he's got anything of real value to leave, but for

Lisbet's sake we'll go. It would be churlish otherwise.'

The next day at noon Gabriel, Eleanor and their children along with six or seven specially invited guests gathered in the parlour of Lisbet's little cottage. There was also old Trenton who Gabriel knew from the bay; he was one of Abner's old smuggling cronies. Jax, always close to Lisbet, was a more welcome guest.

The widow sat at the head of the table in the neat little parlour. The home made will before her was tied with a red ribbon. She laid out several small parcels wrapped in linen and tied with string. The children thought Christmas had come again.

Lisbet passed the will to Gabriel and asked him to read it.

R

'Who would have imagined Abner to be a sentimentalist,' Gabriel said as he looked at the pocket watch which the old man had left him. The watch had belonged to Gabriel's father at one time, but he had given it to Abner in return for a special favour it said in the will. They would never know what the good deed was for whatever it was Abner had taken it to his grave. As it was a particularly good watch it must have been an exceptionally good turn he had performed.

Eleanor sipped the sherry Gabriel handed her. 'I for one would never have expected him to be sentimental. I didn't think he even liked me that much. I always thought he blamed me for telling you about his smuggling, but he had some regard for me after all.' She fanned herself with a pretty whalebone fan he had made especially for her; it had her name engraved on the bone handle. 'It was kind of him to remember Rebecca too.' She had received an intricately carved heart shaped wooden box.

'And as for the twins' faces when they unwrapped their legacies. For certain there will be more death and destruction now,' Gabriel said chuckling. 'Abner was always good with his hands.' The old man had made the boys wooden duelling swords with whalebone handles. They were expertly carved, but lethal to his eye.

'I've told them they aren't toys, they're too finely wrought, the twins would break them in five minutes. For me it was the look on Rose's face as she unwrapped his old spy glass. She's always coveted it ever since he showed her how to use it. Now she can look for mermaids to her heart's content; it's his fault she believes in them in the first place. Nothing will ever dissuade her they don't exist. He told her he'd seen them in his whaling days, said he'd nearly been lured onto rocks on more than one occasion,' she said smiling. 'He was quite a character.'

'He'll be missed for certain. However, I'm not sure he isn't right; I once thought I saw a mermaid here at Westshore, well in the sea that is. I seem to remember her telling me there weren't any rocks to lure me onto, but I'm not so sure. I think I've been enticed once too often. What do you think my love?'

'I think you need to take more water with your rum. You're possibly imagining things.'

He returned to the subject. 'It was almost as if he knew Ginny was going to play a part in his end for of all the little trinkets he left for the staff, Ginny's was the prettiest to my mind. It was certainly the biggest.'

There had been three little wooden boxes with pearly shells decorating the lids given out, but the one with Ginny's name on had the most beautiful shells and it was the only one lined with deep blue velvet. It was also the largest, big enough to hold several pieces of jewellery, if she had any of course.

Eleanor smiled knowingly. 'I think there's been a little, shall we say *rearranging* of labels.'

'What do you mean? Rearranging by whom?'

'By Lisbet of course; I think that particular box was one Abner had intended for Lisbet. I think she wanted to say thank you to Ginny for being with Abner, for staying with him and making sure he wasn't alone when he died.'

'So Lisbet too is sentimental. Under the gruff exterior lies a heart of gold, but then I never doubted it. She's a diamond in the rough.'

'I remember someone saying that about her once. I think it was Charity, though I can't be certain, but you're right. When I came here as a new bride she was kind to me, after we edged about each other in the beginning I mean... she was especially kind after the miscarriage.'

Gabriel let out a long breath. 'The old man must have spent all his retirement making these objects to leave in his will.'

'It seems so.'

Abner had also made Jax a tool for getting stones from a horse's hoof, a sort of hoof pick, but again it was beautifully wrought, ornate as well as practical. Jax had been to see Lisbet every day since Abner's death; she was the ma he had never had. He too invited her to live with him at the stud but he knew she would never leave Westshore again.

Gabriel looked out of the window. 'I think I'll go for a walk my love, the clouds are too high to drop rain now.'

Eleanor stood in front of him and reached up to put her arms about his neck. 'I know this is another link with Jack that has been broken, but try not to let it get you down my love.'

'Must you know me so well? Are you sure you're not a gypsy?' He tried a smile. 'The next blow will be Lisbet... I couldn't believe it when she said Abner was going to be eighty next, she must be a good age too.'

'On a more practical level I'll ask Sam to help her with the tasks she can't manage. I think he already helps by chopping firewood and filling her coal scuttle.'

'We will all help.'

On the beach Gabriel headed north. The wind buffeted about throwing spume into the air as waves crashed to shore. The tide was coming in. He had walked only a few minutes when he spotted Rose sitting in the dunes. She had the spy glass up to her eye.

'Are there mermaids about? If there are I shall have to watch out.' He sat close beside her.

'Not today, but I'm sure I'll see one someday if I look hard enough. Are you still sad Pa?'

'More than a little my love; I've known Abner all my life. It will take some time to get used to him being gone.'

She leaned against him and he put his arm around her and hugged her close. He was glad of her company. 'When I die Rose I want to be buried at sea, remember that. I'd hate not to hear the sea every day.'

Rose looked horrified. 'Don't say that Pa, you're never to die. I forbid it.'

'Very well I'll be immortal like a mermaid.'

'A merman. If I don't see a mermaid I should be happy to see a merman in her stead.'

They sat for a while. She kept him from dismal thoughts with her cheery non-sequiturs and unabashed optimism.

'Pass me the glass Rose. Let me see... I think I've spotted something.' He looked for a long moment. 'There look straight ahead, can you see it?'

He handed the spy glass back to her and she peered out to sea an excited look on her face. 'I see it Pa but what is it?'

'It's a porpoise. Have you not seen one when you've been with Abner?'

'We've seen seals, whales and dolphins but not a porpoise. That's the very first time I've seen one.' She watched it until it disappeared. 'I think Abner sent it to me don't you Pa? We've been trying to see one for ages. He said every time he saw one I was somewhere else. I think he's sent it especially for me. Thank you Abner.' She waved her chubby little hand out to sea. A sudden shower began to wet them, but neither made to move. He hugged her closer. 'Look, you don't need a spy glass to see that, even with your extremely old eyes.' Rose giggled. A rainbow had appeared making a bridge over the glittering sea. 'Abner's sent a rainbow now, he's so clever isn't he Pa?'

'Either that or you have a very vivid imagination my love.'

14

Gabriel looked at his wife and said: 'You're late up this morning. You had a bad night I think,'

'Sorry did I keep you awake?'

'No, no I was concerned for you. Do you have something on your mind?'

'Not especially, I couldn't drop off.'

Gabriel smiled to himself as he ordered fresh coffee for his wife. When it arrived he poured for her.

'Thank you that's better,' she said sipping the strong brew.

Gabriel took her hand and squeezed it. 'When are you going to tell me? Must you keep me in suspense my love?'

'Can't a lady have her secrets?' She looked at him brazenly then shook her head and laughed. 'How did you guess?'

'After almost ten years of marriage I think I know you by now Eleanor.' He cocked an eyebrow. 'The only time you've ever denied me my conjugal rights is in the weeks when you suspect you're with child. A man notices these things. Once you've told me your news normal service is resumed. Why that's the case I have no idea. Is it true my love? Are we to expect a happy event?'

'I think so, but I didn't want to say until I was sure. After all this time I thought our family complete, but it looks like nature has other ideas. Are you pleased? Of course you are I can tell by your face.'

Gabriel knelt by his wife's chair and gazed up at her. 'It's tremendous news. I couldn't be happier, but after the twins I hope you'll take extra care my love. Let's hope you won't be swooning for six months like last time.'

'Yes, let's hope that doesn't happen again.' She drank more coffee. 'As for why I "deny you your rights",' she rolled her eyes, 'it's something to do with protecting the baby perhaps but I wasn't aware I did. Call it a mother's instinct, who knows?'

'Perhaps it is. All I know is that now you've told me...' He smirked.

'You think "normal service will be resumed". She raised an eyebrow. 'And as for your "rights" Gabriel Reynolds what of my rights? Remember I'm mistress here and can withdraw my favours as and when I see fit.'

'Actually you can't. In law a married woman has no rights whatsoever. I can take you whenever I choose; you have no say in the matter.' He enjoyed teasing her. Nevertheless he moved quickly to resume his seat before she could land a blow. From a safe distance he said: 'When a lady marries her body belongs to her husband so it's as well I'm irresistible.'

Eleanor helped herself to ham. She looked thoughtful. 'Imagine what life is like for a woman married to someone she was forced to marry. Picture being married to someone you don't love or even like; Rebecca's poor mother comes to mind.'

'Or Violet - if I was married to her I would be forced to take a lover.' He ignored the withering look his wife sent him. 'Sometimes you're a passion killer, here am I being ardent and all you do is turn the conversation deadly serious. It's a good job I'm man enough for you Mrs Reynolds. There's a time and a place for everything, but for now let's celebrate the new life we're to bring into the world. Can we worry about other women at another time?'

Carver stood by the door. 'Dr Sharpe is here sir. I've put him in the morning room.'

'Dr Sharpe? Why is he here?' Eleanor asked Gabriel.

'To confirm what I suspected of course. I was so positive you were with child I took the liberty of asking him to call to check you over.'

Eleanor pulled a face. 'I see my body is not my own. I feel like one of your brood mares.'

'You're even more precious to me than them my love, more precious even than Falladore.'

'I'm honoured. This is another reason I like to wait until I'm sure.

You'll start fussing, worrying, calling in the doctor.'

'It's only natural to worry about the thing you love most in the world is it not?'

'"Thing" Gabriel? For an eloquent man sometimes you can be inept with the English language.'

'I'll go and speak with Dr Sharpe. Take your time my love, he can wait.'

He kissed the top of her head as he passed by. 'When do you think it will be?'

'December I think if I've got my dates correct.'

'A Christmas present for us all. I wonder what the children will say.'

'The twins won't be too impressed, but Rose will be pleased. She loves baby animals of any description.'

'Now who's inept?'

'How is it inept to say we're animals, are we not animals?'

'I'll go to Dr Sharpe and tell him I suspect you're in foal shall I?'

He saw his wife smile. He hoped for another girl.

Gabriel was pacing in the morning room when Eleanor returned.

'Well? What did Sharpe say?'

'It's as I thought. However he says it is early days so can't say if it's one baby or two.'

He grabbed her hands in his, pulled her towards him and kissed her. 'For your sake I hope it's just one this time.' His face dropped.

'What's the matter? You're about to start fretting aren't you?'

'Not if I can help it.' He furrowed his brow. 'You say it as if it's something I can turn on and off. I can only say I'll *attempt* not to agonize too much. It wasn't that I was thinking of however, it was something I'd planned that will now have to be postponed - again.'

'Tell me.'

'As we'll have been married for ten years in December I had been planning a surprise trip. You always wanted to travel more, but almost every time we plan something it gets scuppered. I'd hoped to take you to Scandinavia for Christmas. I know you prefer sun to snow but when we first met I told you about a sleigh ride in the snow

I'd taken in the Baltics do you remember?'

'Oh Gabriel how wonderful! Christmas with snow guaranteed. I do remember, you said it would have been romantic had it not been taken with your father. You were on a business trip were you not?'

He nodded. 'I thought it would coincide well with our anniversary, but now once again the trip will have to be put off, I'm so sorry my love. I'd thought we could take the children too, not on the romantic sleigh ride of course. Imagine a sleigh ride with the twins. It would be far from passionate and Rose would try to sit between us I'm sure.'

'So the baby is bad timing, I see that. Oh well never mind we can go in a year or two. It was a lovely thought Gabriel and something to look forward to in the future. You are good to me.'

'I try to be, but I wouldn't have the timing any other way. Is another baby not the most perfect anniversary present for both of us?'

'It is I agree, although a sleigh ride in snow with you by my side, sans enfants, would have been perfect too. I can almost hear the sleigh bells ringing.'

She sat by the fire and for a moment she looked distracted. He knew she was torn between wanting the two things, as was he if truth be told.

Like Eleanor he had thought babies were a thing of the past - it had not been for the want of trying, but after all the twins were six now. Their birth had affected Eleanor greatly, both emotionally and physically; it had taken her quite some time to recover, longer than either of them had expected. The pregnancy had drained her, and the birth with its fainting fits had been far from easy.

For the first time in their married life his marital rights had been the last thing on his mind; he knew she would let him know when she was ready. But even though he had been patient, it had taken almost eight months before they'd enjoyed intimacy again. He hadn't cared so long as she was well again. It had been a worrying time for him; all he could do was watch and wait, and cherish her all the more.

Now at seven and twenty she was six years older than the last time she had been expecting, not that she looked it. Her age was something else for him to worry about though he knew better than to mention it. She would have told him she was still young, and she was, just not as young as when she was with child before. To his mind the older a woman was the more danger there was in childbirth. The thought struck him that his own dear mama had died giving birth at the very same age.

Gabriel was roused from his gloomy thoughts.

'I think we should wait to tell the children, but when we do we should tell Rose first. As the eldest I think she'd like that and after all she'll be the one most pleased I'm sure.'

'Of course. The twins will be less than interested as you rightly say.'

'And although I'm eager to tell Rebecca I think it too early. Let's not count our chickens before they're hatched.'

'But you feel well? You will say if...'

'Gabriel!'

R

Lisbet was sitting on the bench by the kitchen door enjoying the sunshine when Eleanor entered the well kept garden of the little whitewashed cottage.

'Good afternoon Lisbet, how are you?'

'Well enough, yer look bonny.'

'Where's my daughter? Have you sold her to the rag and bone man?'

'She's stepped inside to get some embroidery thread from the basket, here she is now.'

'Look Mama my sampler is almost finished. Lisbet says I should give it to Grandmama as a gift.'

'It's lovely Rose, you certainly don't take after me for I find it hard enough to thread a needle.'

'Yer Grandmama Reynolds were a fine needlewoman so it's in yer blood Rose.'

Eleanor sat beside her old cook and squeezed her hand affectionately. 'Have a care for yourself Lisbet. Don't hesitate to ask if you need anything, anything at all. I know Sam does the odd task for you but if there's more you need you'll let us know won't you?'

'Sam's a good lad an' his little lass is a help about the house and in the garden; Beth likes to feed the chickens and collect the eggs.'

'Speaking of birds, you got the goose we sent over earlier I take it? It was Gabriel's idea to help you take some rest. He worries about you since... well you know... he always has your best interests at heart.'

'Thank him fer the thought, but A can manage, not that it weren't a treat. Dora comes over an' helps on her day off bless her, an' Ginny often calls. Folks have bin that kind.' She changed the subject. 'Where's Miss Rebecca this afternoon?'

'She's gone for a walk into Alnmouth. She had an errand to run.'

'She's another one who's bin kind. She comes often fer a dish of tea. She brought her sewing wi' her last time an' A told her stories about Gabriel when he were a lad.'

'Did you now? Perhaps I'll join her next time and find out about his wicked past.'

After supper as Eleanor set up the backgammon board Gabriel massaged her neck and shoulders. 'Is that good?'

'It is, but don't start trying to curry favour. I mean to win and if I do it will be three games in a row.'

'That's only because you're in a delicate condition and I'm going easy on you.'

'We both know that's an untruth.'

'I thought Rebecca might join us. I've not seen her since dinner.'

'I think perhaps she's gone to see Lisbet. Apparently she visits most days and takes a dish of tea. They have what Lisbet says is a chin wag - about you apparently.'

Eleanor put the two dice in the cup and threw two sixes on her home board. She laughed out loud. 'Beat that my love. Oh no you can't can you?'

Gabriel threw a six and a five and grimaced. It meant Eleanor would get the first turn. 'Why would they talk about me?' he asked.

'I think Lisbet likes to reminisce and Rebecca probably wants to know more about her big brother. I think it shows what a kind heart Becky has, visiting Lisbet.'

She threw her dice.

'It does, and at least she's not still mooning over Charles.'

'Perhaps she has a fancy for George Black? Although she still gets correspondence from Kit. He writes a good letter.'

'How do you know?'

'Because I've read them.'

'Aren't they private?'

'Ladies like to share their letters, it's twice the fun.'

'So the letters I wrote to you when we were courting were shared about Whitby?'

'Of course not. Your letters weren't so tantalising. I'm joking of course,' she said when she saw his face fall.

'What are we supposed to do about it if she has thoughts for George, or if indeed *he* has ideas about her? Kit is younger which is a good thing in my opinion. An officer would be a good catch for her do you think?' Gabriel thought about it then added: 'But George is so much older, a widower with a child. I can see how he'd take a fancy to her, he must see how she's situated, how good she is, how pretty but I cannot believe she'd be attracted to *him*. He's hardly on a par with Charles or Kit Eskdale for that matter.'

Eleanor shrugged as she knocked one of his pieces from the board.

'I've said it before Eleanor we choose with our eyes first and as she has two perfectly good ones then I think we're safe from welcoming George Black into the family.'

R

Eleanor was at her desk when Ginny knocked and entered.

'You're not going to like this.'

'What's Haydan done now?'

'He says it was an experiment. However, that's not what Molly and Dora thought it was and they're not best pleased I can tell you.'

Eleanor knew when staff were involved it would need her diplomatic skills to come to the fore to calm troubled waters, and she wasn't in the mood. She'd had morning sickness for the last week and was still, even at midday, feeling queasy.

'You might want to come and see but I warn you you'll need to hold your nose.'

Despite herself Eleanor was intrigued to know what her son had been up to. She hoped Ginny was exaggerating. Sadly she wasn't. As she got to the top of the servants' staircase she met Rebecca who had her hand over her mouth.

'What is that awful smell? It's worse than ever today.' Rebecca wrinkled her nose.

'I've no idea.' The smell assaulted her nostrils, that and the buzzing of bluebottles.

'Is it a dead rat under the floorboards?'

Ginny explained: 'That's what's left after the seagull was removed, imagine the smell before.'

'Seagull? Has one come down the chimney?' Eleanor held her stomach then promptly vomited. 'Oh Lord, there's something else to upset the staff,' Eleanor said as she rushed down the stairs closely followed by Rebecca.

Later a chastened looking Haydan stood before his parents. His Papa was grim faced, his mama pale and feeling decidedly unwell.

'As I understand it you found a dead seagull on the beach and decided to put it in a drawer in an empty room in the servants' quarters to see what would happen to it. Is that the top and bottom of it?'

'Not exactly Papa. It was a scientific experiment I was carrying out. Uncle Wilson has told me about some of the experiments he's done over the years and I thought to try one for myself. I've been checking on the seagull every two days to see how it looks. There's a word, decomp - something or other, which means it's turning rotten. I wanted to see what happens and how long it would be before it disappeared. I hadn't counted on maggots and bluebottles. I'm sorry it made you sick Mama.' For once he really did look apologetic.

'So am I. Did it not occur to you to watch its decomposing body in an outbuilding where the smell might not be so all consuming? The poor servants have been looking everywhere for days wondering where the smell was coming from.'

'It's too cold outside. I think if it's warmer it goes off quicker. The one I put in the barn last winter froze solid and took ages to de - comp - ose.' He slowly sounded out the three syllables of the new word he had learnt.

'You're saying you've done this sort of thing before? Are there any other dead creatures hidden about the house to which you want to own up?' Gabriel asked. Ordinarily he would have found the whole thing amusing, but he had seen his wife's pale face when he had returned home from the bay. He knew she was suffering morning sickness and now this decaying seagull smell was pervading the whole house despite all the windows being thrown open.

'Not now. I threw the frog out last week because I was going to ask Uncle Wilson to put it in some acid or something so I could see its skeleton, but I put it in the tack room and one of Rose's stupid kittens ran off with it.'

Later when Eleanor was laid abed still feeling nauseous, Gabriel perched on the edge. 'I can still smell it and it's making me feel ill so heaven knows how you feel. The chest of drawers which contained the bird has been put in the small barn. It reeks because all sorts of fluids have leaked out.'

'Enough! Unless you want me to be ill again?' She held her stomach. 'Did you do tricks like this when you were a boy?'

'No, never. The only skeletons I was interested in were those of a ship. I used to spend my time designing frigates not dissecting frogs. I never thought being a parent would be so complicated.'

'I was too squeamish and I liked things to be alive. If ever Tomas and I found a dead gull we buried it, gave it a Quaker funeral. Although at this precise moment I could cheerfully strangle my son, I see how he has an enquiring mind. We should talk to Wilson in how best to encourage him with experiments of the less smelly variety. I don't want to stop him exploring the world.'

'So long as he does his exploring outside. And why must the twins be at each other's throats all the time? They fight all the day long.'

Eleanor looked unperturbed. 'That's normal with siblings. Tomas and I used to fight like cat and dog. We still loved each other and would have defended one another to the death. You only find it strange because you didn't have siblings growing up.'

'Here drink this my love. Lisbet heard about what's happened, she's made lemonade. She says she knows it always helps when you feel nauseous.'

Eleanor looked suspicious. 'She means sickness because of the seagull I take it? You haven't told her I'm with child?'

'I didn't have to, she told me. I don't understand it myself because you look the exact same size and shape to me as you've been for the last few years, but yet she says as soon as she saw you on Sunday afternoon she knew.'

'I swear she's a witch. You told her to keep it to herself for now I hope?'

'Of course, and she will. She's often curious but she's loyal.'

15

Eleanor was telling Rebecca about the Hope Ball. 'It's an annual event to raise much needed funds for Hope House. We always need more money, the place is consistently full,' Eleanor said sighing. 'The event is always fancy dress. Your half brother hates dressing up and complains bitterly every year.'

'Really? I think it sounds fun.' Rebecca who had recently received another letter from Kit Eskdale was in a sunny mood. The pair had been corresponding since Christmas. Kit was away at sea and would be for at least another three months.

'Since the first ball Gabriel has been dragged along kicking and screaming, well not exactly screaming, but it's not his favourite event of the year.'

'But because you're the founder he has to go I suppose.'

'He does. Lottie is co-founder but she loves dressing up. Each year her costumes become more and more flamboyant. You need to give some thought to what you will wear. We can go to the costumier or you can have something made. I've already decided on my costume.'

'How exciting, where is it to be held?'

'Since the first ball it's been held at Lottie and Wilson's home, Wooden House. Perhaps you'll help me to deliver the invitations? Then we can make calls and introduce you to more people. That way you'll recognise people on the night.'

'Of course I'll help in any way I can, oh I'm so excited. I shall have to give what I'm to wear some serious thought.'

'Especially as the militia are back in the district; a man in uniform is the best fancy dress I know.'

They were giggling like schoolgirls when Gabriel came to join them. 'What's this you're planning?' he said smiling amiably.

'We were talking about The Hope Ball. I was telling Rebecca how she needs to begin thinking about her costume.'

Eleanor waited for him to start his usual complaints about how he hated dressing up, but he smiled enigmatically instead.

'What does that look mean?'

'Nothing.'

'Nothing? I'm no fool Gabriel Reynolds.'

'Let's just say it's all in hand, so you don't have to bully me into going to the costumier.' He looked decidedly smug. Eleanor was pleasantly surprised then turned to Becky. 'Oh no, he's going as a ship owner! Every year he threatens to go as himself.'

'Surely you have to be more imaginative than that Gabriel. Are you going to tell us what you'll wear?' Rebecca asked.

'It will be a surprise as always.' He kissed his wife's cheek. 'And I hope that on the night you'll see I have used my imagination. Fear not my love, I'm not going as myself.'

'My outfit too will be a surprise,' Eleanor said. 'I can tell you Becky but you're not to breathe a word to Gabriel.'

'Interesting... I bet I can get it out of you before the night.' Gabriel gave his wife a look she understood.

'Oh no you won't, I'm determined.'

'I could go as a flower,' Rebecca said her excitement mounting.

'What's your favourite flower?' Gabriel poured himself a brandy and handed cordials to the ladies.

'Like Eleanor I love roses, but my favourite wildflower is possibly a buttercup. That might work. What do you think Eleanor?'

'That's a lovely idea and better than a dandelion. Mama always said if we picked them we would pee the bed. I think it an old wives' tale.'

'I can guarantee you will learn a lot from my wife Rebecca,' Gabriel said, 'and not all of it useful.'

R

On the night of the ball Eleanor swept into the drawing room brandishing a tambourine. Gabriel burst out laughing.

'A gypsy how apt. I remember I thought you of the Romany persuasion when we met. You look wonderful my love. Red and black, a scarlet woman, again most appropriate.'

'I think so,' she said laughing. 'You look quite good yourself.'

Gabriel had chosen to go as a pirate. He explained his choice of outfit: 'I don't know why I never thought of it before. I told you how I always loved pirate stories when I was a boy. It was Steven who gave me the idea; I told him how I wanted to be a pirate when I grew up.'

Eleanor looked her husband up and down. 'I remember the time when you went as a highway man and Scrabble thought you were a burglar and tried to bite you. It was so funny.'

'He's so deaf these days I doubt he would even notice me, unless I tried to steal his bone of course.'

Rebecca joined them dressed in red silk. She was to go as a flower but poppy not a buttercup.

'You look quite the buccaneer Gabriel. I like the red bandana. How fortuitous that without knowing what the other would wear our costumes all match in colour.'

'Not chance at all Rebecca,' Eleanor said smiling. 'Lisbet engineered the whole thing. She made both our ensembles. She's a good at keeping secrets it seems. I thought you were to go as a buttercup; I bet she convinced you to change your mind to wear red.'

Rebecca giggled. 'You're right of course, I wondered why she was so dismissive of my idea of wearing yellow.'

'Did you really make your own costume?' Gabriel asked Rebecca. 'The flowers almost look real.'

'I had help, from Lisbet of course,' she said giggling. 'I knew not to ask Eleanor.'

The ball as always was a great success. Rebecca was enjoying herself Gabriel noticed; even though this was the first charity ball she had attended she didn't appear at all nervous. Her confidence was growing steadily. His ward was attracting attention both from the ladies and the gentlemen, but especially from the militia.

‘Now the soldiers are back in the district it’s swollen the numbers of gentlemen here tonight which is good news.’ Lottie dressed as Cleopatra observed.

‘Why are they in the area?’ Rebecca asked Gabriel.

‘There’s been unrest. Three failed harvests have meant the price of grain has soared. There are a lot of hungry people in the North East especially away from the coast where at least the poor can catch fish to supplement their meagre diet. By bringing in the militia they hope to keep a lid on the problem. Stop any rioting. The money would be better spent finding work for the people so they can provide for their families.’

Bendor who had been a magistrate for the last four years added: ‘I’m seeing more and more of the lower orders come before me for poaching. I’ve taken to turning a blind eye on my own estate. My gamekeeper thinks me run mad but what are the poor to do?’

A young soldier came to claim Rebecca for the dance he had been promised. Gabriel watched as he led her away. ‘I’m surprised how protective of Rebecca I’ve become. I feel the responsibility to make sure she’s looked after.’

‘Lord knows what we’ll feel like when it’s our own daughters Gabe. There’s a sobering thought; in another eight years or so we’ll be beating the suitors off with a stick.’

‘I know it.’

‘Did you catch his name?’ Eleanor asked.

‘Lieutenant Mangham. I don’t know him from Adam. He looks young for the rank. I suppose he bought the commission.’

‘His eyes are set too close together,’ Eleanor said baldly.

Grace, dressed as Queen Elizabeth, agreed: ‘I was about to make the self same observation.’

‘Poor man.’ Gabriel shook his head. ‘There’s nothing he can do about that.’

‘It’s just that the soldier she danced with earlier was far better looking, so attentive too.’

‘I thought she’d her heart set on a young naval officer from Whitby?’ Lottie asked.

‘Kit Eskdale is away at sea and will be for some time. He writes of course. I think her eye has already wandered... to the soldier you mentioned, Captain Truelove. What a perfect name for a suitor. She’s quite taken with him.’

Lottie said: ‘Absence makes the heart wander then *not* grow fonder. Good for her. No need to get tied down at such a young age, play the field a while is my advice.’

‘I’d be obliged if you didn’t share your views with my ward Lottie. I don’t think my nerves can stand it.’

Just then George Black, wearing a kilt, joined the party.

‘Bonny Prince Charlie?’ Lottie asked.

‘Or any other Scotsman you care to name,’ George said cheerfully. ‘What a good turn out ladies, you must be pleased. Mrs Chaffer do you have room for me on your dance card?’

Later Gabriel watched as George danced with Rebecca. ‘I don’t think he has an especial liking for Rebecca do you? He bestows his favours far and wide by the looks of it. He’s danced with Lottie, Fliss, Mary and the Brophy girl. I think he’s enjoying himself.’

‘He hasn’t asked me to dance. Do you think I should be offended?’

‘If you are I’ll call him out shall I... or should I make him walk the plank? How dare he slight my wife? Come my love, I can take a hint.’ He bowed low and took her hand. ‘Would you do me the honour of dancing with me?’

‘I would. I thought you’d never ask.’

R

The day after the ball Lieutenant Mangham asked to call and see Rebecca. She told Eleanor how she wasn’t keen to meet him again as she preferred Captain Truelove. ‘I don’t think the lieutenant behaved in a gentlemanly way despite his rank,’ Rebecca said.

‘Captain Truelove could hardly get a look in,’ Eleanor agreed, ‘he certainly monopolised you.’

Rebecca had a dreamy look on her face. ‘Was Gabriel the perfect gentleman when you were courting? I bet he was.’

'Erm,' Eleanor was lost for words, 'I don't think you should follow our example Rebecca, for while Gabriel was somewhat gallant I'm not sure he was altogether a true gentleman although he did consider my reputation, more than I did myself I have to say. I was a little worldlier than you of course and the circumstances were different. We knew from the minute we saw each other we had to be together. You know Lieutenant Mangham isn't for you so it's not the same at all.'

Rebecca sighed. 'So it was love at first sight for you and Gabriel, how romantic.'

'It was and I don't think either of us has regretted it, well not often anyway.'

'How did you know? What was it made you realise Gabriel was your one and only?'

'Besides his handsome face and the twinkle in his eye?' Eleanor chuckled. 'It's not something I could rightly explain; it's a feeling, a knowing that without him my life would be meaningless. His eyes, his voice... with other men, men just as handsome perhaps there was no connection, no spark, no longing. Put simply we were meant for each other. He was no saint, nor was I for that matter but to this day I feel the same. And we will have been married ten years on Christmas Eve. It's not always been easy, but we're happy and incredibly fortunate to have found each other.'

'You married on Christmas Eve, how adorable.'

Eleanor thought she was filling the young girl's head with unrealistic notions of romance. She knew how lucky she was to have found Gabriel and knew not everyone had the marriage she enjoyed.

Rebecca looked downcast. 'If only I was blessed enough to find someone to love... and so deeply.'

'You will I'm certain of it, but my advice to you, for what it's worth, is don't compromise. If someone falls short of your expectations then walk away. That's not to say the gentleman has to be perfect, no one is, but love, loyalty and honesty are a priority not an option. However, the most important trait in any relationship, and especially in marriage I've learnt, is trust. Without it there's nothing.

Gabriel and I trust each other in all things. It's not something that came easily to either of us, but we cared enough about our marriage to learn. And by and large we trust each other because we both know that once trust is lost it can never be fully regained. In time you'll fall in love and hopefully your chosen one will love you in return. In the meantime enjoy yourself, within the boundaries of polite society, that is. Have fun, flirt, but don't lead men on if you aren't interested. Why waste time on the Lieutenant Manghams of this world when you might have a Captain Truelove.' Eleanor added: 'Let's hope he is as good as his namesake.'

Two days later Gabriel asked to see his half sister in his study. 'I have had a note from a gentleman asking if he can call on you.'

'Not Lieutenant Mangham.' Rebecca's hands flew to her face.

'A Captain Truelove.'

'Oh...'

'Well, do you want to meet him? I take it the captain isn't as repellent to you as Mangham.' Gabriel smiled.

'No, I mean yes, I would like to meet him if you will allow it.'

'I will allow it but you must to be chaperoned.'

'Of course, I know better now.' She shifted her weight from one foot to the other. 'About the business with Captain Noble. I'm sorry Gabriel I was foolish, I see that. I misread the captain's intentions. My only excuse is that no one had ever paid me any attention before and I was flattered I suppose. Eleanor has since talked some sense into me, and I see if I'm to safeguard my reputation then I need to think more carefully about how I act; once lost a reputation can never be recovered.'

'Very true my dear, but that doesn't mean you cannot have fun.' Rebecca sat down and relaxed a little. 'Can I ask you a question Rebecca? You don't have to answer if you feel it's too personal.'

'Of course, ask me anything.' Gabriel saw Rebecca's open countenance and continued: 'Is Kit Eskdale still a correspondent? I only ask because of this.' He waved Captain Truelove's missive in the air. 'If you're still writing to each other, is there an understanding between the two of you? If there is, and bearing in mind the Eskdales are friends of Eleanor's family, then I think you shouldn't lead Captain Truelove on, it's not fair to anyone. It's clear from what he says in his letter he holds you in high regard, so is it honourable to meet with Trulove if he's only a pastime until Kit returns?'

'There isn't an understanding between Kit and me... I do like him, very much but... well, he's not due shore leave for months and he says there may well be a war with France soon and then he'll be at sea even longer. Truth be told I don't think I'm cut out to be a sailor's wife. All the absences would be trying I think. Not that he's asked for my hand of course. At first it was romantic, him on the other side of the world writing to me, but now it's hard to remember what he looks like.'

'In that case I think you know what is to be done.'

'I do, I see that now Gabriel.'

'Then let him down gently and say perhaps you wish to remain friends. When we're in Whitby we'll see the Eskdales socially, I also do business with his uncle and grandfather. Keep it friendly is all I ask.'

'Of course, I see I still have a lot to learn. I'll write to him at once.'

R

'It's so warm today.' Gabriel flung his jacket on a chair and unbuttoned his waistcoat. 'Who chaperoned Rebecca for her visit with Captain Truelove? Jenny I expect.'

Eleanor passed him a glass of lemonade which he looked at suspiciously before downing it in one. They were in the garden; he collapsed into a chair and watched as Rose made a daisy chain.

'Jenny is to start work as Rebecca's maid next week. I was chaperone. It was... interesting. There's an art to being a good chaperone I think. From experience I remember some chaperones, Attie for example, stick to a person like dog dirt to a shoe.'

Gabriel spluttered then laughed loudly. 'What an analogy! Better not let your sister hear you compare her to - '

'I didn't compare her to, oh never mind. What I'm trying to say is I tried to give Rebecca and Captain Truelove a little privacy, yet still stay within range. I've never been a chaperone before and being an inquisitive sort of person I was interested to hear what they were talking about so I was somewhat torn.'

'A nosy person don't you mean.' Rose draped the daisy chain on his head like a crown. 'Rose never allow your mama to chaperone you when you're older,' he said as she climbed onto his knee.

'Why Pa?'

'Never mind. Get down Rose, it's too hot. Make a crown for your mama.'

'As I was saying, it's a little tedious sitting there so I was sort of eavesdropping. Captain Truelove is a nice young man. Oh Lord, I sound like an old maiden aunt!'

'I suppose we both appear old to Rebecca, I know when I asked her about Kit Eskdale I felt the same.'

'What like a maiden aunt?'

He ignored her flippant comment. 'So what did you overhear?'

'Nothing so exciting. He's an only son, he's three and twenty and has two unmarried sisters. His family are titled, his father is a Lord and they hail from Devon.'

'He would be a good match for Rebecca then would he not? Listen to me. She's taken tea with him once and I've got her half way up the aisle.'

'I liked him and so did Rebecca, but I see he's no different to Kit really. If there is a war then he'll be posted abroad undoubtedly, better not to set her cap at a military man I think, well that's what I advised. I wouldn't want an absent husband, I quite like it when you go away for the night, but I'm always pleased when you come home again.'

'That's a back handed compliment if ever I heard one, but I know what you mean. When I've been away and I round the bay and I'm once again on my own land it makes my heart swell to know you're here waiting for me. A little absence makes the heart grow fonder, but a longer one is not to be borne when one is in love.' He poured himself more lemonade. 'Is she to meet with Truelove again?'

'I expect so, he seemed smitten with her.'

'She's a popular young lady. I wonder if a large dowry is of concern to him. In my experience the landed gentry are often short of ready coin, take the Nobles for example.'

'There you go again. The poor girl will be married before she's eighteen if you have your way. I think she should shop around first, not get too serious too soon. He is handsome though in his regimentals. If only I was in the marriage market.'

ℛ

As George Black was back in the area he called at Westshore one bright and breezy afternoon. Gabriel knew the lawyer was in talks with Saul Coates about combining their businesses and was interested to know how things were progressing.

'Mr Coates and I met again this morning and I think we have reached an agreement. We are to form a partnership.'

'Congratulations. You'll be moving then, making Lesbury Lodge your permanent residence?'

'In time yes, possibly by September we shall have amalgamated the two businesses. After discussing the partnership further Gabriel thought he sensed George was building up to talk about something in particular. He was right.

'Since my wife died Gabriel I have lived a solitary life; just myself, my mother and Sophia. The Hope Ball was the first purely social event I have attended in years.' He shrugged. 'At first, after Augusta died, I socialised for business purposes but very little else. Then gradually as the years have passed I have seen that I am still a young man and would perhaps look for someone to share my life with. It would be good for Sophia too to have a new mama perhaps.'

Gabriel made a few placatory remarks before George continued: 'Since meeting Miss Argyle I have thought of her more than I have thought of any lady since I lost Augusta. Your ward is a sweet natured young woman I think, and quite the prettiest face I have seen in a long time.'

Gabriel was astounded. He had convinced himself if George had an eye for any young lady it was Fliss Coates. Had Eleanor guessed the truth of the matter he wondered.

'My ward may go to finishing school, she's but seventeen and I shouldn't want her to miss out on the experience. What exactly are you proposing may I ask?'

'I understand perfectly Gabriel, and I would not want to stand in her way. All I would ask is that you grant me permission to get to know Miss Argyle a little better. If she does go away to be finished, then perhaps we could correspond. I have not spoken to her; I would not until I had asked your consent. Indeed I am not sure she has any feelings for me. We have met but a handful of times. She seems not repulsed by me at any rate.' He shrugged again. It appeared to be a habit Gabriel thought, shrugging. 'She may not have any interest in me, in which case this conversation will have been a waste of both our time, but I would venture to speak with her if you would allow it. Hopefully I have a lot of life yet to live and I would like to share it with someone, someone like Miss Argyle.'

Gabriel wondered if the man was thinking Rebecca would come with a hefty dowry. Was that also an attraction for George Black? Did he look about for a lady with the biggest purse?

'If things did progress, if you and she grew to esteem one another then I feel it only fair to inform you Rebecca will see no monies from her father's estate.'

'Ah yes, I knew her father by repute, well his business dealings at any rate. He was a wealthy man by all accounts. I read about his tragic death in the newspaper.'

'In confidence George I would tell you that a few days before his death John Argyle cut his daughter from his will leaving a distant cousin the main beneficiary. I don't feel comfortable going into detail about why he did this, indeed I don't rightly know, but any dowry Miss Argyle has will come from my pocket and conditions have been put in place you understand, or at least they will be when the document is finalised. I hope you don't take offense at my frankness.'

'Not at all, I'm reasonably well situated, especially so since Aunt Susan left me all her worldly goods. It is not for her dowry that I would pursue Miss Argyle. I genuinely admire her.'

'My wife had the idea any monies we bestow on her won't be released until after she marries and produces her first child. Any monies will be suspended until then and held in trust for the child, be it a boy or a girl.'

'Your wife is an astute, forward thinking lady.' George smiled making him appear less the lawyer and more the prospective lover. 'It is the sort of plan I propose to put in place for Sophia; stops a man chasing after the dowry does it not?'

'That's what we hope. By making Rebecca's first born the beneficiary we can be sure any man is interested in the lady and not her money. Rose will also benefit from this clause which puts my mind at rest as you can imagine. All too often we hear of a man marrying for love, until he gets his hands on the lady's fortune, then he treats his wife worse than he treats his horses or his hunting dogs.'

Gabriel refilled their glasses. 'Another concern is Rebecca's age; she's still so young and not as mature as one may think.'

'For your information I am nine and twenty next month so although I'm around twelve years her senior I don't think it altogether too big a difference. I've also witnessed how Miss Argyle acts with children. She clearly loves them, as do I. If it turned out we were compatible then she is young enough to have children of her own, with me that is.'

'I'll discuss the matter with my wife and Rebecca, and let you know my decision George. Either way I hope it won't spoil our friendship.'

At supper Gabriel told Eleanor of the conversation with George. He noted his wife looked unsurprised. 'I'd thought he had a special look for her at the ball,' Eleanor said matter of factly. Gabriel let out a low whistle. 'When Rose is Rebecca's age - '

'I'll have built a turret in which to lock her up. How will any man be good enough for my daughter? I know what men are like. As you say in some ways it will be a relief if Rebecca goes away for the next year. I can't keep up; the list of suitors gets longer by the day. What do you think to George's proposition?'

'I think it's fair enough though a lot can happen in a year. If she goes away she'll be a proficient letter writer if nothing else, first Kit now George. Poor Captain Truelove, will he be relegated I wonder?' Eleanor sighed. 'Young love, I remember it well.'

'Do you remember it fondly?'

'I think I put a rosy glow on it. It was full of angst when I come to think of it, especially when I met you.'

'Ah, but then you fell head over heels and lived happily ever after.'

'If you say so Gabriel. Who am I, a mere woman, to disagree?'

R

Gabriel thought to address the idea of Rebecca going to finishing school again, this time with the young woman herself. His talk with George and a chance meeting earlier had put it into his head. He was teaching Rebecca to play backgammon in the library when he broached the subject. Eleanor was at Lottie's playing cards.

'Earlier today I saw Mrs Coates out shopping with Mary. They were buying necessities for Mary's forthcoming departure for Switzerland. She's to leave in September for finishing school as I think you know. Have you thought anymore about going too? It doesn't have to be Switzerland of course you could go to France or stay in England if you'd prefer.'

'I've thought about it but I'm torn and would welcome your thoughts on the subject.'

'Torn in what way? Please don't worry about the cost. You know I'm happy to pay for your education, but if you did decide not to go then that's equally alright. It's your choice. I know your experience of school hasn't been altogether good, but I don't think you need fear. Mary's sister Felicity was at the self same school that Mary is to attend. She enjoyed herself immensely so Mary was telling me today. She can't wait to go.'

'Both those reasons have been worrying me. Firstly you and Eleanor have been unstinting in your care and attention. I don't like to think of you going to further expense on my behalf. And secondly as you say my experience of school so far has been unpleasant to say the least. However, from what you say and from what Mary has told me about the Swiss school, then I think I should enjoy it there. But there's another consideration, another reason I'm undecided about the matter.' Gabriel waited. 'For the first time in years I'm happy. In truth I'm reluctant to leave you all; you, Eleanor and of course the children. Westshore is such a happy home, with such a loving, carefree atmosphere. I've never experienced so much love and consideration before. When Mama tried to show me any affection my... *he* would soon put a stop to it by some means or another. I don't know if I can tear myself away from here.'

'But it would only be for a year then you'll come back ready to take Alnmouth by storm I'm sure. Please don't throw this opportunity away lightly, although of course it must be *your* decision in the end. It's your life and you must live it as you see fit.'

'There's one other concern.' Gabriel wondered if she was reluctant to leave because she had her heart set on someone. Who it could be he couldn't fathom; every time he thought he was abreast of his ward's love affairs Eleanor told him *that was last week*.

'If I go away in September for a year I'll be no help at all to Eleanor. I won't be here for her confinement and I won't see the new baby, in fact it won't be a new baby when I return. Can Eleanor spare me do you think?' Rebecca had caught Eleanor being ill and so she had confessed about the pregnancy.

'I'm sure she can although we feel the same about you. We'll all miss you, even the boys.'

'If I *were* to go at least I'd have a companion in Mary, if I went to Switzerland that is which, by and large I think I'd prefer. Mary is a lovely, kind hearted girl. She reminds me of my school friend Lizzie, the one I told you who was forced into marrying an old man.' She bit her lip. 'When all is considered I think I'd be a fool not to take advantage of your generous offer.'

'Does that mean you'll go?'

Eleanor swept into the room. 'That's the last time I partner Rosalind Coates,' she said hotly and without preamble. 'She's a lovely woman but she can't play whist. She chatters and then forgets what trumps led. It's so frustrating. Sorry, how rude of me to interrupt. Have you two had a good evening? I hope you beat my husband Rebecca?' She nodded towards the backgammon board.

'Sadly not, he's too good for me and I've not played backgammon before.'

'Rebecca, make a note not to play whist with Eleanor. She's such a bad loser.'

'Nonsense, you just need more practise,' Eleanor said to Rebecca pointedly ignoring her husband's jibe.'

'We were discussing Rebecca going to finishing school. I think she has made a decision.' He looked at his half-sister expectantly.

'Good. What are you to do Rebecca?'

'I think I shouldn't look a gift horse in the mouth. If you can spare me Eleanor, I should like to go to Switzerland. To miss such an opportunity would be wrong of me. When I think of my friend married to a man old enough to be her grandfather I think I have much to be grateful for. I ought to live my life to the fullest and be thankful to be able to complete my education.'

'That's wonderful news isn't it Gabriel? Of course I should have liked you to be here with us a little longer, but it's only for a year, it will fly by. I didn't go to finishing school so I'm quite envious. You must speak to Lottie, she was finished in France. On reflection *don't* speak to Lottie, I've just remembered what she told me about her time there. She was dreadfully naughty by all accounts.' Eleanor hugged the girl then sat beside her husband and kissed his cheek. 'Imagine if I'd been finished,' she smiled, 'I'd have been perfect then.'

Gabriel thought it safer not to comment.

16

Gabriel received a letter from Libby saying she was considering sending Steven to Harrow in the autumn. Gabriel was oddly annoyed. It wasn't entirely out of the blue he was forced to admit, as Libby had said at their last meeting her late husband had set aside money for Steven's education.

He had hoped to convince Libby to send Steven to his old alma mater in Alnwick then he would be able to see his son more often. If Steven went to Harrow the boy would be at the other end of the country; he would never get to see him. He had hoped Libby would have consulted with him, his real father, on such an important decision but it appeared not.

He decided he must in that case, go to Whitby in the next few weeks. He would try to change her mind and ask her to send the boy to a school not so far distant. He must go though he didn't want to leave Eleanor in her present condition.

Later after he had thought it through he had talked to Eleanor and she had agreed he should go saying that if it was important to him he must say his piece. He thought, not for the first time, what a remarkable woman he had married. Each time he threw an obstacle in her way she neatly and undramatically side-stepped it; he loved her for her understanding and loyalty.

He decided to kill two birds with one stone and combine the visit to Whitby with business. He had a proposition to put to Ingram Eskdale and now rather than write to him about it, he could speak with him face to face. If he stayed in Whitby for three nights he could be back before Rebecca left to go to Switzerland and at least Eleanor would have company at Westshore whilst he was away.

Gabriel sailed out on The Eleanor Rose on a fine August day

taking the children with him. They were eager to see their grandparents and cousins and he thought it may help Eleanor to get some much needed rest. With the children out of the way Westshore would be quieter.

Having deposited them with their grandparents at Mulgrave House, Gabriel borrowed a horse from the stable and rode into Whitby.

He was shown into the drawing room of Prospect House where Libby was waiting for him. She was alone. 'I thought it best if we talked without Steven present at first, so I could let you know why I decided on Harrow. Steven can join us in a little while. How are you Gabriel? Atalana tells me your wife is with child again.'

'Thank you, I'm well and yes we're to expect another child in December. We're very pleased.' He took the seat he was offered. 'Have you definitely decided on Harrow? In your letter I thought you hadn't reached a final decision.' Gabriel jumped straight in.

Libby outlined her reasons for choosing Harrow adding: 'Also my brother went to Harrow.'

'Fat lot of good it did him! I'm sorry Libby that was uncalled for, I apologise.' Gabriel thought her other grounds not unreasonable in the main and said so, but he needed to change her mind. 'You obviously realise Harrow is at the other end of the country. Steven will spend most of his holidays travelling back to Whitby.'

'I realise this, my brother only ever came home in the long summer vacation, but the school has such a good reputation.'

'I agree, but there are other schools, not as prestigious perhaps, but nevertheless still well regarded. As you may remember I went to Alnwick. I didn't go on to university choosing to go straight to work for my father, but I received a good education there and had I wished to, I could have gone to Cambridge or Oxford. Indeed my good friend Sir Bendor Percy went to Alnwick school and then on to Cambridge. The school is first class. I won't hesitate when the time comes to send the twins there. If Steven were to go to Alnwick would it not be easier for everyone, especially Steven.'

'Especially for Steven? What do you mean? Surely going to one of the top schools in the country would be the best thing for him. Are you sure you're not thinking it would be best for you Gabriel?'

Gabriel thought for a moment. 'You're right of course it would serve me better. I should get to see him in the school holidays. He could break his journey at Westshore then sail on one of my ships to Whitby, better than his school holidays being spent in a carriage. He'd come home to you every term not once a year.' Gabriel hoped to play on Libby's heartstrings.

'I understand what you're saying but... let me think on it further. I must admit the thought of Steven getting ill, the damp weather does his chest no favours, worries me. Were he to fall ill there with only the school matron to take care of him - a stranger looking after my boy is not a thought to be relished.' She sat musing for a moment. 'And as you point out you would be on hand. From that standpoint I think I would feel easier in my mind. It is such a hard decision, I'm glad I can talk it over with you Gabriel. Let me sleep on it. A decision needs to be reached soon of course.'

'What would Steven prefer?'

'He is keen to go to school but not university. He has a fancy to join the navy. He could change his mind of course he's still young. If he gets his choice then I will hardly ever see him. It's hard being a mother. I want the best for him, but selfishly I want him to stay on dry land, be a lawyer, anything with less risk than the sea.'

'Tell me, did you ever consider having more children Libby?' He saw how easily he fell into his old ways with her. He always found her good company.

Libby looked a little uncomfortable. 'My late husband was a Quaker as you know, and when he asked for my hand in marriage it came with certain conditions. I think I told you he offered me marriage, but when I told him the truth about Steven's parentage he changed his mind only to change it back again on his return from his latest mission.'

'Conditions, what sort of conditions?'

Libby bit her lip reluctant to go on but then began to explain: 'Cyrus was a good man, but not what I'd call a romantic or passionate man. Straight-laced best describes him I think. In fact as it turned out he only wanted me as token wife, a wife in name only that is; someone to look after his house in fact. Latterly, when he changed course, had interests other than whaling, I was someone to host his business dinners. There was never a physical relationship between us. Never any intimacies save a peck on the cheek.' Libby blushed.

'I see and yet I remember you as a passionate woman... I'm sorry I shouldn't comment it's just that... you were happy with this arrangement?'

'Somewhat. I didn't love him, but I was hardly in a position to turn him down. My options were few at the time as I recall. Marrying Cyrus was to be the new start I'd been longing for, not that I blame you Gabriel I hope you know that. It's all so long ago, let's leave it at that.' She looked up at him, an embarrassed blush colouring her cheeks. 'But enough about me, we are here to talk about Steven's education.'

Gabriel was also keen to see his son. Libby rang the bell and told the servant to bring tea and to ask Steven to join them.

Gabriel was astonished to see his son had grown a head taller in the months since he had last seen him, but to say so would not be the done thing he knew. Boys of that age were often self-conscious. They took tea and eventually began to discuss Steven going to school.

'I'm excited to be going, but at the same time a little apprehensive. It will be a huge change from the Quaker school where everyone is like-minded, well about religion at any rate. Mama says I shall have to grow a thicker skin.'

Gabriel thought how mature his son sounded. 'It is a big upheaval going away to school, I remember it well. My father was a widower and we were close so I was sad to leave him on his own, but at the same time happy to widen my horizons. You'll soon make new friends I'm sure. I met a lifelong friend at school, we are like brothers.'

Steven helped himself to another crumpet and said: 'I hope so, but at least Mama won't be alone now.' He spread butter thickly on his crumpet then looked up at her and smiled.

Libby avoided Gabriel's curious gaze and poured more tea.

'I remember you saying your late husband's brother had been a help. He'll be company for you I expect,' Gabriel said. He saw an exchange of looks pass between mother and son. A look he didn't fully comprehend.

'Is your wife with you on this trip Gabriel?' Libby asked changing the subject. He explained why it was just himself and the children in Whitby.

The conversation was light and easy for the rest of the visit. Gabriel liked the boy. He was polite and well mannered, but had a glint in his eye that reminded him of the twins. He teased his mother and made light hearted comments about all manner of current affairs. Gabriel could see his son was intelligent but not a braggart. After an hour or so Steven said he had promised to go and help his uncle at the harbour and asked if he could leave the table.

Gabriel, always a tactile man, wanted to hug his son on what might be the last time he would see him in a while, but contented himself with a handshake. 'Goodbye Steven and good luck at school whichever one it is you choose.' He dearly wanted to try to convince him to his way of thinking, but knew it would be disrespectful to Libby. 'I'm sure your mama will let me know when a decision is made.'

'Thank you sir, I'm sure she will. By the next time we meet again who knows I may be as tall as you.' After bowing to Gabriel and kissing his mama he left the room. Gabriel felt overcome with emotion. It was true; he may not see Steven again for some time if he did go to Harrow.

Libby interrupted his thoughts. 'I shall miss him so much, but his needs and not mine, and not yours, must come first. I know this is hard for you Gabriel, I know you feel things deeply but Steven's education is paramount.'

Gabriel stayed standing not sure whether to go or stay. 'Will you perhaps take a little brandy?' She smiled at him warmly. 'I keep a little for medicinal purposes.' She poured a glass and handed it to him. She put a hand on his shoulder and squeezed it before sitting by the fire. 'You know Gabriel you were the only man I ever loved... until now.'

'What!'

'Earlier I told you my marriage was loveless, though not unsatisfactory. As Steven has hinted I've been granted another chance of happiness. I've met someone at the Meeting House and although he's a good man, a kind man, it's a love match this time; we love each other. We are to marry before Steven goes away to school. That's what Steven meant by my not being alone.'

'I thought he meant you had his uncle's support. My wife often chides me for being slow on the uptake; I'm barking up the wrong tree... again.'

'I wanted to put the record straight. I do have his uncle's blessing, but now I shall have a husband's support too. Again I had to chance my arm and tell Samuel about the circumstances of Steven's birth. Again I give thanks to God that my future husband is a tolerant man, most Quakers are I find. His name is Samuel Fishburn and he's a widower. He has a small daughter. We will be a little family together and in time hopefully we will add to it although I'm getting on a little I suppose, but who knows? I'm confident this time around it will be a proper marriage and not one in name only.'

Gabriel was overcome. First with Libby's confession that she had loved him and secondly that she was to marry again. Then another thought struck home; how would another father figure fit with Steven? Would Libby's new husband want to adopt Steven also? Did Gabriel have the right to even ask let alone object? Perhaps this man wanted Steven to go to the other end of the country... he might want someone else's son out of the way.

'Congratulations Libby, if what you say is true and you never loved your husband then you deserve happiness, but what about Steven? How will this affect my relationship with my son? Selfishly I must know; will I still be allowed to see him after you re-marry?'

'I told Samuel how we recently met again and what level of involvement you have with Steven. Sam isn't a possessive, jealous man and he wants only what's best for me and for Steven. Sam won't go against my wishes. He will treat Steven as a step-son but nothing more and I will be his daughter's step-mama. We are both happy with the arrangements so you needn't fear. So long as you stick to your side of the bargain and don't tell Steven you're his real father then we shall carry on as before.'

Riding back to Sandsend he felt the need to call at The Hart to steady his nerves before returning to Mulgrave House. How he wished Eleanor was here to talk over the matter. He knew she would put things into perspective; see the positives, rather than the negatives, dare him to hope Steven would go to Alnwick and not Harrow. He had expected today's visit to be difficult, but with the decision of Steven's schooling still not decided and Libby's impending remarriage he had been thrown into utter confusion. He ordered another brandy, drank it off quickly then rode along the beach before dismounting. He sat on the damp sand and watched as the tide went out.

ℛ

The next day, his last in Whitby, Gabriel met with Ingram Eskdale and put his business proposal to him. To his delight the shipbuilder was keen on the deal, but even this didn't raise his spirits.

He had promised the children a trip into Whitby and so they set off to walk the short distance to the harbour. They called to see Tomas; the boys in particular loved exploring the shipyard. Rose was keen to see Eva at the hat shop as Eleanor had said she could choose a new summer bonnet as a treat. The boys almost had to be dragged into the milliners, but Gabriel was determined they would do as he bid them. They couldn't have everything their own way he told them. Rose was soon sporting a new bonnet complete with yellow rosebuds around the brim.

As they made their way along Church Street, Gabriel was surprised to see Steven coming out of the Friends' Meeting House. His eldest son saw him and waved and smiled. Gabriel advanced and shook hands with the boy, introductions were made. Seeing the twins with their half brother was disconcerting to say the least. He dearly wanted each of them to know they were kin, but knew he dared not mention it. For once the twins stood quietly and looked Steven up and down. Gabriel's heart was fit to burst with pride.

'As we are to leave for Alnmouth tomorrow we are going to choose a gift for Mrs Reynolds from the jewellers across the way. She has a fondness for aquamarines so we thought to add to her collection.'

'As Mama is a Quaker, the only jewellery she has is a wedding band and soon that will be replaced with a new one when she remarries.'

'You like her husband to be?' Gabriel couldn't help himself; he wanted to know what the boy thought of the impending marriage.

'Mr Fishburn is a well respected man, I think he will make Mama happy. Since Father died there have been many changes, not least us leaving America. I think her ready to start a new life in a new country, although she's done it before of course.'

Ruari's ears pricked up. 'You've been to America?'

Gabriel smiled at his son whose eyes were on stalks. 'Steven lived there for most of his life, but now he's come back to England to live.'

'Are you interested in travel young man?' Steven asked Ruari.

'I am, although I've only ever been here to Whitby but one day I want to explore the world.'

'See the boatyard down the estuary,' Steven pointed it out, 'that's Mr Thomas Fishburn's yard. He built the ship that Captain Cook is sailing in now, the one which has recently broken the world record in the South Pole. You've heard of Captain Cook who in 1769 sailed to the east coast of Australia?'

Ruari nodded enthusiastically. 'I have heard of him. He said the Resolution was the fittest for service of any he has seen.'

'That's right and my soon to be step-father's shipyard built her.' Gabriel saw how proud the boy looked. It was a strange sensation. 'I too would like to be an explorer,' Steven added. 'Perhaps I'll gain experience first as a navigator and like Captain Cook join the navy.'

Gabriel looked at his children, all four of them, as they discussed Captain Cook and his adventures. Even Rose was joining in. It was odd seeing *all* of his children together. Talking, laughing enjoying themselves. This may not happen again for years... or ever. Listening to them talk now, he thought, they would each be in different corners of the world if they had their way. It made him want to keep them all close by him while he still could. Sadly this would not be possible with his eldest child.

'I should be off,' Steven said, 'Mama worries if I'm late, she's convinced I'll be pressed into service.' He smiled and Gabriel saw how alike his three sons were.

'She's right to worry, take care Steven you're tall for your age and the gangs won't stop to ask how old you are. We'll walk part of the way over the bridge with you if we may?'

Outside The Angel they said their goodbyes. Gabriel felt overcome with emotion but tried to remain light hearted; it would look strange to them all if he made too much of this last leave taking.

'Goodbye sir, it's been a pleasure to meet your children. I never met twins before, or a prettier auburn-haired young lady.' He bowed to Rose who blushed, and then he sprinted along the harbour and was quickly out of sight.

'I like him, he's nice.' Rose watched Steven go then looked up at her papa. 'I think you've forgotten something. You said we were going to buy Mama a present.'

'So I did, come let's retrace our steps. You can all help me choose a bracelet.'

The next day as they were about to set off back home Gabriel received a letter from Libby. Gabriel could hardly believe it when he read it. It said after giving it much thought she had changed her mind - she had made the decision to send Steven to Alnwick. Gabriel heaved a huge sigh of relief.

R

Eleanor listened as Gabriel told her about Libby's decision. He also told her about her impending marriage and how she had tried to put his mind at rest by saying nothing would change as far as his son was concerned. Eleanor knew he was unconvinced.

'My love try to keep this news in perspective, you have your heart's desire; Steven is to be nearer to you than you ever thought possible.'

'I know and don't think I'm ungrateful, yet I find I'm disconcerted by the thought of her remarrying. Men say things before they're married then change their minds later.'

'Of course I know the Fishburns; they're one of my family's main competitors.' Eleanor jumped in before the conversation took a dark turn. 'Tomas and I went to school with Sam although Tomas was more friendly with him than I. I had quite a fancy for his younger brother Henry as I recall. I remember Mama telling me Sam's wife had died, it must have been about the time the twins were born. At least this time, from what you say, it's a love match for Libby. She deserves the love of a good man. Sam *is* a nice man I think, he'll keep his word I'm sure.'

'I hope so, but in any case Steven will be close by. I know this is an imposition, but would you mind if Steven were to lay his head here for an odd night, when he arrives and departs for school. Say so if you'd rather he didn't, I understand.'

Eleanor watched as her daughter walked down to the summer house. It was a favourite spot of hers. 'Of course,' she said looking at her new bracelet, 'I see now this is a bribe - I'm kidding. He could hardly stay at an inn my love.' She changed the subject. 'And the family are well you say? Little Martha has recovered from her cold? Cora was worried for a time as she showed signs of fever.'

'Everyone is well and sends their love. Rose enjoyed playing with Martha I think. She treats her like her doll but I must get on.' Gabriel kissed the top of his wife's head. 'I have a meeting with Bendor at the stud. I'll not be home for dinner.'

When he had gone Eleanor made her way down to the summerhouse. She had missed her children, especially Rose who was mature enough now to hold a proper conversation. Mother and daughter often talked about subjects close to their hearts. In Rose's case these usually involved small furry animals. She was especially fond of anything with four legs especially if they were injured and in need of care and attention.

'Did you enjoy yourself in Whitby?'

'I did. Grandmama asked Mrs Tibbs to bake scallywags as she knows they're a particular favourite of mine.' Eleanor smiled to herself. Rose's other favourite thing was food. She was a podgy little thing, but Eleanor hoped she would grow out of it as she herself had done.

'We went to Whitby and as usual we went up the one hundred and ninety nine steps to the abbey. The twins had to race of course. Ruari won this time. Pa used to put me on his shoulders to carry me up, but he said those days are long gone. I think he's getting old.'

'Or you're getting too big. Don't let your father hear you say he's getting old or you'll be in bother young lady.' Eleanor tucked a stray curl behind her daughter's ear. 'The bonnet you choose is so pretty. Was Eva well?'

'Yes, but the boys were *so* silly in her shop. Pa made them wait outside after they knocked over a hat stand, then when we came out they got a telling off.'

'Oh dear, I don't know what we'll do with them. Send them to sea I should think.'

'We could send them away to school, to the one the boy might go to. Pa says it's a long way away, which means they would hardly ever come home.'

'What boy Rose?' Eleanor watched her daughter dance her favourite rag doll up and down on her knee.

'His name was Steven. He wants to be an explorer and so he's going to learn how to be a navigator at this school called Barrow. Strange name for a school don't you think Mama?'

'Harrow. Where did you meet him Rose? Did you go to his house?' Eleanor felt guilty at interrogating her daughter this way, but she was taken aback by the declaration.

'We saw him coming out of the Friends' Meeting House. He stopped to talk to us. Pa says he knows Steven's mama because she used to live in Alnmouth, but then she went to America. The twins were excited when the boy told them he'd lived in the New World most of his life. I asked him if he'd seen any Indians and he said he had. He was nice, sensible, unlike the twins who started making silly noises at the mention of Indians. He was a good looking boy I thought. I think Pa must have looked like him when he was a boy. They have the same hair; curly and not combed properly.'

Eleanor was unsure how she felt about this turn of events. By all accounts it sounded an accidental meeting, but if that was the case why then had Gabriel not mentioned it?

Before supper Eleanor decided to walk on the beach to think it over. Was he trying to save her feelings or was he hiding the meeting from her and if so why? She walked north. The evening sun was still warm as it glinted on the sea. High clouds wiped the smile off the sun's face from time to time, but the wind had dropped since the morning.

She had not gone far when she saw Gabriel riding towards her. He dismounted as he drew near. Eleanor often came to meet him on summer evenings, but today she hadn't expected him home so early.

'I miss having you sit up on Copper with me as we did in the past; with the size of your belly her poor knees would buckle.'

'If you're going to be this complimentary you needn't come home at all,' she said trying not to smile. 'Did you have a good meeting?'

He told her about the latest figures which had far exceeded what they had ever imagined. 'And Fashia is in foal again which is good news.' Through the years the stud farm had become renowned for producing race horses of the highest calibre. The foals often sold for hundreds of guineas, especially Fashia's and Falladore's prodigy.

Throughout supper they chatted easily enough, but in the back of Eleanor's mind was the fact she knew about the meeting with the children. She had given her husband ample opportunity to tell her but he hadn't mentioned it. Not a word.

'I'm going to have an early night,' she said eventually. 'My back aches and I can't get comfortable.'

'I think I'll join you my love. The journey from Whitby with the boys misbehaving and an early start this morning has tired me I fear. They were a handful cooped up on board ship, but nothing compared to what they were like in the carriage. I put my foot down in the end so Rose and I at least got some peace. Threatened them with walking behind the carriage; they have so much energy.'

'Rose told me she had to walk up to the abbey, she thinks you too old to carry her.'

'She at least was a model of good behaviour. It's a shame none of it rubs off on the twins.' He chuckled. 'We both know why I can't carry her up one hundred and ninety nine steps. Lord, I'd keel over half way up.'

'Poor Rose, perhaps we should start watching how much cake she eats, but I'm not keen to do so. I was a little tubby as a child, but I think by five or six I'd started to grow up rather than out. I hope she'll shed it soon.'

Eleanor went up to bed and told Molly she would see to herself. She was still thinking about whether to tell Gabriel she knew about the children meeting Steven. She couldn't quite understand why it bothered her so much, but it did. Perhaps it was because, for some reason, he had not told her himself.

By the time Gabriel joined her she was sitting up in bed plaiting her hair. She decided to broach the subject. It didn't do to go to bed on a grievance. 'Rose tells me you all met Steven on Church Street.'

Gabriel got into bed beside her. 'I was going to tell you, but there hasn't been the right moment since we came home. I didn't want you to be upset by it. I wasn't sure how you would feel.'

'Was it a planned meeting? Did you know Steven was at the Friends and you thought to bump into him? I know you wanted to see as much of him as you could while you were in Whitby.'

'It wasn't planned; it was a coincidence we happened to meet. It was most peculiar.'

'In what way peculiar?'

'Six months ago I never expected to see Steven ever again and then there he is in Whitby and talking to our children. I was a little concerned what you would think, but short of ignoring the boy what else could I do? I know this isn't easy for you my love.' He turned on his side to face her. 'I certainly didn't plan it; I wouldn't go behind your back you know that. If Libby had been inclined to let Steven meet the children, which I know she wasn't, then I'd have discussed it with you first.'

Eleanor stared at the ceiling. 'It's a little upsetting. I don't know why because I know you love us and would never do anything to hurt us, but you also love Steven. He's your son, your flesh and blood. How could you not love him, especially now you've got to know him a little? He's part of your life, but not of mine and that troubles me.'

'I have to abide by Libby's rules or not see him at all. Not perfect but there it is. I don't love you or *our* children any less because of Steven. I do love him and *like* him. At first, before I met him, and because he's been brought up a Quaker I thought he might be a little - '

'Like Obed?'

'Well yes, a little dour, but not a bit of it. He's clever and a good conversationalist for a boy of his age. He knows his own mind, appears to know what he wants to do with his life too.' He stroked her arm. 'It's not straight forward meeting him after all these years. It puts me in mind of a hymn we used to sing at school, The Magic Penny song.'

Eleanor was baffled. 'As Quakers we didn't learn hymns. I don't know what song you mean.'

'I can't remember the exact words,' he smiled, 'but it was something about if you gave away love you ended up having more.' He laughed at himself. 'Fancy me remembering that!'

'Fancy!' Eleanor moved closer to him and he put his arm around her. 'What I'm trying to say, via a children's hymn would you believe, is that's how I feel about Steven; loving him makes me love you and the children more somehow. I appreciate all that I have. Seeing the children grow and change, watching how their personalities are forming is a precious thing, well when the twins aren't brawling that is.' He pulled her closer. 'I haven't been able to do that with Steven, watch him grow and change, but at least I know him a little now, which is something I never expected. I'm grateful too that he'll be going to Alnwick School. Now I might see him a little more if Libby will allow it.'

'I think I understand,' she said sighing. 'It's not that I begrudge you spending money on his education if you decide to contribute that is, you know I don't care what it costs, but what about the twins? Will they go away to school, to Harrow or Eton or Alnwick? Ought we to discuss it?'

'Of course; it will be *our* decision not just mine. Who knows what will happen? Even if they go to school in Alnwick, like me, they'll still board. Is that what worries you? The boys being away from home?'

'Partly yes... I'd miss them.'

'As my father wanted the best for me I want them to have a good education too. Whether that means Alnwick I don't know. There are some good schools north of the border which would be further from home but not too far; Musselburgh for instance, although I'd not hesitate to send them to my old school. It has to be your decision too. I don't want them to go soon. We didn't have children to send them away, but I see their needs must be met. I didn't go to university because I knew I wanted to follow in my father's footsteps, yet neither of the twins are interested in shipping at the moment. I wonder if they'll be content to go to school, but not university. I'd like them to go all the same, wouldn't you?'

'I would, I should also like Rose to have a good education, but the best we can do for her is Mrs Grammond's Ladies Academy in Alnwick.' She tutted derisively.

'The boys might want to go to university. Haydan seems of a scientific frame of mind and Ruari says he wants to be an explorer like Captain Cook.'

'Last week he told me he wanted to be a blacksmith because he likes horses. He thought you might give him a job at the stud.'

'Coming back from Whitby I tried to engage them about shipping, but they were intent on trying to throw one another overboard, although they love your father's shipyard, perhaps ship building will interest them more?' He thought for a moment. 'Even Nat remarked that at their age I was asking questions about tonnage and wind speeds. Perhaps they won't want to take over the business. Nat was good with them, kept them amused for a while with his stories. It took me back to when he used to tell me his tall tales, he's such a character. Did I tell you his eldest is engaged to the Timmins boy?'

Eleanor nodded. 'Then we'll let Rose have it, the business I mean,' she said not altogether joking. 'She can make Drommie a captain. She does love that doll, they go everywhere together.'

'Eva gave her a ribbon for the doll's hair. Hair! It's wool for goodness' sake! And why is it called Andromeda? Isn't it a fancy name for a rag doll?'

'She said it's a character from a book Ginny read to her. The girl was brave apparently which impressed our daughter. Before we got sidetracked we were speaking of plans, I remember at Caroline's funeral Padraic said making plans was a waste of time. He said although he was brought up Catholic he was more of a fatalist. He said no matter how well you laid down your plans fate intervened. We might make all these grand plans for the children only for them to eschew them.'

'They might, but we can at least have ambition for them.'

'But not for poor Rose. Mrs Grammond's and a finishing school is the best she can hope for. Why are there not universities for girls?' She didn't wait for an answer. 'In that case I must augment her education myself, teach her to speak Dutch at least and how to balance a cost book. I'll give her life lessons; lessons in how to live life to the full without relying on a man. Rebecca too is well educated, she speaks French, she might teach Rose.'

'No man will touch my poor daughter with a barge pole.' He laughed. 'She will be too clever.'

'And of course there's the spinet, Becky can teach her to play. And commerce, I can teach her about business.'

Gabriel put his hand on Eleanor's bump. 'Man alive, poor Rose. She'll be the most accomplished girl in Northumberland. I hope this one will be another boy.'

ℛ

The day of Rebecca's departure for Switzerland was a crisp, early September day. High clouds drifted amiably across a pale blue sky as Gabriel, Eleanor and the children assembled at the quayside to see her off. Rosalind and Saul Coates along with Felicity were also there to see Mary and Rebecca embark on the first leg of their journey.

At the last minute Captain Truelove arrived to say his goodbyes, which in the end was quite embarrassing for all concerned, as the Brophy boy also came to bid Rebecca farewell; neither Eleanor nor Gabriel even knew he was in the running.

After much hugging and kissing from friends and family, Mary and Rebecca were finally ready to board The Jack and Alice when a messenger arrived carrying a parcel addressed to Rebecca.

Eleanor read the note Rebecca passed to her. The bon voyage gift, from George Black, of scented notepaper was apt. Eleanor thought the present showed a quiet confidence and maturity. She knew they had said their goodbyes two days ago when he had invited them all to sup, so Rebecca had said she didn't expect him today.

The two girls stood on deck waving as the ship prepared to set sail. A second before the gangplank was lifted Eleanor noticed Haydan was missing; he was unceremoniously put ashore by Nat Pearson.

'Like mother like son,' Gabriel said. 'At least your attempt at being a stowaway was more successful.' He clipped his son around the head playfully.

Later back at Westshore Eleanor looked pensive.

'Is something worrying you my love?'

'I was thinking... now Rebecca has gone the house will seem emptier will it not?'

'Yes, but not for long.' He looked at her baby bump. 'I'll miss Rebecca, but it's not forever as we've been keen to tell her.' He put his hand lightly on her belly. 'It's small after the size you were with the twins. I remember you were twice the size then.'

'Thank you my love for those warm words, but I'm grateful I'm not so huge.' She tried to get comfortable. 'If it's a girl I have an idea for a name.'

'Oh, what is it? Not Andromeda for pity's sake.'

She curbed an eye roll. 'I thought it would be nice to call her Eva if it's a girl. After all when you think about it, it's because of Eva we met in the first place.'

'And in the last placc if it's a boy we could call him William because if you'd not seen him with a strumpet we wouldn't have got together at all.'

'Very droll my love, but I like Robert if it's a boy. What do you think?'

'I like Eva and as we agreed a girl would be named after Grace, Eva Grace sounds pretty to my mind. Robert I like also. Robert Reynolds is a good, solid name I think.'

17

Gabriel stood on the quayside as The Jack and Alice berthed. He looked up and saw what he had been waiting for; his son Steven was waving from the deck. No sooner had the gangplank been lowered than Gabriel raced up and shook Steven by the hand.

'Welcome to Alnmouth Steven.' He tried hard to restrain his enthusiasm and managed to stop himself from hugging his son. He tried to remember he was a "friend of the family".

His eldest son was to stay the night at Westshore, after which Gabriel was to escort him to school for his first day of term. He was so proud. He had already been in touch with his old headmaster and told him he would be bringing a friend's son to school. The master had been convivial and asked Gabriel to dine before his return. It would be a chance to visit his alma mater and he was looking forward to it.

The only downside of Steven going to school in Alnwick was that inevitably lies would have to be told about his exact parentage. Eleanor and Gabriel minded not at all about the school, but Eleanor was struggling with her principles where others were concerned. Of course the children were too young to understand the ramifications of the situation, but still it was an insurmountable problem, there was nothing else for it than to carry on the subterfuge. The couple hoped to keep the lies to a minimum. To this end they had only mentioned Steven's visit to Bendor and Grace. The less people who knew about Steven the fewer lies would have to be told.

As they rode the short distance to Westshore, Gabriel asked after Libby and they talked about her recent nuptials. 'I'm glad now I'm to be at school Mama will have company. Mr Fishburn is an agreeable man I think, he's well respected in Whitby.'

‘My wife is from Whitby and knows the family well. Her parents are also shipbuilders and Fishburn’s yard is their main competitor. I think you’re right, your mama deserves to be happy, she’s a good woman.’

Westshore came into view and Gabriel pointed with his crop. ‘The house ahead is my home, Westshore.’

‘It’s magnificent sir and almost on the beach. I would wager your children adore being so close to the sands.’

‘They do and I expect they’ll want to take you rock pooling, but if you’re tired after your journey you must say so.’

Gabriel could see Eleanor waiting on the veranda, her hands clasped in front of her the way she held them when she was anxious but trying not to show it. Before he had left for the bay she had been concerned the visit wouldn’t live up to Gabriel’s high expectations. Gabriel had no such qualms.

Sam and the other young groom led the horses away and Gabriel introduced Steven to his wife.

‘But we’ve met before Mrs Reynolds.’ Steven smiled confidently. ‘I hadn’t made the connection, but I remember you were with Mrs Coffin, outside the Meeting House. Are you not her sister?’

‘Yes I am. We met but briefly I recall.’

‘I normally wouldn’t remember, but you have such distinctive hair. Sorry ma’am I meant the observation as a compliment.’

‘There’s no need to apologise, I took it as one. Please come inside you must be tired after your journey. Dora will show you to your room. When you’re ready come and join us for refreshments, the children are keen to make your acquaintance again.’

‘Thank you ma’am, but I’m not tired, I’ll join you all directly if I may.’ He bowed to them both then followed Dora upstairs.

Gabriel put his arm about his wife’s shoulders. ‘I’m sorry this is a strain for you my love, can you bear it?’

‘Of course, it’s not a problem at all though I did warn you he might remember we’d met before.’ She thought for a moment. ‘It’s a little disconcerting how much he looks like you and the boys, anyone seeing you together would be bound to guess the truth of the matter.’

‘I think not - it’s because *we* know the reality. I’m glad you’re happy, I knew you’d cope, it’s true you do have distinctive hair... how had I never noticed?’ He kissed the top of her head hoping to defuse the tension from the atmosphere.’ Have the twins been pressed to be on their best behaviour?’

‘They have but give them some credit Gabriel,’ she said defensively, ‘they were perfect gentlemen at Rebecca’s goodbye supper. And I said I was fine, not happy... there’s a world of difference.’

‘Of course, foolish of me I only meant - ’

She put her arms around his neck. ‘I’m sorry, I’m a little on edge, I don’t want to spoil your day, forgive me.’

‘It reminds me of when we met him that time, when he was a baby. We’re all trying to do the best we can in difficult circumstances.’

The twins, dressed soberly, entered the drawing room, Ruari fiddling with his neckcloth and pulling a face. They preferred to be in their play clothes, but had been ordered to change. Rose followed them wearing a pretty green dimity dress. She brought Drommie for moral support.

‘I’m dreadfully hungry Mama, will we be eating soon,’ Haydan said collapsing on a sofa.

‘Haydan, sit up straight please. When we have guests you have to behave like a gentleman not like a... ah, Steven... come and join us. You remember Rose, Haydan and Ruari I’m sure. Ruari is wearing a pin in his neck cloth so you may tell them apart; we thought it easier that way.’ Gabriel made the introductions.

They took refreshments on the veranda, it being a pleasantly warm early autumn day. The boys asked questions about America and Steven was at pains to tell them all they wanted to know. ‘It appears you will all be adventurers and leave your poor parents behind,’ Eleanor said after the boys expressed a wish to see the world. ‘Elbows Haydan,’ she added as she saw her son forget himself.

‘I shan’t leave you Mama; I’ll stay and look after you both.’

‘Thank you Rose that makes me feel... better.’

Once tea had been taken the children were excused from the table.

As predicted Steven was asked to go rock pooling. They shed their shoes and stockings, picked up nets and buckets and were about to head to the beach when Lisbet appeared. Gabriel introduced her to Steven.

'Did you make the blackberry tart Lisbet?' Rose asked. 'I bet you did, you make the best blackberry tart in the whole world.'

Lisbet told Rose she had made it especially for her then looked hard at Steven. After welcoming him she said: 'Yer off to school young man. A hope yer learn more than Mr Gabriel did when he were there.'

Steven looked surprised at the woman's forwardness, but made no comment. He ran to join the children and soon caught them up.

Lisbet handed two shirts to Gabriel. 'A brought these back, A turned the collars, they were near to frayin' but now they're as good as new.'

'Thank you Lisbet, what would I do without you?'

Lisbet waddled off. Gabriel watched her go.

'I never thought to see the day when Steven would step over our threshold.' Emotion was close to the surface.

'I know my love, who would ever have thought such a thing possible.' She clasped her hands tightly. 'I must remind Connie we're to sup early so Steven can get an early night. You'll need to be up before the cock crows in the morning.'

Gabriel knew she was leaving him so he might join Steven on the beach; she was so intuitive, so thoughtful. He would tell her later how much he appreciated her.

Gabriel met Rose on her way back to the house, trailing Drommie as she walked. 'Won't the boys let you join in?'

'Oh yes, but Drommie fell in the rock pool and was almost drowned. Steven kindly fished her out for me, but she wants to go home. Ginny will get me a huckerback to dry her off.' He ruffled her hair as she passed by.

The twins, with Steven's help, had netted quite a haul. He was telling them about the different kinds of jelly fish to be found on the beaches of Nantucket Island. When he saw Gabriel he came over to join him.

'Mama said she used to live in Alnmouth sir, might you show me whereabouts she lived? When I write to her I could say I have seen her old home.'

Gabriel swallowed hard. 'I'm afraid that won't be possible Steven. About five years ago when the harbour was made bigger the house where your mama lived was knocked down to make room.'

It was true, but Libby's old house had long since fallen into disrepair, it had probably not needed much of a push to demolish it. Of course he would not have wanted the boy to see it; she had lived in a poor district in those days.

'That's a shame, but never mind. Will we pass by near where she used to live in Alnwick on the way to school?'

'I'm afraid not, it's on the other side of town. I could come over one day later in the term and take you to see it.' Gabriel only knew the address, he presumed it was a good house in a good area, but had never been. He had only ever written to her there, when Steven was a baby, but he kept this information to himself. At least Steven had been spared seeing her humble abode in Alnmouth.

'Time you two were getting ready for bed boys,' Gabriel called to the twins. He tried not to look surprised when they complied straight away. They walked back to the house together laughing and talking. Eleanor was waiting in the conservatory to greet them.

After supping Steven asked to be excused. He suggested he wasn't good at rising early so might need a second knock. As he was about to bid them goodnight, Carver entered and said Mr and Mrs Charles Noble had called and were asking if they could wait on them.

Gabriel and Eleanor exchanged looks. 'I can take my leave sir, and let you greet your guests in peace.'

Eleanor's earlier comment about anyone seeing Steven would instantly see the resemblance came to mind, but undaunted Gabriel said: 'You might find Captain Noble interesting Steven, he was in the navy for nigh on twenty years.'

The Nobles were shown in and introduced, Gabriel explained that Steven was the son of an old family friend who was about to start at their old school.

'Well I hope you enjoy your time there as much as Gabriel and I, we had a good education did we not Gabriel?'

Steven asked Charles questions about his time in the navy. A pleasant half hour passed before Steven begged to be excused and took his leave.

'What a pleasant young lad, with his temperament he'll do well at Alnwick, he'll soon make friends. They were happy days were they not Gabriel, we had quite an education.'

'So you said Charles,' Violet chided her husband, but she was light hearted, a little flirtatious. 'We're sorry to call unannounced,' she continued, 'but as we were passing we thought it rude not to drop in. It's such a pleasant evening so we decided to walk before we supped. However we didn't intend to stay so long and supper will be ruined if we don't set off now.'

No one would have guessed by looking at her that Violet was expecting a child. Charles had told Gabriel she too expected in December. Violet was still stick thin.

'Yes,' Charles agreed, 'our cook's victuals are bad enough without them being burnt offerings.'

When they had gone Eleanor said: 'Violet was almost jolly I think?'

'She was indeed, but did you see the way she looked at Steven? Do you think she suspected anything?'

'Don't be silly, you're letting your imagination run away with you.' Gabriel suspected she thought the same, but was trying to put his mind at ease.

The next morning after Gabriel had supervised the loading of Steven's trunks, father and son broke their fast together then set off early for Alnwick. It was a mellow morning and once the mist had burnt off it promised to be sunny and warm.

As they rode out of Alnmouth they struck up a companionable conversation where the pair exchanged views, talked about Steven's life in America and how he felt about starting a new school. In return Gabriel told Steven about his own life, about his father and how close they had been.

Steven said: 'My father was a good man but he was a little distant. When I was small he was away at sea for months on end of course, but he was never affectionate, nor was he over strict to be fair. I've seen how you behave with your children, he was never so inclined, he'd never have dreamt of going to the beach with me. I would have loved a brother or sister to play with, but it never happened.'

'I was an only child too; I think you learn to be self reliant to some extent, although my father always made time for me especially after Mama died.'

As they were turning towards Lesbury, Gabriel saw a familiar figure. It was Bendor riding towards them. 'I was telling Steven how I met a lifelong friend at school and would you believe it, here you are.'

Bendor knew the real story of Steven's pedigree and so Gabriel felt easy, proud in fact, when he introduced them.

'I'm pleased to make your acquaintance Master Hague. How lucky you are to be going to Alnwick School, it is a good school.' Bendor, who was on the board of trustees, told Steven about the school's excellent facilities and asked him if he was interested in sport.

'Not especially sir, I like to walk, but only so I can collect specimens of flora and fauna. I'm much interested in botany.'

After Bendor extolled the virtues of Alnwick's facilities he said he must be on his way or he would be late for his meeting. 'Well Master Hague I'm sometimes about the school. I'll look out for you, a friendly face is most welcome in one's first term I know from experience. The best thing that happened to me in my school days is sitting a horse beside you; Gabriel and I met in the first week of term and have been brothers in arms ever since. I pray you are lucky enough to meet such a friend. Good friends are beyond guineas. Good day to you.'

Bendor rode past Gabriel and reached out and squeezed his friend's arm. He took advantage of Steven's horse shying away to whisper: 'He's the double of you at that age, poor chap.' He grinned. 'So long Gabriel, I'll see you soon my friend.'

Father and son journeyed on and after a while they reached a declivity. The sun was now high in the sky so they were glad of their water bottles.

'Sir, there is something I would confide in you, something that if I failed to mention would feel deceitful. I've been waiting for the right time and think I must speak now.'

'I see. You may speak freely Steven.'

The boy began hesitantly. 'When you came to Prospect House and took tea with us, you may remember I had to leave to go for my Latin class. I have a poor memory for practical matters I'm afraid; I forgot my exercise book.' He paused and drew breath. 'I came back for it and as the door was ajar I overheard you and Mama talking.' The rehearsed speech tumbled from his son's lips.

'I see.' Gabriel took off his tricorn and mopped his forehead. 'What exactly did you hear?'

'I know you are my real father and that I was adopted by Captain Hague.'

'Is your Mama aware you know this may I ask?'

'She does not know. I think she would be... upset... embarrassed if she knew I'd learnt the truth.'

'And how do you feel about this Steven? Your mama has always had your best interests at heart; she was trying to protect you. We both were. She thought, rightly or wrongly, you'd had enough to cope with what with returning to England and then losing... your father.'

'I don't blame her, or you for that matter, but I wanted you to be aware that I know I'm your son. I'm happy to know you sir and your family.'

'This is some shock, but I'm more than happy the truth is out. You're most welcome at Westshore any time you choose to come, but what of your mama? I should write and tell her, better still I'll go and see her. She ought to know.'

'If you wouldn't mind sir, I'd rather you didn't. I think she would be much troubled. She would wonder why I'd not told her. I found out in an underhand way after all. Not that I meant to eavesdrop at the beginning. I only didn't tell her because she too has had a lot to contend with of late and now of course she's newly remarried. We could keep the information to ourselves.'

'I don't think I can do that Steven, she must be told, it wouldn't be fair otherwise. You found out by accident, it's not your fault.'

'I suppose you're right.' He thought for a moment. 'May I ask you something sir?'

'Of course, so long as it doesn't compromise your Mama.'

'It's regarding Mrs Reynolds. Does she know who I really am, does she know I'm your son?'

'She does. I can't disclose the exact circumstances - it wouldn't be fair to either lady. You were born after I met and married my wife, but she met you, as did I when you were a baby. We met you once before you left for America. I want you to know I didn't abandon you, we were hoping, my wife and I, to be thought of as godparents to you, so we'd have some involvement in your life. But then your mama had an offer of marriage from Captain Hague and she decided to take it. I never blamed her Steven, though I was heartbroken to lose you.' Gabriel furrowed his brow. 'You're too young to understand these things Steven, but please know never a day passed that I didn't think of you. And now to have you back in my life again is more than I ever thought possible. For me it's a dream come true.'

'As you say I'm young and know nothing of the world, but I regard myself as lucky. Some boys don't have a father at all and I appear to have managed to have three.' He chuckled as he looked at Gabriel. They continued their journey each lost in their own thoughts.

After Gabriel had seen Steven safely lodged at school, he made his way to see the headmaster. In truth he wished he could go straight home, he needed to talk to Eleanor. However, the dinner was good and the headmaster not at all how Gabriel remembered him. He had a great fondness for the port bottle. At last Gabriel made business his excuse to get away or he would have been drinking into the early evening.

Passing through Lesbury once again he met with Bendor returning from his meeting. 'Are we not like ships that pass in the night?'

Bendor said. 'Do you have time to wet your whistle at The Coach and Horses?'

Once they were settled Gabriel told his old friend how Steven had learned Gabriel was his real father. Bendor let out a long whistle.

'I'm not surprised. The boy has two good eyes in his head, he could have guessed by looking at you. He's the image of you. When I saw him this morning it was like I'd been transported back in time and was looking at the young boy I first met all those years ago.'

'Steady on Bendor, not all that many years ago.' Gabriel toyed with his glass. 'I'm glad he knows I'm his father, though I don't expect Libby will be at all pleased. She asked me not to tell him, and I haven't of course, but I could hardly deny the truth.'

'Eleanor will be somewhat surprised.'

'That's an understatement, yet as you say Steven and I look so alike... Charles and Violet called last evening and both Eleanor and I were certain they would see the truth, but then it's as Eleanor said we're reading far more into it.'

After talking the matter over further Gabriel was keen to get home, he took his leave and quickened his pace so he arrived home as dusk was falling.

Without beating about the bush he told his wife the news that Steven knew his true parentage.

'It's the sort of thing Haydan would do, listen at doors, we've all done it at times I'll bet. I think you're right however, Libby must be told.'

'One of my ships will be going to Whitby, I'll check the schedules and go and see her. It's not the sort of thing I'd want to put in a letter.'

They discussed the topic for some time and Gabriel was pleased to note Eleanor didn't seem unduly put out by the revelation.

She squeezed his hand. 'He's a fine boy but how could he not be, his father is a good man. All I ever wanted was for you to be happy my love, and now the shadow of not knowing your eldest son has been swept away I think you can be truly fulfilled.'

'I was content before, but I understand what you mean.'

‘Earlier we were talking of people listening at doors.’ She raised both eyebrows mischievously. ‘Lisbet came earlier looking for you. I told her you’d be back for supper. She said it wasn’t urgent, but could you call on her when you have the time.’

‘Was she unwell, out of sorts?’

‘Not at all, I enquired after her health, she’s well.’

He said goodnight to the children then went to see Lisbet. ‘Is that apple pie?’ Gabriel asked as he sat at Lisbet’s kitchen table.

‘You’ll spoil yer supper,’ she said cutting him a slice. It transported him back to when he was a child. ‘They’re fer the harvest supper, but A made this knowin’ yer’d want to mek sure it were up to snuff.’

‘Eleanor said you were looking for me? What’s amiss?’

She sat opposite him and poured them both a glass of brandy. ‘Some years back when yer were first married after poor Eleanor lost the bairn, you two had a fearsome argument, lasted days, yer were sleepin’ separate an’ hardly speakin’ to each other.’

Gabriel saw which way the wind was blowing.

‘What of it, was it any of your business?’ He knew the rebuke wouldn’t deter her, when she was on a mission she was like a cat after a rat.

‘The other night, when A brought yer shirts back, an’ A saw that little lad an’ A thought to maself - ’

A silence opened up between them.

‘Yes Lisbet, he’s my son, not that it’s any concern of yours.’ He was irritated for a moment then saw it was futile to lose his temper with her. She had meant no harm, in all the years he had known her she had been inquisitive, no not that, downright nosy, but never malicious.

‘It was something that became known to us after I’d married Eleanor, and as you say it was all the worse for coming as it did after the miscarriage.’ He told her the bare minimum to satisfy her curiosity knowing as he did she would never breathe a word to anyone else.

‘It were Jax who first med me think somethin’ were goin’ on.’ She refilled their glasses. 'He were up in the hayloft and heard Eleanor say somethin' about a baby boy, he weren't earwiggin', yer didn't know he were there. He asked me about it an' course A knew nothin', but it got me wonderin'. A couldn't mek the pieces fit. Now A understand. How is that lass er yours copin' now he's turned up, it can't be easy fer her.'

'My wife is a tower of strength. I'm not saying she's pleased, but she knows it's something she can't change and so is sanguine, as always.'

'Yer fell on yer feet the day yer met that Whitby lass, yer do know that don't yer?'

'I do and I count my blessings daily.'

ℛ

Gabriel sent a note from Mulgrave House where he was staying with his in-laws asking to see Libby. Eleanor would not accompany him to Whitby as he would only be staying two nights. He would return home straight away once he had delivered his news. It was news he wasn't eager to impart.

On her marriage Libby had left Prospect House to move to Harbourside, the larger home Sam Fishburn had shared with his first wife and daughter. She was waiting for him in the drawing room. He congratulated her on her recent marriage and presented her with a gift. Eleanor had thought it may help soften the blow.

'Thank you Gabriel, but you shouldn't have. Please thank Eleanor for me, how kind.'

'Think nothing of it, I'm sure as you both previously had your own establishments you already have all you need, but we wanted to mark the occasion.'

'It is a kind thought, thank you.'

'Are you settled?' Gabriel looked about the well appointed room. It was quite restrained he noticed. Quaker houses were not known to be ostentatious but the heavy furniture whilst not to his taste was good quality.

'Yes thank you. Hopefully by the time Steven comes home for Christmas his new room will be ready for him.'

'It is Steven I wish to discuss with you.' Gabriel thought it best to get straight to the point.

'He's well, I heard from him only yesterday, but perhaps you being nearer have heard something I have not?'

'No, no he's well, don't worry.' They sat down and reassured Libby sent for coffee.

'Steven says he has met one or two boys whom he thinks might become friends in time. He's so affable; I've no worries on that score at least. I'm sorry Gabriel you said you wanted to talk about Steven, but here I am rambling on.'

Gabriel took a deep breath. 'You said you didn't want to tell Steven I was his father and I accepted your decision, I respected it.'

Libby's eyes flashed a look of antagonism. 'You have kept your word I trust?'

'I have, but to no avail. Steven knows Libby. He overheard our conversation and knows I'm his father.'

Libby was visibly shocked. 'My goodness I can hardly believe it. Why did he not tell me he knew?'

Gabriel explained the reasons Steven had stated.

Libby listened not wanting to believe what she was hearing. 'He's so mature for his age is he not? It is like him to think of my welfare. He's always been a thoughtful boy, but oh how I wish he'd not found out.' She was close to tears. 'I've always had my son's respect, but now, my goodness what must he think of me?'

'He loves you Libby and because you've raised him well, he doesn't judge. Besides he's young and doesn't know the circumstances. That's up to you to decide if and when you tell him. In my opinion he's too young to know of such things. At his age I wouldn't have understood I'm sure.'

'It does complicate matters somewhat. Samuel will be upset too I think. They are only just getting to know each other and now this... this doesn't change things with our arrangement Gabriel. Of course Steven has some say in the matter now he knows, but I would still wish your involvement kept to a minimum, well perhaps not that but I shouldn't want... oh dear if only he'd not found out.'

'But he has and despite all I'm glad, though I understand how you must feel, of course I do, you're his mother but believe me Libby he's still your loving son. Nothing will change that.'

'I wish he was here now, though I've no idea what I would say. Perhaps I should write, but then again how to explain.'

'As you say it will be a difficult conversation but not one you have to have now.' He took another deep breath. 'Steven asked me to show him where you lived, when you lived in Alnwick, it was a childish whim you understand, but I said I'd take him out one day later in the term. If you don't wish it I will give back word.'

She thought for a long moment then said: 'What harm can it do? Having you close by him is a comfort to me and if Steven wishes to have contact with you then who am I to stop him.'

She burst into tears.

'Hey, don't take on so.' He took her hands in his.

'I can't bear he may think badly of me, what if he thinks me a wanton, a trull?'

'You know that's not the case and never could be. Why not go to see him if you're so upset, speak to him and tell him when he's older you'll explain, well tell him as much as you're prepared to tell him. Blame me if you must for I take full responsibility.'

'I would never blame you, you know why. You saved me from a fate worse than death. I'll speak with my husband when he comes home and take his advice. In the meantime Gabriel would you mind leaving me please, I need to think, this has been some shock.'

On the way back to Mulgrave House Gabriel fortified himself at The Hart Inn. He knew he was going to have to have a difficult conversation with his father-in-law. On the journey down from Alnmouth, Gabriel had realised he ought to make a clean breast of things; tell Eleanor's father about Steven. Ordinarily he wouldn't have relished the thought of sharing his past misdemeanours with all and sundry, but there was a particular reason for telling Eleanor's parents.

The Barkers and the Fishburns had always been on friendly terms despite being business rivals. Eleanor had said the friendliness had begun when the Barkers were Quakers and it had survived John Barker's expulsion from the Friends. Gabriel would rather tell the Barkers about Steven himself so there was no chance of embarrassing his in-laws.

He doubted Samuel Fishburn was the type of man to tell the world his business, but if, as Gabriel imagined, Steven were to visit Mulgrave House now that he was a Fishburn in all but name, it would save any awkwardness. Gabriel held John and Anne Barker in too much esteem to embarrass them.

To this end Gabriel asked to see John Barker privately. His father-in-law, who was curious about the request, complied readily enough. Gabriel told his story succinctly and without embellishment.

'I see. This is some shock Gabriel, but on reflection it is not unheard of I suppose. I am only surprised Tomas has not some offspring born the wrong side of the blanket too; who knows one may yet show itself. He was a wild young man at times, hard to believe now he has settled down to become a family man. However, I am not sure why you feel the need to tell me, I presume Eleanor has known from the outset and accepted the situation.'

'She's known all along as you say, but Steven, my son, is now Samuel Fishburn's step-son. That's the reason I thought to tell you. The boy may visit you with Samuel and if it turned out I was here too, you might have been puzzled why we were acquainted. I'm sure Steven wouldn't say what the connection was, he's sensible of his mama's feelings, but he's a child and children are open books are they not? I only think of our relationship John. I would hate to embarrass you and Anne.'

'This cannot have been at all easy for you my son, I do think of you as my son Gabriel, and although I cannot pretend I am not disappointed, especially for my daughter, I am glad you have been open with me.' John Barker thought for a moment then added: 'In fact we have met the boy already. We met at Samuel's wedding. Libby is a lovely lady, a little older than Sam, but they seem well suited in temperament. Now I know the truth of the matter I can also see the likeness; Steven is very much like the twins in looks.'

'I would expect you'll tell Anne, I have no objections obviously. I want to reassure you though Eleanor isn't at all happy about all this she's always been supportive of me, eager for my happiness and well being. She knows I would never intentionally hurt her. As the years pass I love her more and more and I believe she feels the same about me. When I asked for her hand in marriage I had no idea I had a son.'

'I know you would cut off your right hand rather than hurt Eleanor, and what is done cannot be undone, so let that be all that needs to be said on the matter. Come, it must be dinner time.'

18

Two white-wigged footmen opened the door to the newly renovated South Point. Two more, wearing navy and gold relieved Eleanor and Gabriel of their cloaks and led them up the marble staircase to the main reception room. The ballroom, complete with minstrel's gallery, where a quartet played discreetly, was cavernous. South Point's renovations were finally almost complete. Charles and Violet were throwing a ball to show off their new, not inconsiderable home.

As Gabriel and Eleanor were announced Eleanor spotted Lottie and Wilson.

'This house is huge.' Lottie exclaimed. 'I sent my maid to find the retiring room. That was three days ago and I've not seen her since.'

'You are wicked Lottie, but it is impressive I have to admit, so elegant and grand. This is what a house that belongs to the landed gentry looks like I expect. The plasterwork and marble columns are so imposing,' Eleanor sighed, 'and the gold leaf everywhere must have cost a fortune. Is that uncouth to say so?'

'Correction,' Bendor interrupted overhearing Eleanor's comment as he and Grace joined the group, 'this is what the home of the landed gentry looks like when a wife's dowry saves it from falling into rack and ruin.'

'True enough, but it's still much larger and grander than I'd expected.'

'Luckily for me my wife brought other riches on our wedding day.' Bendor squeezed Grace's hand.

Wilson said: 'The servants reflect Charles' naval background do they not? Do you suppose it was intentional?' They availed themselves of wine from a footman again wearing navy and gold and an upright military stance.

'My love, I think we need new livery for the staff at Westshore,' Eleanor said.

Gabriel looked skyward for divine assistance. 'I can see this is going to cost me.'

'I can't wait to see the bedrooms,' Grace burst out. 'We're to stay the night as it's a little too far to travel back to Dunstanburgh. I believe they have all the latest conveniences, including water piped into the rooms.'

'Really, I've heard of this. The pipes are wood are they not?' Eleanor said with a touch of envy. Grace nodded and whispered that the rooms boasted indoor water closets. Both ladies looked impressed. Eleanor looked slightly embarrassed when she said: 'We're to stay too. We could at a stretch have travelled back to Westshore, but when the invitation included overnight accommodation we thought it prudent to stay. It was blowing a gale earlier so I'm glad we decided not to go home and now I've seen the place I'm doubly pleased we're to stay the night.'

Gabriel shook his head. 'Don't start getting ideas my love. Piped water wouldn't be possible at Westshore. Where would we get a water supply from? The sea.'

The ball was well attended and when the dancing began Bendor, always more of a dancer than Gabriel, escorted Eleanor onto the dance floor. They chatted amiably as old friends are wont to do.

As they danced Eleanor noticed a woman had sidled up to Gabriel. She didn't recognise her and wondered who the lady could be. She was stunning and was dressed in the most fashionable midnight blue gown. She wore diamonds as big as gulls' eggs about her throat, wrist and ears. Silky blonde hair was dressed in the latest style and topped with plumes of ostrich feathers... at just the correct angle.

'Who's the lady talking so intimately with my husband Bendor,' she asked as they came together. She noticed the lady was hanging onto Gabriel's every word. 'I've never seen her before; perhaps she's from out of town? She's certainly been dressed in London by the looks of it.'

'Ah, that my dear Eleanor is the not so honourable Lady Berwick,' Bendor grinned. 'Marguerite Strachan was a Percy before her marriage to some aged duffer. She and Gabriel are old friends, or is that adversaries? I'm not too sure.'

The dance precluded further conversation as they moved on to new partners. Eleanor's interest was piqued as she saw the woman laughing affectedly at something Gabriel had said. Her husband on the other hand, looked less than happy which was a surprise to her. He liked a pretty face as much as the next man. Why then did he look taciturn? After all these years together she could read what was in her husband's mind. She thought him not over enamoured with Lady Berwick and was intrigued to know why. Although not in the first flush of youth, the lady was possibly of an age with Gabriel, she had drawn the eye of every man in the room. Why then was her husband seemingly immune to the lady's charms?

The dance ended and Bendor filled Eleanor in. 'Gabriel and Lady Berwick met at a house party at Dunstanburgh, it would have been when he and Caroline had ended their engagement I think because I remember my mother, God rest her soul, was playing matchmaker.'

'Matching him with Lady Berwick?'

'Good Lord no, with Cora or Jane. Lady B had an old rich husband and as she'd provided him with an heir she felt obliged to play the field as it were. Her extra marital dalliances were legendary. She was hardly discreet and quite voracious in her appetites. Not that I speak from first hand experience you understand, but several of my acquaintances would testify to her enthusiasm.'

'I see. So are you telling me Gabriel was one of her dalliances?' Eleanor wasn't sure how she felt about this turn of events. She knew he had a past obviously, and she knew he would have had relationships with gorgeous women before his marriage, after all he was a good looking man, but she had never *seen* any of them... apart from Caroline...and Libby. This was different somehow. Lady Berwick was possibly one of the most striking women she had ever laid eyes on.

'No no no! Quite the reverse Eleanor.' Bendor took her arm to lead her back to her husband. 'Now I come to think of it I remember he'd recently met you. He was quite smitten - with you I mean, but there was some complication or other between you, I don't remember what exactly.'

They'd arrived back at their group. Gabriel looked at her like a drowning man looks at his rescuer. 'Ah, here's the lady in question, Eleanor I was just pointing you out. Lady Berwick this is my wife Eleanor.'

'Gabriel, please are we not old friends? Call me Marguerite. I'm pleased to make your acquaintance Mrs Reynolds.'

The two ladies greeted each other just as Charles joined them. There was much bonhomie as the men in the group ragged him about his magnificent home.

'I don't believe we have been introduced,' Lady Berwick said looking admiringly at her host. 'Of course it was your brother Claude who issued my invitation for this evening, we're old friends.'

Gabriel did the honours. It was perfectly clear to all, there was an instant mutual appreciation the moment Marguerite and Charles were introduced.

'It's quite warm in here is it not Captain Noble? Would you do me the honour of showing me what you've done with the gardens?'

'Of course, it would be my pleasure.'

The rest of the group watched them move off.

'You know Ben, if I'm not very much mistaken that was the same line she used to try to trap me all those years ago!' Gabriel looked astonished then laughed.

'Charles hardly appears trapped Gabe, he looks a willing conspirator to me.' The men helped themselves to more wine. 'I'll wager Marguerite won't be as interested in the plumbing arrangements as our wives,' Bendor muttered under his breath.

Eleanor noticed Violet sitting with her sister-in-law. She had obviously seen her husband head for the gardens with a ravishing lady on his arm. Eleanor thought it the height of bad manners Charles hadn't introduced Lady Berwick to his wife.

'Excuse me a moment my love,' Eleanor said making a bee line for

Violet. Both ladies expected to be delivered of their offspring in December, and so consequently they were both quite noticeably big with child. Eleanor remembered how she had felt the first time she was pregnant; it had done nothing for her confidence. She had often compared herself unfavourably to other women, Bryony Swift sprang to mind. She wondered if seeing her husband escorting a stunningly handsome woman had a similar effect on Violet.

'South Point is a triumph Violet; you must be thrilled with how it's turned out.'

'Thank you, we are but there is still much to do. Not all the rooms are ready but the majority of the building work is done. There is still plenty for the decorators to do and there is also quite a lot of landscaping to finish in the spring should it ever stop raining.'

This gave Eleanor the opening she had hoped for. 'Would you show me what progress has been made in the gardens? It's not raining now.'

The two ladies made their way outside. Braziers had been lit so although it was dark they could see where to walk. Although she and Violet hadn't always got on, Eleanor felt protective of Violet. From what Eleanor had witnessed Lady Berwick's eye was firmly fixed on Charles and if her reputation was anything to go by a mere trifle like a wife would not stand in her way. Charles was as handsome as Lady Berwick was beautiful. They made a quite a pair. Eleanor looked about, but could see neither of them.

After a stroll around the garden with Violet telling Eleanor of her plans they returned to the ballroom. Eleanor excused herself and went back to her husband. He glanced at her suspiciously. 'You've been up to something. Trying to avert a major incident?' he whispered so their friends didn't overhear.

'I know Charles is an old friend, but did you see the way he and Lady Berwick looked at each other? No good can come of this Gabriel if what Bendor says is true. I thought him better than that.'

'His was an arranged marriage and should Violet produce a male heir, well then.' Gabriel shrugged. 'Is it not inevitable Charles will stray from time to time?'

Eleanor knew this to be true. 'But I thought he and Violet were making something of their marriage. Did he not say he was more content than he thought he'd be?'

'He's a man...'

Eleanor could see Gabriel was expecting her to retaliate vociferously, but she was old enough and wise enough to know what he said was probably true so she kept her own counsel. It didn't stop her from feeling sorry for Violet or angry with Charles. If he was going to start a *flirtation* then at least he should have the good manners not to make it so obvious.

After supper the usual set of friends chatted; Cecily and Lady Berwick joined them. Eleanor watched Marguerite Strachan like a hawk for any tell tale signs that she and Charles had planned an assignation. Would he really be brazen enough to consort with another woman under his own roof?

'Might it not suit Lady, er, I mean Marguerite well my love?' Eleanor realised she hadn't been paying attention.

'Sorry what were you saying Gabriel?'

'Marguerite was saying she's thinking of moving from Rothbury to the coast. She's looking for a house to let hereabouts. Now Charles and Violet have moved out I suggested Eastshore might fit the bill.'

Eleanor was horrified but could hardly say so. 'I'm sure it wouldn't be suitable. It's not so big and it's quite dark is it not Charles?' She pierced him with a look.

'We found Eastshore perfectly comfortable. Perhaps it looks dark to you Eleanor because Westshore is so light and airy, but I didn't find the house oppressive, in fact it was quite cosy. The landlady however was a tad exacting.' He grinned boyishly. Eleanor ignored his little joke; she was annoyed with him on Violet's behalf.

Eleanor wondered if Lady Berwick's wish to remove to the coast was a sudden whim brought about by the man she had just met and obviously admired so much or if it was more long standing. She knew which her money was on.

'The landlady? Does an agent not deal with the lease?'

'He does, Charles is teasing you Lady Berwick,' Violent

intervened. 'Mrs Reynolds owns the property, but I can assure you she's nothing but fair. However, I agree with Eleanor, Eastshore is perhaps a little small for you having only twelve bedrooms. Here we shall have over twenty five guest bedrooms available when all the decorations are complete.'

'On the contrary, a small establishment by the sea might be just the ticket. I should of course keep my house on in Rothbury. When my husband died he left it to me along with a hunting lodge in The Highlands and a house in Cork. He also left me a townhouse in Grosvenor Square which is useful for the season. My son is at Harrow so I can see him when I'm in London. If the lease were a short one it would suit me admirably.'

Eleanor was quick to seize the opportunity. 'We only let for a minimum of a year I'm afraid, it doesn't make commercial sense to lease for less.'

Although Violet wasn't exactly a close friend it still rankled that another woman should try to steal Charles away, if of course that's what Lady Berwick intended.

'A year would be perfect. Let me think on it... perhaps after a good night's sleep I shall be clearer in my expectations.'

Eleanor was furious; she guessed the last thing the woman had her mind on was sleep. Somehow Eleanor had been backed into a corner by this odious woman. She had a good mind to tell the agent not to let it to her.

Gabriel came to her aid. 'May I suggest Marguerite you approach the agent? For all we know he may have someone else already lined up, he's a good man, works hard on our behalf. Perhaps I spoke out of turn.' He cast a look of apology at his wife. Eleanor knew he hadn't meant any harm by the suggestion so she forgave him and smiled back.

Later Gabriel, Wilson and Bendor found themselves without their wives on the terrace.

'So Marguerite is thinking of removing from Rothbury to avail herself of the sea air, or has she run out of conquests in her own environs I wonder?'

Gabriel said: 'I knew her husband was ancient, but I didn't know he'd died, you never said Ben.'

'Why would I? You never had any interest in that direction. He's been gone three, maybe four years. She's been abroad, for her health... if you get my drift, perfecting her craft, learning foreign ways.' He raised an eyebrow. 'She's a distant cousin Wilson and one with a bit of a reputation where gentlemen are concerned.'

'So I gathered. She's clearly taken a fancy to Charles. She's striking I have to admit.' At that moment the man in question came to join them. 'Do I hear my name being mentioned? Is it in vain?' he asked jovially.

'You'll be hearing your name mentioned a whole lot more if you take up with Lady Berwick. I don't think Marguerite is known for her discretion. Indeed she possibly has a scoring system set up. I'd watch out, you might come down the list. She probably broadcasts her rankings to her friends so they can compare notes.' Bendor punched Charles on the shoulder playfully.

'I've no worries on that score, I've picked up a few tricks of my own on my travels,' he said laughing. 'But what's a man to do when he finds himself without? Vi's bedroom door is not just locked to me it's bolted for the duration of her confinement.' He winked at his friends. 'Surely you've *wandered* when your wives have been in the family way. A man has needs, needs that are used to being fulfilled. Of course I'd never force myself on Vi even though I'd be perfectly within my rights but when I was in the navy there was always another port and another woman. I'm not used to short rations.'

'My wife's door is never locked, she knows when she's well off,' Bendor quipped, 'but had it been I still wouldn't have strayed. It's different for you Charles, you didn't marry for love whereas I did.'

'You must admit the lady in question is a stunner.' Charles glanced to where Marguerite stood, a crowd of admirers surrounded her. 'She tells me she met you before you were married Gabriel. Did you venture there? I got the feeling you didn't get on board though I can't imagine why you wouldn't avail yourself.'

'She's a striking woman as you say, but we all have different tastes. As I recall I'd just met Eleanor, briefly that is, and I was like a love struck puppy.' He thought it not to anyone's advantage to say he thought Lady Berwick attractive but arrogant and self entitled; both traits he had found off putting. Gabriel saw George Black out of the corner of his eye.

'George come and join us,' Gabriel beckoned the lawyer over. He introduced him to Wilson and Bendor. He had already met Charles at Saul Coates' house. After he had thanked his host for the invitation and after praising South Point he turned to speak with Gabriel. 'Thank you again Gabriel for allowing me to correspond with your ward. I shall write to her shortly, thought I would give her chance to settle in first.'

'Thank Rebecca not me. I asked her if she minded and she said not so there it is. Only time will tell whether anything comes of it I suppose. How are you settling in George? I hear you've removed to Lesbury Lodge.'

'Sophia and I feel at home already thank you. You must come to sup again soon.'

'And our daughters must meet up too, Rose would like that I know.'

The evening came to a close and Eleanor and Gabriel retired to their allotted bedchamber which was in fact a suite of four rooms consisting of two dressing rooms, a sitting room and a bedchamber the size of the paddock at the back of Westshore. Eleanor was vastly impressed.

R

The next morning, Eleanor was aggrieved to observe, Lady Berwick failed to make an appearance at the breakfast table. Gabriel had told her about the time the lady had tried to seduce him. She had tied a ribbon to her door handle so he would know which room was hers. Eleanor wondered if there had been any nocturnal wanderings and ribbon tying the night before. She hoped not for Violet's sake.

Eleanor and Gabriel left South Point a little before midday and arrived back at Westshore to find Rose had a sore throat and a chesty cough. Eleanor immediately felt guilty for leaving her child overnight. She sent for Wilson who prescribed bed rest and linctus.

'Is it quinsy?' Eleanor asked.

'I don't think so; I can't see anything to indicate the condition. Fear not Eleanor, it's just a sore throat, Rose is prone to them I fear.'

Eleanor agreed she was and was pacified. She tried not to fuss but stayed within earshot of her daughter for two days.

On the third day Lady Berwick was announced much inconveniencing Eleanor. Rose was much better and back at her lessons with Mr Pater but Eleanor had had a disturbed night as the baby had been particularly active recently. She felt tired as a result. The thought of a morning call from a beautiful woman was vexing. The two ladies sat either side of the blazing fire to drink tea.

'I came to say, as I'm sure you must be aware, that I have taken Eastshore. I'm thrilled with the house. I expect your agent has informed you Mrs Reynolds.'

Eleanor was annoyed with herself for not getting in touch with Mr Clark. She had meant to tell him not to let it to Lady Berwick under any circumstances, but with Rose being ill on their return from South Point it had gone clean out of her head.

'I've been staying at North Point with Claude and his brood, but I'm keen not to put upon him for much longer. I'm to move into Eastshore on the first of November, in two days time.' Eleanor was angry but it was too late to do anything about it now. 'As we're to be neighbours please call me Marguerite.'

Eleanor remembered her manners and tried to be more civil. 'In that case allow me to welcome you to Alnmouth. Marguerite is the name of a flower is it not?'

'It is. It is in the daisy family. Daisy was my late husband's pet name for me.'

'Our daughter is named after a flower, she's called Rose. Flowers make for pretty names do they not? Charles' wife also has a flower name. She's called Violet but I expect you remember that from when you were introduced the other evening.'

Eleanor looked pointedly at her new tenant but Marguerite only smiled sweetly.

'Shall you call your next offspring by a flower name if it's a girl? You could have a whole bunch of them.' Marguerite was amused at the idea.

'We have a name in mind but if it's a girl she won't be named after a flower this time.' Eleanor shifted her weight, which in this blasted woman's company felt immense, to try to get more comfortable. 'I understand you have a son?'

'Geoffrey was named after his father. He's going to be thirteen in December, how time flies. He's at Harrow so I don't see him as often as I would like. Such a lovely boy; I dote on him as you must with your sons. Your husband tells me you have twins in addition to your daughter.'

'The boys can be boisterous at times, they're spoilt I fear. Have you never thought to marry again Marguerite?' Eleanor poured more tea.

Lady Berwick looked sceptically at her new neighbour. 'Why on earth would I do that Eleanor? When my husband passed he left me a wealthy woman. All that I own will one day be left to my son. If I remarried all my worldly goods would then be bestowed on another man to do with as he wished. Who's to say he'd take care of my fortune and more importantly a step-son? Another reason I'd never marry again, an exceedingly important reason I might add, is I shouldn't want my freedom curtailed. I'm my own mistress you understand; I come and go as I please without anyone telling me what to do, or where to go. I married for position and now that I have it I'm not about to surrender it. Why would I?'

'I see your point. If, God forbid, something should happen to my husband I'd not marry again either. No one could ever match up to Gabriel. He's a wonderful husband and father, there's none better. We both married for love of course.' The baby kicked making Eleanor almost spill her tea. 'I don't blame you at all for not wanting to marry again for the reasons you've stated, I should feel the same in your position, but are you not lonely without someone with whom to share your life?'

Marguerite smiled emphatically. 'My dear, I'm never without company if I want it... and I often want it I find. I've been in Venice and I had as much company as a lady can manage I can assure you.' She smiled knowingly. 'In fact I came home to get away from *too* much company.' Again the tinkling, confident laugh. 'I intend to take things easy for a while here in Alnmouth, after I've given a little party at Eastshore to get to know my new neighbours.'

R

Gabriel strode along the quay towards The Hope and Anchor. He had thought to slake his thirst before going home to dine when he saw Charles coming to greet him. The two friends settled themselves at a corner table where there would have been a view along the bay had it not been for the rain lashing against the window.

'What brings you here this wet and windy day? I'd have thought you would be tucked up in your warm, dry palace.' Gabriel took a gulp of his porter. 'Eleanor was most impressed with South Point and is now planning all sorts of improvements at Westshore, not least of which is new livery for the servants. Thank you Charles, it's going to cost me a packet.'

Charles shrugged and laughed. He looked through the dimpled window as the rain splattered hard against it. 'You know it's odd, but even in this weather I miss the sea. I've never been on dry land for so long; well not since I was fourteen anyway. Lately I've often wished I'd not resigned my commission. I've an idea to get in touch with the Admiralty, see if I can't be of use somehow. There's trouble brewing with France again.'

'There's always trouble with France. When you say offer your services in what capacity do you mean? You'd go back to sea?'

'Before we wed I promised Vi I wouldn't sign on again so no, but in another role perhaps. Men will be needed to see what's happening on the ground in France I'd wager.'

'Spying you mean.'

'Observing,' he said wryly. 'Reporting back *unofficially* about what's being planned.' He sighed and drank off his rum, then raised his hand to order more. 'I lack stimulus now South Point is almost finished. The plans and the building have kept me occupied for months but now I feel at a loose end and believe me when I get bored... '

'What, you chase women to alleviate the tedium?'

'Something like that.' Charles gave his friend a sideways look.

'Anyone caught your eye Charles?'

'I'm far too discreet to say Gabe.'

Later when he arrived home late for dinner Gabriel noticed Eleanor looked tired. He knew she'd had a sleepless night.

'I had a visit from Marguerite Strachan this morning,' she told him not looking at all pleased. 'She's taken Eastshore.'

'You should be happy, since you bought the place it's been let all the time. That's a good return on your investment in anyone's book. How's Rose?'

'Back in the schoolroom I'm pleased to say. The linctus Wilson gives her usually does the trick. Last winter she suffered sore throats, but the medicine cleared it up quick enough. She had a good night's sleep, unlike me. I think this baby is going to be a street fighter. It's never still of late and for some reason it's awake when I'm trying to sleep.'

'Poor you. Why not have a lie down after dinner, put your feet up.' He stroked her arm. 'Charles and I met up and went for a drink and like our unborn child he too is restless.'

'In what way restless?'

'He's thinking of taking on a role at the Admiralty, not joining up again but perhaps working in a different capacity.'

Carver brought a note which curtailed their discourse. 'It's for Charles from South Point, asking him to go home straight away, Violet's labours have begun. I thought she was due at about the same time as you?'

'That's true. She's premature in that case. Oh dear, I hope she and the baby are going to be alright. Still she's only four weeks early so there should be no real danger; perhaps she got her dates mixed up.'

'Charles should be home by now, when we parted he said he was heading straight for South Point. I'll send a note and say he should be back within the hour although he'll possibly be home before my note gets there.'

Carver announced Wilson Chaffer who had come to check up on Rose. Gabriel excused himself to write the note.

'I'm so sorry you had a wasted journey Wilson,' Eleanor said, 'she's much better thank goodness. The linctus did the trick again.'

'No matter, I was passing anyway. I've seen three cases of septic throat this week and I wanted to make sure my goddaughter wasn't suffering. If as you say she's at her lessons she must be well enough.'

'I'm surprised you're not attending Violet Noble,' Gabriel said on his return. 'Her baby is on its way apparently, we just had a note from South Point. Charles is missing in action, but why they thought he was here I've no idea, though I did see him earlier at the bay.'

'South Point is a little too far from Wooden House for me to consider her as a patient. I said I'd gladly wait on Violet but suggested they'd do better to engage Dr Elgar as he's practically on their doorstep. She's early is she not Eleanor?'

Carver brought another note. 'It's like Whitby harbour here today!' Gabriel said as he read the note. 'It's from Lottie; she says there's a message from South Point asking if you can attend Violet as Dr Elgar isn't available.'

'Oh well, the best laid plans... I must be off then. I told Lottie I was calling to see Rose, she remembered it appears.' He downed the rum Gabriel handed him.

'I'm sure someone will let you know when Violet is delivered. It will be some time yet I expect. First babies like to dawdle in my experience.'

R

It was just before supper the next evening when a message arrived from South Point saying Violet had been delivered of a boy weighing less than five pounds. The note said although Violet was well the baby wasn't expected to live. He had been born blue and was struggling to hold onto life.

'I should go to see Charles, he'll need all the support he can get I imagine, poor Violet.'

Eleanor sank onto a chair, visibly shocked. Gabriel took her hand. 'Hold hard my love, I know this is upsetting news but try not to get agitated.'

Eleanor's pregnancy so far had been straightforward, unlike when she was expecting the twins when she had swooned for months before the birth. Gabriel saw her take a long steadying breath.

'What a nightmare for them, let's pray the baby pulls through. By all means go and see Charles, you're right to think he may need a friend to lean on.'

'I'll go after supper. I don't want to leave you now. I want to keep my eye on you. After we sup you could get an early night.'

Having persuaded his wife to go to bed, Gabriel arrived at South Point in a howling gale. The white-wigged footman showed him into the study where Claude was availing himself of the port.

'Good of you to come Gabriel. Charles is aloft with Dr Chaffer who's still here keeping an eye on mother and child. For how long there will be a child is anyone's guess. They've told Violet to expect the worst and Charles says she's taken the news well considering.'

'How devastating for them; as fathers you and I know what they must be going through.'

Wilson, looking dog tired, came into the study and collapsed into a chair. He had slept not at all for thirty six hours. 'I'm heading home to get my head down, but I'll be back in the morning. I've told Charles not to hesitate to send for me if there's any change.' He hauled himself from the chair with difficulty.

'Thank you Chaffer, sterling effort.' Claude showed him to the door. 'Leave your horse here, I've had the carriage readied, I don't want you falling off your nag in this weather. Go home and get some well deserved sleep. Send your bill to me.'

When they were alone again Claude shook his head. 'Charles is feeling bad of course not to mention a little guilty.'

'Oh, why's that?'

'When Violet began her pains her errant husband was nowhere to be found. Turns out he'd been in the throes of passion whilst his poor wife had been in the throes of childbirth.'

'With whom, dare I ask?'

'Lord knows - I'm no model husband but I'm only glad I'm not in his shoes. Charles is a good fellow; he'll take it hard if the boy doesn't survive.'

Charles, tired and pale, joined them. 'Gabriel, you shouldn't have come on such a vile night, but I thank you all the same. Wilson gave Violet a draught and she's sleeping, she's done in. However, he thinks she's out of the woods. Wilson said rest will see her right.'

'And the baby?'

'Charles, for that is the name he's been christened, Vi couldn't rest until the vicar was sent for in case... Charles is still struggling on although he has better colour than when he was first born. You know Violet is a remarkable woman; she won't hear of the baby... well you know. Says her son is a fighter. I only wish I had her faith for he looks a sickly little thing to my eyes.' He fell into a chair and put his head in his hands.

The three men drowned their sorrows as a vigil was kept for the baby.

Much later back at Westshore, Gabriel tiptoed into the bedroom. He needn't have bothered as he found Eleanor wide awake. She struggled to sit up.

'What news my love?'

'You should be sleeping. He took her hand as he sat on the bed. 'Violet is rallying, but the

boy is clinging on so far thank God, but for how long is anyone's guess. Why are you awake?'

'Ask the bruiser in my belly. I've had not a moment's peace for the last two hours, before that I did sleep a little. Under the circumstances I'm not complaining as it shows the baby is strong does it not?'

‘We can but hope.’

He undressed and climbed wearily into bed. She snuggled into him. ‘Try to get some sleep Gabriel, you look worn out too.’

He told her about Wilson’s dedication to duty.

‘Knowing him he’ll be back at South Point at the crack of dawn, unless of course he’s sent for before.’

In the event the good doctor got a sound night’s sleep. When he arrived at South Point the next morning he found a well rested new mother and a baby who had fed from his wet nurse twice during the night. Although Wilson was encouraged by the progress and wanted to say there was every reason to be hopeful, he knew from past experience not to say too much. Often sickly, premature babies looked about to pull through only to fade quickly and die. He kept his own counsel and was thankful Violet at least appeared better than he had dared hope. It had been a difficult birthing, and although she was a strong woman, if he wasn’t very much mistaken her ordeal was not over yet. There was the threat of childbed fever for a few days to come.

In the event this time, unusually, the good doctor’s prognosis was wrong.

R

A week later when mother and baby were gaining strength daily, Eleanor sent a basket of fruit and asked when she could visit the newborn. Charles sent a note by return thanking her but saying Violet was not quite up to callers just yet. He said she sat by her son’s crib from morning until night and he would let her know immediately when Violet was receiving visitors.

Reluctantly Eleanor decided she ought to return Lady Berwick’s call instead. She knew it was bad form not to, especially as that morning they had received an invitation to a supper party to be held the following week.

Eleanor was shown into the morning room at Eastshore. Just as before when Violet had been in residence Eleanor was irrationally surprised to see another lady, other than Caroline, presiding over the tea table. After greetings and pleasantries had been dispensed with Lady Berwick, dressed elegantly in a deep purple day dress that fitted her curves perfectly, astounded Eleanor by saying she was to go to London for a month or two after next week's party.

'Oh, I imagined you'd stay in Alnmouth a little while as you've only recently arrived. I'm surprised.'

'My son will be home from school for the holidays so we can stay at Grosvenor Square for the festive season.' She looked a little on edge. Eleanor noticed the lady's eyes kept flitting to the clock on the mantle shelf. 'Geoffrey would spend half his holiday in a carriage otherwise. I shall return in January, weather permitting of course.'

Lady Berwick patted her perfectly coiffed pale-blonde hair even though there was not a hair out of place. An uneasy silence fell as the ormolu mantel clock struck the quarter hour. It sounded unnaturally loud to Eleanor's ear. She had the distinct impression Lady Berwick was expecting a caller; a gentleman caller perhaps? Eleanor hoped it wasn't Charles, though she thought perhaps it was. If it was Charles then Eleanor would be aggrieved; she had always liked him, but now she was perhaps seeing him in a different light. If he was conducting an affair with Marguerite Strachan then he had gone down in her estimations. He would no longer be noble by name and noble by nature in her opinion. To have an affair at any time was despicable to Eleanor's mind, but to have one when your wife was recovering from delivering a son and when that son had been at death's door was reprehensible.

After a few desultory comments Eleanor made to leave. 'If you need anything please don't hesitate to let my agent know. I'll take my leave and see you next week, thank you for the invitation Marguerite, goodbye.'

Relief spread across Lady Berwick's face like a cloud revealing the sun on a rainy day. Eleanor was shown out by the faithful Ribble. As he helped her into her carriage she tested the water. 'How are you finding your new employer Ribble? A change again is it not? First the Nobles and now Lady Berwick, but at least they have kept you employed which is something.'

'It is indeed Mrs Reynolds. I cannot complain.'

'It looks like you'll have an easy time over Christmas. Lady Berwick tells me she's to be away until late January.'

'I hadn't heard, but I'm sure the staff will be pleased to hear it. Lady Berwick is not a hard taskmaster, but I'm not used to staying up late to see guests in and out at all hours.' He coughed awkwardly realising he had said more than he ought. He thought to make amends. 'Lady Berwick, like a lot of her class I assume, likes to keep London hours. My lady receives callers much later than we are used to in these parts.'

'Is that so? Gentleman callers would that be Ribble?' She slipped a coin into the footman's hand.

'Ladies hereabouts don't tend to keep such late hours Mrs Reynolds as I'm sure you are aware, especially not on cold winter nights.'

'Indeed. And is the caller always the same gentleman or...?'

'So far as I am aware the caller has been the same gentleman Mrs Reynolds, but then Lady Berwick has only been in residence a short while so who knows, she may yet have need of a change.' He struggled to keep the smirk from his face as she took her seat.

'She may well indeed.'

Eleanor knew she was no wiser; she still didn't know for certain it was Charles who was the late night visitor. But if not him, then who?

R

On the night of Lady Berwick's supper party Eleanor deemed herself too large to be seen in public. She also felt too tired to go so asked Gabriel to give her apologies. Eleanor persuaded him that one of them should attend so as not to appear rude. Not keen to go alone, he said he would not stay late.

In the drawing room of Eastshore, Marguerite Strachan was surrounded by a group of men all eager for her attention. Gabriel didn't recognise any of them. She waved her fan in his direction in way of a greeting when she saw him. Gabriel made a bee line for Saul Coates and his wife Rosalind. Their daughter Felicity and George Black were also in the group. After they had asked after Eleanor's health, Gabriel mentioned he had received a letter from Rebecca.

'We had one too, from Mary,' Rosalind said. 'They are enjoying themselves I think Gabriel?'

'It appears so. They're busy preparing for a ball, it all sounds incredibly grand.'

'It's The Autumn Ball which the school holds every year,' Felicity said. 'The one I attended was magnificent. There were sleighs to take us to the chateau in the mountains and ice sculptures on all the tables. I'm quite envious they're getting to experience it all.'

'You attended the same finishing school Miss Coates?' George asked.

'Two years ago sir, it was on my recommendation Mary and Rebecca went to Switzerland.'

At supper Gabriel sat next to a pretty blonde he had never met before. She was a friend of Lady Berwick's from her days in Scotland it appeared. While she was not a patch on her friend, Margaret Lacy was a pleasant enough supper companion. Felicity was placed next to George and Gabriel saw they were getting along well. He had always liked Felicity and wondered if she had hopes where George was concerned. She must be over twenty now and would be looking to settle down perhaps. Did he have an eye on Fliss Gabriel wondered. Perhaps since their discussion about Rebecca he had changed his mind, after all she would be gone a year and Fliss was here and seemingly available. Gabriel wished Eleanor was here; she would have been able to tell in one glance what was on George's mind, whether he was flirting, or merely being attentive to his new business partner's daughter.

After supper the men took their port. Charles and Claude who had arrived late headed straight for the library where gaming tables had been set up. There was also dancing for those who were so inclined.

Marguerite, along with her friend Margaret, joined Gabriel and

George as they entered the drawing room. Gabriel thought it was almost as if the pair had been lying in wait for them.

'Why I wonder,' Marguerite said to Margaret in what she thought was a playful manner, 'do the men linger over the port so long when there are ladies waiting to attend them? Is it not a mystery?'

'It is no mystery Lady Berwick. You should consider providing a more inferior port then the gentlemen would be eager to leave it,' George said.

Lady Berwick looked George up and down. 'I think there's a compliment in there somewhere Margaret, but we'll forgive you both as you're here now and that's all that matters.'

George asked the hostess to dance and was accepted. Gabriel, who wasn't intending to make a night of it, wasn't keen to dance. He saw Margaret look at him expectantly, but he wouldn't be drawn. He glanced about the room looking for a friendly face. He was saved further embarrassment when Saul and Rosalind joined them. Saul asked Margaret Lacey to dance and led her off.

Rosalind watched George dancing with Lady Berwick. She leaned into Gabriel. 'They make a handsome couple do they not?' Her tone of voice told him she didn't approve. Perhaps she was hoping Fliss would catch the wealthy lawyer herself.

'There's nothing to worry about in that regard Rosalind, Lady Berwick isn't the marrying kind.' Rosalind's eyebrows shot up. Gabriel could see he had been a little too forthright. He must have caught it from Eleanor. He tried to make amends. 'I thought George was charmed with Fliss at supper. They appeared to be enjoying each other's company exceedingly well.'

'Indeed they did. He has dined and supped with us often over the past months whilst he's been meeting with my husband over the merger. He's shown a keen interest in Felicity but I'm not sure how serious he is in his attentions. Fliss says he has been complimentary, but who knows with men these days. If he pays my daughter notice tonight Saul will expect him to speak his mind otherwise people will begin to talk.'

Gabriel decided not to mention George had also dined at

Westshore on occasions and had been similarly disposed towards Rebecca. He was glad his ward was abroad. At least if George had turned his coat she would not be witness to his duplicity. Much to Rosalind's consternation George danced two more dances with Lady Berwick before finally asking Felicity to dance the gavotte.

After a hand or two at cards Gabriel made his excuses to leave. He began the ride home in a thoughtful mood. Something strange had occurred to him as he pointed Copper in the right direction. If he wasn't very much mistaken it was not George Black Marguerite Strachan had her sights on. Gabriel had seen the knowing looks pass between her and another gentleman and both had appeared to understand their meaning. He wondered if Eleanor suspected. On reflection he thought not.

19

December roared in with heavy snow which came early for this of part of the North East coast. Often they avoided snow all winter, but if it did come it usually came in January. By the end of the first week rain washed away any remnants of the white stuff which the children had enjoyed so much. There had been snowball fights and snow castles built in the garden. The last time there had been this much snow the twins had been too young to appreciate it, but this time the children enjoyed themselves enormously.

One foggy day Eleanor was surprised with a morning call from Violet Noble. Since the birth of baby Charles this was the first call Violet had made on Eleanor for a long time.

Violet wearing a well cut, but mud splattered riding habit, strode into the morning room. She looked mannish rather than elegant. After pleasantries had been observed she sat awkwardly on the edge of a sofa. She was also wearing a fur hat which sported three pheasant feathers; they made her look tall even though she was sitting down. Her boots would have given Rebecca's a run for their money; the ones Becky had walked miles in when she had run away from school that is. Violet's wary eyes stared at her host. Eleanor wondered if Violet had been to finishing school. She thought not because she was sure they would have told her it was rude to stare. Violet removed her hat and placed it on the sofa beside her. It looked like something she had shot on the way.

Since getting to know her a little better at various house parties, Eleanor realised what others saw as aloofness was possibly a lack of confidence. A socially awkward appearance meant people did not warm to Violet, not like they did to her husband. The people hereabouts liked Charles; he was one of them. They tolerated Violet because she was his wife. It was, as many commented behind their fans, a strange coupling; Charles was easy company, socially competent and likeable. Violet was prickly, uncommunicative and appeared to look down her nose at everyone. Eleanor wondered why she had been honoured with a visit.

'You're soon back in the saddle. Charles Junior is doing better I hope?' Eleanor ventured.

'We both are, and he's as fat as a pig ready for market.' Eleanor noted Violent didn't suffer post baby weight; she was ramrod thin.

'Thank you for the fruit basket, it was thoughtful.' Violet strived for a smile, but didn't quite manage to find one. Another thing about Violet was she found little to smile about. Again this was contrary to Charles as he was full of good humour and fun. Eleanor noticed Violet didn't ask after her own health or about the health of her family. There was never any idle talk where Violet was concerned, she was unaffected by stony silences. Eleanor knew she was the one who was going to have to keep the conversation afloat or it would sink without trace.

'I hear Charles is thinking of becoming a ship broker.'

'Is he? I had no idea. What is that?'

'He'll sell space for cargo.'

Violet looked nonplussed. 'Why I wonder would a gentleman seek work when he has the means to please himself. He hasn't told me of his plans,' she said shrugging.

'He does not discuss his thoughts with you, ask for your opinion?'

'Why would he? I'm his wife not his steward.'

'I don't know... Gabriel and I share everything, views, opinions, plans, ideas. It's what marriage is about.' Eleanor then felt she had spoken out of turn; Violet's marriage wasn't a love match, it had been arranged and so it was probably conducted on very different terms to her own.

Violet broke a biscuit in half and crumbled it in her napkin absentmindedly. She swallowed hard as if deciding whether to speak then at a rush said: 'Charles doesn't need to consult with me about anything, especially about becoming a merchant. Why would he? He doesn't care what I think. Charles is amicable, thoughtful to some extent, and adores the baby, but how to do that, how to get Charles to talk to me about anything but the weather?'

It was the longest speech Eleanor had ever heard Violet utter.

'Forgive me, but I think you're wrong, he does care.' Eleanor remembered Charles had said he admired his wife and that his marriage was far from the disaster he had thought it might be. It was damning with faint praise but nevertheless Eleanor had thought he meant it. 'Perhaps he doesn't *show* he cares, most men don't. They're strange creatures sometimes.'

'Oh.'

'Can I be forward and ask you what you may think is an impertinent question?' Eleanor asked bravely.

'Very well, but I reserve the right not to answer if it's too impudent.'

Eleanor stopped herself from sighing. 'The question is Violet do you want to have a happy marriage or are you content to live separate lives in the same house?'

Violet looked suspiciously at Eleanor. 'I don't know what you mean, who says we aren't happy?'

'Can I then ask another question?' She didn't wait for an answer. 'Charles appears a good man, he's attractive, fun loving. Might you love Charles, love him enough to ask him *his* thoughts and feelings? Enough to find out who your husband really is? Behind closed doors I mean.'

Violet thought for a long moment. She sat up straight and put her tea down, spilling some of it on the tablecloth.

'Love? I admire Charles in some ways, he is as you say well respected, liked, but tell me honestly would you, in my place, be predisposed to love a man who married you for your dowry? Would you fawn over a man who didn't notice you were in the room? Pander to his vanity? It is beneath my dignity. Under those circumstances would you risk an attachment, risk loving someone who had the capability to hurt you? I would feel it beneath me to give him the satisfaction of knowing I had any regard for him. We know little about one another but I believe he is content with the marriage.'

'But are *you* content with your marriage? It seems you do have *some* feelings for your husband as you are a little protective of your heart, a little frightened to show your hand in case you're rejected.' Eleanor realised the woman was about to either blow up or storm out of the room. The look on her face was hard to read. Undeterred Eleanor ploughed on. 'Marriage is forever and building on flimsy foundations might be costly. Does he tell you he loves you? Oh, I'm sorry Violet that's none of my business, I go too far. Forgive me I beg you.'

Again there was a long pause while Violet thought about what Eleanor had said. 'I believe marriage is about compromise, on the woman's side that is, men can do as they choose.' Violet looked thoughtful. In almost a whisper she said: 'He *says* he loves me, but it's just his way. I know there's no feeling behind the words. He says what he's expected to say. Don't all men? I'm his wife and he says and does what a husband should within the confines of his home. What he does beyond South Point is not my business. At home he's a gentleman and treats me as a lady expects to be treated.'

'Why do you not believe him when he says he loves you? How do you *know* he doesn't love you?' Eleanor waited until Violet had drained her dish of tea.

'He can't love me, why would he? I don't possess ladylike accomplishments. I ride, hunt, shoot arrows, but I don't sing well, sew or prattle on about the latest fashions. I don't know how and I don't care to know how, that sort of thing bores me. I'm not delicate; I don't need pretty words, especially if they aren't true. I'm not the sort of woman men admire and I don't particularly care what people think of me.'

'Good for you. That's precisely why Charles married you I expect. Can you see him being happy with some empty headed, dizzy chit of a girl? He admires you for yourself not whether you can hit the right notes or sew a tablecloth.'

Violent took in air. 'Another reason I know he doesn't love me is because he has a lover. But I don't care, I expected it. I can see how men need to... anyway there it is. A handsome man such as Charles will always have lovers. I wouldn't mention it, but you must know... the whole of Alnmouth must be talking about it. Let them talk if they will, it's not I who is at fault after all, it doesn't reflect badly on me.'

'If they are then I've not heard the gossip. It's news to me. Has he told you? Have you asked him?'

It was true Eleanor had not heard any gossip, but she did suspect Violet was right. She felt nothing but pity for the poor woman; imagine being married to such a man as Charles and knowing he took his pleasure elsewhere. Then she thought again. If he was such a rake then he wasn't loveable was he? If it was Lady Berwick he was consorting with how could any women match up to her beauty and elegance? Eleanor looked at the woman sitting opposite her, her hair looking like a crow's nest, stubbornly adamant her husband didn't care about her. Perhaps she was right and Eleanor was interfering when she should know better. There was another long silence that eventually Eleanor, once again sought to fill.'

'You and I are different people Violet, but if I were you, and I know you say you don't care, but I think possibly you do, then I'd have it out with him. Ask him if he has a lover. *If* he does then I think at least he's being discreet as I can honestly say he's not the talk of the town and Alnmouth is such a small place that once word gets out then everyone knows your business.'

'As you say Eleanor we are not the same. How would I even broach the subject when I find it hard enough to talk to him about anything other than mundane matters? How am I to even think of such a thing? I couldn't possibly ask him and to what end anyway? Surely he would deny it. It's not like I didn't expect my husband to stray, most men do exactly what Charles is doing, whether it's an arranged marriage or not.'

'I suppose you're right. I think I'm lucky - my husband and I are the exception to the rule.' Eleanor shifted in her seat. 'Would you care for more tea?'

'Thank you no, I've taken up too much of your time already I'm sure.' She sat grim faced, but made no effort to leave.

Eventually Eleanor said: 'I realise your marriage is none of my business, but I only want to help if I can. I think you do like, or even love Charles in your own way, but won't allow yourself to let him know. I understand your reasoning and I admire you for it, loving someone is a risky business, but aren't you hurting anyway? If you told him, showed him how much you cared perhaps you might reach an agreement, know each other's ways a little better, not only for your sake but for your son's too. I know this sounds wrongheaded, but perhaps he thinks not to bother you, thinks to take his *pleasure* elsewhere because he thinks *you* don't care for *him*.'

Violet stood up abruptly. 'Are you mad? She retrieved her hat which she had been about to leave behind. 'Now I really must go. Good morning Eleanor.' She strode towards the door then stopped abruptly. 'I hope when the time comes you are delivered safely Eleanor.' There was a moment's pause. 'I don't know you particularly well, but I hope I can trust you not to discuss what we've talked about here this morning with the "friendly sociable ladies" hereabouts.'

'As you say Violet you don't know me at all well, because if you did you wouldn't need to ask that particular question.' Eleanor struggled to her feet as her belly threatened to overbalance her.

Violet turned back. 'Forgive me please, that was rude.'

'Of course, it's forgotten. Good morning Violet, I hope you enjoy your ride home.'

Eleanor let out a long breath. Why is it that each time I begin to like Violet she then says something to put my hackles up again Eleanor wondered as she watched her ride off. Violet Noble was indeed a complex woman, a spiky one but Eleanor couldn't help but like her.

R

By mid December Eleanor was listless. With her due date passed she was eager to get the birth over and done with. She felt well enough, but tired easily and had taken to breaking her fast in bed and later than was usual for her.

For the past week Gabriel had been reluctant to leave her despite him only being a ten minute ride away at the bay. She tried to reason with him. 'When my labours begin it will be hours before anything happens so if I send for you the minute I feel the first twinge you'll still have time to call for a fortifying brandy or two at The Hope and Anchor on your way home.'

'As if I would!' He was horrified at the suggestion. 'If you're sure you'll be alright I'll go, for I see I'm getting on your nerves. Stay abed and see if you can't get some more sleep.'

'I may break my fast first, I'm starving.'

'Over the last month or so you have said nothing else. This baby is as greedy as Rose.' He leaned over and kissed her. 'Send for me the minute you feel a pain, promise me Eleanor.'

'I promise I'll send for Ivy and then for you. After all she'll be more use to me than you.'

'I remember I did quite well last time. By the time Ruari was born I was an expert.'

'So you were. I wonder if there are any kippers left, I fancy a few kippers.'

'What is it about smoked fish? That's all you eat of late, are you not bored with the taste?'

'Not yet. I like kippers.'

'So do I, but not morning, noon and night.'

'You exaggerate. I only have them for breakfast.'

'I've noticed,' he smiled then kissed her. 'This baby will come out kippered.'

As he left the bedroom Molly popped her head around the door. 'Good morning, are you getting up or breakfasting abed first?'

'I'll powder my nose then you can ask Mrs Madison to send up my breakfast.' Eleanor heaved herself to a sitting position then slid her legs out of bed. As she stood her waters broke. 'Oh Lord! At last... I thought this baby would still be in here at Christmas.'

Molly helped Eleanor to sit on the side of the bed. 'I'll go and get

Mr Gabriel, he can't have left yet.'

'No don't.' She grasped her maid's arm. 'It'll be hours before anything happens and you know how he worries. Let him be spared, let him go to the bay. He'll be back for dinner so that will be soon enough for him to be told. I'd rather you sent for Ivy. Similarly we'll send for Dr Sharpe when Ivy has assessed the situation.'

'As you wish, I know better than to argue with you. I'll send to Hope House.' She headed for the door. 'I'll send Dora to - ' She waved her arm at the wet patch on the rug.

'Oh, and get someone to bring the kippers. I still fancy them and they'll sustain me during my ordeal.'

'Shall I bring the brandy wine too and you can have a little party?'

Ivy arrived within the hour. 'It smells of kippers in here.'

'That's because a while ago I broke my waters and then my fast,' Eleanor said a mischievous glint in her eye.

'Looking at you A'd guess this was a false alarm, but you say you're over your time so A'm not sure what to think. How are the pains?'

'Manageable, but gaining in frequency.' She glanced at the clock. 'It's almost midday and I started my labours long before ten.' A contraction took hold and shook her body. Panting she said: 'That's the first proper one I'd say, dear Lord I'd forgotten how they hurt. Stop your ears Ivy, I feel cussing coming on.'

Ivy sent orders for towels and hot water. Eleanor was surprised to see it was Lisbet who brought them.

'A'd a feelin' today were the day so A thought A'd pop over an' see if yer needed a hand.'

'Are you sure you're not a witch Lisbet?' Eleanor asked as another pain started.

'Shall A send for Dr Sharpe? Ivy asked. 'A don't think this baby's going to hang about now it's decided to come, A bet it's a girl.'

'I hope so, but as long as it's healthy we won't mind.' Another spasm surged through her like a riptide. 'Does all look well to you because if it does I'd sooner manage with you if you can cope? You dealt with the twins admirably on your own, or should I say with

Gabriel's help.'

'Lisbet's here now so between us we can manage. A never have a doctor at Hope House unless A have to send for Dr Chaffer when there's a problem. It's all the same to me but you're not a village girl if you see what A mean. Will Mr Gabriel be mad if you don't send for the doctor?'

'Leave Mr Gabriel to me Ivy, he'll be pacified when he's presented with a baby,' Lisbet said firmly.

The next hour saw the matter progress swiftly. It wanted ten minutes to two when the mewling of a baby could be heard. 'You have your wish Mistress. It's a girl, an' she's a good size by the looks of her.'

Eleanor fell back on the bed exhausted. 'Let me see her, oh, she has dark hair and so much of it.'

'A'll sort the baby out and then Lisbet can look to you. A'll get the boy to fetch Mr Gabriel. He's going to be that mad you wouldn't let me send for him sooner.'

'He'll be taken aback but happy to have a daughter.' Eleanor let her old servant sort her out. It was nice having the two women look after her, though she would have dearly liked her mama present. 'There's no point in sending for him now he'll be on his way home for dinner. Send Molly to make me look presentable please Lisbet.'

'When the master comes home he'll have an early Christmas present,' Lisbet said chuckling. 'She has her pa's hair fer sure. I'll make yer some rosehip syrup later. That'll buck yer up, not that yer look like yer need reviving.'

At the same time as Eleanor was readying herself for her husband, Gabriel was riding into the stableyard. Sam came out to greet him. 'I don't remember a colder day,' Gabriel said shivering. 'I'm frozen to the bone. There's no wind to speak of but it's bitterly cold. Look, the frost still hangs on the branches.'

'It's true, the pump's frozen and at this time of day. Even that bit of watery sun isn't helping.'

Gabriel decided getting to his fireside as quickly as possible was expedient. He flung his gauntlets on a chair, warmed his hands by the fire then threw on another log. Finally he went to pour himself a brandy. He was wondering where Eleanor could be when Lisbet came in smiling.

'Ah Lisbet, fancy a tot to warm you up? It's blithering out there as you would say.' He poured his old retainer a snifter.

'Aye it is that.' She took the proffered brandy. 'Congratulations,' she said raising her glass. A tear fell from her eye. 'Don't just stand there yer great lummox go an' meet yer new bairn.'

'What in God's name?' Gabriel took in a deep breath then realised Lisbet's meaning and made for the stairs.

Eleanor was sitting up in bed smiling radiantly. He saw she was holding a bundle.

'How did this happen?'

'In the usual way I expect.'

'Of course, but I mean you weren't in the throes when I left. Why did you not send for me? You promised me faithfully this morning. How can it all be over so quickly?' The words tumbled from him. He hadn't decided yet whether to be angry or thrilled.

'On the first point I did my old trick of crossing my fingers so the promise didn't count, you really should have learnt to check after all this time. And secondly you had hardly stepped out of the door when it all started.'

She looked up at him and his heart melted.

'Stop lecturing Gabriel, and say hello to your daughter Miss Eva Grace Anne Reynolds; all seven pounds and six ounces of her. I think she can accommodate my mother's name as well as she's a good weight.'

He reached down and lifted his daughter into his arms. 'She's beautiful... let's keep her.' He looked sidelong at his wife. 'She's not like Rose at all - black hair like my mother. I can hardly believe it. I go to the bay only to come home for my dinner to find the latest member of the Reynolds family has arrived at last. Better late than never baby Eva. I expect you wanted to make up for lost time by coming so quickly. At any rate you're more than welcome.' Ivy stepped into the room and Gabriel thanked her. She didn't blush at all he noticed. 'Where's Dr Sharpe, don't tell me he was otherwise engaged like last time?'

'Don't blame me Mr Gabriel, you know your wife can be obstinate.'

'We managed well enough with Ivy and Lisbet. It was a drama free birth, no swooning and no dark premonitions from the mother. It all happened so quickly we hardly had time to draw breath. If you want me to see Sharpe then by all means send for him my love, but I feel perfectly well, or I will be when I've had a rest.'

'Ivy, have Mrs Madison feed you before you go back to Hope House, then the carriage will take you back when you're ready. Do the children know?' he asked.

'I'll send them in on my way out,' Ivy said.

A few minutes later the three children filed in led by Rose. Even Haydan looked impressed.

R

Two weeks after the delivery Wilson Chaffer stood by Eva's crib.

'You say she's well in every other way?'

Eleanor had called in Wilson; she was worried Eva wasn't putting on weight as quickly as she should. 'She is, but she doesn't feed at all well. When the twins were ready for a feed they screamed the house down. Eva has such a polite little cry as if she doesn't want to bother anyone. Then she'll feed for a while then go straight back to sleep, even before she's been winded sometimes.'

'I've examined her and can see nothing wrong. It's normal for some babies to lose a little weight after they're born, but you say she's only put on a couple of ounces.' He looked sideways at the anxious mother. 'Have you noticed how long she is? I think she's growing long rather than fat,' he joked. 'She's going to be tall like Gabriel.'

'Long and thin if she doesn't soon take to the breast.' Eleanor puckered her brow. She was trying not to worry, but not quite succeeding.

'There is one idea you could try but you won't like it.'

'Tell me, I'm willing to try anything.'

'When the twins were born Sharpe suggested a wet nurse to ease your burden as you had a difficult birthing; why not try that again? What harm can it do?'

'It may help? Perhaps I don't have enough milk?'

Wilson continued: 'There's a young woman at Hope House who's had her baby adopted. She's a strong healthy woman, not so young, in her mid twenties perhaps, but I think you should engage her. Give her a try for the next couple of weeks and see if there's an improvement. If the baby starts to gain weight all well and good, if she doesn't then we'll try something else. There's nothing to lose as I cannot see anything else amiss. The saving grace is she's not losing weight which would be a worrying development.'

When Eleanor and Wilson joined Gabriel in the drawing room he asked: 'Well do you know what the problem is Wilson? Is she ailing?' It was on his insistence Wilson had been called in. Eleanor was concerned, but she wished she had not shared her worries with him. She knew he was beside himself, over anxious.

'There's no sign of infection, no fever and her temperature and pulse are all normal.' He sighed. 'Some babies are greedy and others not so. She's made a tiny weight gain, but as I said to Eleanor I'd be more worried if she was losing it. Eleanor has agreed to give a wet nurse a try to see if that makes a difference.'

'Have you? Good I'm glad.'

The next day Bessie Blunt, large and rosy cheeked, began her duties as wet nurse with immediate effect. Within the week Eva had put on five ounces. Bessie was a round woman in all respects; round red face, round short body and eyes and a mouth that appeared as if she was permanently startled. Eleanor was suspicious of her the minute she laid eyes on her.

'When the twins had a wet nurse she was a sweet little thing, do you remember Sarah?' Eleanor didn't wait for her husband to reply. 'But this woman is a different kettle of fish.'

'Will that be a kettle of smoked fish, herring or mackerel perhaps?'

Gabriel was more at ease now Eva was improving. His wife's penchant for smoked or salty fish had disappeared since the birth he was pleased to note. 'What's wrong with the woman, why have you not taken to her?'

'I don't know. She's polite enough I have to say and friendly, perhaps a bit too friendly. Molly thinks the same. She's not rough with Eva or anything like that though she's not as gentle as I am. Helps herself to whatever she fancies from the kitchen which doesn't go down well with our cook of course. She told Mrs M I said she was to have whatever she liked, which I did, but according to the food constable, Mrs Madison, Bessie Blunt never stops eating, or drinking for that matter. Apparently she likes a drop or two of dark stout. Says it's good for the baby. Poor Eva will be a drunkard when she grows up.'

'I don't care if the woman eats us out of house and home so long as Eva continues to gain weight. Are they the only reasons you can't like Bessie?'

'Aren't they enough? I didn't say I didn't like her, but she's not the sort of woman I would have chosen. Had Wilson not suggested her there were a couple of others at Hope House who would have been infinitely more suitable. Anyway I'm going to pour oil on troubled waters and try to calm Mrs Madison's temper. Wish me luck.'

Gabriel put aside his book as Wilson was shown in. 'Is this a social call or are you come to check on Eva?' He poured his friend a glass of rum.

'Both as a matter of fact; I hear the wet nurse is proving a success, Eleanor will be relieved, and you too of course.'

'We're pleased, though Eleanor for some reason isn't keen on Bessie.'

'Ah I see. I wondered if they would get along. I don't think under the circumstances Eleanor was going to like anyone other than herself feeding Eva.'

'Why do you say that? She put up with Sarah.'

'She did but Eleanor was in poor health for a while after the twins if you remember. However, after this birth she's bounced back to full health quickly.'

'She has. Being able to sleep through the night is helping.'

Also Eleanor is more mature now, with this pregnancy she took advice, took rest, ate little and often. Took to lying abed in the morning which as you know she wouldn't do with the twins. I think she had a little scare then and was determined to do all in her power to have a safe delivery this time.'

'It was certainly a quick delivery which again put less strain on her thank goodness.'

Wilson had helped himself to more rum when Eleanor joined them.

'Is Mrs M pacified?' Gabriel explained Eleanor had been on a mission.

'Anyone would think the cook paid for the food herself,' Eleanor said exasperated.

'Bessie is a large girl is she not?' Wilson crossed his legs and chuckled.

'She certainly is but then I remember always being hungry when I was feeding Rose so I can hardly blame her.'

'Eva is thriving,' Wilson said, 'don't give up on Bessie. Is it not worth a month or two of the wet nurse if your daughter benefits from her attentions?'

'Of course, as you say Eva's needs must come first, but months? I doubt I shall need her that long.'

ℛ

A few days later Eleanor was in the scullery looking for her pruning shears which Sam had taken to sharpen for her when she heard Bessie talking to Dora. The maid of all work was hanging washing outside the laundry room. Eleanor peered through the small window and saw Bessie eating a pie as she leaned on the wall.

'So you know who it were that made you with child?' Dora asked looking scandalised.

'Course A do, what do you tek me for? Fat lot of good it did me.' She laughed raucously. 'A told yer he's gone missin' which is strange ’cause he were a man of regular habits, well afore he met me that is. She put a hand in her apron pocket and brought out another wedge of pork pie.

‘All A’m sayin’ is that we all knew what time it were ’cause at seven sharp every night he set off to go to Lindy Moran’s cottage and just the same we knew when it were ten ’cause that’s when he came back. Everyday like clockwork an’ we all knew what he got up to there.’

‘Was he courtin’ her then?’ Dora looked confused.

‘Courtin’! Yer don’t call what they were up to courtin’. A’m not sayin’ money changed hands, but she were paid in kind p’haps. She allus looked fligged up an’ she had no other money comin’ in since her husband went down with The Altogether.’ Bessie guffawed coarsely, pastry crumbs flying from her mouth. ‘A wonder if they did it in “the altogether”.’

Dora knitted her brows together. She clearly wasn’t as worldly wise as Bessie, but then Dora was only fifteen.

‘An’ you say this is the man who made you with child? A don’t get your meanin’ Bessie. Were this Toby your husband? Was he untrue?’

‘Untrue! This were *afore* A took up wi’ him. Keep up droopy breeches.’ She shoved the last of the pie in her mouth and wiped her hands on her apron. Eleanor made a mental note to make sure Bessie changed it before feeding Eva.

‘A soon put a stop to his wanderin’s when we started walkin’ out, an’ for about a year we were happy. He said we could be married, but when A told him A was expectin’ he took to his old ways. Why he’d want to go back to Lindy Moran is anybody’s guess. She must be forty if she’s a day and she has caterpillars for eyebrows. A never saw a hairier woman.’

‘So then what did you do? Could your pa not mek him marry you?’

‘Pa weren’t keen on me marryin’ him in the first place, said he were a fly by night so he did nowt but tell him to pay up or else. Pa’s a big man and he’s handy wi’ his fists. Toby din’t have a choice.’

‘Pay up for the bairn do you mean, towards its upkeep?’

'Pa went to Toby's cottage down by Pease Lane. Took ma Uncle John wi' him, he's built like a... any road Toby said he'd pay instalments when the bairn were born. He's not daft he din't want a good pastin' markin' his handsome face.'

'He were good lookin' then?'

'Passable handsome A'd say. Not too tall, but all his own teeth an' hair; A sweet talker right enough. Anyhow it were all arranged, but then the next thing we know Toby's disappeared. Like A said at the start it were odd. He's not bin seen since. It's strange 'cause all his belongin's are still at his cottage. He's disappeared. Puff just like that. Gone. Doesn't even know he has a son. Wi' him gone A had no choice but to have the bairn adopted. All done proper like it were. The Mrs, Doctor Chaffer's wife that is, found 'im a good family to live wi'.'

Dora picked up the basket, but her way to the laundry room was blocked by Bessie's bulk. 'So he never paid any money to you or the bairn?'

'Not a penny an' Pa said as he couldn't look after us. He's got a new wife an' two bairns under four himself. A had no choice but to go an' throw maself on the mercy of Hope House. It were that or the workhouse an' that weren't a choice anybody in their right mind would pick. Without Hope House A don't know what would've happened.'

'An' you've not seen him since?' Dora looked crestfallen.

'A telled yer, he's disappeared off the face of the earth.'

'Not Toby, the bairn.'

'Course not. He's away in Seahouses wi' his new mam and dad.'

'Do you not miss him? The bairn A mean.'

There was a long silence. 'Course A do, but it were fer the best. What could A do? A can barely look after maself. How could A work? Mrs Chaffer said as we could stay at Hope House an' said the lad would've bin taken care of, an' me an 'all but,' she sighed heavily. 'A did what A thought were best fer the bairn in the end.'

'What did you call him?'

'A called him Simon. A thought he suited it, but who knows what he's called now. His new mam and dad have probably changed his name. It makes no difference though 'cause when A say ma prayers at night A allus ask God to look after ma Simon.'

The pair moved off into the laundry room.

Eleanor realised tears were wetting her cheeks.

R

'Why is the post still on the hall table? Gabriel asked as he handed three letters to his wife and opened the one addressed to him.

'I took them from Carver, but I was arranging the flowers on the hall table and then I must have forgotten to pick them up. This one is from Papa. He doesn't often write to me himself, he usually adds a postscript to Mama's letters but this is his handwriting, I'd know it anywhere.'

Gabriel was reading his own missive. 'This is from Rebecca, she's well, happy.' They were each absorbed in reading their letters when Eleanor exclaimed: 'Lord Gabriel, Mama has had an accident. She's had a fall.'

'Is she badly hurt? She's not so young anymore.'

'She doesn't have fifty summers until May, but yes I think she's injured herself badly. Papa says they were walking on the cliff tops when she stumbled and fell. She knocked herself out and has a lump the size of a plum on her head.'

'I hope she hasn't lost her memory,' Gabriel said ironically.

'She was soon awake again Papa says, but she put her arm out to break her fall and instead she's broken her right wrist so she can't write. She's also injured her knee which was twisted and it's all the colours of green, purple and yellow. It's very badly bruised. Poor Mama, it's times like this when I wish we lived closer.'

Gabriel could see his wife's calculating brain working overtime. She was trying to see if there was a way she could go to Whitby to see her mama he knew. He sympathised but would not have her racing off so soon after giving birth.

'I know it's hard but you can't go shooting off now. It'll be

Christmas soon and they're coming to stay with us. You can look after her then, smother her with love and good intentions.'

'That's just it. Papa says she can't travel, she's won't be well enough. Gabriel they aren't coming for Christmas. They say they are so upset not to meet Eva, but Doctor Burns has said she shouldn't consider travelling in winter weather.'

'Eleanor I'm so sorry, I know you were looking forward to it, as was I. I know we weren't going to do anything grand for our tenth wedding anniversary, but it would have been nice to have them with us.'

He could see she was close to tears. 'Try not to upset yourself my love, I know it's hard not being able to see her, but we'll still have a good Christmas. You surely wouldn't go to Whitby now? Does your Papa ask you to go? Is she so bad?'

'He says expressly *not* to go as he knows I'll want to see her to put my mind at rest. He says she would be too uncomfortable being jolted about on the long journey.'

'Then you must do as we both ask. You wouldn't leave Eva and we couldn't take her with us. I know we took Rose to Whitby when she was a new born but that was in summertime.'

Eleanor sighed. 'As you say it would be hard to travel with Eva. Papa said he'll send straight away if she's worse, but he says she'll soon be on the mend and suggests we go to them at Easter.'

'Easter is early next year I believe. If the weather doesn't turn too bad in February we could consider going then and stay for Easter.'

Later after Eleanor had written to her mother she went to the nursery. Bessie was about to feed Eva. The new mother resented the fact someone else was doing the job she ought to be doing. She loved feeding her daughter; it was a special time for her where the two of them could strengthen their attachment. She hoped in the next day or so to resume some of the daytime feeds once again.

'Good afternoon Bessie.' Eleanor looked in the crib where Eva was sound asleep. One hand was made into a tiny fist by her head and her eyelids were flickering.

'She's a good sleeper. A came to see if she were awake, it's more

’en four hours since her last feed,’ Bessie said.

‘She is good and putting on weight now thanks to you.’ Eleanor noticed how pleased Bessie looked. ‘You have been an invaluable help. However, from tomorrow I thought to take over some of the day feeds again myself. You would still be kept on of course.’

‘Thank you. Whatever you say Mistress Reynolds.’

‘I know it’s some way off, but what will you do when you leave us Bessie? What work did you do before?’ Eleanor was mindful of the story she had heard Bessie tell Dora.

‘A were a kitchen maid, but then when A ended up in the family way A was let go. A hope to find kitchen work again when ma job here comes to an end.’

‘Where did you work before?’

She mentioned the name of a large house that was on the way to Warkworth. Eleanor knew it belonged to a clergyman. As she went down to the kitchen she wondered if Lisbet knew the cook there, wondered what kind of a worker Bessie Blunt was. Lisbet knew most of the local cooks from what Eleanor could see. In fact she knew most people in the district to hear her talk. Eleanor believed her.

When she reached the kitchen Mrs Madison was bent over the oven taking out a tray of biscuits. The delicious aroma made Eleanor’s mouth water.

‘Oh, I didn’t see you there.’ The cook began to lift the biscuits onto a tray to cool. ‘Is there something I can do for you ma’am?’

‘Good morning Mrs M. I’m sorry to say my family won’t be coming to stay for Christmas after all so you might want to cancel some of the extra hands. By all means have one or two extra village girls if you think it would help, but it will only be us for Christmas Day. We’re to entertain Sir Bendor, Lady Grace and their children on Christmas Eve, but that will be the extent of our entertaining I’m afraid. They’ll dine and stay for an early supper before going back to Dunstanburgh. This should lessen your work load I think.’ Eleanor eyed the biscuits. ‘Connie has been with us for quite some time has she not? Do you manage well between the two you?’

'We can always use more help as you can imagine, especially at busy times like Christmas. I've booked extra staff like you asked, but there's a lot to prepare beforehand. Christmas isn't the only time we're shorthanded.'

'I was thinking perhaps we could promote Connie, give her a little more responsibility if you think she's ready?' Eleanor wondered if the biscuits were too hot to eat.

At that moment Connie came in from the yard.

'Might I have a word?' the cook said casting a look at Connie, 'privately if you will Mrs Reynolds.'

Mrs Madison loaded a plate with the still warm biscuits and asked Connie to take them to the schoolroom for the children's break. Eleanor watched them pass by enviously.

'What is it Mrs M? Do you not think Connie ready for more responsibility?' From what Eleanor had seen Connie did the majority of the work these days.

'I wasn't going to mention it until after Christmas, I didn't want to worry you but I was thinking of going to live with my sister, the one who lives in Amble. Now she's a widow she's asked me to go and live with her and I'm not getting any younger myself. I thought to retire.'

'Oh, I see.'

'There's no rush and I shouldn't leave you in the lurch, but I was going to suggest Connie take over from me when I go. She's as ready as she'll ever be in my opinion; I can't teach her anymore. She'll be able to cater for the family's needs day to day or for a ball of one hundred I should think. She needs no direction from me now.'

'We shall be sorry to lose you, but everything has fallen into place has it not? When you go we shall only have to find an assistant for Connie, that is if you think she will be agreeable to taking over the kitchen?'

'I'm sure she will. Of course I would serve my notice Mrs Reynolds. Perhaps I could leave in the New Year if that would be convenient?'

'It would I'm sure, but let me speak to Connie first to make certain we aren't being presumptuous.'

Later that morning Eleanor summoned Connie to the drawing room and offered her the position of head cook at Westshore.

'A should like nothing better Mistress Reynolds but there's, well there might be a fly in the ointment. It's not the work you understand, A'm more than happy to run the kitchen it's just that, well A'm to be married in the spring.'

'Married! Oh I had no idea... congratulations Connie. Why should I know, of course it's none of my business.' Eleanor thought at one time there had been more than a spark between Connie and Jonty Walters, but perhaps she was wrong.

'Me an' Sam have been walking out this last year an' more. A would have married him long ago if he'd had his way, he's a kind man, forbearing, but A love ma job. Any road he won't be put off any longer so A was going to serve notice in February if that's convenient Mrs Reynolds.'

Eleanor was stunned. She was to lose two cooks. Then she had an idea. 'I know it's customary for the head cook to be unmarried, but would you consider staying on after you marry? If you live in Sam's cottage you'll be on hand after all. Of course in time if there's the patter of tiny feet we will have to think again, but I'd be prepared to keep you on if you would consider staying. Speak to Sam and see what he says by all means.'

'If there was only me to think of A'd say yes straight away, there's nothing A'd like better, but there's Sam's two kiddies. A'll have them to look after.'

Eleanor chewed her lip. 'I've been thinking for a while now about Davy and Beth's education. They're of an age with our children and I thought Mr Pater can teach five children as easily as he can teach three. I spoke of it with my husband only last week and he was going to speak to Sam. Knowing Mr Reynolds as I do he'll have forgotten.'

Connie was smiling broadly. 'It would mean working different hours, but A reckon as Lisbet minds the children oftentimes if she were to carry on an' they went to have lessons then it might work. A'd need an assistant though of course, A can't manage on ma own.'

'Mrs Madison said earlier that sometimes you're stretched in the kitchen, especially when we entertain. Perhaps you could have two assistants, an under cook and a pastry cook. Let me think about it. Speak to Sam and let me know what he thinks and we'll talk again.'

After Connie left, Eleanor made her way to see Lisbet where she asked her if she knew the cook at the vicarage. Lisbet said she did, they were old friends. Eleanor told her of her plan.

Later that afternoon Lisbet, driven by Sam in the pony and trap, called to see Mrs Chalmers the cook at the vicarage. By four that afternoon Lisbet was back and full of news.

'Mrs Chalmers were most put out when Bessie Blunt were forced to leave.'

'Oh really, was she not a good worker?' Eleanor's face fell. She was hoping to offer the woman the job of under cook. She hoped she had not run off with the silver.

'Just the reverse; Mrs Chalmers has five under her.' Lisbet bristled possibly because Westshore had never had so many kitchen staff for her to call on when she had been cook. 'She'd made her mind up to raise Bessie up to be the pastry cook; Mrs Chalmers says she's the lightest hands where pastry's concerned, but then the daft thing gets herself up the duff.'

Eleanor looked askance. 'Up the duff?'

'In the family way. Agatha says if yer thinkin' of hirin' her then she'll vouch fer the girl and you can't say fairer than that. She's a hard taskmaster is Aggie Chalmers. She liked the girl, though she said Bessie's a bit rough around the edges, she can read enough to follow a receipt an' she uses her initiative. There now, what do yer say to that?'

'I say we may have found ourselves a pastry cook. All we need now is an under cook. Thank you Lisbet.'

'A know yer said you'll hire another girl, but if only A were twenty years younger.'

'Perhaps you can help me find another girl to complement the other two, that is if Bessie agrees to take the job. I trust your judgement Lisbet and there's isn't a rush as Mrs Madison won't be leaving Westshore imminently. Perhaps you'll cook us a goose at Christmas, Gabriel always says no one cooks one like you.'

A few days later all was accomplished to everyone's satisfaction. Bessie had jumped at the chance of a new job, Connie had persuaded Sam she could stay on after they married, for the time being at least, and Lisbet had found a friend of hers who had a daughter looking for work so she was hired. Gabriel was the only one with reservations it appeared.

'So all this change is to happen in the New Year, well most of it. I see the young kitchen maid has already started work. What's her name did you say?'

'The new girl is Mary. She's a quiet little thing. Her mother says she's fourteen though she looks like she's not seen eleven summers to me. Possibly it's because these village girls are undernourished, a few weeks of good food should help fatten her up.'

'If she can wrestle it out of Bessie Blunt's hands,' Gabriel said laughing. 'Bessie will probably cost us a fortune in extra provisions, but all I care about is that Connie can produce my favourite puddings to the same standard as Mrs M. From what you say she's being doing the lion's share of the work for a while now anyway so hopefully I won't notice the difference.' Gabriel, who was writing to Rebecca, stroked his cheek with the quill. 'Did you know Sam and Connie were walking out? I never expected Sam to re-marry, I don't know why but there it is.'

'I thought once there was something between them, but then I thought Jonty Walters was her beau. Who knows? I'm so busy these days I haven't the time to follow the staffs' romantic affairs.'

'Jonty was interested in her I remember him telling me, but he's a bit of a lad and possibly expected more than Connie was prepared to give.'

'It was ever thus Gabriel, it was ever thus.'

ℛ

Eleanor entered the study and stared at her husband. His crossed ankles were resting on the corner of his desk as he lay back in his chair, his hands folded across his flat stomach. He was sleeping.

Since his accident he sometimes had a nap in the afternoon after he had dined, but usually only if he had something on his mind. Eleanor wondered what might be bothering him. He must have sensed she was looking at him for he woke, stretched and yawned.

'Were you watching me?'

'Not watching, looking. Am I not allowed to look at my husband?'

He put his long legs to the floor and yawned again. 'Excuse me, I feel better for that. A cat can look at a King I suppose.' He ran his fingers through his hair. 'When I was in Italy years ago, I noticed the locals had a sleep in the afternoon. It was at the hottest part of the day and they would stop work, close the shutters and sleep for an hour or two. It's quite a civilised idea I think. It had a name but I can't remember what it was called.'

'Is it a siesta?'

'No, I think that's the Spanish equivalent.' He rubbed his chin thinking. 'I was in Northern Italy where it's called... riposo, I think it's called something different in the south but I can't remember what.'

Gabriel stood and stretched again and moved to stand by his wife's side. She was looking out of the window. 'Have you something on your mind my love, do you want to talk about it?' she asked.

Gabriel sighed, took her in his arms and kissed her forehead. 'Can a man have no secrets; am I such an open book?' Eleanor waited. 'Earlier I had a visit from Mr Tripp.'

'The baker? What did he want?'

Gabriel drew in a long breath. 'To put a loaded shotgun to Jonty Walters' head quite possibly.'

'Oh no, I can guess why.'

'It appears he's got Tripp's youngest, Sarah, in the family way and wants to know what Walters is going to do about it.'

Eleanor scoffed. 'Knowing him it will be nothing at all if he can get away with it. I like Jonty, he's personable and good looking, but therein lies the problem. The village girls queue up for his attentions.

He breaks hearts for a hobby but what does Mr Tripp think you can do about it?'

'Talk to him I expect. At any rate I said I would speak to Jonty, try to persuade him to do the right thing. Like you I'm fond of him. He's good at his job; conscientious, hard working and he's easy to get along with which is important with one's valet.' Gabriel laughed. 'Listening to his exploits helps pass the time when he's shaving me.'

Eleanor tutted. 'So you live vicariously through your valet?'

'Are you saying I don't have a life of my own?'

'Not that sort of life I hope.'

'He certainly gives the girls around here a run for their money, not to mention Sally Slide.' He mentioned the Madam of the brothel in Amble. 'I should pay his wages directly to her and cut out the middle man - or woman.' Eleanor saw him grin. She held back a tirade but if he made a joke about the baker's daughter having a bun in the oven she wouldn't be responsible for her actions. She merely tutted again then said: 'It's all well and good Gabriel but I run a charity rescuing girls from the likes of Jonty Walters. It's no laughing matter. Poor Sarah must be at her wits' end.'

He pulled the bell and asked for Walters to be sent to him. 'No time like the present.'

'Should I stay or go?'

'I'll speak to him man to man I think.'

Eleanor left the room muttering under her breath: 'Man to man indeed, all boys together...'

Walters was coming down the stairs as she passed through the hall. He looked handsome and smart in his new black uniform.

'Good afternoon Mrs Reynolds. I get the feeling I'm in trouble, I've never been summoned to appear before the master in all the years I've worked here.' He smiled as if it were some amusing joke. No wonder the girls found it hard to steer clear of his flattery and charm.

Eleanor inclined her head. 'Good afternoon to you too; it's been nice knowing you Jonty,' she said cryptically and smiled as she saw the look on his face change from cheerful to something resembling anxiety. She put on her hat and went out.

Gabriel sat behind his desk whilst Walters stood before it, straight and tall, his hands clasped behind his back. Gabriel was reminded of a soldier. No wonder the girls hereabouts fell at his feet.

'I'll come straight to the point Jonty. I've had a visit from Mr Tripp; I understand you're acquainted with his daughter.'

'I think I might know what this is about. She told me last night she has a bun in the oven.'

Gabriel didn't smile. 'It's not a laughing matter Jonty, the girl is beyond worried.'

'Sorry, I know, we talked about it and I said I'd think what's to be done.'

'You have only two options as I see it. You either pay for the child's upkeep in keeping with the bastardy laws or you marry her.' Walters let out a long breath. 'Her father favours the latter option of course, as does the young woman I assume.'

Walters bit the inside of his cheek and thought for a long moment. 'As would I... although I never thought I would ever think such a thing. Sarah is a looker as well as a sweet natured girl but there's another matter, a more important issue I think.' He waited.

'Tell me.'

'I chose to be a valet for a number of reasons, one of which was that valets are always single men. It was a good excuse when a girl started making hints she wanted things to progress further you understand. It was my get out clause.' He grinned. 'But now, well I want to marry Sarah, do right by her but here's the rub. I'd lose my job. A valet is needed morning, noon and night, they're always bachelors and always live in.'

Gabriel picked up a quill and began twisting it between his finger and thumb. 'I see,' he said thoughtfully. 'Sarah is a respectable girl, from a good family. Her father is mortified. The Tripps have had the bakery for generations I think.' He continued to twirl the quill in his fingers. 'The other half of Sam's cottage is, well in a poor state, though the roof is sound enough. In a few years I'd thought to knock through so when Sam's children were older they'd have more space.

If you did right by the girl and married her then you could have that for as long as you work for me. You would still be here on site but would go home to Sarah instead of living in the house. I can't see why it wouldn't work if we adopted this plan. My habits are fairly routine so what do you think?'

'I think I'm about to put my head in the noose and without a single shot being fired,' he said as if he could hardly believe he was going to be married. Thank you, I appreciate the gesture.'

Gabriel poured two glasses of rum. 'Congratulations Jonty, welcome to the club.' He grinned at his valet. 'You know I hate change, I'd hate to lose you and besides with a baby screaming the house down you'll be here more than you are already. Now what are you waiting for man? Go and put the poor girl out of her misery and give her the good news.'

Gabriel thought about all the recent staff changes. Westshore now ran like a well oiled machine thanks to Eleanor. How different to a decade ago when it was himself, Lisbet and Abner. Now with indoor staff, cooks, grooms, and gardeners he had more than a dozen staff on the payroll, more at busy times. He was relieved Jonty was staying.

Later after Eleanor returned from her walk, she sat drinking tea with her husband.

'I never thought to see the day when Jonty Walters got caught. I take it Sarah accepted him?'

'She did and they will be married as soon as the banns have been read.' Gabriel sniggered.

'What's so funny?'

'Mr Tripp had anticipated Walters might lose his position and so offered him a job as a miller. Can you imagine Jonty milling flour?'

'I certainly can't see him with flour in his hair and calluses on his hands,' Eleanor said laughing at the idea. 'I take it he wasn't tempted by the offer then?'

'Not a bit of it but who knows what might happen. Sarah is one of three daughters; there are no sons to carry on the bakery or the mill. He may have fallen on his feet when the old man decides to hang up his apron.'

Eleanor said: 'Are you pleased you won't lose him?'

'Of course, we get on. You know what it was like when Charity left you, well it's the same with a valet. You know I don't like change, there's been enough change in staff recently for my liking, and if I had to find someone new then I would have been put out.'

Eleanor pulled a currant out of the scone she was eating, examined it then ate it. 'Hayden calls them dead flies - currants I mean. There's a lot of work to be done on the cottage if it's to be ready for the happy couple. I'll ask Dora to look out some curtains and rugs, there's bound to be things we can supply. It'll be nice to have another baby at Westshore. Wait until Lisbet hears Jonty is to be a father.'

'Are you getting broody already my love?'

'Not at all.' She laughed. 'Don't you start getting ideas, it's far too soon.'

'I'm perfectly content with what we have, but you're right about the cottage. Tomorrow I'll get the men to make a start on the renovations.'

'Perhaps Sam will make them a small piece of furniture as a wedding present; he's good with his hands. One thing's for sure, Lisbet will be sewing layettes before you know it. I'll have to think what we can get them for a wedding present.'

'We're giving them a cottage, isn't that enough? I think the girl's parents are comfortably off so they'll have a good start to their married life, better than most.'

'Jonty Walters married. Three words I never thought to hear in the same sentence,' Eleanor said laughing.

R

Christmas was fast approaching and Gabriel was looking forward to Steven coming to stay. It had been arranged that the night before travelling on to Whitby for the festive season his eldest son would stay at Westshore. From now on this would be the pattern of things

Gabriel hoped. Eleanor had suggested they held a small celebration, nothing too fancy as Steven was, after all, being raised a Quaker.

'Will we not be able to give him a gift?' Gabriel asked in consternation.

'If it's modest and useful perhaps.' Eleanor had told him.

To that end Gabriel had found his son a book on botany which the bookseller had assured him was the most up to date. Steven's visit was brief, but welcome nonetheless. Having all his children together under his roof had been the best Christmas gift Gabriel could have wished for, besides baby Eva of course. He felt truly blessed.

That night in bed Gabriel said: 'Steven told me he's enjoying school. He's made a friend too, a Scottish boy named Hamish.'

'Good. At least when the twins go away to school they will have each other for company. I wonder if my parents will see him over Christmas. It was good of you to think to speak to Papa, I know it can't have been easy for you.'

'It wasn't, but your parents are good people, I'm only sorry I had to embarrass you.'

'I don't embarrass easily my love, you should know that by now, and they know how the world works. As Papa said it could well have been Tomas who presented them with a... well you know my feelings about men and their dalliances.'

The rest of Christmas was a quieter affair than usual, but nonetheless enjoyable. On Christmas Eve Gabriel had given Eleanor a stunning diamond necklace for their tenth wedding anniversary. She had been stunned by its brilliance. He had also given her an eternity ring to match. She had worn both to supper with Bendor and Grace where they toasted their good fortune.

For Christmas the twins each received a rocking horse; two identical black stallions. They had spent each wet day riding imaginary races. Their screams and shouts could be heard all over Westshore. Rose had a real pony, a bigger pony whom she named Smoke as she was a dappled grey and remarkably pretty. Baby Eva had a silver rattle though she was still too small to play with it.

Eleanor had given Gabriel a new saddle made of Spanish leather. It was exceptionally ornate and he said it was the finest saddle he had ever owned. Eleanor had worried he might think it too fancy, but he convinced her it was the best Christmas present he'd had in years. This pleased her though she knew the greatest present he had received was the visit from Steven. She didn't resent it; not at all, she was only pleased her husband had all he had ever wanted.

As expected the snow returned in January but this time it was accompanied by strong winds which embayed all Gabriel's ships for two weeks. Blizzards rattled Westshore's windows and the wind was so fierce it lifted part of Lisbet's cottage roof off so she had to move into the main house until it was repaired. Then in the last week of January the rains came. Torrential downpours lashed across the beach so it was hard to discern the sea from the sky. The twins rode more races which became more raucous each day. Rose was frustrated and a little annoyed not to be able to ride her new pony.

'Spring is just around the corner,' Eleanor told her pouting daughter though she didn't believe the statement herself. 'Soon you'll be able to ride out, you'll see.'

'But I want to take her in the paddock. Every day I groom her so she shines, but I want to *ride* her. I know she's bored too, she told me so.'

Eleanor smiled at her daughter's lively imagination. 'Did she also tell you she didn't want to drown, for I swear if either of you went out in this weather you'd be washed away.'

When Gabriel came home from the bay that evening he was so wet he had to change the minute he walked in the door. 'Man alive, pass me a hammer I need to start building an ark, the weather is biblical out there.'

'Did The Jack and Alice make port?' Eleanor knew he was late home as he was waiting for her to dock. Steven was returning to school and had boarded her in Whitby.

'Not yet. I'd thought she might make it before dark, but it's not to be. The weather isn't helping of course. Have you waited supper for me?'

'I have.' She rang and supper was served. 'Was she not expected yesterday?' Eleanor asked. 'I thought maybe you would have had Steven in tow.'

'As did I but this weather is exceptional. Who knows when she'll reach safe harbour? Perhaps she's put in somewhere more sheltered along the coast and is waiting out the storm. It's happened before, but not for many years. It would have been in my father's time if I remember rightly. I hope Steven has good sea legs.' He poured himself a large glass of claret. 'Were the boys boisterous again today? They hate to be indoors do they not?'

'They were, but thank goodness they have their rocking horses. They're worth their weight in gold; they've kept the twins entertained since Christmas. I only hope when they begin to ride real ponies they're a little less enthusiastic.'

Gabriel poured himself another glass and offered the bottle to her, but Eleanor declined. 'They're a little too animated. I told Haydan he would break the rockers if he rode so hard. Clearly he took not a bit of notice.'

'They get carried away, but it wasn't the rocker he broke.'

'Oh... '

'They "borrowed" two crops and were whipping the horses so hard one of them broke. I almost felt sorry for the horses.'

'I expect that was Haydan?' She nodded. 'I'll have a word in the morning and see if I can't convince them to calm down. In the meantime I'm so tired I think after supper and a game of backgammon I'll be in the arms of Morpheus. I hope Steven will be alright.'

'He will be, his father is a good sailor and so was his grandfather.' She put her arms around his waist. 'You're tired are you? And I was hoping you'd be in my arms not the arms of some mythological god,' she said. 'It's not just the children who want for exercise.'

The next day The Jack and Alice made safe harbour. Steven, a little green about the gills, was glad to make dry land.

20

The spring of 1776 was one of the warmest Gabriel could remember. The sun shone in a clear blue sky and the sea was as still as a mill pond. In fact it was the warmest spring since the year he had met Eleanor. He remembered coming back from Whitby after meeting his Whitby Wench in The Fleece Tavern. He remembered how hot he had been tramping up the beach pondering why the red-haired stunner had run out on him. It seemed like a lifetime ago, but a good lifetime.

From the conservatory Gabriel saw Charles riding towards Westshore. They were to sup together. Eleanor was playing whist at Wooden House with Lottie and a few other ladies, it was something they did on a regular basis, so it would be just the two of them who sat down to eat.

During supper, after they'd each discussed the matters of the day, the talk inevitably turned to their families. Both men's youngest children were of an age so for a time they talked proudly of their offspring's merits. Gabriel was surprised Charles was so attached to his son; he had never had him down as a family man. An heir was always longed for by the nobility in particular, but Gabriel thought that would have been as far as it went with Charles. Apparently he had been wrong.

'Perhaps when Eva is older she and Charles might come together. It would be a good match would it not?' Charles said.

'God forbid Charles. I mean no offence but the trouble it caused between Caroline and I. We would do well to leave well alone. Trying to please our fathers almost caused a rift between the families.'

'I didn't know that,' Charles said. 'Perhaps you're right.'

Gabriel changed the subject. 'So how is married life suiting you these days? You've been married for over a year now, are you used to each other's ways yet?'

'Thanks to your wife's marriage counselling, it's better than before thank you.' He grinned slyly.

'What has Eleanor to do with anything? What can you mean?'

'A while ago she had a talk with Vi, suggested she ask me if I was having an affair.'

'I'm sorry Charles, I had no idea.' He was a little embarrassed. 'My wife has especially modern views about how marriage should be conducted, but I'm not sure she should be inflicting them on other people. She will have meant no harm I can assure you, but once she gets an idea in her head, well she can appear opinionated, blind to others' points of view. But as I say, she will only have been trying to be helpful.'

'And she was. Vi challenged me, asked me about Marguerite Strachan. I assured her I wasn't having an affair with anyone.'

Gabriel helped himself to more beef. 'Marguerite has moved back to Rothbury I know. Eastshore is let again, to a retired army officer.'

Charles laughed loudly. 'So you too thought I was carrying on with Lady Berwick? Does everyone assume this to be the case?' Gabriel inclined his head and cocked an eyebrow. 'Not I but I know Eleanor thinks that.'

'How funny. After what Bendor said about the lady's lack of discretion I thought to give her a wide berth. I admit when we first met I was taken with her, who wouldn't be, she's a stunning looking woman, but I do have some thought for my wife. I shouldn't want Vi looked down on because of my indiscretions.'

'There have been indiscretions then, I remember Claude remarking when baby Charles was born how you couldn't be found.'

'Yes, and I can't begin to tell you how I berated myself afterwards, but well, what can I say. Vi's bedchamber had been out of bounds to me for months.' He looked thoughtful. 'Then her time came sooner than we had imagined and well... that day we met at The Hope and Anchor I picked up the bar wench after you had left. It was my one and only fling since my marriage.' Gabriel looked surprised at the confession. 'As I said I'm grateful to Eleanor. My wife and I are now in accord; within reason she will accommodate my needs and in return I won't stray. That's the deal. I hope, and I think it's already working, that Vi will soon be as keen as me in *that* direction, she's already begun to unbend. We're getting along well, both in and out of the bedchamber. We've been at cross purposes. Vi thought once I had a son and heir I'd not be bothering her again, and I thought she wouldn't want to be troubled as she would think she'd fulfilled her end of the bargain. We were both wrong. There has been a lack of communication in my marriage.'

'I see. That's good news for I knew you had to marry for reasons other than love, and I felt for you. But now, if you have some regard for one another then your home life will be all the better for it.'

'I said when I married Vi she wasn't my type, but she wasn't empty headed and that was one of the things I liked about her. She has spirit. Like your own wife, Vi is unconventional, you've made a success of your marriage, why then shouldn't I? I think the seeds of love have been planted and with tender care and attention they will flourish.' Again he laughed loudly. 'How could it not? Aren't most women powerless to resist me, this one just took a little longer to germinate.'

Gabriel poured his friend a glass of claret. 'I'm pleased for you both... but there's something else puzzling me, something I think I know the answer to, but then again Eleanor always says I'm slow on the up-take in such matters.'

'Are you going to start dispensing marital advice too?'

'God forbid, I still need guidance myself on occasions. Sometimes my wife has the most extraordinary ideas. No, no it's that I think I know who Marguerite was having a fling with.' He repeated the story Eleanor had told him about a regular late night gentleman caller at Eastshore.

Charles took a long drink then sat back in his chair. 'Man, I thought everyone knew. Why, you're right it was Claude of course.' He grinned. 'He doesn't give a fig who knows either, neither does

Cecily so I'm surprised it's not all over the county. I told you before they go their own ways. He's a randy old sod, and Cecily's not much better.'

'Well then the lady is more discreet than we all gave her credit for because I'd not heard, and believe me I hear all the gossip at the bay, or at least in the tap room of the The Hope and Anchor.' He in turn grinned. 'Eleanor will be furious.'

'Furious, why?'

'Because she didn't know who the man was, well she didn't look further than you to be honest.'

'I see, wait until I see your errant wife, I might have some fun with this... with your permission of course. Perhaps I'll pretend to make a play for her, make out I'm the love rat she thinks I am.' He helped himself to more claret.

'Man alive, it would end in tears... no not tears, death and I'm not quite sure whose.'

'Speaking of misdemeanours, what's all this?' Charles asked. 'Why have you not shared your news?'

'News, what news? I'm not in an entanglement.'

'Not now you're not, but way back, surely it was a different matter then.'

'Way back we all had our moments, I'd not deny that. What are you getting at?'

'When Vi and I called that time and the young lad, Steven I think you said he was called, was staying here. It was like looking at you on your first day at school. Come on, out with it, he's the fruit of your loins is he not?'

Charles, who was in his cups, suddenly realised he had been crass. 'I'm sorry Gabriel, take the decanter away it makes me run at the mouth. Accept my apology I was out of order.'

Gabriel hauled in a long breath. 'You're right of course, but I'd appreciate it if you kept it to yourself. I'd rather not go into details, there's Eleanor to consider in all this and she's blameless as is Steven. You're correct, he is my son. That's all I want to say on the matter.'

'Of course Gabriel, it's none of my business and as you'll be aware my wife cares nothing for gossip so I shan't be sharing this news with her, rest assured.' He shuffled in his seat. 'As a matter of fact the same thing happened to me five years ago. A pretty little French girl turned up at my digs with a daughter in tow. Said the child was mine - looking at the child I couldn't deny it. I saw her a few times, helped pay the girl's bills, but then my daughter died. She had barely three summers, the sins of the father eh Gabriel?' The mood had taken a melancholic turn. Then Charles roused himself. 'I'll tell you one thing I envy you for my friend,' he said, 'and that's your cook. We haven't been so fortunate. Vi sends more food back to the kitchen than she eats, not that she doesn't have a good appetite, she does. In the navy I was used to mediocre fare, but now I'm running my own establishment I'd like the food to be at least edible, especially when we have guests.'

Both men were glad to change the subject and lighten the mood. The dessert wine was brought in along with the puddings. Connie was proving to be a good head cook and when Bessie's sweet pastries and apple tart arrived Charles was in seventh heaven. 'How much do you pay your kitchen staff? I might offer more to try to tempt them away to South Point.'

'That's the handy work of Bessie our pastry cook, she's quite an appetite herself. She could eat and drink you and I under the table.' Gabriel cut them both another slice of the tart. 'I never had you down as a gourmet Charles, as you say short rations, ships biscuits and weevils were your usual fare on board ship.'

'Ah yes, but when in port we officers went to the best places to eat, especially in France.'

Stuffed to the gunnels they retired to the library. 'Tell me Charles, last year you were talking of applying to the admiralty for a position *observing* I think you called it. Have you given up on the idea?'

'I'm glad you raised the point, I was going to mention it, quite the contrary, I am to go to London next week. I'm to be deployed in Paris for the summer. At least I'll get good food, even if I do risk getting shot. There's major unrest in the big cities.'

'It's in the papers daily. I'm pleased for you if that's what you want to do, but a shame you'll be away from Violet for so long when you're beginning to get along together.'

'Not so my friend, Vi is to come too. It's good cover to be travelling with one's wife. She's only coming of course because it's out of season for hunting. It's the one thing we can't see eye to eye on; the amount of time she spends chasing damn foxes. No sooner had she given birth to Charles she was chomping at the bit to get back in the field. Do you know she's bought two of your hunters in the last six months? Says she needs different mounts for different terrain and so that she can rest one and ride another. Some women waste money on fancy clothes, mine wastes it on horses. Then again, technically it's her money I suppose to do with as she will.'

As the evening drew to a close Gabriel bid his friend goodnight and awaited his wife's return. He did not look forward to telling her Charles had guessed their secret about Steven's parentage... but he couldn't wait to tell her she had been wrong about who was having an affair with Lady Berwick. Then again perhaps he would tell her in the morning otherwise it might be him on short rations.

R

The next day Gabriel was in the stud farm office looking over the accounts when Bendor entered and threw himself on the chair opposite.

'Well are we to sell the family silver in order to survive?' he said laughing, knowing the converse to be true. 'Have you seen we have an order from the palace? One of our horses will run in the Prince's colours, how impressive is that?'

'It's tremendous news, the order will really put us on the map. Who would have thought such a thing possible eight years ago? Not I for one.'

'What started out as a small concern has grown exponentially year on year. We're now the most highly regarded stud in the north, famed for race horses all over the country and now to have an order from on high, well it's the utmost accolade is it not?'

'It most certainly is, wait until I tell Eleanor.' He laughed. 'In the beginning she accused us of starting horse breeding as a hobby, a pastime. Yet the income the stud generates now is on a par with my shipping line. Far from costing us money it's making us a fortune.'

'Grace thought the same, said we were throwing money away, but now the stud helps support the estate. It truly is a success story. It's as well under the circumstances.' Bendor poured them both a good measure of rum to celebrate.

'What circumstances?'

Bendor grinned. 'There's more than one stud around here my friend, I'm proud to announce I've sired another offspring.'

Gabriel slapped his old friend on the back. 'That's tremendous news Bendor, when will the happy event happen?'

'In the autumn, October or thereabouts. Grace is doing well and is of course like myself, hoping for a son and heir. However if it's another filly we shan't mind so long as it's healthy.'

Gabriel knew his friend wanted an heir to carry on the family name. In part because Bendor had done what a lot of the landed aristocracy had failed to do in recent times, and that is made his estate not just pay but grow and prosper. The stud farm had indeed contributed to this success.

Gabriel said: 'I think it time Jax was recognised for his contribution to our enterprise. Now Hodges is to retire I think Jax should be promoted to stud manager. He's the best man for the job - knows more about race horses than we two put together.'

'I thought the same thing myself. He's been loyal and hard working and he loves the place as much as we do. I'd also thought to reward him with shares in the company. What say you?'

'That's a wonderful idea and one I know he'll appreciate. To think how far he's come from the scruffy urchin who washed up on the tide all those years ago.'

'All thanks to you Gabe. I know his freedom came at a terrible cost, but it was one worth paying in the scheme of things.'

'I suppose so, but it's still something I'd rather not dwell on. I almost lost my liberty remember. Sometimes, even after all these years, I wake in the night and - '

'Enough, this is a celebration. Don't start putting a damper on the proceedings.'

There was a knock at the door and Jax stuck his head around it.

Gabriel advanced to his old groom jovially. 'Come in Jax, have some rum. Sir Percy and I have good news for you.'

Epilogue

Gabriel swam for the shore with long even strokes. The May sun had risen two hours ago, it felt pleasantly warm on his back as he padded up the beach and retrieved his breeches. He saw Eleanor walking towards him her red hair blowing in the breeze. She was carrying baby Eva who at five months was growing fast. Eleanor laid the child on a shawl on the sand.

'You were keen to leave our bed this morning, am I such a sight first thing?' She held her hand to her eyes to shield them from the sun.

'A sight for sore eyes as Lisbet always says.' He kissed her then bent to stroke Eva's dark hair. He grabbed Eleanor and spun her around so she was facing Westshore keeping his arms about her waist. 'I'd thought to bring you breakfast in bed as a treat on this momentous day.'

'Momentous? What's momentous about it, although every day is special I don't see how this one is any different.' She held his hands.

'It's eleven years exactly to the very day since we met.'

'Eleven? That's an odd anniversary. How do you know and why have we never noted it before?'

'I knew we met in May, but I couldn't have told you the exact date, but then I was looking for some paperwork to do with The Eleanor Rose. I noticed a receipt for the first instalment I'd paid over to your father and it was dated the seventh of May 1765. After I had paid him I went to The Fleece for my supper and ended up with more than I'd bargained for.'

She nudged him lightly in the ribs as he kissed the top of her head. 'And the rest,' she said, 'is history.'

'Eleven years and four children later and I love you still. More than

I ever thought possible.'

Eleanor turned in his arms. They kissed. The unmistakable sound of Haydan mimicking a kiss by sucking on his own hand could be heard. 'Yuk,' he said before throwing himself into the sea.

'Good morning,' Ruari shouted as he raced past his parents and leapt into the water. Rose, wearing only her shift, smiled at Eva as the baby kicked her fat little legs in the air. 'Good morning Mama, Pa.' She joined her brothers for an early morning swim.

Wrapped in each other's arms they watched as their children frolicked and played, laughed and generally made as much noise as possible.

'Why are the children up so early? It must be the light mornings.'

'I've no idea but I don't mind, they'll be ready to break their fast after a good swim.' They watched the children still entwined in each other's arms. 'Eleven years of marital bliss... some heartache, but then in all lives a little rain must fall.'

'I've no regrets.' Eleanor sighed.

'That's the only way to live, without regret. When I've been away, even if it's only been for one night I love to come home to Westshore and know all my most precious ones, bar one, are inside. I never thought to know Steven of course and even that is a blessing now he's a regular visitor.' Eva cooed contentedly. 'No matter what happens we've always got each other. The shipping line and the stud may wither and die, but we'll always have the most precious gift a couple can have here at Westshore - love. The house my father built hoping against the odds to fill with children never happened for him, but it has happened for us and here we are, happy anniversary my love, we've reached safe harbour.'

'Happy anniversary and many more of them, I love you Gabriel Reynolds.'

'And I love you Eleanor Barker.'

The End

A Message from Jane

Dear Reader,

I just wanted to say a big thank you for choosing to read Safe Harbour. If you enjoyed it, I'd be grateful if you could leave a review on Amazon, or mention it to your friends and family. Word-of-mouth recommendations are so important to an author's success, and doing so will help new readers to discover my work.

It would be lovely to hear from you too, either via my website, or on Facebook, Twitter or Instagram. Safe Harbour is the third and concluding episode in the Reynolds Saga but there are plenty of other books to come so please join me for what I promise will be an exciting adventure.

www.janefenwick.co.uk

About the Author

Jane Fenwick lives in the market town of Settle in Yorkshire, England. She studied education at Sheffield University gaining a B.Ed (Hons) in 1989 and going on to teach primary age range children. Jane decided to try her hand at penning a novel rather than writing school reports as she has always been an avid reader, especially enjoying historical and crime fiction. She decided to combine her love of both genres to write her first historical crime novel **Never the Twain**. Jane has always been a lover of antiques, particularly art nouveau and art deco ceramics and turned this hobby into a business opening an antiques and collectables shop in Settle. However her time as a dealer was short lived; she spent far too much time in the sale rooms buying items that ended up in her home rather than the shop! Animal welfare is a cause close to Jane's heart and she has been vegetarian since the age of fourteen. For the last twenty years she has been trustee of an animal charity which rescues and re-homes cats, dogs and all manner of creatures looking for a forever home. Of course several of these have been "adopted" by Jane! Although she lives in the Yorkshire Dales Jane is particularly drawn to the North East Coast which she knows well; often visiting Whitby, Sandsend and Alnmouth for research purposes. When she isn't walking on Sandsend beach with her dog Scout, a Patterdale "Terrorist" she is to be found in her favourite coffee shop gazing out to sea and dreaming up her next plot.

Printed in Great Britain
by Amazon